ONE WAY
THE BUS FOR GUS

A Novel By:
C. John Coombes

COVER DESIGN, PAGE LAYOUTS,
AND TYPESETTING BY:
C. JOHN COOMBES

BOOK PUBLISHED BY:
C J COOMBES STUDIO
PRINT ISBN 978-1-941623-60-2

EDITED BY:
MARIA DENBOER

CONTRIBUTING EDITORS:
C JOHN COOMBES
NANCY BURKE SMITH
MARTHA HART

First Edition

ALL RIGHTS RESERVED BY C. JOHN COOMBES
COPYRIGHT 2017

1

There was pain. The *first* awareness.

Pain at the front of the head, at the back of the head, at the sides and all places in between pain that might have started or stopped at the skull after a circuitous journey through every bone in a stiff, aching body.

As he reclaimed his senses, he grappled with an increasing state of agony that seemingly had no beginning or end. It just was. Although he possessed sufficient wit to appreciate his wretched condition, he lacked the least understanding for the reason behind his misery.

The pain Gus experienced was excruciating. But *was it really pain?* It was a measure of distress to be sure, but as his mind cleared, he wondered if he suffered something less a state of pain and more a state of transformation—*brutal* transformation. Possibly a return to head-splitting sobriety following a night of guzzling cheap bottom-shelf whiskey—brew he fondly called *anti-freeze*.

Underlying this hell of sobriety, or transformation, or whatever, was a notion that he had narrowly escaped some traumatic event... or had he? Maybe he was not yet free of the harrowing experience. Everything seemed wrong. He was badly shaken, anxious, disoriented. He felt blistered, as if burned by a hard rub, a soul scraped raw by some closely hidden world of mistrust and mayhem.

No, no... he was not in that world of woe anymore. He could feel the change. The fog of fright was dissipating, the nightmare receding, growing distant, feelings of dread fading from his awareness. He was somehow unreachable from that place, safely beyond the grasp of something worse than wicked. He seemed free of all save a few unsettling sensations bleeding through like bad dreams.

Whether day two, week two, or year two, when came the *second* awareness, it arrived as noise. It grew increasingly louder as it worked its way along canals to strike the drums within his ears. The sounds pounded erratic rhythms deep into his awakening consciousness. For Gus, it was easier to listen than look. Noise eased anxiety. Noise was distracting. Mentally, it drew him away from his torments.

Only to Gus was the sound that swirled about something more than an invasive clamor of traffic. For him, the spectrum of mechanical notes was as full and familiar as the song of his life. The howl of passing tires, the blare of horns, the staccato exhaust of heavy haulers, the echoes of an expressway; it was a chorus of trebles and basses, rhythms and chords. It was the melody of liberation.

Rather than shun the din, Gus longed for the highway's *song* as if it were a mother's lullaby. The drone of traffic soothed him. It could send him to sleep like a rickety old fan. For reasons unknown, Gus sensed that he was no stranger to life on the curb. Spontaneous horn-blasts and tire-screeches thrilled him. They fired his imagination about faraway places—places that held promise.

The harsh crescendo titillated him, whipping up emotions eager to burst free of his subconscious. Gus knew the highway was there to awaken him, to lead him away or lead him astray. It would spare him the crushing pressure of responsibility. It would free him from accountability. In some manner, he knew that in the worst of times it would provide a way out of town with life and limb intact. It would keep him a step ahead of paybacks from a past of bad checks, bad choices, and debts due in blood.

Only the road allowed Gus the option of never looking back, *and he never did.* For behind him, maybe within that hidden world just departed, a storm of memories threatened to rain down and drown any hope of peaceful sleep. Haunted nights were held at bay only by the light of dawn, where road met horizon and a rising sun. The highway was his salvation, always had been, always would be.

Gus did not *specifically* remember that the highway was his life. He did not *actually* recall that houses, apartments, hotels, and motel rooms were nothing more than doors that opened and closed in the darkness of night. There were no memories to spell out the reality that no matter how stationary, secure, or tranquil were these shelters, they were but addresses, stop points, pushpins stuck in a mental map that marked the extent of his wandering and foul deeds. For Gus, there was only a gut feeling that he was always on the run.

Maybe it was in hope of gaining a foothold or stopping his mind from spinning out of control that the *third* awareness, sight—the light of day—came to be. It might have been an hour, or a year, or maybe a thousand years later when Gus opted to open his eyes the least possible amount for the briefest of looks. A pale gray light hung over him as he pried his swollen eyelids apart. In ever-longer steps, he forced himself to investigate the dull illumination that his dilated pupils waded through without joy.

Now, Gus needed answers. He stared with clouded vision at a line.

Am I a chicken gawking at the center stripe of a country road?

No, he did not think so, not a chicken.

Is that a crack in the sidewalk?

No, he did not think so because he felt to be lying on his back looking at the sky.

Maybe he was looking at a power line high in the air, or a telephone line, or possibly cable TV strung overhead. Maybe a clothesline pulled taut between two trees, tight against a prevailing wind while awaiting the next wash.

No, there's no wind.

Whatever it was, Gus focused on the line as if beholding the fulcrum upon which all of reality teetered. The line might well have been the chain of a swinging watch, for his eyes held to it as if in hypnotic trance as he unglued his lips and peeled his tongue off the roof of his mouth. He sucked in a single spastic breath. It entered as a rush and exited as a pathetic moan. As his lungs filled, an onslaught of sensory input prodded him to realize a basic fact.

Apparently, I am alive.

The conclusion felt more remarkable than consoling. A faint smile crossed his face as the slits before his eyes closed. Gus preferred darkness to gloom. The mysterious line could wait until a later time.

It was only natural that upon his awakening, upon piecing together fragments of his visions, Gus would begin to align random thoughts into a string of sensibilities. He would wonder where the road had brought him. Where had he laid his weary head? Curiosity was merciless, and pushed him to give the day-world another chance. Again, his eyes opened. This time they shifted about.

Gus was now certain that he was alive, but that was about all he could figure. He was moaning and uttering nonsense as he confronted the all-too-familiar confusion that greeted him on this latest of awakenings. He was stiff; he was cold.

It must have been a hell of a night. Am I alone?

He slid his arm across—

What the....

Gus turned his head to the left and sighted along his outstretched arm. As the distance came into focus, he noted where fingertips ended; there were no sheets, no blankets—no whores. Only an uncomfortably cold, hard, and perfectly flat expanse of featureless gray concrete.

Gus rolled his head back. His upturned face stared into the gray heavens that now looked much more like a concrete ceiling than an overcast sky. As his focus sharpened, he recognized the line of an expansion joint passing directly above him. It annoyed him.

"Powerline? Huh. Clothesline? You *fucking* idiot," he whispered.

Gus's self-imposed reprimand reverberated more inside his head than out.

This is special. How not to start a day.

Braving a skull-splitting migraine, he raised his head to look around further. Randomly parked vehicles surrounded him. Apparently, he was lying on the inhospitable floor of a parking garage. His eyelids again drifted shut as his head dropped back to the unforgiving surface. He took another deep breath.

"So.... Where am I?" he asked aloud.

A garage floor. A good place to get mowed over by some idiot chick driver. No place to nap.

Unnerved by the thought, Gus slowly rolled over onto his belly. Soon after, he struggled to raise himself slowly onto all fours. Doing so took all the willpower he could muster. He swayed as he came to his knees. He fought for balance. Once on his feet, he wobbled like a spent toy top leaning in all directions as he battled to stay upright. Because he was baffled by a clumsiness that only added to his confusion, his questions quickly piled one atop another.

Did I get stoned last night? Am I still high? Am I alone in this place?

The only people lying about parking garages are druggies, expended prostitutes, and stiffs spread around to make a point.

His last insight jolted him back to something inexplicable. Filled with a sudden rush of urgency, he spun around as if preparing to dodge a bullet. He sought and studied the many dark crevices and shadowed corners that formed the perimeter of the garage. He changed positions to see around concrete columns and supports that obstructed open views. He listened with intent, but heard only the noise of the highway. Those reassuring sounds that calmed him. He stood unmoving a good while before he settled. He concluded he was not about to...

... take one for the team.

"Whoa!"

What do you mean, "take one for the team"?

Gus's eyes dropped from viewing dark corners to viewing his chest. He looked down his arms. He inspected the length of his legs, both front and back. He patted down his frame until certain he was not shot, knifed, tortured, or otherwise mortally wounded. However, that brought to mind a question in itself.

Why would anything like that happen to me?

Gus frowned. How odd to have been struck with these thoughts. Even odder was his not having any other thought—*of any kind*. The first wave of panic now washed over him. He dropped his head into his hands. He massaged his temples slowly with his fingers. He sucked in air until his chest pained. He let loose the breath hoping to relax and get past the hurt that was apparently clouding his mental acuity.

"Where the hell am I?"

Eyes again closed. Gus's hand fell away. He rolled his head around repeatedly, believing that at some point the doors to his memory would swing wide open and allow the light of his life to come pouring back in. He strained to remember what he had been doing the night before.

Where was I partying last night? Did I bone anybody? Something here's way outta whack. I never forget the faces of women I bag. Although... I might have slept alone. I mean, who wants to get laid on concrete? Good point—

The second wave of panic hit Gus head on. It was not fun. A massive rush of adrenaline caused him to tremble violently. This was not about remembering a great set of tits, where he was, or what he did last night. This was not about remembering everything; it was about remembering *anything*. Remembering what his name was, for example.

"...good point— For chrissakes, c'mon! Good point—"

Gus's hands quivered as if ninety years old. His insides filled with a poisonous mix of fear and apprehension. There was frustration, desperation, and finally exasperation. Thrash about as it might, his mind's search for anything, anything at all, the slightest clue to what was happening proved pointless.

Gus felt as if somebody had slammed a door shut behind him. He felt as if a lock had twisted to trap him inside one of those small roadside churches with stained glass windows. A sanctuary to the rest of the world, but a place Gus did not belong. A place that imprisoned him behind windows of color and texture that distorted every memorable image entering his mind. He could perceive light and dark, or smears of color. He could perceive movement and shape, but nothing more—nothing with clarity.

He strived to make sense of the present by busting open his past. However, "past" revealed little more than disjointed, incomprehensible artifacts, a realm void of anything useful. In stark contrast to the lack of any logical or coherent memory, his emotions, every one, remained intact—*especially fear*.

When a memory passed by close enough, or pressed up hard against the windows of distortion, it was easier to extract. Unfortunately, as if by design, that only occurred when he needed to recall what a thing was, or how it functioned, or how he should proceed to face his environment. It was never a revelation about him. He was to remain a stranger to himself.

"C'mon, c'mon, gimme a break. My... name... is...."

Gus was certain his name would automatically roll off his tongue, but no such luck. Then....

My wallet.

The thought brought a badly needed ray of hope. His hand raced around to the back pocket of his jeans only to discover it empty.

"Damn it!"

Then another thought as he stared across the sad assortment of long-unused, dust-covered vehicles, hoping to find one that was familiar.

Keys.

Gus checked his side pockets. They also were empty, not as much as a ball of lint.

"Figures," he whispered.

Gus's hand moved from the back of his pants to the back of his head—to the hurt. There was a massive lump. He looked down at the concrete pavement. He focused on a dot of pink gum. From there, his eyes followed paths of mini-cracks past chip-outs, oil stains, and irregularities of a well-worn surface. He scrutinized every square foot, groping for clues—something dropped, something discarded. Anything to shed light on his situation.

He arranged what little information he had into a reasonable order.

Okay. Let's think about this. One, I woke up on the floor of a parking garage. Two, my head is killing me. Three, I thought I had a watch, and that's gone. Four, my pockets are empty, my wallet missing. Can only mean one thing.

"I got mugged," he said in amused disbelief.

"I'll be damned. No wonder I'm thinking about guns an' shit. I got mugged." He rubbed the lump at the back of his head. "Pistol-whipped from behind. I'll be damned. I got mugged. Unbelievable."

Gus shook his head and quieted.

Hard to believe, but a pistol whipping would certainly explain my wound.

Ironically, instead of fright, the supposed misfortune greatly reduced his anxiety. He relaxed. He fell back against a concrete column and stared out across the parking garage. His mind was blank, but at least for now, at least for the first time, sensible explanations were at hand to calm his fears.

For Gus, the possibility of a mugging would work well until something better came along. It was more than just plausible. He was entirely comfortable with that idea, yet, he felt certain there was still something... something else—something weird. He felt... he felt... disheartened. In some strange fashion, he felt almost depressed.

He felt as if he had lost a great deal more than just his wallet. He could not remember. He could not put his finger on it, but it was there just beyond the tinted, textured, metaphorical glass sheet barrier. It was there just beneath the surface of his awareness. Yes, he was dead certain he had lost something major, something he would surely come to regret.

While pondering the extent of his losses, Gus stared blindly at a nearby wall. It showed the same gloomy, featureless gray as the floor, as the ceiling—as his recollection. He looked around the garage and it seemed darker. It felt to be filling with shadows. The place was suffocating. He tried to catch his breath. He inhaled as before, drawing air deep into his lungs before letting it slowly wheeze out. It suddenly seemed dank. The place was unhealthy.

Gus turned to face a slightly brighter shade of gloom that streamed down the slope of an entrance ramp. The weak light flowed into the parking garage from outside. Gus was gaining a sense of his whereabouts.

I'm below ground. I'm in a parking garage, or a storage garage below ground. This place is as depressing as a mausoleum. Get me some air. Fresh air. Get me some sunshine. Get me the hell outta here.

Sensing a mounting fear, Gus started for the ramp. He yearned for the meager light penetrating the coffin-like chamber he hastened to leave behind. He staggered up the incline. The climb was taxing. At the top, Gus swerved to find a wall against which he could lean. The only thing racing faster than his heart was his mind. Again, the questions.

What the hell happened to me? Where the hell am I? What was I doing last night? What's my name?

Again, no answers, only exasperation and distress.

"Damn it all."

Gus closed his eyes. He was panting hard and felt the sweat break out across his brow. He scraped his mouth with his tongue and spit out a thick, near dry wad of saliva. He waited for the pressure in his chest to pass. His struggle to scale the ramp nearly accomplished what the fear of a bullet had not.

Clearly, dodging exercise is as sensible as dodging bullets.

At this moment, Gus believed every word. His jaw hung slack. He drew in badly needed oxygen. His mouth dried further, but he relished the relief of open air.

Gasps for breath shortened and soon passed. Gus raised his face skyward in hopes of finding something in the brighter haze overhead that might press warmth into his chilled soul. A semblance of strength returned to drive his corpse-like muscles, stiffened by too much sleep on a cement bed. Slowly, he pushed himself off the wall and instinctively pointed his feet toward the beckoning sounds of a highway still unseen.

Having emerged from below ground, Gus assessed his surroundings. The streets were empty, not a soul in sight.

So... where is everybody? Where is this place?

The light of day felt scarce but for divided rays of sunbeams that fanned out to cut across an early morning sky. The glow was greatest in the direction of the highway sounds.

The radiance was far more appealing than the shadows at his back. There, a pallid, depressive atmosphere heavy with airs of persecution draped off structures to pool in the street and choke out life like bad gas. He wanted no part of it. Compelled to get away, Gus started forward along the abandoned street with renewed drive. There was no sign of life. It was deathly quiet, and he thought this to be another clue.

It must be Sunday—church day.

2

The roar of the highway was like nothing Gus had ever heard. It ricocheted off columned structures faced with cold but perfectly aligned rows of black opaque windows. Each window mirrored an opposing window in the crowded spaces overhead. The roar echoed in and out of alleys. It echoed up and down the vacant side streets he passed on foot.

The noise was to his ears what beacons of light were to the eyes of lost sailors. The sounds guided him through the unease of this place, this neighborhood that appeared heartless and uncaring. Every shadow seemed a threat. He felt exposed as if prey in the open, but at the same time tethered, or worse, bound helplessly to the shadows he was desperate to leave. He was not afraid, but the whole of it unnerved him to no end.

More than ever, Gus wanted to reach that highway. More than ever, he wanted to run to the sounds that heralded a better place, a place of life, a place fresh with movement and activity. With utmost determination, he sought what seemed the best means of escape.

Along the street underfoot, it appeared that ages ago something dark had dragged down anything remotely uplifting. There was no happiness. There was no soul. The street appeared to be little more than an extension of the deserted parking garage he had rushed to exit. He now walked a street that was as steeply inclined as the parking ramp, and it kicked his ass every bit as bad. The sidewalks should have been stepped. It was like scaling a cliff, an exaggeration to be sure, but a fight nonetheless. Everything encountered was an obstacle, either physical or mental—barriers preventing him from rising above the wretched place.

Gus looked back over his shoulder. He looked down into the encroaching gloom that filled the spaces, gloom that flowed like ground fog to cover his tracks. The street channeled a storm of familiarity that alarmed him. The storm felt like a lifetime of sin—obscured memories best left buried in the murkiness. Fear closed in to breathe down his neck, to whisper in his ear that the collector of debts was at his heels.

Gus shuddered. His hair stood on end. He was quick to turn away, to look ahead. He focused on the upper ridge lined with buildings like a fortress and the promising light beyond. With renewed vigor, he picked up the pace. Intent on leaving his apprehensions behind, he absorbed the sound of traffic. It was a perfect prescription for all that ailed him. It brought his soul relief, forcing out the pervasive sickness that worked to drain him.

An overwhelming sense of liberation accompanied Gus upon cresting the hill. He stood on the upper expanse, sensing the nearness of the highway. Before him stretched the shadowed side of a fortress-like row of structures that both lined the ridge and shrouded the highway.

The buildings pressed tightly against each other to enclose the rushing blood of life, the pulse of humanity. They stood as watchtowers high over the side streets that fell away into abandoned neighborhoods before disappearing in the distance and dark obscurity of lower elevations. They stood guard along the ridge to contain the light of life and drive back the dread of dark.

Gus's fixation broke only once, and for little more than seconds when he dared to look behind one last time. Briefly, he stared back along the narrow, barren side street that dropped precipitously from where he stood. It had been a tough climb out of the swirling nightmare.

From the height of the ridge, he viewed the flood of ominous churning mist that concealed everything, that lay claim to all, a mist that gave up nothing, including a part of him. He felt anything but free of the fearful sight, the turmoil, the trepidation, the unwanted connection to something in his past. The feeling was more than disturbing, it was crippling in every way.

"Good riddance to that hell."

Gus turned his back on the unholy place with great relief. Looking ahead, he knifed his way through the barrier of buildings. He managed his way forward until halting in stunned amazement. Now, only a single line of ramshackle shops and stalls remained. They butted up end to end to form an inner wall that bordered a highway unlike anything he had ever seen. A highway of such magnitude, a structure so colossal, it defied not only description, but also mental assessment.

"*Wow...,*" flowed a single fitting word of expression, nearly indistinguishable as it exited on his breath.

The highway was dead straight, straight as the beams of sunshine that traveled back along its length from the horizon. The morning sun obliterated all detail, turning everything ahead into black outlines and silhouettes. Its brilliance blinded all, and prevented Gus from defining anything in the distance before him.

Gus noted that the freeway was raised above all else. It stood proudly like a pier over water. Countless side streets similar to the one Gus had ascended from the parking garage scaled the steep slope at regular intervals for the whole of its visible length to meet the thoroughfare.

The highway shoulder was a wide, hard-packed dirt surface. It was dry and dusty due to a crowd of many thousands hiking upon it. The shoulder was a lateral extension of the freeway, just as flat and running parallel like three or four unofficial lanes for the benefit of pedestrians. Its edge dropped gently toward the inner wall of shanties and then leveled out beneath the fortification of buildings along the ridge.

Now, he absorbed all before him that was alive and upbeat. He looked in both directions along the highway and reveled in the midst of life that appeared nonsensically vibrant. There were thousands of people, tens of thousands, possibly hundreds of thousands streaming along the shoulder of the road.

Persons of every size and shape, every color, race, and age, streamed by. Families, couples, friends, people dressed in fashions as colorful and diverse as their heritage and homelands bumped into one another, all jostling for space and carrying on, all conversing in various tongues and contributing to the collective energy. The abnormality of the scene was astounding, entirely overwhelming, but certainly consoling to Gus when compared to the wasteland of empty streets back in the depths.

In spite of all the commotion and distraction one might envision, the highway is what most held Gus's attention. It surpassed everything. Having reached it, he stood with toes at curb's edge and studied every detail of the thoroughfare. It was like something out of an epic science fiction story. If symmetrical, he estimated the highway to be at least fifty or sixty lanes wide. He could not say for sure because it was difficult—no, impossible—to see anything beyond the center lanes.

The traffic on each lane moved at distinctly different speeds. Vehicles using the outside lane traveled the slowest, engaged in curbside parking, pick-ups, and deliveries. The closer a lane of traffic to center, the faster it moved, faster and faster until reaching the centermost lanes where vehicles were but passing blurs of motion.

They must be traveling four or five hundred miles an hour...or more, maybe way more.

Gus noted how speeding vehicles prevented anyone from crossing the street. Not that anyone would consider such a feat in the first place. It was simply too outrageous an idea. It was as if looking at a dozen airport runways butted up side by side with traffic every bit as fast and loud as jets under way.

Whereas it was impossible to make out the shape of anything traveling down the center lanes due to speed, the vehicles that traveled the outer lanes were nothing if not thoroughly bizarre. Buses and motorhomes converted for the long haul far outnumbered cars. Gus could only compare the scene to those movies made in the Australian outback.

Australia? How weird that he should suddenly remember Australia. *Balls ablaze, am I in Australia? I gotta be in Australia*, he thought to himself.

"No shit."

God, what a relief.

Gus wanted to drop to his knees and pray for forgiveness, pray for his memory... pray for his sanity.

This has to be another clue. Am I Australian? Am I from Australia? Is this Australia? Is it Sunday morning in...?

A horrific screech of brakes obliterated the tortured ponderings within Gus's head. One of the bus-like vehicles came to a squealing, pitching stop directly in front of him. The door opened and narrowly missed knocking him off his feet.

"Balls ablaze!"

Startled by the near miss, Gus was about to unleash the anger that quickly welled up. He opened his mouth but went silent after meeting the gaze, the scrutiny put upon him by the driver. The man's face was black as pitch and showed a bleach-white set of block teeth that stretched his lips thin as he grinned. His portrait appeared nested, settled upon an outlandish multicolored bandana wrapped repeatedly about his neck.

A departing rider stepped into the doorway, blocking the driver from view. Gus closed his mouth and backed away from the open door as the rider, an older man possessing a large and imposing frame, descended to the curb. The man was dressed in a collection of well-worn off-whites. White slacks, shirt, and jacket. A chiseled white beard. A ruddy, sunbaked complexion shaded by a white cowboy hat that shielded black eyes looking directly at Gus. The man raised his hat to acknowledge, or possibly study, Gus briefly before winking and turning away to disappear in the crowd. It was but a glance, but one that bore clean through him. It was chilling, and caused Gus to suffer a wicked rash of goose flesh.

Gus rubbed his arms briskly as he looked back at the driver, who yet sported the devilish grin. The man's eyes never swayed. The tension across his lips gave way as he spoke.

"You look like you could use a lift."

"Uhh...."

"Com' on. This bus has your name all over it. Get on."

Sorry, bud, but you're a bit too pushy, too demanding for my liking. Besides, I don't know where I am so why would I wanna jump on a bus or whatever it is you're driving?

Gus looked up at the marquee. It read BUS 7 CHARTERED.

Seven's lucky. A good sign. But I must be here because this place or someplace nearby is where I belong. There has to be a connection, some clue around here to who I am. I'd better stick around.

"Thanks, but no thanks. I'll walk," Gus answered.

"You're sure?"

"Yeah."

"Suit yourself."

As the driver reached for the lever that triggered the door to close, his eyes never left Gus. As if to mimic the rider in white, from behind the door windows, the driver also winked. The bus pulled out into the mayhem of passing vehicles, leaving Gus with nothing but portraits of two disconcerting strangers slotted into a perfectly uncluttered and useless memory.

Gus took to walking the bank. He gave thought to the bus driver, who was peculiar to say the least, but the old man in white haunted him. The man in white was long gone, but the image of his face looped through Gus's mind repeatedly. A snapshot of that moment when the stranger tipped his hat to reveal a swarthy, well-traveled, and weathered face... and the *other* thing. *A scar.* No, it was too perfect for a scar—*a tattoo.*

The tattoo that slipped into view beneath the brim of the old man's hat was one of a crescent moon breaking out over a bank of clouds... *right in the middle of his forehead.* It was plain as day, and worse, just plain scary.

If only I could remember, Gus thought.

3

BUS 7 CHARTERED disappeared into the distance, leaving Gus standing alone and wondering what next to do. He took stock of his surroundings. A river of humanity coursed alongside the road as far as he could see. Its momentum pressed, passed, and finally dragged him shoulder to shoulder alongside uncountable strangers in an intimate hustle. The flow wedged wayfarers between the curb and the endless inner wall of shanties butted end to end. The structures were irregular and appeared placed strategically to crowd the crowd by design. Hordes of travelers funneled past structures displaying goods for sale, food to eat, or services at call.

At the very least, the whole of it was entertaining. The bustle gave Gus a chance to enjoy a distraction from his presently screwed up situation. With an eye to the left, he watched the stream of vehicles race impatiently toward the horizon. With an eye to the right, he observed the myriad of items and services giving rise and reason to the infinite hedge of cobbled structures. The unending stream of peculiarities and strange sights laid waste to his sense of time. He continued to walk for what might have been hours gone days, gone weeks, gone time unknown. It was not until he spotted a half-full pitcher of water sitting on a table that he slowed.

Unlike most of the three-sided shanties that lined the highway, Gus happened upon a relatively open space occupied by a fully enclosed structure that resembled an old western tavern. The walls appeared shabby, cracked, and smeared with dirty pinkish-white stucco that fell away to expose unpainted patches of mortar. The place presented a sense of privacy and exuded a *members only* atmosphere that seemed to hold the world of hawkers at a distance.

However, the look was deceptive, reason being size. The building was far too small for members. The construction was no more than five long strides across the front. There was one door on the right, one window at center, one table beneath the window, and one old man under a white cowboy hat sitting at the table.

Gus stopped.

He recognized the man at once.

Balls ablaze. If it isn't that fearful old fart with the crescent moon tattoo.

There was one empty glass, one empty chair, and one inviting pitcher of water.

The second Gus laid eyes on the cool, perspiring pitcher, he grew oblivious to the crowds bent on reaching some unknown destination. He learned quickly that he was but one lost face in an infinite number of travelers. It was for this reason that his preoccupation was no longer with those colliding bodies, but with the lay of the land, the bigger picture. Therefore, it was somewhat startling when the old man seated at the table beneath the window singled him out to address directly, for if ever in Gus's existence he was a nameless nobody, it was now.

"You thirsty, son?"

At the mention of thirst, Gus's insides became as desiccated as the clay dust covering his shoes. The air was suddenly hot, very hot. His attention zeroed in on slices of lemon trapped amid chunks of ice jammed into that pitcher of water. With a swollen tongue, he licked his shriveled, paper-dry lips.

"I'm so thirsty; I couldn't spit to save my soul."

"Ha!" the old man cried out with a deep, resounding laugh. "In this heat, savin' a soul sounds like way too much work. Been a scorcher, yes siree—sweltering. If ya care t' join me, I believe this glass has yer name on it."

Gus could smell the chilled water, crushed ice, and vibrant yellow fruit as the mix spilled from the pitcher into a waiting glass. The old man returned the pitcher precisely to a wet circular track that marked its resting place. He then picked up the glass and offered it to Gus.

"Enjoy. Have a seat, my friend. Ease the load. Face it; the day's too hot an' too long t' fight the crowds or, as you said, save souls."

Gus lost all former unease about the old man as he grabbed the glass thankfully and downed the water without taking a breath. He lowered the glass to the tabletop. Gus stood suspended as the cool liquid slid down his esophagus, passed through his stomach, and spiraled deep into his gut. The relief was a godsend that made the heat markedly more bearable.

"Damn, that's good. I didn't realize how thirsty I was."

"Well, have some more. I got plenty."

The old man poured. Gus took up the invitation to sit, and collapsed into the opposite chair. As soon as the glass was full, Gus grabbed it and guzzled it down.

"Where ya from, stranger?" asked the old man in a deep voice.

"No idea. No idea at all."

"Humph. Don' mind me sayin', that's a bit odd. How 'bout, where ya headed?"

Gus shook his head.

"No idea."

Gus studied the bottom of his glass. His fingers dug through the ice to retrieve a couple cuts of lemon. He inserted them into his mouth as if fitting dentures and bit out the pulp. His face suffered the consequence.

"Oh, shit, that's tart. Mmph."

"Here, lemme top that off."

The old man filled his glass a third time.

"Thanks. Who knew water could taste so good?"

"I hear ya. On a day like this, ain't nothing better."

Satiated, Gus tossed the stripped rinds onto the table, sat back, and let out a moan. The two men sat quietly watching the assortment of strange faces stream past, leaving Gus to wonder.

Where in hell are all these people going?

"Sure are a lot of people out walking," noted Gus.

"Yup." The old man nodded.

Gus continued. "I been watching that highway since I got here, and I've never seen a road that massive. Must be fifty lanes or more... and the speed. Balls ablaze, how fast are they going in those center lanes? Three, four hundred miles an hour?"

"Fast. Faster'n you could know."

"I'll bet. It's unbelievable, that's for sure." Gus shook his head in wonder. "You know... the other thing that really gets me is the way everybody's going the same direction—one way. Everybody." Gus looked at the old man. "What's with that? Is it always like this? I mean, it's just so weird. Do they all come back, you know, walk in the opposite direction at night?"

"Nope. They don't come back at night. They don't like the Lingerin'."

The old man's comment was a bit odd, but something more pressing distracted Gus.

"Can I ask you a personal question?"

"Have at it," said the old man.

Gus snickered. "I gotta ask. What's the story behind that tattoo? I mean it takes serious balls to sew a patch on the forehead."

"Not a tattoo. No sir. It's a scar."

"What?!"

"Yes sir. A scar it is."

"No shit!" exclaimed Gus. "That's what I thought! But then I'm thinking, *no way*. Can't be. Too detailed for a scar. And you're telling me that crescent moon, the clouds and all.... It's a scar. Huh. Unreal. That has to be the most perfect scar ever."

"The only perfect thing 'bout my scar is the way the crescent moon matches the diameter of a broken beer bottle. A Goddard's Belgium Blue. Never saw it comin'. My shredded skin formed them clouds—broken glass skiddin' 'cross my skull."

"Jesus." Gus winced. "That must o' hurt. Bloody mess I'll bet. I'll say this, scar or tattoo, I knew there had to be a hell of a story behind it. Wow." Gus shook his head in awe. "Okay if I have another glass of water?"

"Help yourself. Like I said, got plenty more inside."

"So, what's the deal with your voice? You a singer or something? I mean, you should be. Like the best bass singer in a barbershop quartet. If you aren't, I can tell you this. You'd blow 'em away. Take my word for it."

"Nope, don't sing, never did."

"If I'm being rude, I apologize. I don't mean to be, but… you have throat cancer or something like that? You know… something that trashed your vocal cords all to hell? Well, I don't mean trashed…."

"Nope. Just a deep voice. Since I's a kid. Always boomed like an empty barrel."

"Damn. Take it from me; you should be making records. Changing the subject, you said, *you* got more water inside. The way you said it. That means like you own this place or something?"

"Yup, sure do."

"Damn. Must be one hell of a moneymaker. You're right in the thick of the flow. I mean, how do you get past this place without trippin' over it?"

"I s'pose the right man could turn himself a tidy profit. Never been my ambition. Don't need much. Money, that is. Prefer to sit out here an' watch the crowd go by. It's peaceful in a way. Always entertainin'. Never know who you're gonna meet. Take you, for example."

"I suppose. Hey, you need any help around here?"

"Help? Help doin' what? Watchin' people go by?"

"No. Hell no. Help, like working for you. You know, cleaning up... waiting on tables.... Well, I assume you have more tables inside."

"You wanna work fer me?"

"Sure, why not? No offense, but c'mon, at your age, you gotta be thinking about retiring. Maybe we could work something out and over time I'd buy the place." Gus looked around. "I like it. I like the feel of it. It's a great little place. Besides, to be honest, I got nothing better to do. Might as well hang around and do something useful."

"Humph."

"What? Bad idea?"

"Gimme yer name, friend."

Gus went silent. The two men stared at each other briefly, before Gus turned away. An expression of frustration crossed his face as he stared into the crowd.

"No idea."

"Meanin' what?"

"Just that. I don't know my name. I got some kind of amnesia or something. I woke up this morning flat on my back—on a parking garage floor, and couldn't remember my name. That's all there is to it."

"Recall where you're from?"

"No idea."

"So... lemme get this straight. Ya don' know from where ya come. Ya don' know yer name. But you're talkin' 'bout buyin' my place." The old man looked across at Gus through squinted eyes. "Ya get where I'm comin' from, son?"

"Yeah.... I hear ya. Sorry. I know. Sounds stupid." Gus let out a breath. "It was just a thought."

"Well, I give ya an A for ambition, but now I gotta ask you somethin'."

"What's that?"

"What about the Lingerin'?"

"The what?"

"The Lingerin'."

"What the hell's that?"

The old man removed his hat and sat it upon the table. He ran his fingers through a thick salt and pepper head of hair. His brow arched beneath the crescent moon.

"How long ya been here, boy?"

"I don't know. I can't remember anything before this morning."

The old man fingered his hat. He raised it off the table, picked at the brim, brushed away dust, and shaped it. He spun it in his hand as he mulled over some thought. He placed the hat back on his head, carefully positioning it before turning to face Gus directly. The brim sliced across the man's forehead, covering the scar and causing his eyes to look dark and sinister in its shadow. They bore through him—just like at the bus. Gus's hair stood on end—just like at the bus. The old man leaned in as if to stare him down.

"Tell me somethin', friend. What d'ya see behind me?"

The bar owner tossed his head back over his shoulder.

Gus moved forward in his chair to look beyond the old man. He looked down the road past a horde of faces stretching into the distance.

"I don't know. I see a shitload of people. All walking this way." Gus looked back at the old man's expression. "I take it, you mean besides that."

"What d'ya see in the sky?"

Gus sat up taller in his chair. He looked off into the distance a second time. He looked around. He looked overhead. He looked back at the old man.

"You mean like a plane or something?"

"No. I mean like the sky itself. The sky. Look at the sky."

Gus looked behind the bar owner a third time, now focused on the horizon.

"Well.... At the horizon, I see some nasty-looking storm clouds. Is that what you mean?"

"Yeah. Exactly. What're ya gonna do 'bout that?"

"Old man, I don't know what you're gettin' at. But if it's gonna rain, I'll step inside. Why? What are you gonna do?"

"I'm just gonna sit here, but I been through it a time or two. Sounds to me like you ain't."

"You're playing games with me, right? I can't remember anything I've done. I can't remember my name. But something tells me that a storm is rain and wind, some thunder and lightning; it comes in fast and moves out just as fast. So what's the big deal?"

"It's not that kind o' storm."

Gus looked back at the horizon. The clouds were black and swirling. They were coming toward him and the old man at a notable clip.

"Are you sayin' that it's full of... you know... ahhhh.... What are them things called? You know they spin in circles...."

"Tornadoes?"

"Yeah, tornadoes! That's what I'm thinking, tornadoes. Is that what you're going on about?"

"Oh, no-no-no. Nope. Not at all. The storm you see a-comin' is way worse than tornadoes. It's way worse than hurricanes or cyclones or haboobs. It's a different kind o' storm."

"What the hell, man? You playin' with me or what?" The two men stared at each other. "Hey, if you got something to say, old man, spit it out. Just say it. If you don't want me to work for you, just say it."

"It's full o' fear, son, an' I don't want ya t' work for me."

"What?"

"Said, I don' want ya t' work for me."

"No, the other thing you said."

"It's full o' fear."

"What's full of fear?"

"The storm."

"What the hell's that mean? *Full of fear....*"

"Jus' what I said. It's full o' fear."

"Fear?" Gus snickered.

"Fear. If ya never been through it, ya won't understand. It ain't like no regular storm. No sir."

"I thought you said you're just gonna sit here and ride it out. For a storm that's full of fear, don't look to me like you're shakin' much."

"Yup," the old man nodded. "I did say that. But I also said, I been through it a time or two, an' you ain't."

Gus looked past the old man. He studied the sky. A third of it was now lost to the blackish-orange swirling clouds. They did look ominous, that was for certain, but he looked back down at the old man calmly sitting in his off-white garb.

"Fear, you say. Humph. I'll tell you something, ya old geezer. You don't look too concerned. Not from where I'm sitting. And if you got the balls and whatnot to sit it out, so do I."

The old man started laughing. He lowered his hat onto his lap. Again, he ran his fingers through his hair. He looked up at the clouds. As if on cue, a large bolt of lightning arched across the sky. There was no thunderclap, only a static-like crackle followed by a ground-shaking rumble. Attracted by the flash of light, Gus followed the old man's gaze upward. He observed the threatening clouds as the old man quipped.

"I guess I'll get us another pitcher o' water."

The old man placed his hat back on the table. Gus did not respond. It was with a mild sense of apprehension that he continued to look upward. But that changed the second the old man rose from his chair and disappeared into the shack.

It was then that the black swirling nightmare flooded over Gus. He clenched his teeth. He clutched the arms of the chair. The fear was intense, inexplicable, but invasive to the extreme. He looked at the white hat on the table and desperately wanted the old man to return. And he did, but when he stepped back out of the shack, Gus went numb. He was speechless. He could only stare.

The old man towered over the table. He looked down at Gus and then out across the highway. He raised his arm and made a large sweeping arc. He spoke, but this time his voice went from deep, to ground-shaking, to soul-shattering. His voice pounded the inside of Gus's chest.

"They're all gone. You see. They know."

It took all the courage Gus could muster to glance away from what stood before him. In a fraction of a second, he observed that the highway was empty, not a vehicle to be seen. The crowds ceased to exist—vanished. There was not a sign of life other than the fiend standing an arm's length away.

The demon held up the fresh pitcher and began pouring the water across his smoldering chest and shoulders. There was no hint of a white jacket or shirt. There was no hint of clothes. Just black, cracked, crusted skin upon which the water vaporized on contact. Great clouds of steam rose off the creature, but the worst part was the sizzling sounds and smell of burnt sulfur that made Gus want to vomit.

The thing looked down at Gus. Its eyes were the color of burning coals. The crescent moon appeared white-hot behind black clouds.

"You want some more water, Gus?" he thundered.

Gus was unable to answer. The demon poured boiling water out of the pitcher into his glass. The cubes of ice exploded as the slices of lemon summersaulted in the overheated currents. The demon then emptied the pitcher's remaining water over his head and shoulders, again sending up large plumes of steam.

"Tell me something, son. If you were walking along the highway, what direction would *you* go?"

The demon turned to look into the storm. Gus followed the creature's gaze and understood at once why the crowds traveled in one direction. He trembled as he looked down the highway from whence came the maelstrom. He wished he had not. Moving slowly toward him along the shoulder of the road, past the now vacated stalls, was a scattered pack of black wolf-like creatures. They were sniffing, probing, dashing in and out of the empty stalls, clearly in search of something as they drew closer.

Gus watched the hellhounds emerge from the black turbulence that roiled across the entire width of the now abandoned highway, across all the lifeless lanes. The unnatural four-legged beasts appeared to be searching for leftovers, for signs of prey. Their heads hung low as if sucking in scents close to the ground. Their forms lacked light or color and so they repeatedly emerged and fell back to disappear into the black churning fog. What did not disappear were their glowing eyes, eyes identical to those of the demon that now bored holes into Gus's soul.

Gus looked back at the demon that awaited his answer. Finding a voice was impossible. Gus simply raised a hand in order to answer the question. He pointed back over his shoulder in the direction that crowds of people, all smarter than him, had headed in haste. The demon nodded in agreement and spoke knowingly.

"You don't sit and linger in Locum Veniae, my friend. There's no salvation here. Nothing exists behind that storm but fear, no highway, no nothing. There is only one direction, only one way."

The demon raised his hand and likewise pointed in the direction of crowds and traffic long since passed. Gus did not know his own name. He did not know from where he came. He did not know where he was or how he got here. What he did know was that he had shit all over himself and the demon was pointing. Gus jumped up from the table. Instantly, a thousand hellhounds raised their heads to focus on him.

Gus bolted. He ran for the last remnants of sunshine that remained far up the road beyond the hellish line of roiling clouds that stretched across the sky. He looked back over his shoulder and panicked. His movements attracted the beasts. He was certain they were altering their course, coming together, gathering speed to take him down.

Gus feared to look back a second time. He knew it was pointless. He knew he would never outrun the nightmarish creatures. He fled the openness of the highway and ducked between the stalls. He left the shanties behind as he bolted toward the fortress wall of buildings that edged the ridge. Gus stumbled down the steep grade of a side street. He disappeared into the shadows of structures built to last, maybe for eternity in obscurity. Ironically, the very gloom he had been desperate to leave now was most inviting.

It began to rain—*hard*. Gus scoured the street, straining to see through the mix of darkness and downpour for an open door, a haven, anyplace that offered shelter from the scavenging beasts. He came upon a formidable bank-like structure that appeared secure because of its barred windows and solid side doors. Frantic, he scrambled along its exterior walls feeling his way until finding the main entry doors. He pushed and pulled with all his might until the doors broke loose and slowly parted. Once opened enough for him to pass through, he slipped inside greatly relieved.

Inside, it was difficult to see, or maybe Gus saw with something other than his eyes. He studied the massive doors in search of the locking mechanisms, and when found wasted no time throwing the latches. Afterward, he stumbled about, circling the inside of the building, assuring himself there were no other points of entry aside from an emergency back-door fire escape. Feeling more secure after the perimeter check, he returned to the lobby. Gus leaned against a window ledge to look out glass panes divided by heavy steel bars and streaked by creeping raindrops. Sickened by anxiety and apprehension, he stood, waited, and watched. Had he watched for hours, days, or years, he could not say.

In those fleeting moments between downpours, Gus could glimpse along the street and up the hill toward the highway. It was then he spied the first set of fiery eyes coming over the crest to begin the descent. In quick succession, there came a second set, a third, a fourth, and soon too many to sort out. Even more chilling was the appearance of a single set of scorching eyes above the rest. Like a shepherd, the old-man demon with the white-hot crescent moon walked in their midst. He walked slowly toward Gus as he tended to his cursed pack of four-legged minions.

The rain started back up, falling by the bucket loads. Gus's blood went cold as he watched enormous clouds of steam rise off the demon and his rabid beasts. Not daring to move, he watched the ghoulish horde approach the building. Eventually, their lot arrived to stand before the massive entry doors. They, along with the doors, were now beyond the view of the window, and so Gus backed away from the ledge and moved across the lobby to observe the entry doors with intent. The large wooden slabs were all that separated him from the horror that stood opposite. He had no plan. He had no idea what he might do other than await the outcome.

Gus stared at the wooden doors. Had it been hours, or years, or eternities, he could not say. He waited and watched their composition change over time as heat radiating from the devil's spawn slowly turned the impenetrable panels of oak into charcoal. In stark contrast to the eternal wait, as quick as the snap of a finger, the doors dropped to the floor in a heavy collapse of ash and dust.

The demon and his hounds stood in the blinding downpour and sizzled. All eyes focused on Gus as the legion moved to enter the building. Gus fled toward a set of interior stairs that led him up many floors until arriving at a steel fire-escape door that opened to the rooftop. Barging through the portal and into the downpour, he crossed the flat roof until reaching the farthest parapet at the back of the building.

Taken by a delusional sense of hope, Gus leaned over the parapet to look down. He then turned to his left and ran along the roof's perimeter desperate to resolve the impossibility of his situation. If he had hoped to wake up from a bad dream, or find light or a fire escape, he was mistaken. The winds overhead were howling and blowing with enough force to push the rain up along the sides of the building. Gus slowed to a walk as his eyes followed the shower of rain upward where it disappeared into an atmosphere that was not as much clouds as twisting and boiling black currents.

Gus had no idea where he was to end up, but he knew this chapter was about to be closed. He came to a stop at the farthest corner of the roof and turned to look back into the murky fog slithering across the tarred, undulating surface. He watched as the muddy cloud was sliced open by blasts of steam that billowed outward toward him. Preceded by the smell of sulfur, in short time the first set of eyes emerged. Then the second, the third, and so on.

Gus watched the demon come into view. The rooftop was flooded with ankle-deep water that boiled at his feet. The sound of the sizzling body again drove fear to the core of his being. He turned from the nightmarish scene to lean over the parapet. He stared downward. There was nothing other than the featureless churning dark.

It's better to be blind.

Gus knew he would jump. It was his fate. The fact brought with it a sense of relief, a sense of peace. As soon as the demon's heat was upon him, he held out his arms and fell forward, allowing the poisonous winds to carry him to his death. During his last seconds, he hoped to see the memories of his life flash by before him. There was nothing.

Gus had no memories.

4

The return to street level was fast and brutal, but not at all what Gus expected. Instead of flesh pressing through a sieve of cobblestones, he plunged into the blind depths of deep water. He had landed in the flooded truck well of a loading dock. The impact knocked him senseless, but the water about his nose triggered an auto-response that kept him from inhaling. A few seconds later, his body convulsed as he regained his wits along with a sense of up. He began kicking, reaching upward with flailing hands for the feel of air.

Gus surfaced with a mighty gasp followed by uncontrollable choking that served to impale his lungs on broken ribs. It was painful to breathe. It was painful to move. It was painful to be alive, and so once surfaced, he did little more than float—and yell.

"Help! Help! Can anybody hear me? Help! I need help!"

At first, Gus twisted his head about in a frantic search of all four directions, but it was impossible to discern features of any kind. He listened for any hint of voices, responses to his pleas, but the storm concealed everything. There were no voices, no buildings to see, no shore, no sun, stars, or points of reference, nothing but the water immediately about him. Later, with the passing of time, his pleas stopped. He searched less often and resigned himself to an unknown fate.

Gus had no way of knowing how long he struggled to stay afloat. Time seemed somehow different in this place. Whether he bobbed in the flood for days, weeks, months, or more, he could not say. He might well have entered an ocean by this time. It was only when his foot struck something, dragged across something below, that he could appreciate movement. He realized that he was not just bobbing about in place, as if in the middle of a lake, but that he was moving at good speed. He believed himself to be floating in the runoff, the current of a swelled river.

Gus welcomed the thought of a fast-flowing tributary putting distance between him and the demonic horde. However, the sense of escape was short-lived, replaced by other thoughts that were discouraging in their own right. He wondered if he was floating away from the storm and toward the light, or farther into the clutch of his nightmare. There was no way to know. He could not tell, but the signs were not reassuring. The rain pelted him mercilessly. Its force agitated the water's surface to such an extent that to inhale without choking was a challenge with every breath.

Aside from the single strike to his foot, Gus remained oblivious to movement. The perpetual drifting in an endless racket of splashing water numbed all sensory input. His mind no longer possessed its bearing. There was no up or down, no in or out. There were only hallucinations, some confusing and insignificant, others terrifying to the extreme. The bad ones were so unnerving Gus wondered if they were really figments of his imagination.

What is that? There! There! It's watching me. Shit! I'm done. Dinner. Where'd it go? It's below me. Shit. It's gonna eat me. It's coming up. It's coming up!

"No! No! Get outta here! Go! Leave me alone. Ya hear me? Get outta here. Please, just go eat something else."

Gus shuddered at the thought of his legs leaving him to dangle so far above or below a line that separated the air world from the water world. He stopped kicking to avoid attracting anything horrific. He floated in a state of paralysis, in a sea of pure fear, exhausted by stress until coming to accept the futility of hope. If slated to be dinner for heartless monsters lining up and licking their chops, he could do absolutely nothing about it.

It is what it is, he thought to himself. *It is what it is.*

Gus remained suspended in a state of equilibrium, not rising, not sinking, not doing anything but float upon the overspill of a monsoon. His world was one empty of everything until disturbed. On rare occasion, a rogue wave would pass to startle him. The disruption was unwelcome, for not only was it a wave of water, but it was a wave of terror. Then there was only panic. His mind would explode. His head would snap in semi-circles desperate to thwart an attack from behind.

What was that? What caused that wave? Did it come a long way, or did something dreadful just swim by?

For Gus, status quo was good, even if it meant floating for infinity without any connection to reality. He wanted no part of change or any introduction to something unknown and alarming. Going unseen, going unheard, remaining hidden in the black fabric of the storm was safe. Gus liked safe, and he strove to become invisible.

For that reason, when Gus thought he had glimpsed something besides water before him, he was unnerved. All the flags and alarms swayed and sang out in his empty head. He supposed he saw something far in the distance. It was an impression of something large, possibly a hill or bank. It had been a fleeting image. A dream. Surely another of his countless hallucinations. Surely a swirl or formation of the black clouds that engulfed all.

Gus blinked hard to force out the water in his eyes, to dispel the illusion he suffered. It was but the briefest of sights. His inability to sense direction or movement left him with no idea if he was approaching this supposed vision, retreating from it, or simply passing by it in the eternal night. With an awakened awareness, Gus gained focus and grew ever more desperate to believe he had seen landfall. He spun himself around slowly, straining to see something other than the splash of rain-pelted horizons. His perseverance paid off when a brief flash of something large showed itself a second time.

Gus filed the near imperceptible scene to memory at once. He closed his eyes and studied the vision with utmost intent.

Am I dreaming? Is it an illusion? It seems different. I'm thinking it was real.

He reopened his eyes and glanced about. He waited. He studied the featureless dark. He waited. Hoping to confirm his intuition, he waited impatiently for the smallest sign.

There it is! There it is! Yes! I saw it. It's real. It's real. I saw it. I saw it. I know I saw it.

When the third appearance came, Gus compared it to what was in his memory and dared to believe that he was drifting closer to a landmass. He sensed hope. Hope was beyond his ability to control. Hope made him giddy, but at the same time frustrated him.

Don't fall for it. Big mistake. Get your hopes up. Stupid. Stupid. Dangerous to hope. Be smart. It's nothing. It's nothing. It's nothing at all.

It wasn't nothing at all. It was the first feature Gus had seen in a span of time he could not measure. The feature was mesmerizing. The visions of land appeared and disappeared so many times it was difficult to know whether he spied a single mass or a multiple of islands. The currents continually rotated Gus. Each time he would see land, he would have to reposition himself in hopes of looking in the right direction for the next appearance. In time, he gained confidence by learning the land was large, singular, and growing closer. With a little luck, a beach or bank would free him from his water-hell.

Determined, Gus focused on the only thing in his world that was not himself, air, or water. He soon realized that the flow was not only moving him toward land, but it was doing so quickly. He could no longer remember if his ribs were broken. He could no longer tell if he was or was not in pain. It did not matter. If he could get close enough to shore, he would use his arms and legs for whatever thrust needed to beach himself. Better to die of re-awakened pain, no matter now excruciating, than live lifeless.

Gus was fixated on land that was now a certainty. In the murkiness of black air and rain, it appeared somewhat lighter, somewhat sandy colored as if void or stripped of vegetation. The mass began to take form, shaping itself into a vertical wall, a cliff of sorts that protruded upward from his plane of vision. The closer Gus approached, the more formidable and unwelcoming were the mountain's dimensions.

Balls ablaze, that thing is high. There's no climbing that cliff. I can't see the top. I can't see ends. I can't see anything but wall, wall, and only wall in this storm.

The currents carried Gus closer. He observed a narrow dark band that stretched the width of the cliff as far as he could see.

What's that? What's that? That ain't cliff. And... that ain't water. Is that.... Oh, tell me. Please tell me that's a beach front. Please let that be a beach, a safe spot. I don't care how small. Anything that keeps the rocks from pulverizing me. Anything I can rest on. Anything between water and wall.

There was no sign of rough water or turbulence or pounding surf to pulverize him. All appeared peaceful. It was only a matter of waiting to arrive. Gus was grateful. In spite of the eternal storm, the hammering downpour, and the infinite water, he allowed his spirits to rise cautiously as the current carried him toward the landmass. Wishing to be prepared, he scrutinized every detail in search of the wrench, the pitfall, the unexpected glitch. Maybe it was not a good thing that he did, for he soon realized he had considered every setback but one.

A terror equal to the demon and dogs, to the unthinkable monsters swimming beneath, was suddenly before him. The dark strip at the base of the landmass was not beach, rocks, or vegetation. It was not anything. It was a black horizontal void. A cave. *Cave* was too kind of a word. It resembled a massive gaping mouth set wide open to devour whatever the currents brought to bear.

"No-no-no-no-no. Not this. Please, please, not this. Not this."

Gus cried aloud. He prayed to all and any god that would listen, but the hard rain drowned out any sound of his plea. There was no miracle. There was only the towering vertical wall and the infinite horizontal crack. He watched in numb, helpless terror as the massive opening sucked in all that the river brought—*including him.*

Gus entered the bowels of earth.

For all of the darkness mustered by the storm, it was like a white Christmas when compared to the black reserved for his grave. As he drifted deeper into the rock, the roar of the storm outside changed to sounds that lacked depth. It was the type of sound remembered from childhood when hollering through long sections of sewer pipe. The longer the pipe, the tinnier the voices, until sounds subsided and there was only the black and the silence.

Gus could only cry. He was insane with fear of what horrible end awaited him. The echo of his sobs grew closer the farther in he floated. He raised his hand and confirmed the expected. The worst. The ceiling was now less than an arm's length above the water that dragged him into his grave. Strange sensations caused him to sweep his hands across his body. Lumps covered his skin. At first confused, he soon realized that leeches were seeking him out. They were under his clothes. They were impossible to remove. Successive passes of his hand revealed the degree to which they swelled.

Whether hours, days, years, or eons, Gus did not know, but the sensation of a foot dragging across the cave bottom jolted him back to a semi-reality. It happened a second time and then a third. Above and below, the cave was closing in. When both of his feet touched bottom, he thrust his hands upward and planted them firmly on the ceiling. He halted his forward motion.

Why? Why prolong the inevitable? Why suffer? End it. End it. Let it go. End it.

Gus quickly appreciated how cruel was this joke, the likes of which only Satan could devise. Gus could stand firmly against the flow of water for as long as his strength remained. It was not long. And so Gus was forced to walk farther into the cave in order for his arms to drop lower and reduce the strain of holding them up.

By doing so, the distance was reduced between water and ceiling. When exhaustion finally won out, Gus had walked far enough to allow his forehead to press against the rock overhead and hold him in place. His arms dangled at his sides, swaying in the current. His neck cramped painfully under the strain.

Gus's existence reduced to a single objective—*breathing*. Keeping his mouth above water. Breaths.

One—two—three....

The small space open to him was a gravy of air and mosquitoes, mostly mosquitoes. Thick with mosquitoes. Millions of blood-starved mosquitoes. They covered his face like fur. They entered his nostrils. Their proboscises passed through his eyelids in search of blood within his eyes. He used his teeth to strain them out of his remaining gasps for air. They were far more of a torment than the bloated leeches below that competed for whatever blood remained. Gus wished desperately to pass out prior to letting loose his grip, prior to suffering through his own demise. The amount of blood lost to leeches and millions of ravenous mosquitos nearly facilitated his wish.

Nearly, but not quite.

5

The first awareness was pain. It seemed to come from every direction. It permeated his body—arms, legs, torso, but most notably his head. His head felt as if it was being hacked in two with a dull cleaver, brains splattered with every blow. For Gus, finding his way back through the labyrinth of oblivion grew more painful with every turn toward consciousness. Each step closer to light was a step that notched his agony upward. He understood he was suffering. He did not understand why.

At first, *pain* was the only term that came to mind. Initially, it best described what Gus believed was crippling him. As he gained additional wit, he sensed there was more. Pain felt to be one of many afflicting layers. It was closest to his awareness, and therefore easiest to label, but he sensed other levels of misery that existed deeper in his subconscious.

He might well have used the term *pain* to describe a physically excruciating change of state. Such as awakening sober to a decimating hangover. Such as vomiting for relief while trying not to break a rib. In any case, his was such a miserable state that for the sake of simplicity, *pain* would remain the preferred word. The only solace for Gus grew out of a gnawing fear, an awareness that he awoke just out of reach from something or someplace far worse.

At least, for Gus, there was one particular blessing in the waiting. It came as a chorus of mechanical sounds, un-pretty, disorganized, invasive, but in every way perfect as a distraction from his trauma. There was a reverb, an echo, to the sounds as if they raced across walls that surrounded him. An audience of one, centered in a large hall, he recognized the erratic melody as the noise of traffic.

Contrary to expectations, the sounds of traffic did much more for Gus than distract him. The barrage of highway sounds lifted his spirits. The song of the highway was nothing less than the song of the piper. It beckoned him to wake up, to leap up and away from the shroud of despondency. It unshackled his soul and set him free. It filled him with happiness and a will to thrive. He needed to find the light and instinctively willed his eyes to open.

Groupings of flutters followed by consecutively longer intervals marked progress in Gus's return to the brighter side of existence. How bright was altogether another matter. The last opening of his eyes was long enough to sponge up a sickly illumination that might have acknowledged he was alive, but barely.

As Gus regained an awareness of his being, he also gained a sense of curiosity. His brain was beginning to work as designed. In spite of the monotone of grays that surrounded him, details came into view. The foggy sky was acquiring texture. Lines were passing overhead. Beams were coming into play. The features were harsher and unlike the gentle mid-morning surroundings of overstuffed pillows and bedsheets.

Gus began working a clenched jaw. A vacuum held his tongue firmly to the roof of his mouth. It separated only for the sake of air wedging its way in. Delayed and long awaited, as if drowned and revived, he sucked in a single convulsive breath. It entered as a rush to press against his ribs and so remained until exiting in a death-like moan.

The inrush of air ushered his awakening to a higher level of awareness. An onslaught of sensory input assured him that although clearly not well, he was functioning. The thought was calming, and so the slits before his eyes closed. Gus wanted the darkness to strengthen his thoughts. He needed to focus on recent events. He awaited enlightenment, something to spell out where the road had brought him to rest his drunken or wretchedly stoned head.

Thoughts of the bedroom steered Gus to wonder if he was alone. Curiosity prodded him to give the day-world another chance. Again, his eyes opened. This time they shifted about. He rolled his head from side to side, but made no sense of what he saw. It was like an endless stretch of sheet pulled tightly over a hard bed. A bed with no pillows or blankets. No wonder his head hurt. No wonder he was cold. He was still moaning and uttering nonsense as he confronted the all-too-familiar confusion that greeted him on this latest of awakenings.

Balls ablaze. What a night. Am I alone?

Gus reached out to his side. He turned his head to the left and sighted along his outstretched arm only to see an uncomfortably cold, hard, and perfectly flat expanse of colorless concrete.

Ahhhhh. Do I know this place?

He rolled his head back. He stared up into the gray heavens that now looked much more like the bottom side of an upper concrete floor than an overcast sky. He pondered the line of an expansion joint passing directly above him. There was something about that line—*that joint.* Something that stirred something about something in the back of his head. Something like déjà vu.

Weird.

Gus pried his eyes away from the ceiling overhead. Braving a skull-splitting migraine, he raised his head to look around. Apparently, he was lying upon the inhospitable floor of a parking garage. His eyes drifted shut as his head dropped back to the unforgiving surface.

This was special.

He took another deep breath. Again, he sensed a familiarity with the place. He knew this place. He was sure of it. The familiarity was nagging. He paused, believing it was about to come to him. He struggled to bring it about. He waited for it to pop into his head, but nothing.

"So. Where am I exactly?" he asked aloud.

Gus's head pitched back and forth slow as an old lady rocking. His eyes rolled around like marbles on the loose. He assessed his surroundings. One thought prevailed.

A driveway is no place to nap.

He felt uncomfortably exposed. Gus turned over onto his belly and slowly raised himself onto all fours. He swayed as he came to his knees. On his feet, he struggled for balance, stumbling about with little if any control over his shaky legs. It added to his confusion. Gus had a head full of unanswered questions.

Balls ablaze, I'm screwed up. What the fuck did I do last night? Am I stoned? Am I still high? Why am I alone? The only people found alone on concrete are junkies and stiffs.

This last insight jolted Gus back to something inexplicable. Filled with a sudden rush of uneasiness, he turned around slowly to study the dark crevices and shadowed corners. He changed positions to peer around concrete columns and shafts that obstructed an open view. He listened with intent, but heard only the noise of the highway. Those reassuring sounds that calmed him. A moment or two passed before he settled.

I guess it's just me down here. Probably best that way. Safest.

Gus's eyes dropped from viewing dark corners to viewing himself. He looked down his arms and legs, twisted his limbs to inspect front and back.

Humph. No holes, no cuts, scratches, bruises—no memories....

Closing his eyes, Gus cupped his face with his palms. His fingers pressed his forehead and massaged it. He worked to wring out some hint of the night passed, some recollection of value.

What the hell's going on here?

Dropping his hands, Gus bowled his head about in large circles and listened as the sound of gristle squeezed by vertebrae snapped and popped. He believed at some point the doors to his memory would swing wide open and allow the light of his life to come pouring back in. Meanwhile, he felt uneasy, panicky. A mix of adrenaline and fear was building as if he had just broken the law and narrowly escaped.

Why the anxiety? Adrenaline? Maybe. Maybe not. Feels like something else. Something more. Something bad.

A lack of memory, no matter how short-term, was unsettling. He strained to recall what he had been doing the night before.

Where did I go? Who did I meet? Was I partying with friends or... was I on the run?

Gus was now fighting panic head on. It was not fun. His eyes narrowed as he stared hard toward a featureless wall.

"All right, that's it. Enough is enough." *This ain't about what I did last night. This ain't about remembering where I put my keys. This is about remembering my fucking name—remembering fucking anything.* "...for chrissakes, c'mon!"

Gus focused on the past as he tried to make sense of the present. But the past was a world of subconscious images spread helter-skelter through his head in fragmented, meaningless details. He felt mentally imprisoned behind panels of fluid, elastic color that misrepresented every image or view entering his mind. He could not see past or around the perceptions of light and dark, or borderless smears of color. He could perceive movement and shape, but nothing more, nothing with clarity.

"Balls ablaze, will ya gimme a break? My... name... is....

My wallet!"

The thought brought a fresh chance. His hand raced around to the back pocket of his pants. Nothing. It was as gone as were his memories.

"Damn it!"

The thought of keys came to mind. Gus's right hand slid around to his pockets.

Nothing. No keys, no change, no receipts, no anything. Nothing-nothing-nothing.

His eyes drifted toward the few cars scattered about the garage. They looked dusty, unused, as if abandoned.

"Gimme a break," he whispered.

Gus rubbed the back of his neck. He tried to work out both the tension and stiffness from sleeping on the ground. His eyes shifted to the concrete floor. He looked around.

Okay, buddy. Calm down. Just calm down. Get ahold of yourself. There's got to be something. Something dropped. Something tossed aside. Something, anything, that might help me work out this mess.

Gus analyzed what little he knew.

One. I woke up on the floor of a parking garage. Two. My head is killing me. Three. I can't believe I forgot my wallet, but it's gone. Four. Nothing in my pockets. Not a thing. Five. Tan lines on my wrist means I had a watch. Six. There's no tan line on my ring finger. I'm not married... unless I got married last night. I can't believe I wouldn't remember that. Seven....

Then came an idea worth merit.

Seven.... I got mugged. I got mugged....

"Balls ablaze! I got mugged! That's gotta be it," Gus said aloud. "No wonder I'm on edge and all panicky. I got mugged. Maybe they pushed me out of a car—left me for dead. That's would make sense. I guess. I don't know. Yeah, why not?"

Gus rubbed a tender spot at the back of his head.

Ooooooo. That don't feel good. Swollen. Must've slammed my head on the concrete. Or... maybe I was pistol-whipped. A mugging makes perfect sense. A pistol-whipping would certainly explain my amnesia.

Instead of being upset, Gus felt relieved. He relaxed. He leaned against a support column and stared at nothing. His mind was blank, but calm.

Gus could live with the idea of a mugging. In some peculiar way, it was a resolution to his problem that made perfect sense. He accepted it on a gut level. What did not make perfect sense was the haunting perception that this was only the tip of the iceberg. The loss of something on a much grander scale plagued him. It was not anything that he could finger or articulate. It was simply something he could feel. He feared it might be something devastating. Whatever it was, it remained just beyond his reach, most likely for the better.

To gain additional insight was about as impossible as eyeballing holes through the wall at which Gus stared. The wall, the floor, the ceiling, his memory, all shared the same featureless gray gloom. He looked around the garage and it appeared to be growing darker. It was filling with shadows. The space harbored an oppressive atmosphere that seemed bent on suffocating him. He tried to catch his breath. He opened his mouth, sucking air deep into his lungs before slowly setting it free.

"I gotta get outta here."

Gus needed the freedom of open space. A brighter light seeping into the garage attracted him as it flowed down an entrance ramp from above. Without thought, he already seemed to know that he was below ground level. He felt the pressure of the earth closing in on him. It was impossible to linger any longer. Something compelled him to move on.

Gus started for the ramp. He was reeling, trying to manage his legs. He staggered up the incline. The climb was taxing. It left him surprised at his obvious weakness. Once scaled, he backed into a wall against which he could lean. His heart pounded, raced, outpaced only by his mind, which continued to ask the same unanswerable questions.

What the hell happened to me? What was I doing? Where am I?

"Forget it, man. It ain't coming. Just get on with it. Just wait it out. Something's bound to come up."

Sweat broke out across Gus's forehead. As he waited for the burn in his lungs to subside, he closed his eyes and forced out all troubling thoughts. He rejected anything that interfered with calming down. He worked to settle himself. He raised his face and looked skyward to enjoy a brighter haze. Its meager glow improved his state of mind and tortured soul. His jaw fell away to free the air flowing to his working heart. In time, his gasps for breath shortened and passed. His strength returned. Shaky, but confident, Gus pushed himself off the wall. He set course for the beckoning sounds of a highway still unseen.

Having emerged from below ground, Gus instinctively studied his surroundings with a wary eye. The place was odd. Maybe most odd because it seemed familiar. He raked the buildings with his eyes. He sighted up and down the streets.

I swear I know this place.

He tried to imagine walking these sidewalks at some point in his past. It did not help. In his gut, he could feel the essence of this place but he could not put a name to a street, or a shop, or the neighborhood. *Neighborhood* was too good a word.

Where is everybody?

There were no neighbors. The streets were vacant, not a soul in sight. In fact, no hint of any life in any form. Not so much as a rat. Even the light of day felt scarce. The only blessing in this faceless place were rays of sunshine that emanated from beyond a ridge in the direction of the highway sounds.

Gus turned to look behind. The sight of a dark, uninviting fog jolted him. It clung to the structures and obscured the features at his back. Gus felt himself shrivel before whatever was creeping toward him. There was no explanation for his need to run, but he did, pushing forward with fresh determination.

6

The roar of the highway was unlike anything Gus could recall. It reverberated between the brick- and stone-walled structures that lined the empty streets. It brought badly needed sounds of life to a lifeless world. The growl of an unseen road seemed to be the only thing that could penetrate the oppressive gloom. If echoes passed along the alleys, or up and down the vacant streets, they went unheard but for the force of their source.

Gus shuffled his feet faster and faster toward the sounds that beckoned him. He was fearful that it was all a mirage, that it might escape him. He feared the last bus would pull out without him. He needed to see the jostle of crowds, the jabber of shoppers and merchants—a place fresh with movement and activity. A place that was obnoxiously full of life.

The lifeless street fought to keep him. It battled him physically. It grew steeper by the step, far worse than the garage ramp that first stole away his strength. He now walked a street that caused his legs to burn. While his mind was fearful, urging him to escape, to run, his body pressed him to halt. The sidewalks should have been stepped. The struggle was nothing short of climbing a cliff, a fight to the finish. Whether physical or mental, it was ironic that the road leading to a better place was also the obstacle preventing him from rising above the vile environment that fought to keep him.

Gus dared again to look back over his shoulder. He peered down into the encroaching gloom that filled the spaces and flowed like ground fog to cover his tracks. The sight channeled a storm of familiarity that frightened him on a deeper level. It was an unreasonable fear. Something about the clouds closing in brought on a cold sweat.

Whether a lifetime of sin or a single terrifying memory that remained hidden for the sake of sanity, he did not know. He knew he was afraid of something breathing down his neck, whispering in his ear that the worst of the worse was drawing near. Taut as a drum, Gus's skin caused every hair on his body to stand on end. He shuddered. His throat tightened, constricted by panic. He was suffocating in air thick with dread.

Gus spun to face the light. He bolted forward to fight the climb, the pain, the fear—the forces holding him back. His eyes, opened wide and wary of the unseen, remained fixed on the crest of the hill and the only hope he could reckon. He soaked up every note of the overpowering roar of traffic. The din increased to deafening magnitudes. He could feel its protection. It blanketed the sound of his shuffle from whatever listened. It kept secret his movements.

By the time Gus crested the hill to stand on the upper expanse, his legs felt heavy, immovable, as if cast in lead. By contrast, his heart felt light as a butterfly, fluttering like the wings of a bird. A burden of unknown quantity, but massive to be sure, was leaving his charge. Now, he needed only to proceed forward through the sprawling row of structures that he was certain marked the way of the thoroughfare.

The erections were akin to castle walls that shunned all things fearful and offered hope and confidence to those within. Believing his goal was within reach, he walked forward with a confident, measured pace. His eyes took in every revealing detail until the vistas beyond were his to witness in full.

Gus stood in stunned amazement. His eyes never wavered from the wonder before him. It was beyond anything he might have dreamed. It defied description.

"Balls ablaze. Where is this place? Who would believe this? Why am I here? Is this home? Do I know where I am?"

He voiced the questions aloud, but the thunder of traffic drowned him out. The questions were far more significant than Gus realized. On a conscious level, he merely asked about a scene that left him speechless. On a deeper level, a subconscious level, in spite of the odds against it, he considered the possibility of past connections.

The highway was a marvel of engineering. Dead straight. Straight as the strand of web above a dangling spider. Straight as a sapling's reach for the sun. If a curve, a bend, or a dip existed, it was lost in the distance along with files of speeding traffic. The moving world headed directly for a brilliant rising sun that obscured all signs of their existence.

Unwilling to risk staring into the radiant orb, Gus lowered his gaze to the area before him. He noted that the freeway stood proudly above the line of shanties. The shoulder on his side of the road was flat and wide, and could easily have handled two or three, maybe even four, additional lanes of traffic had it been paved. It fell away to the level of ground that supported both the shanties and taller buildings afar. At the outermost walls of the taller buildings, the ground dropped off cliff-like to enter the regions of darkness.

Countless side streets, similar to the one Gus recently battled, intersected with the highway at regular intervals. Each side street struck out perpendicular from the highway to pass first through the shanties and then the multi-storied structures that marked the fall of the cliff. Much like the steep banks of a river or lake, or the shores of a sea, those structures on the ridge confined the black waves of dread to the lower elevations.

"What happens in Hell stays in Hell. Thank god for that. Humph."

Gus turned his back on the broad underworld of profanity. Now, he welcomed all before him that was vibrant and cheerful. As his soul lifted, his step lightened. He meandered along the highway and allowed the flood of humanity to usher him away.

Immersed within the safety of an unending parade of people, Gus felt secure. The massive display of life buried the day's earlier plague of fears. Thousands of people from every race, every walk of life, traveled the side of the road. Families, couples, friends, all bumping into one another, all jostling for space, laughed and conversed in various tongues. The scene was straight out of a drug-induced fantasy. It was astounding. It was overwhelming. Compared to the black void of the depths, it was a crisis of pure joy.

And yet, in light of the joy, the jubilance, the frenzied conversation and riotous laughter, it remained the highway that reined in Gus's attention. With toes to the curb, he studied everything about the thoroughfare. It was science fiction at its best. It was the future now. If symmetrical, he estimated the highway to be dozens of lanes wide. In fact, it would never be more than a guess because it was impossible to see beyond the center lanes.

Those center lanes ferried vehicles at an alarming rate of speed. Gus figured hundreds of miles an hour…or more, maybe much more. Blinding speeds assured nobody dared cross the road. Not that anyone would relish the idea in the first place. It was simply too far a distance and much too dangerous. He thought of himself trying to swim across the Mississippi, dodging barges at every stroke. It was foolish and suicidal at the least.

The screech of brakes obliterated Gus's mental ramblings as a bizarre bus-like contraption approached with an apparent determination to run him over. He leapt backward from the curb as an opening door passed by, missing Gus's head by mere inches. The driver, sitting in a captain's chair, was about to say something but didn't get the chance.

"Need a—"

"Balls ablaze, man! You *tryin'* to kill me or what?"

"Truly sorry about that. Thought you were in need of a ride."

"Not on the grille! Ya damn near ran my ass over."

"Said I was sorry. You need a—"

"I don't need anything. Now, get that goddamned heap out of my face! Get it outta here!"

Gus slapped the side of the opened bus door with the palm of his hand. He struck it hard enough to unfold and snap shut almost as fast as an expression of anger streaked across his face. His temper begged the driver to reopen the door and his mouth. Gus was itching to come unglued.

The driver did reopen the door, but to Gus's surprise, the driver said nothing. The man simply smiled as he stretched his neck while adjusting the fit of his multicolored bandana. In the meantime, eight or nine passengers standing in line to exit now stepped down to merge with the crowd. As they passed, they looked at Gus with some disdain. There were three boorish-looking men, a couple of women, a blonde and a red-head, among others. They all shared one thing: they were clearly unimpressed with his show of anger.

Once the last two passengers disembarked, a woman followed by a small Asian man, who nodded toward Gus as he walked by, Gus stood alone to stare down the driver. Instead of encouraging a row, the driver winked at Gus and broke into a ridiculous grin that stretched across his face. The driver hammered down on the gas pedal and never once looked forward while pulling away from the curb to merge with traffic. His eyes remained locked onto Gus as he disappeared into the flow of speeding vehicles. Gus made note of the glowing green letters scrolling across the marquee, which read *BUS 7 CHARTERED.*

As if to spite the driver, Gus turned to walk away in the opposite direction. He struck out against the flow of life. He may have lost his memory, but something of his character appeared to be intact. He was not one easily pushed around. He disliked getting bumped or jostled. He expected his space, and spared no effort to make the fact known.

"Hey! Watch where you're going," he fumed.

"Sorry."

"Hey! D'you mind?" Gus barked.

"My apologies, sir."

"What are you doing, man? You blind or what?"

"So sorry, it's the Lingering. You know."

Gus was getting hotter with every step. He was no longer swearing *under* his breath.

"Get the hell out outta my way!" he snapped.

"Pardon me. Gotta go, I gotta go."

Gus could feel himself boiling over.

"Go *where,* for chrissakes?" he hollered.

Gus turned to await a response from the last person to careen off his shoulder. It never came. He stood half-twisted about, watching the stranger disappear into the distance before flipping the man off behind his back.

"That's for you, buddy."

With nothing to hold back a bad attitude, he resumed his belligerent charge into the oncoming crowd. The more Gus pressed against the crowd, the angrier he became and the louder he cursed. The more resistant the crowd, the more determined he was to plow his way through. A buried facet of Gus's nature was to push back, to be contrary. That concealed part of him lived for confrontation. It needed the fight. It thrived on the rush. Opposite of most others, for Gus, a fight relieved stress. It made him feel alive. It made him competitive to his last breath, to the death if need be.

To his delight, Gus sensed a win. He expected nothing less. A faint smile crossed his face for having overcome the odds. At a thousand to one, he watched the wave of humanity circle around as he stood his ground. He refused to give an inch. He stood. He glared. He dared. Whether hours, days, or years, he did not know, but eventually the crowds thinned as if conceding the battle. Their numbers fell to handfuls. Space opened all about him. Finally, he was able to breathe freely, or so it seemed.

Once Gus settled down and recovered his senses, he realized that as his anger retreated, fresh concerns advanced. One facet perfectly replacing the other. It began with an inner fear, something in his gut. He could not explain it. Likewise, he could not explain the expressions of alarm smeared across the faces of what few stragglers remained to scramble past ground Gus proudly held.

What's with these fools? Gus thought with a frown. *They look terrified. Maybe I got this wrong. Maybe they're not running to catch up. Maybe they're running to get away.... Running from what? They keep looking back. Humph. Strange. What's with that?*

Only when Gus looked past the last few faces of dread to search the distance did he consider the sky. Only after his fit passed along with the last of humanity did he fully appreciate what blanketed the distant horizon. Something that started out as a horizontal band of dark clouds easily dismissed changed into numerous churning towers webbed with frightening flashes of light and soaring to incalculable heights. Their innards were a muddy orange glow of strobing explosions. It was as if Hell had flipped above ground.

For reasons that defied his understanding, the clouds instilled an immediate and intense terror that shriveled his entire being. He shuddered for reasons he could not comprehend. He looked to the passersby for a possible explanation, but there was no longer a crowd for him to stand against. There was no longer any living thing before him. His guts twisted into a single massive knot that might well have doubled him over.

Something's tellin' me something, and it can't be good.

Gus was convinced this storm was not about rain or thunder. It was not about the threat of tornadoes or straight-line winds. This was something far worse.

This is end-of-the-world bad.

There was no desire to question, no need to know what or why. There was only a primal instinct to survive. Gus spun around, and like all the others, wearing faces smeared with terror, he held his breath and ran like hell. He was not about to be the last man running.

7

Gus strained his eyes to keep in sight what few scattered souls remained ahead. Their numbers were few and distant. In groups of two and three, they left the shoulder of the abandoned highway to follow the side streets, disappearing between the shanties and buildings beyond. Gus's lungs felt shredded as he struggled to catch up. He closed in on the last visible group just as they passed through the tall buildings that edged the cliff. He watched with distress as the last two or three strangers headed down toward the gloom.

"No! No! Don't go down there! Stop! Stop! Stay with the road! Stay with the road! Follow the highway! Stay with the road!"

Gus gave his all in an attempt to dissuade anybody who might listen. He continued to yell, but his cries faded before his exhaustion.

"No. Don't go that way. Don't go down there. Don't...."

Gus had to stop. He was sick with fatigue. Panting hard, he bent over, bracing himself with hands upon thighs. Slowly, he dropped to his knees.

"Why?"

The question was barely audible. Gus looked up. A young woman accompanied by a small Asian man half her size stood before him. The two had stepped back from the gloom to hear him out. They acted like a couple, or close friends. Their faces appeared troweled with grooves, expressions of fear and confusion. The woman spoke.

"I can't decide if we should go down there or not. We've gone up and down two or three times. Now we're up. Tell me why we shouldn't go down there, but make it fast."

Before Gus could speak, another voice sounded from the gloom. This one unseen and unpleasant.

"Yeah, tell us why we shouldn't go down and take cover."

Three hard-looking men had followed the couple out of the dark mists. The leader of sorts wasted no time addressing Gus.

"Okay, bud. Let's hear it. You got ten seconds to explain yourself. Spit it out or shut the fuck up before you get these people killed while they listen to your crap."

"You can't go down there," Gus insisted.

"Yeah, we got all o' that. Now tell us something we don't know."

"I'm trying to tell you, it's not safe. I mean, I don't think it's safe. You have to follow the highway. The light. You have to stay with the highway and—"

Gus grew apprehensive as the three walked directly toward him with a menacing demeanor. In spite of his temper, he held his tongue when the stranger in front interrupted him.

"What d'ya mean, ya don' *think* it's safe? Ya don't *think* it's safe?" asked the loutish-looking leader.

"Do *you* know what's down there?" asked a second man.

Gus advanced his concerns with care. "No, not exactly. But I just came up from down there, and it's really uhh, uh...."

"Uh? Uh, what?" asked the brute in his confrontational manner, or maybe it only seemed that way to Gus due to a fear shared by all.

"Look, I know I'm not being clear. I uh... don't know how to answer. I'm just sayin' I don't think going down there is a good idea. You need to stay on the highway—stay ahead of the storm. Catch up with the light."

"Well, let me ask you something, stranger. See that?" The man pointed at the sky above them. Everybody looked up. Gus observed the roiling brew moving overhead. It was unnerving. "You're way too late to catch light, buddy. You think staying up here is a good idea? You honestly think it's smart to stay on the road out in the open with that over your head?"

"I'm not sure," answered Gus.

"Not sure? Not sure! There's no time for not sure. Can't you feel it? Where's your instincts, man?" The brute stopped talking for a second, just long enough to study Gus. "You don't even know what that is. Oh, man. You don't even know what the fuck that is. It's the Lingering, man. It's the Lingering!"

Gus struggled to turn away from the vision of fury bearing down on them in order to face the brute. The light was fading fast, and he felt pressed to focus all attention on the sky. Options were about zero, but he loathed any thought of going back down into the gloom. He finally looked at the five now looking at him and awaiting his reaction.

"The Lingering?" Gus repeated.

"Holy shit, man. Yeah. The Lingering. The Lingering. You can feel it here. Right here in your guts!" The brute slapped his torso hard with the palms of his hands. "I know you feel it. I can see it in your eyes. Hey, maybe you got balls the size of boulders, but I don't. I admit it. So, stay up here and face your fate, but do it alone. Don't drag these folks into that hell. Join us if you want. Your choice. We're outta here."

The man ended the conversation abruptly as he turned to leave Gus to his decision. The brute broke into a run. The other two cohorts were fast behind, heading down the side street without hesitation. Within seconds, they were back in the gloom. Without warning, the woman ran off after the men. Only the Asian remained to consider Gus and the fear of the storm. The Asian looked at the sky and the impending hell about to break loose. He shook his head, signaling Gus not to risk the maelstrom.

"Lo ti' wai' a-roun'." The man shook his finger. "Rook." The man pointed at the sky. "We go. Ya? You lo stay. You fo-rrow me. Come. Come. Fo-rrow me. We go togetter. You fo-rrow me laow o' you wi-oh die. I sink you wi-oh die."

Again, the Asian wagged his finger as he spun about and chased after the rest. His small frame was quick to vanish.

For Gus, explaining his dislike for the gloom was straightforward. He had just come out of it. The memories were fresh. It was not a pleasant place. On the other hand, he hardly doubted his deep-rooted fear of the sky. The stranger was not kidding about gut feelings. Indeed, his guts were squirming like an agitated pit of snakes. He could feel the fear carving up his insides, but he had no idea why. One last look overhead convinced him to go with the lesser of two evils, to go with the crowd, to seek shelter in the gloom. There was a sense of security in numbers. One thing more, he thought he recognized these people as having gotten off the bus. It was a long shot, but maybe one of them knew something about him. He broke into a run.

"Wait up! I'm coming! I'm coming. I'm coming!"

The farther Gus ran downhill, the harder it was to see. Glimpses of the group would come and go. At one point, Gus lost sight of them too long for comfort and found himself overcome with anxiety. He focused on the sound of voices that echoed the distance of an empty school corridor. He hustled fast as he dared and was relieved to catch up with the couple.

A group had formed into a queue of panicky people waiting to enter a building. Gus was the last person in line. It made his being back in the gloom worse. He disliked his inability to see what lurked at his back. He wanted to push forward, to reach the middle, to immerse himself in the safety of numbers. He wanted the support of a hundred other eyes. Instead, he looked over his shoulder into the mists, repeatedly searching for signs of unwanted movement.

His guts continued to squirm. Gus wondered what was worse, that which was behind or that which was ahead. Restless, he complained aloud mostly to himself and the Asian man standing second to last in line. The Asian was also scanning the surroundings as if expecting something to leap out of the fog.

"What is taking them so long to go inside? I feel like shark bait standing here."

"Ya. Lo goo. Lo goo. Soon we go in-si," said the Asian.

The line barely moved forward. It might have been hours, or days, or centuries for all that Gus knew. However, the queue did dwindle over time, growing shorter, until he remained the only person outside awaiting entry into the gray featureless structure. At this point, anxiety forced him to turn his back to those in line and face whatever might be out there watching him. In the herd, whatever was last was lost.

The group spoke only in whispers, which served to accentuate the oppressive atmosphere. From where Gus stood outside, the whispering sounded more like an ongoing hiss. Fortunately, enough space opened for Gus to enter the shelter. He was grateful beyond measure to finally stand inside the building and relax.

Inside, there was no light, and yet there was. A near non-existent bluish glow appeared to seep between the walls and circulate about the rooms. There was no discernable source, but it was sufficient to illuminate the corridors once Gus's eyes adjusted to it. The line continued to move forward in somewhat less of a single file. Yet, most had one hand clenched to the shirttail of another and a second hand outstretched to forewarn of unseen obstacles.

It was not long before the crowd stopped to gather in a space large enough to hold their number. Gus estimated the gathering to be about twenty or thirty, possibly a few more. They reminded him of passengers departing a chartered bus. Chatter was incessant. It revealed the collective uncertainty about what to do next.

Gus followed the Asian, staying close behind as the man moved to stand alongside his female friend. The three of them did as the rest. They waited for someone to make a decision. Gus hoped a natural born leader would step forward with an air of hope. Someone who would pass out instructions and make demands that the rest would be eager to fulfill in order to lessen the rampant anxiety. Someone of strong character. Maybe the brute and his cohorts. For now, there seemed to be no such person, or if there was, news never got back to him.

While Gus waited, he noticed a number of people waiting to use a restroom. The sight made him realize how bad he had to piss. He left the Asian and his female friend to end up last in line for a second time. To make short the wait, he addressed the man standing ahead of him.

"So tell me, friend, do you have any idea where the hell we are?"

"Nope."

"Have you heard anything about what the crew's gonna do next? Anybody in command here or what? Do you know?"

"Not really. But you can bet we're not safe from the Lingering as long as we stick around here. We're headed deeper. You wait, you'll see. By the looks of it, they're getting about ready to head down now. I think they just stopped a moment so everybody could catch up. They won't be hangin' around here. Not this close. You'll see."

"The Lingering. Yeah, everybody's been talking about that. Do you mind telling me—"

Gus stopped mid-sentence as the man broke away to enter the restroom. Gus waited for him to exit. He wanted to know more about the *Lingering*, but the man shot out the restroom in a different direction. Everybody sensed a stirring, the group growing restless and about to move on.

Gus shrugged and entered the restroom. As soon as he pulled open the door, the smell nearly dropped him. It was noxious. He used an elbow to pry open the door enough for him to lean into breathable air. The open door might have allowed the blue glow to enter, but not as far as Gus could tell. He could only just make out the white shape of a toilet bowl and nothing else of the room. His lungs rebelled, forcing him to lean out for another breath that failed to stop him from gagging. A blind man could tell what he stood in. He touched nothing. He unzipped his pants, pulled out his penis, and let loose. He was not sure if he was pissing in the pot or on his shoes. He hardly cared. Well, he cared a little, but mostly he wanted out of a room that wrapped around him tighter than a shit-filled tortilla.

Indifferent to modesty, Gus burst out of the restroom gasping for air before his pants were zipped. There was no chance to be embarrassed. Not because it was dark, but because there was no one about to look at him. The crowd had moved on. The adrenaline was quick to arrive. He felt the panic starting to slosh about his insides. The only thing worse than being in this place was being in this place alone.

Risking a fall, Gus sprinted in the direction where he had last seen the group. He stopped to look in all directions. They were gone.

"Damn."

For a second time, Gus found himself listening for the sound of voices. He strained to hear the hushed whispers of a group that survived in a perpetual state of fear. The idea of raising a voice or calling out was unthinkable. The whole point was to hide, to shrink from the awareness of the Lingering.

Whatever the hell that is.

Gus tried to calm himself. He tried to think rationally. It was difficult. He did not know who he was, or where he was. He could not remember anything but... but....

That guy said we had to go deeper to be safe.

Gus looked about the room, and based on the position of the restroom, he was able to sort out the direction from which he came and the direction the crowd must have headed.

That way. They must have gone that way.

The slope of the floor supported his conclusion. With arms outstretched, he started in the downward direction as quickly as he dared.

In time, Gus determined that he was searching through something more than just a building.

This has to be a chain of basements or something strung together because these corridors go on forever.

Another alarming aspect of this place was that although there were plenty of steps to descend, every passage between staircases sloped downward. It made the rate of descent significant. He felt like he was negotiating a footpath down the side of a mountain.

Balls ablaze, this going down is creeping me out. What goes down has to come up. Going back up these corridors will be as bad as scaling the road from the garage to the highway. The longer I walk, the more tired I'll get. The more tired I get, the easier to walk downward. The farther downward, the harder back up. It's like getting sucked down into quicksand. Wonder if I'll ever get back up to that highway?

Where the hell did those guys go?

Gus stopped. He listened. He went on. The only thing worse than understanding the perils of going deeper was suffering the anxiety of doing so by himself. It was far too easy to lose one's mind in this place. In the dark, the voice of another could very well be the only voice of reason. He was desperate to find someone. In spite of his fear to go deeper, he quickened his pace.

Gus rounded a corner and glimpsed a flicker of white light far in the distance.

What was that? I'm too far below ground to see daylight. Wasn't daylight. Too white. Bluish white. No warmth. Besides it was strobing. What strobes? Mechanical stuff.

Whether he walked toward the light for hours, days, or years, he could not say. However, as Gus neared its source, he observed the flickering to be emanating from an opening, possibly a doorway or corridor on the right side of the passage a fair distance ahead. The light was striking the wall opposite. It was the reflection, and not the source of light that he saw from afar. A welcome surprise awaited Gus as he closed in on the supposed opening.

Voices!

He first picked up a drone of echoes, but was unable to make out words. The cadence was one of speech, broken by what was clearly laughter. He was heartened, and picked up the pace. There was no hesitation in his step as he rushed forward, at least not until puzzled by the sight of dank, peeling, olive-green wallpaper. It covered the side of the cave near the light source. It had a heavy Victorian look to it.

With the wallpaper now at his left, Gus came upon a doorway to his right. The door was open and exposed the interior of a room in shadow. A single light glowing dull amber barely reached drab grayish-green walls smothered in dust and indistinguishable black damask patterns.

Peering into the room, Gus noted that the voices were coming from a vintage television. It was a steel box-like thing with rabbit ears resting on top that extended out a good arm's length in each direction. The screen was small and square-ish with rounded corners. A large golden "V" stood proudly upon a grille mounted on gold-colored cloth.

A colorless image lacking warmth jerked across the glass bubble-like surface. Thick black diagonal lines split the frame as they moved slowly from top to bottom of the archaic cathode tube. The contrast between bright whites and dark shadows hurt his eyes. They projected posterized movements that jittered across the dreary walls.

Gus shifted his focus from the television.

Why is there a kitchen window on that wall? Underground? Weird.

The double-hung window centered on the wall to his left was not the type of window used for observing workers in a plant. It had curtains like a residential window. At first, Gus saw nothing outside the window but the black of night. Then beyond the panes of glass, a sense of movement riveted his attention. Gus stared through the pane into the dark beyond.

I woulda swore I saw something move past that window. This place is so bizarre.... Maybe an overactive imagination. Maybe.

The harder he looked through the window the less he saw. Whatever Gus thought moved did so at the periphery of his vision, glimpsed from the corner of his eye.

Could that storm, that black roiling mess, somehow be outside that window? Am I somehow back at the surface? Is that possible? Maybe my senses are getting screwed up down here. Maybe I've been going up. Fooled like one of those gravity rooms at a carnival. Maybe I have walked to the side of a hill. That would make sense. Yeah, that could be. What a relief that would be.

Gus returned his attention to the room and noted that the only things of consequence besides the television and window was a large over-stuffed chair that faced away from the door and toward the TV. It had enormous wing-like side panels.

Is anybody here? Anybody sitting in that chair—a maintenance man living life in isolation, perpetually on call—a security guard monitoring the void beyond the window?

Gus was uneasy. He had no desire to interrupt anybody's privacy.

"Hello? Hello?"

Even worse, he did the unthinkable. He stepped through the portal. Gus entered the room out of desperation. In contrast to the dank chill of the underground passages, a welcome warmth greeted him inside. As he neared the high-back chair, he looked down at a small round wooden side-table situated alongside the right arm. There was a delicately laced doily centered upon it.

Gus cleared his throat and called out in a respectful tone.

"Excuse me. Excuse me?"

"Yeah."

The response startled Gus. Maybe, because of the doily, Gus expected to hear the voice of a woman.

Definitely not a woman. Hardly sounds like a man.

He was at once wary, but pursued his business.

"I apologize for the interruption, sir, but I noticed your door was open. I was wondering if you happened to see or hear a group of people pass down this corridor."

"I did."

Gus was so overjoyed at the news, he unintentionally blurted out his relief.

"Oh, thank god for that. That's great." Recovering quickly, he continued. "I don't suppose you can tell me which way they went or how to get out of here. I am seriously lost."

"Lost? Where were you going?"

"You know, outside. Up, I guess. Upside. Topside. Whatever you wanna call it."

"I don't understand."

"Oh. Well, long story short, I got separated from the group I just mentioned. Don't ask me how. I went to use the restroom, I came out and... I don't know. They were gone. I've been trying to find them but I am *so* lost.... I mean, I am *totally* lost. Not just a little bit, I mean *totally*. So, here I am. If you could just tell me which way is up, or which way they went, I'll be on my—"

"I don't understand."

Gus frowned. The response was all wrong. A red flag began to unfurl.

"Oh. I'm sorry.... I thought I was clear. I'm lost and—"

"Yeah. I heard that. I don't understand where you would go if you left here. Where else is there?"

The sound of the occupant's voice bouncing off the walls or coming from the walls or from inside his head or whatever, coupled with quizzical answers, sent that red flag in Gus's head from waving to whipping every which way. Instead of responding, he stood in place with mouth shut, silent, confused, and contemplating.

As if to speed up the process of enlightenment, an eruption of sizzling sounds followed by a large plume of steam soaring toward the ceiling caused Gus to jump back away from the chair. Immediately thereafter, an appendage of burning embers and black cracked skin oozing red liquid fire reached out from the chair and placed onto the doily, perfectly centered, a large near-empty pitcher of water, ice, and slices of lemon.

Terror paralyzed Gus. His legs locked and seemed unable to move him. It took all the will power he could muster to flee the room. He felt as if thick strands of glue pulled his feet to the floor. The more the fear, the stringier the glue.

Gus had no idea what sat in that chair. It made no difference. His subconscious, his instincts, ordered him to run. It was not a matter of choice. The fear was as intense as the storm overhead.

8

It was impossible for feet to move faster. Gus ran like a spooked stallion, like a rat racing for a hole. Downward he ran, always downward, descending in a perpetual fall. Whether he sank for days or weeks, or longer, he could not say. He had no sense of time. No sun or moon arced a sky to offer clues. This was a lifeless place of unnatural light, of unnatural night. A cold colorless stone tomb bathed in barely perceptible hints of blue. There was one other thing, something unseen. Rolling randomly through the passageway from end to end, in complete contrast to the crushing silence, was a rumbling.

The sound slowed him. Gus no longer ran like a maniac. He did continue to jog, putting as much space possible between him and that *thing* watching television. He kept up the quickened pace until arriving at another of the many sets of steps. Its presence braked him to a walk and eventually he halted.

"Balls ablaze. I'm not liking that," whispered Gus.

Unlike all steps before, this was a circular stairwell. These steps were dangerously narrow and hugged the inside wall of a sizable, round, silo-like room as they spiraled down to disappear into obscurity. Gus stood at the top landing, and peered over the edge. There was no railing. One misstep would end his life. He edged closer. He stood with eyes fixed on the bottomless void of the waterless well. It was while scrutinizing the depths that a flicker of light shredded the darkness far below.

Gus tensed up. Vivid memories of light flickering from an old television remained fresh and raw. He could still see the harsh black-and-white images playing across the drab-papered walls. He was yet unnerved and possessed little desire to revisit that scene.

Spare me a round two.

For now, the light below him was too weak and infrequent to assess. It barely reached the upper landing. Gus seated himself cautiously on the ledge and looked down past his dangling feet. He waited for another flicker of the light, and then another. If he waited for hours, days, or years, he could not say. Time was hard to figure out. The light was hard to figure out. Even the rumble was perplexing. Sometimes it preceded the faint flashes of light, sometimes not.

In spite of grave apprehensions about both the light and sounds, Gus was unable to turn back. Back was impossible. Before him, although farther down, was activity of some manner. At this point, even horrible activity held some attraction after wandering for so long alone.

Gus rose to his feet. He moved to press his back tightly against the circular wall. He slid along that wall until lowering his foot to the first step. He tested it. He lowered his body. Slowly, he took another step down, followed cautiously by another. Wood, steel, stone, at such heights, he did not trust the integrity of anything. For that reason, the descent went at a snail's pace for what seemed to be ages, a long time. There were no side passages, no doors, and no way to alter direction. There was only down.

Always down.

During the descent, Gus saw nothing. He noted nothing. There was nothing besides an awareness of the deep, the faint blue light, and the increasing intensity of the flickering light and random rumbling.

Thunder and lightning.

That is what came to mind. His fractured memory revealed memories of thunder and lightning. As always, he remembered whatever he needed to function. He remembered everything aside from who he was.

"It can't be lightning," he said aloud. "How could I see lightning at this depth? How could I hear thunder? Impossible."

Then came a concern.

If thunder and lightning could reach me down here, then what about the Lingering?

After counting many hundred steps, Gus lost track. He lost track of time. It may have been days, or weeks, or even years before he neared the bottom of the circular stairway. During his time sinking, the growing intensity of the flickering light eventually exposed the floor of the well. It was now two or three hundred steps below his feet.

After descending all but the last three steps, he halted. He was wary. He could see six passages surrounding him at the bottom of the well. Each headed in a different direction. Unlike all the corridors prior, these were cave-like tunnels, chiseled out of rock. He noted that light only illuminated one tunnel—the tunnel that rumbled.

Gus eased himself carefully off the last step. He tested the feel of the stone floor until convinced there was no trickery. Gaining confidence, he set off to enter the cave that channeled the light. Its attraction was impossible to dismiss. With him went the fear that whatever found might well be worse than existing alone, even if forever, but his yearning for companionship was unbearable. He was willing to take the risk. He placed one foot before the next, repeatedly, a thousand times, a million times, all the while staring into the gloom, drawn by shards of intermittent flashes until he heard a voice.

He stopped.

Gus held his breath. He closed his eyes and listened. He waited. He turned his head slowly from left to right, trying to zero in on what he thought he had heard. He opened his eyes and quietly exhaled. He strained to see farther into the gloom. At that moment, there came another flicker of light. This time it was bright enough for him to see clearly how the cave ahead pitched downward. The walls narrowed at the place where the floor fell away. There were large boulders strewn about. It had the appearance of an unused passage that led to even deeper unthinkable depths. Gus ran forward as fast as he dared until reaching that place where the floor pitched steeply downward. There, he stopped. He listened. He waited.

As hoped, in time there came another strobing of light with the expected rumbling. Only this time, the rumble finished with an air of voices. A rush of hope filled Gus. He was both thrilled and perplexed because the light, the rumble, and the voices reached him from behind. He twisted his head around, searching for details in the passageway. He saw nothing. Puzzled, he turned about, intending to walk back up the grade, but discovered to his amazement that there was no up. The floor of the cave continued downward. The fact would likely have driven Gus mad, had it not been for the joy of voices that overshadowed all else.

As he backtracked along the passage, another flicker of light appeared. This time he focused precisely at the place where the light entered the passageway. He picked up his pace. His right hand dragged along the rough stony surface of the wall. As he closed in on the area of light, an unexpected vertical streak of brighter gloom showed itself on the wall to his left. The brighter gloom emanated from a narrow crevice.

How did I miss that? How was that possible? How many more of these narrow passages have I missed in the dark? Maybe that's how I got separated from the group. Maybe they passed through a crevice looking for the source of the light, a crevice that I missed.

Gus faced the narrow passage and placed his hands on the interior walls to assess width. There was not much. Gus turned himself sideways in order to enter. The fit was close and unsettling. The walls of the passage were not jagged or rough-hewn like the cave, but relatively smooth and uniform, similar to the corridors of upper levels. He thought of these walls as the footings of a foundation.

A protracted strobing of light backlit the far end of the crevice. More importantly, no rumbling ensued, but rather a collection of voices that flowed freely between the walls. He heard them clearly while standing in the crevice. The group was near, but he feared to raise his hopes. He found himself trembling. He called out meekly at first, but quickly changed his tune, hollering for all he was worth.

"Hey! Can you hear me? Hey! Can anybody hear me? Hello!"

He listened. There was nothing. He hollered again.

"Hello! Hello! Can you hear me?"

Again, he listened. There was nothing. Not even the random mix of voices that he had heard moments before. His heart sank fast. He felt the sweat of desperation erupt across his forehead. He was anxious. He couldn't allow himself to fail. He couldn't fathom the thought of losing this chance to be found, and so he hollered with renewed determination.

"Can anybody hear me? Can anybody hear me? Hello! Hello! Can you hear me? Lord, let someone answer. I'm begging."

There was no response. Gus laid his head against the wall. He was so near the others. He stared along the length of the crevice. He feared the impossibility of squeezing his way through the cranny. His heart was heavy when a single voice, that of a woman, reached his ears.

"Hello? Hello?"

Gus exploded to life.

"Hello! Hello! I hear you. Can you hear me? I'm here!"

"Yes, we can hear you. We can hear you. It took us a moment to figure out from where your voice was coming. Are you alone? What's your name?"

Gus cried silently. The crevice channeled sound, and her voice carried through the crevice as bright as sunlight.

"Yes. I'm alone. It's just me." Gus gave thought to the brute calling him Bud. It was as good a name as any. "Bud. I go by Buddy. I don't know where I am. I've been trying to find you guys for a long time. A very long time."

Gus had no idea how long he had been alone and searching for the others. Time escaped him. It might have been days, or weeks, or years.

"Can you make it through the crevice?" asked a man. "We will wait if you want to try."

"Please wait. Please don't leave. I'll try. I don't know. It's narrow. I can try. Just don't leave. Please don't leave! Even if I die, please don't leave. Don't leave me to die alone. Please, I'm begging."

"We won't. Don't worry. We'll wait. We'll wait for as long as it takes," assured the man.

There were numerous voices in the background. All were faint, but powerful for a soul in desperation. Gus was ready to claw his way through the crevice if need be. He studied the walls more by feel than sight. He could not see far into the crevice unless the bright light came flickering through. One thing was for sure, it was not going to be easy physically or mentally.

Gus started. He stuffed himself farther into the crevice. After about twenty feet, claustrophobia began to take its toll. He felt blessed that he could not see his situation clearly. In fact, he found it better to keep his eyes closed. He slid his hands along the wall and kept his chest pressed tightly against it. He tried to be calm while praying that he might never feel the opposite wall brush against his back. He continued to pray and slide for what seemed like months, or years, or maybe longer.

"Are you still there?"

"Yes," came the answer every time.

"Please don't leave."

"We won't. Be careful. No need to rush. We'll wait."

"I'm coming."

Sliding hands and chest along the wall, Gus inched his way toward the voices. A wave of welcome relief swept over him when he realized that he could see a hint of brighter gloom that outlined the opposite opening to the crevice. Now he could make out the movement of people beyond the crack when the flickering light erupted.

"I can see you! I can see you!"

"That's good. Take your time. We'll wait."

Gus could feel tears leaking into his eyes. The only thing that mattered was to be in the company of others and spared the loneliness of his hell. He was now able to discern the movement of people. He was now able to follow much of conversations spoken in normal tones. In fact, he could make out whispers, which proved to be gut wrenching.

"It's too narrow. He'll never get though. He'll never make it. Can we widen it? How?"

The hum of conversation moved past him as did the wall against his hands. He refused to accept what he was hearing. Step after careful step, he inched his way closer to the group.

And then... he felt it.

The back of his shirt lightly snagged the surface of the opposite wall for the first time. Out of dread, he stopped at once.

Was it a lone high spot? Was it just a fluke, or is this the end? Maybe I just swayed.

Gus dared a couple more steps. The drag worsened. His question was answered proof-positive. There would be no reaching the others. He took a deep breath, which only emphasized the press against his ribs. At that point, full-blown claustrophobia engulfed him. Swamped with adrenaline, he shook uncontrollably. Sweat broke out across his forehead and flowed down into his eyes. He hyperventilated, each breath expanding his chest to press harder between the walls and exacerbate his condition. The futility of his situation caused him to sob and cry out.

"I can't do it. I can't go any farther. It's too tight. It's the end."

Panic ruled Gus. He could feel the paralysis of fear overtake his body. Only for the sake of a voice....

"Listen, Bud. Relax. Just relax. Tell me, can you get lower? Is the passage wider down by your waist or your knees?"

The question distracted Gus. Focusing helped him evade the insurmountable fear.

"I don't know. I would have to back out. I'm pretty much stuck here."

"All right, back out. See if there is more space by your feet."

Following the advice of the crowd, Gus backed away until he reached a place where the wall released his shirt and afforded him some freedom of movement. However, dropping to his knees was impossible. There had never been room enough for them to bend. He had only one option. He had to lower himself onto his side. Using hands and elbows as brakes, he allowed himself to topple over in a controlled manner as best he could.

Gus lay on his side. It was not good. There was more distance between the walls at this lower level, but without the ability to use his arms, all attempts to move his body forward were extremely difficult. He managed to get his arms over his head and wiggle. Inch by inch, he wiggled forward. He did so for hours, or days, months, years, or maybe eternity.

"Keep going, Bud. You're getting close. We can almost reach you."

Everybody now spoke in a natural voice. No hollering. Nothing that might elevate anxiety. Gus wiggled until the walls again prevented him from moving any farther.

"That's it," Gus cried. "I'm stuck. I can't go any farther. I'm stuck. I can't go forward. I can't go back. I can't breathe. Please don't leave me," he whispered in a voice of defeat.

"Just relax, Bud. First, we won't leave. And second, you're only a few feet from us. We'll figure out something. We'll get you out. All we need is for you to relax. Do you hear me? Bud? Do you understand?"

"Yes," he answered with eyes closed and lips pressed to the ground.

The crowd did their best to soothe Gus. They discussed the situation among themselves and then one came to the crevice and spoke.

"We're going to send someone in to help you squeeze through. He's small boned and shouldn't have any trouble reaching you. Hopefully, he can pull you through in some fashion. His name is Sang.

"Now, listen to me, Bud. Just try your best to relax. Sang is going in now to meet you. Do you understand?"

"Yes."

Sang entered the crevice and did reach Gus. He grasped Gus's outstretched hands and the two men locked wrists. Gus was unable to contain his emotions at the feel of Sang's grip. It filled his soul with relief. Sadly, the relief was short lived. Sang attempted to let loose his grip. An effort that Gus fought the best he could.

"Hor on, Bu. Hor on. Le-lax. I com-ba'. I com-ba. I pom-ise. I com-ba."

The Asian worked to free himself from Gus, but Gus refused to give him up. He remained clamped onto the small man's wrists.

"Eet goo'. Eet goo'. Okay?" said Sang with confidence. "I ge-you-ou'. I com-ba'. I pom-ise."

"No, don't let go. Please, don't let go. Don't leave me."

"Lo pro-brem. You okay. I com-ba'. I com-ba. You see."

Gutted by doubt, Gus eventually let go, allowing the man to work his way back to the opening. A few minutes of discussion ensued. Gus watched the movements beyond the crevice. He also happened to notice that the light was getting brighter in the chamber beyond. There was something more than just the gloom.

The man blocked some of the light as he reappeared in the opening, but this time he was also on his side. He was placing clothes on the ground, carpeting it with shirts, blouses, and the like. He then placed his arms over his head. Another man carefully pushed him into the crevice. He slid forward until he reached Gus's hands.

"Pu' tis a-loun' yo' han'. A-loun' bot' han's."

Gus wrapped the straps around his wrists as instructed. The Asian checked the straps by feel and then turned his head back over his shoulder and hollered out.

"Okay, pu-oh! Pu-oh me ou'!"

As others pulled on Sang's feet, he allowed the belts to slip through his hands. He moved away from Gus until free of the crevice. The belts had been buckled together to form long straps that reached Gus from outside the crevice where a man called out.

"Okay, Bud. We've got you secured to the belts and we're gonna pull gently to drag you out. You will probably have to wiggle to help lessen the drag. Are you ready?"

"Yes."

"Okay, then. Here we go."

With great care, men in the chamber began to drag Gus toward them. The plan did not go as well as hoped. The walls were unwilling to give up their hold. They pressed tighter until the squeeze was unbearable. Each exhalation shrunk the size of his chest, allowing him to move farther forward, but causing him to breathe shallower until he could feel himself suffocating. He barely held enough air to voice the words of his plea.

"I... can't... breathe. I can't... breathe. I can't...."

9

Gus opened his eyes. He was laying on his back listening to the cheer of a crowd. People were standing in a tight circle looking down at him. They quietly applauded his return to consciousness. It took Gus a moment to remember what had happened, to remember the crevice, and, most importantly, to realize he was free. He sat up. Those standing near slapped his back and congratulated him on his success. Sang was standing next to him. Gus reached for Sang's hand and clasped it tightly between both of his.

"Thank you, Sang. Thank you. I can say it a thousand times and you will never know my appreciation."

"Eet ok. You goo'. I do lo-tin'. You tank Car-ly an' Jer-ly fol' pur-ring you ou'. I lo can do alone. Eet no zus' me."

"Yes, yes. I understand. Thank you, Carly and Jerly, or whoever that was, whoever you are, for everything. Thank you for saving my sanity."

"I'm Cary, and you're welcome."

"I'm Jerry, and the pleasure was ours. Glad to see you're safe."

The bystanders laughed. One moved in closer.

"Can you get to your feet?"

Gus worked to get up. He felt a little shaky but stood without help. Another reserved cheer went up from the crowd. Gus smiled a smile that was difficult to see, but felt by all.

"I guess I'm okay. Where are we?"

"We're not sure," said Cary.

"Why is it brighter in here? I noticed that from inside the crevice. What's the deal with the flickering lights? It reminds me of lightning."

The crowd went silent.

"It is lightning," offered a voice in the dark.

"Oh, my god. Thank you, thank you for that. Please tell me we're free of this grave. Lightning. I thought it was lightning.

I kept telling myself that it seemed like lightning and thunder. I just didn't dare to believe it. I couldn't figure how— Wait.... I don't get it. Are we no longer deep underground? How is that possible?"

Another voice responded. "There's a shaft up ahead."

"A shaft? What do you mean a shaft? A shaft to the surface?"

"Yes."

Gus was stunned.

"To the surface?" he asked again in disbelief.

"Yes," affirmed a few.

"We think so," said another.

The idea of returning to the surface was a hope all but lost until this moment.

"Balls ablaze.... Is there a ladder or some way out?" Gus asked, barely able to contain his excitement.

"Yes."

"Can we get out? Has anybody gone?"

There was a notable hesitation to respond.

"We don't believe it's possible."

The answer tamped down the joy. Gus could feel the somber mood as he glanced at the shadowy figures surrounding him.

"But you didn't say it was impossible. You didn't say that. So, is there a plan?"

This time there was total silence. Gus knew whatever came next would be crushing. He struggled to keep his hopes from being dashed. After coming through the crevice, this seemed unfair, or worse... cruel.

"I take it there's no plan."

"It's an awful long ways up," a woman answered.

"I'm not surprised," said Gus. "We're an awful long ways below ground."

Again the silence.

"I don't know if I'm groggy in the head or what, but I can tell that I'm missing something. Something big. What is it you don't want to tell me?"

"Do you want to see the shaft?" someone asked.

"Hell, yes, I want to see the shaft. After feeling buried alive in that crevice, I wanna see the shaft more than anything in life."

The gathering broke apart and drifted along the passageway. In short time, the crowd came to a set of large doors. Gus determined they were made of iron or some kind of metal. He noted that time had frozen the right-hand door shut. The left door was partially open but immovable. Gus followed as one by one the procession of people squeezed through the partially opened portal. Finally, Gus had his turn to step across the threshold.

On the other side of the doors was a different light, unlike the blue light that permeated the depths. This light was slightly more natural, faint but natural, faint but uplifting. From high above, it reached down to the bottom of the shaft and bathed Gus in its feeble presence. His smile was short-lived. The snap of harsh light flooded the well and obliterated the pervading blue glow. He was unused to light and found himself instantly blinded.

Gus waited impatiently for his night vision to return. At that point, he looked up and what he saw was an opening so small due to its distance that it explained the apprehension of those standing about him. The distance to the surface was staggering. He knew he had been walking downward for a very long time, but to see the jagged streak of light snap past the opening to the shaft was nothing if not utterly sobering. He was lost for words.

"Now do you understand?" asked one of the men.

Gus stared upward. He remained silent.

"There is no way the women in our group would ever be able to make that climb. Frankly, I don't believe any of the men could. I know I couldn't, and I'm one of the stronger men. The fact is we're too weak. We're just too weak. A climb like that would be certain suicide."

Gus grabbed the styles of the ladder and climbed up a couple of rungs.

"It'll be a challenge," Gus conceded.

"Challenge?" The man snickered. "When I think of challenge, I think of chess. This, my friend, is hopeless. This is the devil's work. A tease. A view of the world through a tiny window for those locked eternally in Hell. The pain your hands and feet—your legs, would have to endure is unimaginable. I suspect your muscles would cramp to the point of being useless long before you made it a quarter of the way up. So there it is. Our window to freedom is one that we can look through, but never reach. It's like looking through the porthole of a sunken ship."

The group stood quiet, not a whisper made. For Gus, mentioning the devil immediately brought back visions of something unholy seated before a TV. It was enough to convince him that he wanted out. He would rather die trying to exit through this shaft than spend eternity sharing this gloom-filled grave with a demon. If there was a way out of Hell, this shaft looked like the best bet. If this was the only bet, he had no choice but to take it. Gus addressed the crowd, but it was a comment meant for his own benefit.

"I can only speak for myself. I can only say that in my mind, this place is unholy. Why is it we don't get hungry? How is it possible that we aren't dying of thirst down here? We're prisoners. We're trapped in some strange state of suspension. Maybe the blue glow keeps us going, keeps us nourished. I don't know. I really don't care. I just want to know why."

There was no answer given, no answer to echo through the dark of the tunnels. Gus looked back up toward the spot of light.

"How far up do you think it is to the top?" he asked.

The answer was slow in coming. The idea that anyone would ask such a pointless question after viewing the impossibility of the situation spurred murmurs of disbelief to circulate. Finally, someone offered an opinion.

"I'm guessing.... I don't know, maybe a couple of thousand feet. Probably more. Probably a lot more. Who can say? How can you judge the distance of a speck of light? What I do know is that nobody here could endure such a climb."

"I'm thinking this could be done," said Gus to the contrary. "We could get out of here. It wouldn't be easy, but it can't be any worse than drifting aimlessly through these tunnels and sinking farther into the bowels of Hell. Nothing can be worse than that."

"Not true," piped a man.

From his perch on the second rung, Gus looked down and around at the faces that were all studying him.

"What do you mean?" he asked.

"We came here to get out of the storm. We knew we had to go deep to be safe. It's dangerous just standing here looking up at that opening."

"I don't understand. I mean, I don't doubt you. The storm was bad, I could feel it in my gut, but I don't understand what you mean by dangerous. Why is standing here dangerous?"

"The Lingering."

Gus recoiled. It was something of an involuntary action that caused him to step off the ladder and back away.

The Lingering. There was that word. The sound of it curdles my blood. But why? What is it? What does it mean? Why does it upset me?

"Bear with me, folks. I'm not sure how many of you know that I have no memory. For those of you who didn't know, now you do. I can't remember anything, but all of you go on about the Lingering, like it's a demon hunting you down. I feel like I'm familiar with that term, and right now to hear about it frightens me, but I don't know why. What exactly is the *Lingering*?"

Gus raised his voice to emphasize his exasperation.

"Shush! Keep it down. You might be heard," said a frightened woman.

Gus could not see their eyes, but he felt the fear that permeated the air.

"C'mon. Tell me. You folks brought it up. You folks always bring it up. I need an answer.... Anybody?"

The crowd grew restless. They looked at each other. There was more murmuring.

"Shush!"

"Shush? Why am I being shushed?" asked Gus. "Does *anybody* know what the Lingering is? Is it a myth that you keep alive by constantly referring to it? Is it a tool of fear, of doubt, to keep me from climbing to the surface? I need an answer. Is it a myth or not?"

Gus knew before asking that the Lingering was no myth. He had felt its crippling effects in his gut. There was no forgetting the intensity of the fear. Not by anyone.

The responses were as inconclusive as Gus imagined. It appeared that nobody really knew anything about the Lingering other than to give it wide berth. To stay clear at all cost. The voice that brought the storm to their attention broke out from the silence.

"The Lingering is the worst possible thing to get caught up in. It'll scare all hope of sanity out of you. It's pure fear."

"And you know this, how?" asked Gus.

"I've heard folks speak of it many times."

"But do you know this personally? Have you experienced it yourself?"

"No. Well, not exactly."

"You see, there's the problem. You don't really know. Tell me. What do people say?"

"They say nobody escapes the Lingering. They say that's why the crowds all run one way. They aren't going someplace, they are fleeing."

"Fleeing what?" asked Gus.

"The fear."

"Balls ablaze. You keep saying fear. Fear of what?"

"No one knows. It's not like the fear of a thing, an animal, or fire, or something. It's more like... the fear of... *nothing*. I can't explain it. I can tell you this. It's a fear worse than anything you can imagine."

"And you know this from what people have said?"

"That and the fact it nearly overtook me once. It was a long time ago, but there's no forgetting. I was so mortified that I dove into the depths of the gloom to hide. Same as now. Being in these tunnels is comical compared to that storm. Up there, there is no shelter. No place to hide."

Another man spoke up.

"He's right. I disregarded the warnings handed me and suffered the same fate. Mine was only a brush with the darkness, but it laid me to waste. I sensed the fear was not of this world. It was... how would I describe it? Ahh... universal? A universal fear. Does that even make sense? All I know is that it's better down here. Here, we're safe."

Gus was not so sure. He could not dismiss their warnings because something in his gut told him that the storm, or Lingering, or whatever, was terrifying not just beyond their ability to explain, but beyond the ability of words to express.

"One last question. Did any of you see or meet anybody down here. Did any of you see anything strange?"

The consensus was negative. Gus chose not to mention what he had glimpsed in the room with the television. He had no desire to dwell on the matter.

"So. What's the plan? If you choose not to climb the ladder, then what? The farther you walk in these passages, the deeper you go, the less chance you'll ever get out. You keep saying that nobody gets out of the Lingering. How do you know you aren't already lost within it?"

The thought was so close to their reality that hearts sank in unison. Gus continued to speak.

"Listen. I'm not like you. Wandering these caves for eternity is an unknown, and not about to become my fate. If I'm not already dead, then I would rather die making my escape. I refuse to walk deeper into this grave."

The level of murmuring rose as Gus walked back over to the steel ladder and studied its mounting to the side of the well.

"I'm going up. It's my only chance. It's *our* only chance."

The murmuring reached a crescendo.

"You'll die for sure," said one. "You need to reconsider."

"We all die. One way or another, we all die. I just don't choose to die your way. I may be wrong, but the way I see it, your only hope for rescue is if I make it to the top. I don't see where you have anything to lose so... will you help me or what?"

"You would risk your life, most certainly die, just to help us?" asked the strong man. "Hard to believe. You know the storm is up there. I can't understand why you would do it even for yourself."

"Well... what am I supposed to say? Yes, I know the storm is up there. I do it for myself because I'm scared shitless both above and below ground, but down here I feel like I'm already walking around in my grave. I'd rather die in the open spaces. And for what it's worth, yes, I would risk my life for the lot of you. I'm not a glory boy, but I'm also not selfish. I don't need to take all the risk for me. I'm happy to add another what... dozen?"

"Sixteen," came the answer from somewhere in back of the crowd.

"Sixteen? I'm glad you keep count. So, I take it you knew I was missing?"

A chorus of snickers arose in the dark.

"Yeah. That's what I thought."

Then a man from the crowd cautioned, "I guess it's your call. I'm not sure how we can help. We're stuck down here with nothing. Nothing to make a climb like that."

"Well, for starters, if I'm to attempt this climb, I'll need a couple of good strong belts. Something I can use as a safety strap. I know you've got a couple because you used them to yank me out of that crevice. I'll need some heavy shoes, you know, like work boots. Something with thick soles that will keep the rungs of this ladder from cutting into the soles of my feet. It's not like standing on the flat step of a stepladder."

The low sound of quiet conversation moved through the crowd.

"We have the belts, but nobody here has boots or work shoes," said a voice.

In response, the woman who had shushed him spoke above the rest. "Hon, what if we filled your shoes with sand? There's plenty of that."

Gus thought about what she suggested.

"Silly as that sounds, it might not be a bad idea. The more I pack between my feet and the rungs, the better. Let's give it a try."

"Here's the belts."

"Make sure you sift that sand perfectly clean. The last thing I need is a pebble stuck in a shoe when I'm ten stories up the ladder."

The others laughed.

"Let us have your shoes."

A man interrupted. "Why don't you take mine? I wear a size twelve. You can put a good deal of sand in them."

Gus looked at the man and answered. "But that would leave you barefoot down here."

"Well, not to be callous, but if you don't make it to the top, the shoes will end up back down here anyway. And if you do make it, then you can just drop them back down to me."

"Blunt, but you can't argue with the logic," said Gus.

"I have some extra thick socks, if that will help," came another voice.

Gus sat down to remove his shoes. "Anything will help." He began untying the laces. At the same time, another man handed him two coils of belts.

"These are the strongest we have."

Gus ran his fingers along their lengths to get a sense of their sturdiness. They seemed up to the task.

"They should work. Thank you."

Gus finished pulling on the thick socks, when two women approached him with a pair of shoes over-filled with sand.

"Here ya go, hon."

"No pebbles, right?"

"No pebbles. Pour out what you must to make your feet comfortable."

Gus did just that. He carefully poured a small amount of sand out of each shoe until both feet were inside without discomfort.

He tied the laces loosely and then stood up and began strolling around.

"Definitely feels weird, but I don't think the steel rungs will split my feet in half."

Gus walked over to the ladder. He climbed a few rungs. He bounced on his sand-packed shoes.

"Perfect."

"Hon, do you mind if I ask you a question?"

"No. Go ahead."

"I listened to what you said before, but I still don't understand why you would risk your life going up this ladder. It would kill any of us, and I am certain we all believe it will kill you as well. Why are you doing this?"

"No one else volunteered," Gus quipped.

"Oh, my word. No one volunteered because it amounts to suicide. Hon, I don't mean to be ungrateful, but are you sure you don't have a death wish? I, for one, would much rather you stay here with us."

Gus did not answer right away. He thought about what the woman asked.

"Listen.... It's like this. I have no memory. I got hit on the head or something. I don't know what happened to me. I do know that I have no idea who I am. I have no idea where I am, or where I'm going. I don't even know my name. Someone here called me Buddy, so I go by Buddy. I woke up on the floor of a parking garage with a splitting headache. I assume I was mugged, and that's all I know. Do you understand? I can't tell you my own name. So... the way I see it, if I can scale this ladder and save all our necks—why not? If I don't make it, what have I got to lose? My connection to loved ones? My memories? I have no memories."

Nobody commented. Gus turned to step up onto another rung. He bounced lightly. He started laughing.

"Works like a charm. I take my hat off to the lady with today's best suggestion. We have a winner."

"Hon, I wish you all the luck."

Gus could not make her out in the gloom but recognized her voice.

"Thank you, ma'am. I'll take all I can get."

Gus next fitted the belts together and adjusted them. He grabbed the ladder and, with arms forced straight, he pushed himself against the strap to test it.

"Looks good to me," he assured the others. "Time to go."

"Good luck. God bless. Be careful," the crowd spoke in unison.

One woman stepped up to the ladder and placed her hand on his arm.

"Thank you. Thank you for doing this. For us. I don't want to stay down here in the dark. We know we're going to die. One by one. We don't say it, but we all know it. I pray you can at least save yourself."

"I'll see you again, one way or another."

"Okay, let the man be on his way. Good luck to you, sir."

"And to you."

Gus glanced around and saw Sang watching from the shadows. Gus smiled as he addressed him. "I com' ba', Sang. I com' ba, okay?"

"Ha, ha. Ya. You go. I wa'."

With that, Gus took another step. Then a third, and a fourth.

"I feel better already. Each step on this ladder lightens the burden on my soul."

At about a hundred steps, Gus stopped and looked down. A flash of lightning caused the group to leave an erratic trail of movement. He hollered down.

"Hey! I can see you're still down there. Don't stand around the bottom of the ladder. If I should fall, or if I should make it out and throw down some supplies or items of use, anybody standing around looking up will surely end up brain dead."

"Understood. But how will we catch you if we aren't looking up?" asked a new voice.

For the first time, genuine laughter erupted. Even Gus laughed.

"You won't want to be catching me. My shoes are full of sand. They weigh a good ten pounds apiece. That's a serious kick to the head."

The laughter came again and raised everyone's hearts. Gus looked up at the flickering dot far above his head. He dropped his gaze to the wall before him and went on to climb the ladder. Only the occasional flash of lightning allowed him to see the ladder for any distance, or the wall in front of his face, or the illusion of people yet watching him from below.

Because of the darkness, Gus had no need to open his eyes. There was nothing to navigate. His hands raced up the stiles as his feet pushed against higher rungs. Hand over hand, the same sliding, the same stepping. Every twenty-four steps he had to unbuckle the strap and pass it from below a ladder mount to above. He re-attached the belts and continued upward with eyes closed for another twenty-four steps.

It did not take long for Gus to sink into a routine. A routine that lasted for months or years, or for however long it took a universe to form and die. Occasionally, he would open his eyes to look above and below. Below was nothing but impenetrable gloom. A dark void. It was disheartening for him to know there were souls lost deep in that hole.

Above Gus, the opening was growing larger. The lightning was flashing brighter. He wondered if the storm ever passed. He recalled the words of the man who said *nobody escapes the Lingering*. He wondered if there truly was escape from the hell that gripped them. He closed his eyes and continued to climb for another eternity.

Gus opened and closed his eyes to assess his position many times. More frequently, he stopped his ascent to rest, but rest was impossible. There was no comfortable position, no manner of relieving the burn in his thighs. He no longer felt his blistered and bleeding hands. He no longer felt his feet or shins. He would move upward when his muscles allowed. He would remain stranded when they did not.

Often, when he reached a ladder mount, he would pull half the belt across the top of the mount and slip the opposite half under his buttocks. With a prayer on his lips, Gus would sit on the strap and give his legs a break for however long he was able before the strap cut all circulation to his legs. Repeatedly, he reminded himself of the souls far below whose fate hinged on his success. Repeatedly, he prayed for strength before continuing his climb.

And so it went for weeks, or months, or years. It went this way until Gus opened his eyes to see the rim of the opening just overhead. Seventy or eighty feet, but not much more. Bugs twittered about the wall, snails raced, moss grew, all things that moved faster than he. All signs of life. To the observer, Gus appeared dead still, frozen in place. Mummified. Only in his mind did he appreciate how long and how fast he proceeded to scale the steel ladder in order to reach the surface. He closed his eyes and continued to climb.

The next time Gus opened his eyes, it was not to assess his progress. It was an involuntary action as he screamed out in pain. Something landed on the top of his head and ran down the back of his neck. The fluid seared his skin. It was excruciating.

Gus looked upward to see the ember-like eyes of a hellhound looking down at him. The demon was salivating at the sight of him. He was only about twenty steps from the opening, but the creature's saliva was acidic and scalding hot. It streamed along the demon's jaws and dropped in stringy lengths to crisscross Gus's frame. It was sticky, and much like hot glue; it fused to his skin.

Gus attempted to back down, but no distance was sufficient. A second and a third hound appeared. The three drooled in unison. Soon after, more hellhounds arrived to pack tightly together. Shoulder to shoulder they stood around the rim of the shaft with eyes trained squarely on his being. Heads hung low, the beasts leaned into the well with a wanton desire for his soul.

In Gus's hasty retreat, the safety strap snagged on a mount, preventing him from moving farther downward. He rushed to unbuckle the straps. With fingers too numb to feel, too numb to grasp, he was only spitting distance from freedom when the belt slipped from his hands.

Gus fell backward into space.

His last vision was a circle of light rimmed with the black silhouettes of hellhounds and the television man standing over them as he sizzled in a fall of rain. It was at that moment he recalled a prior encounter with an old man dressed in white, the driver of hounds. It was then he understood the severity of the storm.

Against all odds, Gus had reached the top of the shaft. It was an iron will and the burden of lives clinging to his success that propelled him to the surface. Now, as he exploded across the stone floor at the bottom of the well, in some inexplicable manner while disintegrating into a bloody mist, he found himself approached by the souls he had attempted to save.

In a single file, they passed by him just as they did when they stepped off the bus, the brutes, the woman accompanied by the small Asian man, and all the others. Each conveyed their gratitude for what he had done. They were all smiling and comforting him. Some placed hands on his shoulders. Others cradled his face. The women kissed him.

Each soul that turned to leave said two things to Gus.

"I forgive you," and then with a smile of gratitude, "I gotta go."

10

The first awareness was pain. It assaulted every inch of his body. It paralyzed him. He wondered if some bastard had embedded an axe into his skull. The closer Gus moved toward awaking, the tighter pain wrapped around him.

He understood he was suffering. He did not understand why. *Pain* was the obvious word for what would surely drive Gus into his grave. Only after regaining some of his wit did he sense subtle differences. Pain was all over the surface of his misery, but Gus sensed he might have brushed up against something far worse. However small, there was solace in believing whatever he had left behind was for the best.

For Gus, there was only one meager blessing. The noise of traffic. That obnoxious, invasive din of disorganized mechanical melodies that bounced back and forth between a hundred walls of brick and glass before finding the garage floor where he lay flat on his back. The barrage of highway sounds beckoned him to wake up, to leap up, and to discard his shroud of despondency. The ruckus nagged him to open his eyes and find the light.

As if floating upward from the deep, Gus returned to a brighter side of existence. How bright was debatable. A sickly illumination acknowledged he was alive, but barely. In spite of the monotone of grays that surrounded him, details came into view. His surroundings were acquiring perspective and texture.

Gus began breathing deeper. The additional oxygen swept through his brain, increasing awareness to the point of realizing he was more miserable than alive. His head felt about to explode. Incoming light only added to the pressure. It was better being blind. He closed his eyes. His thoughts shifted to the joy of aspirin.

Gus remained laid out corpse-like upon the concrete until curiosity prodded him to give the day-world another chance. He adjusted his eyelids to meter in the least allowable light. Fortunately, the light was dim and indirect, thus shortening the time needed for his eyes to begin shifting about. Soon after, his head tilted from one side to the next, but made no sense of what he saw.

Initially, Gus thought he awoke on the hard, uncarpeted, floor of a living room, or on bathroom tile.

Whose house is this?

It took a minute for him to focus clearly enough to appreciate the size of the floor.

This ain't a bathroom. Ain't a living room. More like a basement or garage. Concrete. No wonder my head hurts.

Whose garage?

Gus turned his head to one side and sighted along his outstretched arm. He noted the distance to the far walls. He noted a number of parked cars, all of which he was viewing from below.

This is one big garage. Big.

For a moment, he thought he recognized the place. He worked his mind to place it, but to no avail. He rolled his head back. He recognized the line of an expansion joint passing directly above him. Braving a skull-splitting headache, he eased his head up off the concrete to gain a better view of the surroundings.

What the hell...? This ain't no home. A garage. A big garage. A public garage? A storage garage? Do I know this place?

Where the hell am I?

Gus raised himself slowly onto all fours, then gradually stood up. He stumbled about, lacking control over his legs. He had no recollection of ever being so hung over. At this point, he had far more questions than answers.

Did I get stoned last night? Am I still high? Where am I?

Feeling uneasy and vulnerable, Gus turned around slowly to study the dark crevices and shadowed corners. He listened intently for sounds of movement, or anything that might be a threat. There was nothing to hear aside from the noise of the highway. There was, however, a strong sense of familiarity about the place that overrode much of his anxiety. The feeling of familiarity lowered his guard, allowing him to accept he was reasonably safe.

Gus dismissed much of his concern about surroundings in order to inspect himself. He looked down his arms. He inspected the length of his legs, front and back. He patted down his frame until certain he was okay. Aside from a crippling headache, finding no broken bones or bruises left him at a loss to explain his situation. His fingers tracked in a tight circular pattern that gently massaged his temples. He worked to ease out something of value.

What the hell happened to me?

Gus closed his eyes. He believed at some point a switch would flip and allow his memory to kick in. It could not happen soon enough. He felt panicky. A mixture of adrenaline and fear was fermenting inside his bowels. He felt as if he had broken an unknown law and narrowly escaped capture. His lack of memory, no matter how short-term, was unsettling. He strained to recall what he had been doing the night before.

Balls ablaze, what the hell did I do last night to deserve this? Where did I go? Who the hell was I with? Was I driving? I don't think so.

It did not take much time before Gus found himself confronting panic head on, and it was not fun. He was shaking his head back and forth, immersed deep in thought.

No, no, no. This ain't about remembering where I stuck my shoes. You understand? This is about remembering anything. Anything. This is about remembering my fucking name, for chrissakes.

"C'mon, gimme a break," he pleaded aloud.

Gus whacked himself on the back of the head two or three times in hopes of jostling something back into place.

It works for pinballs, maybe pinheads....

It didn't. It did raise his awareness to a sensitive spot at the back of his head. A quick check revealed a sizable mat of coagulated blood and hair. The sight of fresh blood smeared heavily across his hand drove him to resurrect anything, the smallest detail, from the past night to make sense of the present day. But the past night, past week, past everything, remained a meaningless mess of blurry images. He could perceive light and dark, or smears of color. He could perceive movement and shape, but nothing more, nothing with clarity.

"What the hell is my name, for chrissakes? My... name... is...."

He waited. Nothing came.

"My wallet!"

He blurted out an inner thought that brought fresh hope. He reached for the familiar bulge inside his back pocket. Nothing. It was as empty as his head. He checked all his pockets. Nothing. No change, no receipts, no keys, no clues of any kind.

Keys? Car keys?

Gus's eyes narrowed as he passed his focus from one vehicle to the next. Unlike the surroundings in general, nothing specific looked familiar. Certainly no car belonging to him. The vehicles had one thing in common. They appeared un-driven for eons, and offered up no clues.

"Shit," Gus cursed in exasperation. "C'mon.... Gimme a break," he whispered a second time.

Gus broke from his world of problems to focus on his condition. He was constrained by stiffness. He twisted his frame to the left and then to the right. He placed his hand across the top of his head. He pulled it to one side. He pushed it to the other. He rubbed the back of his neck, careful to avoid the slop of blood. He threw his skull backward and then forward, at which time his eyes shifted to the concrete floor. He noted a small puddle of blood. He looked around, hoping to spot clues—something dropped, something tossed aside. Something, anything, he could work with that would help sort out this mess.

Again, that sense of déjà vu. He could not place his surroundings, but he was certain he knew the garage. To some extent, that brought him relief. He relaxed. He leaned against a support column and stared at nothing. His mind was blank, but calm. He listened to the sounds of traffic. They drew his attention to a brighter light that entered the underground parking level by way of an entrance ramp that descended from somewhere above. The feeble light struggled to hold the darkness at bay for Gus's sake. He sensed that there was something foreboding within the shadows. It was not that he remembered anything specific enough to give him anxiety. It was more of an instinct to avoid them.

"I gotta get outta here."

Gus started for the entrance ramp. He staggered up the incline. The climb was taxing. At the top, he backed against a wall. His heart pounded, raced, outpaced only by his mind, which continued to dig for memories.

Where the hell am I? What was I doing? What's my name?

Sweat broke out across Gus's forehead. He closed his eyes. He dismissed anything that might interfere with his calming down. He raised his face skyward to enjoy a brighter haze. Its meager glow improved his state of mind. Shaky, but more confident,

Gus pushed himself off the wall. He set course for the highway, still unseen.

Having emerged from an underground sanctuary of sorts, Gus studied the open spaces with a wary eye. The place was odd. The streets empty. No life found. The light of day was scarce. The only positives were rays of sunshine that reached him from the ridge, the sounds of a highway, and a weird familiarity about the street that signaled memories should return in short order.

The positive signal ahead was very different from the negative signal that followed on Gus's heels. A look behind showed a foreboding fog. It clung to the structures and appeared to suffocate everything it covered. Gus shuddered at the sight and grew single-minded.

I'm outta here. Now!

11

The roar of the highway made Gus jumpy with excitement. It was insanely loud, unlike anything he had ever heard. The sounds roared down empty streets, slamming into old brick and stone structures in need of a jump-start back to life. The snarls and squeals of passing traffic seemed to be the only thing that could penetrate the repressive gloom. If echoes were present, they went unheard in the background of their source.

The traffic sounds signaled Gus to safe harbor. He listened to the roar and rumble that reached deep into the vagueness of this place, this neighborhood of nothingness, in order to draw him out. The highway was all that mattered. It was essential.

He hustled toward sounds that meant freedom, a ticket out of town, or at least out of this place seemingly bent on keeping him. The road out battled him physically. The route grew steeper by the step. It caused his lungs and legs to burn with fatigue. His mind, uneasy about what lurked behind, urged him forward. His body, full of pain, urged him to turn back and stop the torture. Whether physical or mental, it was ironic that his path to freedom was also his greatest obstacle.

He watched warily for unseen inhabitants fixed on sucking the soul out of him. His suspicions were without merit, without proof or explanation, but overwhelming nonetheless. All the while, he looked ahead and he looked behind at clouds that crept forward ever faster to close in and unnerve him.

Gus saw more than eyes alone could witness. He wished the images to be sensory mirages, meaningless. The creeping mist was putrid, like pus oozing from wounds inflicted by a lifetime of sin. He sensed shameful memories, an unsavory history that held claim to his soul. The clouds possessed a fear that could strangle him, a dread that licked at his heels as he struggled to climb the road. They stood his hair on end.

Gus pressed onward with resolve. His eyes focused on the crest of the hill, his ears tuned to the roar of traffic. The louder the din, the more his relief, the faster his steps. He hoped to move unnoticed, unheard, drowned out by the clamor washing down through the uninhabited streets.

Gus reached the hilltop none too soon. The climb reduced his legs to a rubbery state that barely supported his weight. He had used his right hand as a crutch, leaning on the walls of vacated storefronts to keep himself upright and moving forward. His gasps sounded painful as he crossed over the crest to stop and stand bent over atop the high ground of the ridge. Now, Gus could rest. He leaned back against a building and looked around as he removed his shoes. He slapped the soles together and shook out a notable amount of sand.

Sand. That's strange. Sand. Humph. Was I at a beach? Highly doubt it. The desert. Was I in the desert? Possible. Makes more sense. Why would I be in the desert?

Gus noted another possible clue as he stepped back into his shoes. Before moving on, he took what he hoped would be his farewell view of the dreadful place below. His spirits rose considerably. He felt free of burden and pain, free of fatigue. The load lifted was much heavier than flesh and bones. It was something more, a weight of considerable measure that had beaten down his will to exist. Although invisible within the gloom, he sensed the force was ever-present and potent.

Gus felt invigorated and unstrapped. For the moment, nothing pulled at his back, nothing hindered his movement forward. The buildings along the ridge, although shabby in every regard, possessed a sense of protection as if castle walls. They shielded all within from the fearful things beyond and below. They gave a sense of security, offering hope and confidence to those afforded protection within.

Gus passed through the ridgeline constructions and then through a line of shanties and lean-tos that paralleled the highway. There he encountered an immense crowd of people walking toward the sunrise. He stood in awe. His eyes absorbed every detail of the landscape and the flow of souls that stretched out before him. The spectacle was beyond words. The whole of it defied description. The only thing to dampen the magnitude of what he observed was the sensation that it was somehow familiar. A feeling of frustration that he could not shake.

"What is this place? I know this place. I'm certain I know this place. Why can't I nail this down?"

Instead of becoming speechless by the sight before him, in shocked amazement, Gus milled about the crowds, talking unabashedly to himself. He had no concern about what others thought of his ramblings. He was overwhelmed, bewildered. There were likely those that noticed his lips moving, but none could hear his confused words above the intense blare of traffic. As always, the highway had his back.

"Balls ablaze. Look at that highway. Who could forget that? I know that highway. I know that highway… but I can't remember it. How is that possible?"

The thoroughfare was a feat of engineering that left Gus awestruck. It was as straight as laser light. Straight as a beam of sunlight passing through the clouds in the distance. Nothing indicated that a curve or bend, a hill or valley of any sort, might disrupt its line of perfection. The highway appeared infinite, disappearing into the brilliance of the morning sun.

Unable to look into that brilliance, Gus turned away to observe the many features close by that caused long shadows in the early morning sunlight. He noted first that the freeway stood proudly above all else. To stand on its shoulder was to stand on the top of the world.

The shoulder was a flat, wide, hard-packed surface of dirt. It equaled the width of two or three lanes. It was level across its width, after which it fell gently to a lower level that supported the endless row of shanties. Beyond the shanties, the ground held flat as it spread out to support the taller buildings that edged the ridge. From the ridge, the ground dropped away sharply. Side streets similar to the one Gus had battled earlier rose from the murky depths to section the bank, the buildings, and the endless row of shanties at regular intervals.

The ridge acted like an earthen dam to hold back the impenetrable clouds of despair that lapped at it from the lower elevations. Gus couldn't see their presence in the lower depths from where he stood, but he remained entirely conscious of their existence. The ridge divided all that uplifted his soul from all that dragged him down.

Good riddance to that dismal hellhole.

Gus faced the traffic and smiled. He soaked up the bright and cheerful atmosphere that flowed with the crowds and passing vehicles. He allowed the flood of life to wash over him. It brought him a sense of peace, a feeling of security through belonging, as if he were the starling centered in a murmation. He was at center, surrounded by a kaleidoscope of color and cultures. Whether single, or in groups of two, ten, or twenty, people moved in unison, bumping into one another, jostling for space as they walked the banks in haste. The energy thrilled him.

In spite of the fascination and all else offered by the crowd, nothing surpassed the highway. It was mindboggling. Too wide to see across, too long to fathom, the highway disallowed any appreciation of size. It belittled all who stood at the curb in wonder. The number and speed of the vehicles in the innermost lanes was so outrageous that the distance appeared to be a stream of liquid. It was hypnotizing. Gus was quickly lost to thought while staring at the moving expanse.

Out of the expansive flow came a nerve-curdling screech of brakes that obliterated Gus's hypnotic fixation. Convinced he was about to die, he leapt sideways from the curb, hoping for safety over sorrow. As he passed through the air in a panic, he glanced over his shoulder in time to see an opening bus door coming directly for him. It stopped short of knocking him on his ass by less than the width of his palm.

Gus was pissed. The man sitting behind the wheel, wrapped up in a cartoon-like bandana, as if mimicking a baked pig's head nestled in a bed of colorful vegetable trimmings, just handed him an open invitation to explode. He let his fury fly.

"Balls ablaze, man! Are you fucking crazy!? Are you kidding me? What the hell are you doing? Who drives like that? Are you picking passengers up or picking them off? You son of a bitch! Step out here! I dare ya. Step out here. C'mon. You wanna knock me on my ass? C'mon. Step out here, you chicken shit. I'll lay your ass out cold."

The rush of fury made Gus go physical. He slapped the side of the open door so forcefully that it snapped shut. The driver did not accept Gus's offer to step out, but smiled instead. He winked as hit the gas and left Gus at the curb. As Gus backed away, he noted the bus ID, and hollered out as it disappeared into the traffic.

"BUS 7 CHARTERED! I got your number, ya shithead! I'm reporting you! Bet on it!"

Whereas the bus joined the flow of traffic, Gus moved to oppose it. Without thought, he stepped out against the crowd. Shoulders began to collide.

"Hey! Watch where you're going," he fumed.

"Sorry. My apologies." The man sprinted away.

Gus slammed into another. "Hey! You blind or just asking to get pounded?"

"So sorry, the Lingering. You know."

Gus was swearing up a storm, and getting hotter with every step.

"Get the hell out outta my way!" he snapped.

"Pardon me. Gotta go."

Everyone had to go. Everyone was in a rush. Everyone was suddenly pushy and crowding his space. Gus was boiling over.

"Gotta go? That's your excuse? Gotta go *where*, for chrissakes?"

Gus hollered obscenities, but as always, the highway was at his back and drowned out most of his indignities. He pressed against the crowd for no reason other than belligerence. He reveled in his anger. He preferred it to the confusion that filled his head. Anger felt real. It was his weapon of choice, if not his only weapon. And so, pitching shoulders in a fit and swinging arms like clubs, Gus continued with his tantrum until looking beyond the hundreds of wary faces staring at him—the crowd he was primed to battle. At that point everything, especially his attitude, changed dramatically.

It happened at first notice of the distant sky. On the horizon was an ominous horizontal band of churning clouds. Dark sprouts erupted from the band and soared to towering heights as if volcanic plumes pumped blackened ash and soot miles into the atmosphere. At the earth's edge, fire seemed to devour the ground itself. The sight instilled fear far beyond the image before him. He shuddered for causes he could not comprehend. Gus stopped in his tracks. Having no need to experience more, he turned to join the flow.

The frustration, the belligerence, the swearing and anger subsided. People were still bumping into him, but now it only prodded him to move faster. More importantly, instead of blaming others, he wondered why he had fought the crowd in the first place.

Where was I going anyway?

Having fallen in step with the others, something bizarre occurred. The moment Gus turned from the storm, the moment he stopped fighting the crowd, stopped going against the flow, was the moment he began to feel better. He not only felt better, he felt remarkably better. In fact, he felt *too much* better. It was logical to feel better when you stopped running against the wind, but this was different. This was profound.

Gus was sharp enough to appreciate the futility of battling a crowd simply for the sake of battle. One would never win; one would never get satisfaction. A sensible person would step to the side or fall in step as did he. The problem with Gus was his compulsion to fight the crowd, or anybody, or anything just to awaken himself. He needed the anger to feel alive. He needed the adrenaline.

Yet, walking *with* the crowd felt so relaxing that he wondered, what was the point of getting angry under any circumstance? It was not logical. He drifted into deeper thoughts. One such thought had to do with his outbursts. His temper surprised him. In fact, he made a mental note of it.

Gus felt as if he was at the top of his game. Strong. Fearless. Unbeatable. It was as if a switch switched and instantly transformed everything in his world, including him, to the better. Walking with the crowd was more than agreeable. It was closer to euphoric. Maybe he was confused. Maybe he was lost. Maybe for reasons unknown he had no memory, but for now, strolling down the road with strangers was all he wanted. He felt fulfilled.

"I gotta go! I gotta go!" said a man running hurriedly past.

The man interrupted the tranquility of background noise that offered Gus a moment's reprieve. Gus's eyes followed the man as he sped ahead and disappeared into the flow. He smiled.

Again, out of the noisy surroundings came the teeth-shattering squeal of brakes. Gus snapped his head toward the street and viewed the same eight-wheeled piece of bus-junk pull over to the curb. The doors flew open.

"Sure you don't need a lift?"

Gus noticed it was the same driver as before or his twin. But the probability of two idiots with bad taste in bandanas driving buses was so infinitesimally small that it came as a shock. *Improbable* was too weak a term, not just the bandanas, but the impossibility of a bus looping back around that fast on a highway this crazy. Yet, there the driver sat smiling from the captain's chair and asking for a second time if he needed a lift. It was as if the bus reappeared out of thin air.

Gus looked up at the green-lighted sign to be sure. It read BUS 7 CHARTERED.

Impossible. How the....

Gus backed away from the bus as if burned by it. He had no idea how the driver had brought that bus back around in barely a moment's passing, but any sane person knew that couldn't happen. He glanced up and down the road. He looked back at the sign. BUS 7 CHARTERED. There was no question.

Gus backed farther away from the driver, or demon, or whatever unholy time traveler beckoned him. A woman exiting the bus briefly blocked the visual exchange between Gus and driver. Gus and the woman did a brief side-to-side two-step-dance step. She never looked up.

"Excuse me."

"Sorry."

Gus apologized for standing in the way like an insensible idiot. The incident was just enough to break the spell. He retreated deep into the throng of passersby where he shrank out of sight.

12

The return of the bus nearly drove Gus over the edge. He suffered enough wondering about his sanity without facing magical buses that could disappear and then miraculously reappear in the blink of an eye.

He chose not to deal with the impossibility, not to even think about it. Instead, he continued to walk, keeping his head low and eyes to the ground. He spotted a discarded red-and-yellow wrapper from a snack or candy bar that the masses trod upon but failed to bury in the dust. He bent over and picked it up. He studied it. Yellow letters across a red background spelled:

ONE WAY

Beneath, a smaller line of black type read:

A PUSH FOR THOSE ON THE RUN.

Gus glanced around at the number of people streaming past. "Must be a hell of a seller."

Gus let loose of the wrapper, watching it return to the dusty earth. A stab of guilt caused him to glance around for a trash container. He saw none. He was free to step forward and place his shoe squarely upon the wrapper as he walked away. He wondered how many thousands of people had zeroed in on the wrapper for the sole purpose of stepping on it.

Gus also wondered if they did so because they were hungry. The wrapper caused him to realize that he was starving. Until viewing the wrapper, he had been so distraught and confused that the thought of food or eating had never entered his mind. Now he was famished. He looked along the row of open-air stalls, and spotted a food counter located less than a stone's throw ahead.

It was an odd establishment, but so were they all. Most obvious was the way in which many of the structures only had three walls. They were similar to open-air fruit stands, the kind one might find while driving through farm country. Those seasonal stands sporting flat roofs that leaned low in back to shed water. Simple structures built with minimal framing and sheets of white painted plywood to form walls, they stood out from the darker mature green of surrounding fields. Inside, there were always bushels of summer peaches and muskmelons, or autumn apples and various squashes, pushed up against counters covered with mismatched trays of produce and whatever else would trade for cash.

Whereas those farm stands were simple affairs, these structures were at times extensive, shallow in depth, but so long in length that faces in the distance faded to a blur. With dozens upon dozens of stools, the counters or bars were the longest that Gus had ever seen. In spite of their enormousness, crowds packed the shacks to overflowing.

"I gotta go!"

His face aglow, a man blurted out his duty to a waitress as he jumped up from a stool. The server wished him the best and waved him on with a smile as he disappeared into the crowd. Gus was quick to grab the seat. The server was quick to offer him the same inviting smile as she greeted him while placing a menu, silverware, and an empty glass on the counter before him.

"Good morning."

"Good morning. Ahhh.... Didn't I just see you get off the bus up there at the end of the street?"

"Good chance. Do you know what you'd like, or do you need a minute?"

"Oh. Ahhh.... Why don't you let me have some—"

Gus stopped short after instinctively reaching for his wallet and remembering with dismay, he no longer had one.

"Shit."

"Don't think so. Not on the menu. Problem?" she asked.

"Uhh, yeah. I lost my wallet and—"

"Here."

Before Gus could explain, he saw a bill flash before him and settle on the counter. A man sitting at the next stool pitched it without blinking an eye or glancing in his direction. Gus turned to face him.

"Hey, you sure?"

"Can't have a man go hungry. Can't have that."

The man, looking to be living in an overcoat, and roofed by a hat pulled low over his brow, never looked up from his meal to acknowledge Gus. Unlike the server, he wore no smile that Gus could see.

The server, on the other hand, most certainly smiled. A man could see her smile a mile away. A smile that begged a kiss. Gus snuck peeks at her eyes as he struggled to overcome one more *"give me a break"* event—one more outrageous coincidence.

A million people.... We meet at the bus; we meet at breakfast. Just go with it. It is what it is.

"Ya know what ya want, hon?"

Not only was the woman attractive, but she exuded a warmth that drew others to get close. Gus was no exception. It made him uncomfortable. He found it hard to stay focused. He snapped up the menu in order to bury his face. He scanned the print and then tossed it back to the counter.

"Ahhh.... I really don't want to read this. Honestly, I can't think of anything I want more than a straightforward, traditional, no-nonsense, no-surprise plate of eggs, bacon, and American fries—over easy, crisp, and onions if you got 'em."

"Juice?"

"Orange."

"Coffee?"

"Absolutely. Black. The blacker the better. In fact, today I don't think you can make it black enough."

The server laughed, and for Gus, it felt like an injection of ecstasy. She might as well have smothered him with the embrace of her bosom. It eased his inner tension.

"On its way, hon."

"Thanks."

Gus looked over toward the man sitting next to him.

"Just want to say how much I appreciate the save. Do you mind...?"

Gus reached toward a pitcher filled with crushed ice and slices of lemon. The man didn't answer, but gestured his approval. Gus grabbed the pitcher and poured the fresh water into his glass. Setting the pitcher down back in front of the stranger, he picked up the glass and chugged heartily.

"Lord, that's good. Didn't realize how thirsty I was."

Gus tipped the glass upward to coax a piece of ice into his mouth. Looking past the glass, his gaze remained fixed on the server who was scribbling down another order. The smile never went away.

I don't know what it is about that woman, but she sure appeals to me. Maybe it's all about the smile. I wonder if some people are always happy?

As the server headed down along the counter, a patron jumped up from his seat and called out in surprise.

"Gotta go!"

The server's eyes brightened.

"God speed, hon."

"Thanks. Thanks for breakfast."

The man appeared supremely happy as he also sped away into the crowd. Gus slouched over the counter, supporting his head with his hand. Unconsciously, he fondled the wound at the back of his head while contemplating the insanity that surrounded him.

Gotta go where? Where is everybody going? Am I supposed to know where that guy is going? Should I know this?

He was learning firsthand how badly the loss of memory could screw up his life. It was as if all the dots were there but....

The stupid line is missing.

There were very few connected dots in the world of Gus. It was like buying a best-seller after reading the back cover synopsis only to discover the book was a collection of blank pages. His cover looked great, a semblance of his life, but the details were missing. The inside was empty, the contents gone.

While Gus waited for his meal, his thoughts centered on one of his most confounded observations. He sat up and looked over his shoulder. He slowly twisted around on the stool. He leaned back, resting elbows on the counter, and went numb as he attempted to fathom the mass of humanity rushing past.

What started out as a notion, an utterly absurd impression that the world was leaving him behind, suddenly appeared all too factual. This massive march of people was going *one way*. It was too ridiculous to consider.

The absurdity of a demented mind. Allow me to introduce myself.

Yet, from where he sat facing the highway, the crowds migrated from his left to his right for as far as he could see. To his right, there was not a face in sight. If ever there appeared to be an exodus—

"Here ya go, hon."

Gus spun his stool around to eye a great-looking heap of food. The sight and smell of breakfast made his mouth flood with saliva. His obsession with the *one-way* crowd gave way to instant gratification. He did his best at using a traditional plate of eggs and bacon to isolate him from his nightmarish reality.

Oh, yes. Perfect.

Each savory forkful returned him closer to that place of sanity he desperately sought. The eggs arrived on time, fried over-easy to perfection. The bacon, crispy just as ordered. The potatoes, ringed with crunch, boasted Vidalias—sweet as apples. He shoveled it in, all of it, the food, the drink, the feeling. The coffee mug steamed and never emptied.

Gus reveled in this opportunity to drive out the confusion in his life with the simplest of hearty fare. He would have stretched out breakfast for days. He closed his eyes and enjoyed the bliss of a full stomach. He might have fallen asleep upon the stool had it not been for the interruptions of traffic and crowds driving his mind back to the strangeness of his surroundings.

With coffee in hand, he twisted his stool about to again face the hordes. For a second time, Gus tried to make sense of this massive flow that only went one way.

Everybody is walking to work. They're all poor and nobody drives. Except people are driving on the highway. Maybe they're all going to work. And work is that-a-way. It doesn't make sense. None of it makes sense. Is there one, just one, a single solitary face looking back my way? Anybody?

Gus grew determined to spot a single soul walking against the crowd. He scoured heads just for the hell of it. In those thousands of people, not one face looked back. The sight of everybody walking away left him with a deeply unsettled feeling. A feeling of being last in line, of being left behind, of separation from friends and family; it was about *not* getting on the bus. The feeling made his insides squirm.

Jesus, c'mon, c'mon, c'mon. Anybody.... Ah! Aha! Yes! Finally. Thank you, Lord. Thank you for that.

Gus let out a deep breath. It was all in his head. First one, then a second ...a third—there were those rare few walking against the crowd, but they appeared disruptive. It was obvious that the crowd was motivated to move toward the morning sun. They walked alongside traffic that raced by, leaving them to move like snails by comparison. Buffeting winds, turbulent air stirred up by passing vehicles nudged the pedestrians on their way. After some thought, a reasonable explanation for this directional flow came to Gus.

It's because I can't see across the highway. If I could, people would be walking from my right to my left. The opposite of what I see. On this side of the highway they walk to my right. Across, they walk to my left. I just can't see it. That has to be it.

But... Australians walk to the left. Now how the hell would I know that? Balls ablaze. Will someone give me a break? Fine. So I'm not in Australia.

Gus looked over to the Good Samaritan seated next to him. He noted how oddly the man was dressed in his overcoat and fedora. The man wore his overcoat collar raised as if expecting a storm. Between the collar and hat, little more than his nose was visible. The man pinched a cigarette between fingers on a hand raised high above his elbow. It further blocked Gus from seeing his face clearly. The smoke rolled up and around his head. He had that Bogart air all about him. Gus leaned his way.

"Mind if I ask you a question?"

"Not too much."

"Thanks. Where am I? What's the name of this place?"

"Not sure. I'm just passing through. I think it's called Locum Veniae. I think I saw a sign that said Locum Veniae."

"Locum Veniae. *Locum Veniae*.... Hmm... that just doesn't ring a bell. What state is this?"

"What?"

The man's head turned slightly; his eyes shifted to the corners nearest Gus. An unseen expression expressed what was not said. Gus quickly jumped tracks.

"Can you tell me where's everybody going?"

The man's posture remained unchanged and intimidating.

"How would I know that?"

Gus had no answer. The stupidity of his question was immediately apparent.

"Well... what I meant to say is, why is everybody going *that* way?"

Gus nodded his head in the direction of the flow. The stranger on the stool frowned.

"What's the point of going the other way? All you're gonna do is fight the crowd."

"I see what you're saying." For a man who made no sense, the stranger was perfectly capable of making Gus feel like an idiot. "Thanks for breakfast."

"Like I said, can't have a man go hungry. You want some more ice water and lemon?"

"Oh, thanks, but no thanks. I'm good."

The man's demeanor was suddenly fatherly. He rose from his stool and placed his hand on Gus's shoulder. He looked down at him and for the first time hinted at a smile.

"God speed, son."

It was with a perplexed expression that Gus looked up into the stranger's face. There was a scar or something etched into his forehead behind the brim of his hat.

"Thanks."

Gus watched the man walk away and lose himself within the swarm of wayfarers. He continued to stare at the crowd long after it swallowed the man.

"How's that coffee?"

Gus turned to capture the brilliant smile.

"Great. Better than great."

"Lemme top that off."

"Thanks."

Gus did his best to extend the pleasure of breakfast. He insisted on peace of mind. Governed by a full belly, he sat immobilized on the stool, satiated, lazy, sleepy. His eyes closed. His head dropped forward. The world might have thought him to be praying, giving thanks for his food, or just sleeping. It did not matter. At this moment, for Gus, everything was about as close to normal as normal could get. Everything was good. It was all good.

"Bullshit."

His eyes opened.

It might be good if I could remember my stupid name.

Gus wiped his mouth and tossed the napkin onto his cleaned plate. He stood up from the stool.

"Finished?" asked the server, who somehow always managed to be standing before him smiling.

"Yeah, yeah, finished. Uhh, thanks. Breakfast was great. Uhhh, better than great. It was fantastic. What do I owe ya?"

"Ten."

Gus handed the woman a twenty. She returned promptly with two fives in change.

"Thank you."

"Here."

Gus left a five on the counter. He looked up, and by chance caught her glancing his way. She smiled. Gus placed the second five atop the first and returned the smile.

"Thank you again, and God speed, you hear? God speed."

"Yeah."

Gus plowed headlong into the mayhem, wondering aloud if everyone here was a Christian or what. Ambitions to cross the road returned and he fought his way to the curb. He started and stopped; he sidestepped; he danced back and forth until he stood squarely on the concrete lip, evaluating the fearsome traffic. It was insane. At least, he only had to worry about traffic coming one way, but the speed of the vehicles, the number of lanes, the congestion, the whole of it made any attempt to cross certain annihilation.

"Balls ablaze. People gotta cross a road, no?"

Gus looked high and low for a pedestrian crossing, or a traffic light, or a skywalk—anything that would ferry the suicidal to the other side safely. Nothing. He shook his head in disbelief. He looked at the crowd flowing toward him, flowing around him, and he decided to throw out a question.

"Hey, excuse me—"

"Hey!"

"Hey, can you tell me where to cross—"

"Sorry, sir...no time, gotta go."

Gus confronted a man square on.

"Excuse me. Can you tell me where I can cross the road?"

The man looked at him with an expression of misunderstanding.

"Did you say cross the road?"

"Yeah, cross the road."

"Why would anybody want to cross the road?"

"How about to get to the other side?"

Confused, the man looked across the blur of traffic.

"I don't understand. What's over there?"

Gus stared at the stranger, who finally apologized.

"I'm sorry, sir, but I gotta go."

Gus gave up. The world was in too much of a hurry to give him a moment.

Why does everybody gotta go? Where does everybody gotta go? Why the rush?

Feeling mildly annoyed, he turned aside from the crowd to teeter on the curb again—to rock lightly back and forth on the balls of his feet while pondering the impossible lanes of traffic and what lay across the road.

Gus turned his head to the left and gauged the onslaught of vehicles. He looked for gaps. He looked for the breaks. He searched for a pattern to the flow. He waited and he waited. He waited. He became obsessed, and he could feel himself getting pissed. There would be no break in the traffic. It never came.

Gus turned his head to the right. His eyes followed the legions of peculiar-looking contraptions that were passing him by. He wondered if any of them had license plates or working taillights. He tried to glimpse through the windows at riders inside, but the vehicles appeared covered, front to back, in the kind of thick dust that takes months and miles, thousands of miles, to accumulate.

Gus inhaled deeply and then exhaled with exasperation.

Fucking eh. These fools all drive like maniacs. The way they swerve back and forth, the way they cross lanes, and speed up and slow down.... They are out of their minds crazy.

The vision of recklessness produced a string of images in Gus's mind.

"Mexico."

Gus seemed to understand that Mexico referred to a place that was hot and desert-like, a place where drivers might be this insane, a place where nobody gave a shit how anybody drove.

Now that's a possibility. That might be a clue.

The smallest fragments of memories trickled through Gus's mind to assemble a vague impression of industry and massive highways baking in the heat. He felt as if he had traveled many a mile on such sun-bleached pavement.

Could I have been mugged in Mexico? Is Locum Veniae in Mexico? Sure sounds like it. Makes perfect sense.

Gus leaned his head back and looked up into a brilliant blue cloudless sky. He tried once more to remember something of value, anything, anything at all, but there was nothing. Not even his name.

My head is as empty as that sky. Unbelievable.

13

Gus was looking at the backside of passing traffic when he nearly wetted himself. The unmistakable screech of brakes belonging to the same eight-wheeled monstrosity again halted within a spit's distance of his face. BUS 7 CHARTERED. The same door snapped open, and the same driver sat looking down at him from the same captain's chair, from the same embarrassing bandana. It seemed obvious the driver wished to harass him until....

"C'mon, Gus. Get on the bus."

Before he could even think of going into a rage, Gus was struck numb, dumbfounded—*astonished*. He did not know whether to cry or get on his knees. Should he bow and bestow copious amounts of gratitude on this driver or what? His mind shorted out. He just stared at the man.

"Well, are ya gonna get on board or what?"

"Do you know me?"

"Should I?"

"What?"

"I said, should I?"

Gus was as much annoyed as confused.

"How the hell do I know? Are you playin' games with me, or what? You called me Gus. It was a simple question. D'you know who I am or not? Balls ablaze, man! Just answer the question."

The driver studied him.

"Well, that's your name isn't it?"

"Mister, I don't know what the fuck my name is. I don't know where I am or what I'm doing, or fucking anything. I don't know why you keep parkin' this piece of rollin' shit in front of my face. But I do know that you called me Gus. Now, do ya know me or not? Just answer the question."

The two men studied each other in a brief moment of silence before the driver spoke up.

"Well...that's what it says on your shirt."

Gus looked down so fast, he nearly snapped his neck at the joints. There, just above his left side breast pocket, was a label. It said GUS.

"What the hell...."

No way. No way. Impossible.

He refused to believe that after all he had been through, his name was right there, embroidered across a blue background, in bright golden-yellow thread.

"Bullshit."

"Pardon?"

He looked up at the driver utterly frustrated, utterly lost for words—*almost.*

"I give up. I flat out fucking give up."

Gus dropped his head. He closed his eyes. He shook the confusion out of his mind. He opened his eyes to assess the step.

Might as well climb aboard. I've been in the hands of fate since I woke up.

Gus boarded the bus. The door closed behind him. Gus reached for the handrail and pulled himself up the step. He was facing the driver with a full measure of suspicion. He wasn't sure why.

"It's okay, man. Take a seat. Relax," said the driver.

Gus stepped past the driver to face the aisle. To his surprise, the passengers were studying *him* with full measure. Theirs was not a blind stare that routinely assessed the features of a boarding passenger. Theirs was a wanton stare, a busload of eyes boring into his soul. Oddly enough, most were smiling, many with ear-to-ear grins. Many nodded his way as if knowing him for years. He wondered, what were the chances? He desperately wanted to ask if anybody knew him personally, anything about him, but after the humiliation of the nametag, he decided otherwise.

The vehicle lurched violently, forcing Gus to clutch the handrail with a firm grip. The vehicle sounded like a washing machine agitating cases of empty beer cans. Outside, the horrible sound would go unnoticed, lost in the clamorous din. Inside, it was a brow raiser.

"Jesus," Gus whispered under his breath. He then spoke up. "Hey, Driver! Am I safe on this thing? You sure this wreck's gonna make it to the next stop?"

"Ya-hah!" The driver laughed. "This wreck, as you call it, has millions of miles on it, more miles than you might imagine. She ain't never let me down. Not a once, an' I don't think she's about to any time soon."

"Well, I'll give ya this. She *sounds* like she's got millions of miles on her, *more than I can imagine* is right."

"Ya better find yourself a seat, son."

"No kidding."

Gus plopped into the first available seat—A1. In spite of the digs, he decided if the driver was not concerned about the wreck breaking down that was good enough for him. He already had plenty to worry about as it was. Why add to it?

Once the doors closed, once the brakes released, he started to mellow out. Actually, he began to feel rejuvenated, invigorated. After all of the screwed up, mind-warping, nerve-racking incidents, his subconscious felt relieved to be heading down the road. In spite of seeing himself as a man without options, a hostage pressured to board a bus, he could not have felt better.

Gus looked out the window with a lightened heart, an inner peace, not a lot, just enough to smooth out the hard lines crossing his forehead. He felt oddly safe on the bus, safely separated from the mayhem outside that now passed by at ever-increasing speed. The apprehensions and peculiarities of the crowds, the eateries, the stands, the shops, all of it turned into a blur. None of it could reach him now. He closed his eyes and quickly drifted off to sleep.

14

Gus's head hammered the window—the glass pillow. His eyes heavy, weary, occasionally startled open to view the passing scenery. Day had turned to night. Gus slowly came to his senses while gazing out the window. An unending cornice of gaudy multicolored signs showered fake sunlight from shanty rooftops. The stands, still jammed tightly together along the shoulder of the highway, remained a part of the landscape and appeared intent to border it forever. He gazed past the amber glow of low-wattage lights to observe the silhouettes of structures that lay behind the stands, those unlit vacated buildings that edged the ridge.

Gus noted upon awakening that the pain in his head was barely noticeable. He reached back with his hand to feel the wound. He looked at his fingers and saw they were dry. No hint of blood. A good sign that added to his feeling better. Maybe something about being on the bus appealed to his subconscious, like enjoying a little personal space between him and the rush of humanity. Or maybe it was just the aftermath of a great breakfast and napping on a full belly. Did it really matter? He felt better. For now, what else was there?

Gus stared upward into the night sky, mesmerized by the explosion of stars and galaxies that encircled his little smear of existence. These were far from the simple black-and-white heavens that had captured his imagination as a child. These heavens were glorious, iridescent vistas, layered with rainbows that glowed and held him spellbound like a twinkling Christmas tree in the dead stillness of night. Gus was disappointed for being unable to find words that might express such splendor, such radiance, such...such....

"Unnatural magnificence," he whispered, his breath collecting on the window.

The awe of the heavens made his problems seem small. It made him feel humble. It quieted the storm within. He raised his head off the window to look forward along the aisle, first at the driver, and then through the large windshield of the bus. The world was black as black could be except for the shimmering heavens and two distinctly formed rows of light. One made by a stream of amber glow that emanated from the thousands of small stands and structures bordering the highway and passing by on his right. The other by a stream of red taillights that passed by him and those that shared a ride on the slower-moving bus.

Similar to the runway lights of an airport, the rows of sparkling luminance shot forward until merging at a point on the distant horizon. There, all detail disappeared amid a riotous explosion of color. Clusters of stars and galaxies that could only be the work of a great god, a supreme designer of fireworks frozen in time and space, spread silently to embrace a soul's attention for eternity. The ultimate beacon.

Gus contemplated how the highway resembled a bridge that spanned a great divide. From where to where was anybody's guess. He could only express it as a spiritual experience, crossing an infinite universe from the shores of darkness to a distant gloriously welcoming light.

"Driver? Where are we?"

The driver did not respond. Instead, he hit the pedal that produced that horrific spine-chilling squeal. Gus lurched forward. Whether the driver did not hear him or simply chose to ignore him was unclear. Either way, Gus redirected his gaze through the windshield toward a black silhouette backlit by the shanties aglow. A woman had caught the driver's attention—a lone woman standing on the shoulder of the road. The bus stopped. Gus fell back against his seat, and the doors opened with a "clack."

The woman stepped up from the curb, her face hidden from view by the hood of a mottled brown sweater. Gus contemplated a pleasing figure that the sweater failed fully to conceal. The woman nodded at the driver as if knowing him. The driver returned a smile. The doors closed.

Gus noted the woman paid no fare as she passed by the driver. He figured she was a regular, possessing a card-pass or something of the like. As she walked past him on her way down the aisle, he thought about calling out to her, inviting her to sit with him.

He would never do it for real because, in reality, it was one more pressure he did not need. However, to enjoy a private desire, a diversion, a mental romp to pass time imagining the thrill of cuddling up against her—that could be fun.

Gus turned back to view the heavenly vistas. A smile crossed his face as he went on to imagine looking into her eyes, smelling her scent, feeling the warmth of her, but it was short-lived.

"Mind if I sit here?"

Gus's head spun around. She was standing over him. The request caught him completely off guard. He tried to make out her face, but the hood kept it in shadows. Her voice resonated within his head. It seemed familiar, and for once, familiarity meant comfort instead of confusion.

"Uhhhh, yeah, I guess.... Sure. Please... sit down."

The woman sat down close, too close. Had she been a man, Gus would have demanded his space. But she wasn't. She seemed fixated on the road ahead, so Gus chanced looking her over. He was certain she was attractive. He wondered why she sat next to him. He looked back over his shoulder. He noted there were a couple of empty seats she might have chosen. He also noted that everybody seemed to be looking at him, well... maybe at her. He wondered why they were smiling. He wondered all kinds of things, but mostly he wondered why, in view of the empty seats on the bus, this woman decided to sit next to him—a man. He wondered why her leg pressed up against his.

The hood prevented Gus from gauging age or reading expressions on the woman's face. Nevertheless, based on the way she carried herself, the sound of her voice, and the confident manner in which she asked to sit next to him, Gus believed her to be mid-thirtyish. He sensed the strength of maturity.

In a likewise manner, the hood also prevented the woman from seeing Gus watching her. He was free to study her as much as he wanted. Her fragrance was seductive. It washed over him. He breathed it in with pleasure. Her attire was more conservative than not. It was fresh and clean. He stared at her for some time. He realized that something about her called out to him. Just her presence seemed to beckon him. Curiosity finally drove him to open up.

"Ma'am, I'm sorry to bother you. But that perfume.... It's uhhh... lovely... alluring. May I ask the name?"

At first, the woman turned only enough for her eyes to meet Gus's, and he knew he should have kept quiet. Then, unexpectedly, the woman dropped her hood and faced him with a smile. She tilted her head to the side and began fondling an earring. She twisted it, turned it, jostled it about her finger, as she looked at and through Gus.

"Sins of the Past. It *is* my favorite."

Straight away, Gus recognized her as the counter girl who had gotten off the bus earlier and served him breakfast. Unfortunately, that obscure eatery was all of a day's journey and a zillion miles back. Those facts made this encounter impossible. Yet there she was leaning against him with that heart-stealing smile.

Gus was more than stunned.

Here comes another one of those bloody mind-fucks.

The rush of adrenaline was sickening. His complexion went white as his mind teetered. A fist to the face would have been easier to handle. He might have run had she not pinned him between her leg and the window.

"How are you, Gus?"

"Huh?"

"Been a long day, hasn't it?" she continued. "You look pale. I remember you from this morning. You weren't looking so hot then either. I remember that. Worse for wear. 'Bewildered' I think best describes it. I'm sure breakfast did you good, but honestly you need more. Maybe a good night's sleep."

Gus was numb. He fought plunging into another mental abyss, some black crack with no way out.

What are the chances this chick gets on the same bus as me? What were the chances she would sit in the same seat? We gotta be twenty hours away from where she worked. How can that be? What are the chances? Zero. Absolute zero.

Gus's wits snapped back at first scent of a set-up. The smell of a trap was second nature to him.

First the driver, now the server. I need an escape route.

He glanced around in search of a way out, but for now, he was trapped like a rat between the window and the waitress.

"Do I know you?" he asked.

The woman studied his face, all the while smiling.

"You mean other than the eatery?"

"Yes."

"Possibly... but only you would know."

She shrugged her shoulders. Gus flinched.

"You called me Gus—"

"It's on your shirt." She pointed at the patch.

"Of course," Gus stammered. "What I should have asked was do you know me? That's what I meant to say. Do you know me? You look so familiar, but I can't remember.... I can't remember anything. I believe I have amnesia or some kind of temporary memory loss."

"That's unfortunate. What happened? Did you fall—hit your head or something?"

"I'm not sure. I don't think it was a fall because I no longer have my wallet or my watch. I'm thinkin' I was mugged."

"Mugged? Really? Wow, that's terrible."

"Yeah. Well... it is what it is."

"I'm sorry."

"Not your fault."

There was a pause in the conversation. The woman returned her attention to the road ahead. Gus continued to look at her.

"I remember watching you behind the counter this morning and thinking there was something about you, something familiar, something warm, like maybe we were friends or something. It feels like years ago, but it may have yesterday. I can't tell. Any chance of that?"

She gave him her full attention. Their eyes locked as if the two were looking far, far beyond any wall, any defense a soul could muster. In a meshing of the subconscious, they were momentarily one, twirling, falling endlessly deep into each other's awareness. Then she shook her head.

"You know.... Like I said, I meet so many...."

Gus's soul collapsed. After drowning in nothingness, rising to the hope of belonging, and disappearing back into the empty depths, it cried silently for help.

"Oh, yeah. Of course. What am I thinking? I'm sorry. I know, I must sound crazy—crazy man on the bus crazy. Please...."

Gus avoided her eyes by turning to look out the window. He wanted to end it. Whatever it was, he wanted it to end. He stared into the darkness behind the row of stands that bordered the highway. It was immediate and intense, the desolation of the desert. He looked back to the heavens, his only solace. He sought the comfort of its splendor as he began to speak indirectly to the woman.

"It's like I'm a kid standing in a kitchen where the air is thick with the smell of freshly baked dessert. A smell that invades every pore of my body as it surrounds me. I inhale the aroma as deeply as I can. I inhale until I'm dizzy with hunger. My mouth drowns me with saliva. I want so bad to savor that dessert, but it'll never happen. It'll never happen because I can't reach it. The table, or counter, or cupboard is too high. It's just too high. That's what my world is like. My life is all there. It surrounds me. I know everything is there. I can sense it. I can smell it. I just can't have it. I just can't have my life. I'm not sure why."

Gus's reflection ended with the all too annoying squeal of brakes. He turned away from the window and saw the woman stand up from their seat. She looked down at him. Her face wore an expression of pity. When his eyes reached hers, she spoke.

"Where are you headed, Gus?"

Gus shrugged his shoulders.

"I'm not sure. Honestly..., I don't know. Drover might know."

"Drover?"

"Yeah. A joke. My joke. When I dozed off, I was thinking about how river was like a drover herding lost souls through the heavens. Don't ask me why I would think that. I just did."

"I see." The woman stood in place studying him, looking into the heart of him. "All right, you listen to me. I want you to understand, this is not what I do, but I feel for you. If you would like to walk with me, I can offer you a cup of coffee and maybe something light to eat if you wish. You may spend the night, and get yourself a shower and a good night's sleep off the streets. Lord knows, you need it. But don't forget what I said, this is not what I do. This is one night. After that you get back on the bus."

The offer was heartfelt, but came unexpectedly. So much so, that Gus stalled before answering.

"Uh... uhh...."

"Well, don't let me pressure you, Gus." She smirked. "I can see you've got it good sitting here alone, hungry on a bus."

"Sorry. I'm an idiot. I'm just astonished you would offer me that. You know, me being a stranger and all. But I accept. Sounds good. No, actually..., it sounds great."

Gus accepted the invitation, almost without choice. There was not much room for questions. His answer was less an acceptance than an agreement. A part of him was intrigued. Another part of him from a past place and time understood his nature, and the risk she was taking.

"How do you know that I won't rob you, or rape you, or do something worse?"

"I don't. I guess I have to trust my instincts. I look into the eyes of a thousand customers a day—day after day after day. Believe me, that sharpens one's instincts. Mine rarely let me down. Right now, they're telling me you have a good side."

A good side? What the hell did that mean? I must really look shabby—a bum, a drunkard, a... whatever. Jesus, what is it about her? Something so inviting. So receptive. Sensual, almost sexual. Almost, but....

"What's your name?" Gus asked.

"Does it matter?"

"Does to me."

"I would rather not know names."

"But you already know mine."

"True, but I didn't ask for your name, and I don't go around with my name stitched on my blouse."

Out of context, her response would have been a hard rub, a snub, but now it was simply truth.

"Fair enough. I guess it really doesn't matter." Gus chuckled. "Okay. Beautiful savior, like you said, this has been a day. The least confusing thing I might imagine is a quiet cup of coffee with a good-hearted gal. Thank you."

The honesty of Gus's admission was clear in his eyes.

"Just remember, coffee, a bite to eat, and no more. One night. No more."

The woman raised her index finger to accentuate the point.

"Understood," said Gus. "I already owe you for breakfast, the only sanity thus far in this day."

He slid across the seat and stood up behind the nameless woman. She led the way. Before stepping off the bus, she acknowledged the driver with a nod. He nodded back with a grin. The bus door was yet open for Gus to pass, but before he did, he turned to the man behind the wheel, who habitually fidgeted with his bandana.

"What do I owe you?"

"Don't worry about it."

"Don't worry about it?"

"I think you need the fare more than me. Take care of yourself. Be good to the lady. She may be your ticket out of this place."

Gus stared at the driver.

What does that mean? Out of what place?

"Out of what place? I take it you know her?"

"Locum Veniae. I know only that she seems willing to show you some kindness, and that's not something you can afford to waste. Go! I can't sit and chat. Go."

Gus was lost for words. He wasn't sure what to say, or what to think about the woman, the fare, the driver, or anything else for that matter.

"Yeah, sorry. Thanks. Thanks for picking me up."

"I'll see ya around."

The driver split his face with a smile. Gus turned and stepped off the bus into the crowd. He walked in the direction of the woman who was waiting and watching.

"The driver wouldn't take my money."

"Must be he likes you."

"I doubt it. Why would he risk his job to do that?"

"Do what?"

Gus frowned. "Not take my money."

The woman looked at him, also with a frown.

"Why would he lose his job? He's driver."

The woman walked on. Gus stood. He looked down and shook his head. He was hoping to see insanity fall out of his head.

No such luck. Obviously, nothing is going to change. Even with her. Don't say anything. Don't pursue the conversation. She'll just make me feel stupid. Everything about the day has made me feel stupid. Keep the mouth shut and nobody knows I'm an idiot.

If nothing was ever to go right, at least being close to the woman brought him comfort. He felt as if he could breathe easier. At first, it was enough just to be near her, just to walk with her, to watch her, just to accept the balance of reality that she brought him. Now it felt like more. He could not explain it. He wanted to uncover something he could not explain.

"Are you really not going to tell me your name?"

"I would rather not."

"Why? You know mine. Doesn't seem right."

"Yours is on your shirt."

"So you've said."

"If I give you my name, I give you something personal. I am serious about us going our separate ways in the morning. You will have nothing, not even a name to look back on. If that is disagreeable for you, then you are free to get back on the bus."

"That bus is long gone."

"I doubt it."

"It is as far as options go. I chose the pretty lady."

"Don't forget that was your choice."

"Yeah."

Gus was following her along the lane, when she unexpectedly turned about to face him.

"Maybe this isn't—"

Gus did not give her the chance to finish. He worried she was annoyed.

"Okay. I won't press it. I promise. It's just that I don't know what it is about you that makes me feel... I don't know... worth something. Uhhh. I can't explain it. I've only been around you twenty minutes, and I feel like a new person. You see? There it is. Feelings. Feelings that I don't understand. Why would I feel that way? Something about my past that—"

"Do you like fish?" This time she cut him off.

"Fish?"

"Yes, fish. Have you eaten since this morning?"

"No."

"Well, then we'll pick up some fish for dinner."

She charged through the shanties and headed for the ridgeline buildings. She was unconcerned about what Gus might have said. Gus skipped ahead to catch up. She passed through the tall structures and without hesitation started down the steep incline of a side street. He was quick to call out with concern.

"Wait! Wait. Are you sure about this?"

"About what?"

"Going down this street. Going down this hill. I don't like leaving the highway. It makes me uncomfortable—really uncomfortable. And to be honest, that's putting it mildly."

She halted her charge to look at him.

"A rather odd thing to tell me."

"Odd or not, it's true."

"I don't know what to say other than stay with me, and you'll be fine. We'll buy some dinner and go to my place."

The instant she uttered the word *dinner*, the air grew heavy with the aroma of grilled meats and savory side dishes.

"I gotta go!"

Out of nowhere, a man raced past. Gus reached out to shield the woman, and then twisted around to watch the stranger head uphill for the highway.

"C'mon," said the woman.

Gus watched the runner.

"Hey, I said, c'mon."

"Yeah, yeah, I'm coming."

The woman, unbothered by the runner, demanded Gus's attention and beckoned him to follow her into a grocery store. Inside, a dozen customers were making requests to a line of cooks standing between meat counters and a row of deep fryers. It was a busy affair. Gus stood at her back as she signaled a nearby cook.

"Two pounds of today's catch, please."

"You got a number?"

"Yes, right here."

She held up her number, and Gus wondered where she got the ticket. He had followed her into the store and had no recollection of her picking off a ticket.

"Two pounds of catch coming up."

The woman turned away from the counter and walked toward the produce aisle. Gus followed.

"You like salad?"

"Yeah, it's okay."

"Great. I always have fresh salad with my fish."

Gus watched the woman carefully test the produce for freshness. After selecting and bagging a variety of ingredients, she motioned him to follow her back to the fryers. Within minutes, the cook placed a bag filled with fried fish on top of the display counter. Steam rose from within and carried a whiff of vinegar as it passed through the air. The woman grabbed the bag and started for the street.

"Wait, wait...," Gus called out.

She turned to acknowledge him.

"Didn't you forget to pay for that?"

"Pay for what?"

"The fish."

"The fish?"

"Yeah, the fish."

"No."

Gus frowned. "Don't you have to check out or something? Let somebody know what you've got?"

"No. Why would I have to do that? C'mon, before the fish gets cold."

Gus stopped short of whatever else he felt compelled to say.

"Sorry. I thought we had to pay for that. I don't know why I thought that, but I did."

His apology receded into a mumble, but it did not go unheard.

"You don't have to pay for food."

"Oh." Gus was lost. "Wait a minute. This morning when I had breakfast, you said I owned you ten dollars."

"That's because you asked."

"Because I asked? Because I asked?" repeated Gus. "What does that mean? Are you sayin' that if I hadn't asked, I wouldn't have owed you anything for breakfast?"

"Exactly."

"Then why did you take my money?"

"Because you wanted to give it to me."

"Really? How come I didn't know that?"

"Why would you?"

"Why wouldn't I?"

"What do you know? Anything?"

Gus went silent. She had him there. He had no idea about anything. He did not even know his own last name. The woman could see the frustration in his eyes.

"Relax, Gus. Remember, you've lost your memory. You don't know how this works. What you think is, isn't. What you think shouldn't be, is. Just go with it. If I'm going to get you into trouble, it won't be over fish. Okay?"

"Okay." Gus let out a breath. "I'll work on that. Easier said than done."

The woman opened her purse and pulled out some cash. She sorted out two five-dollar bills. Gus watched as she folded them into quarters. She looked up at him.

"Here. Take this. You gave it to me this morning, and now I'm giving it back."

"I can't do that."

"Why?"

"It wouldn't be right."

"Why?"

"Why? What do you mean, why? Because you worked for it. I can't just take your money."

"I've already said that you gave me this money for only one reason. You asked me how much for the breakfast. I said ten. If I said it was free, you wouldn't have given me anything. Now take it and shut up."

Ouch.

Gus let it slide. His head felt like it was spinning. He needed a distraction and reached for her bags.

"Here let me take those."

"It's fine."

"No, please. I want to. I want to do one small thing to feel worthwhile—normal. Maybe at one time I was a gentleman."

"Let's hope so."

The woman looked Gus in the eyes. Her glance was cold. Gus felt the change at once. He was suddenly unsure of himself. She looked down at the bags. She raised the bags as she raised her eyes and the folded five-dollar bills. This time she smiled.

"Fine. Take the bags."

Gus took the bags, the bills, and the baggage. Serious baggage. Something just happened. A door went ajar; a curtain blew back; a lid knocked loose. His spirits sank. He quieted. He walked with her down the side streets, past softly lit shops, deeper into the shadows, but he stayed a half-step behind. He was keenly aware of the dimming glow of highway lights fading into the distance. It unsettled him.

"You've grown quiet. Are you okay?" asked the woman.

"Something about the shadows makes me nervous. I don't like to leave the lights of the highway and the stalls."

"It's nothing more than nighttime. It's dark. There's supposed to be shadows."

Gus stopped walking. The woman did likewise. She turned to await him, and noticed his expression.

"What's the matter?"

"Should I be afraid of you?" asked Gus.

"Silly question. Tonight, I am saving you, aren't I?"

"Are you?"

"More than you know. But you're free to go off on your own. Free as a bird. You're not leashed to me."

"See... this is what slays me. What does that mean, *more than you know*? Why would you say something like that? Why do you make me feel like I'm always one step behind? Always the idiot? Always the one being played?"

"How about because you are totally lost, totally hungry, totally exhausted, and totally paranoid. I think that pretty well sums it up."

Gus wanted desperately to believe her. He allowed a small wave of relief to wash over him, but he still looked around to assure himself nothing more sinister than the *good fairy* lurked in the street.

"I suppose."

Gus continued with a lighter step, but remained a wary soul nonetheless as he moved deeper into the depths.

"We're here. This is where I live."

"Couldn't be soon enough for me."

"Why?"

"This neighborhood makes me nervous."

"Are you on the run from something?"

Gus thought about that.

"Sure feels like it at times, but if I am, I don't know it."

"Not the best answer, but honest. I guess it works."

The woman unlocked the main entry door. She opened it and then stood aside so Gus might pass. He entered the lobby of the building and began looking around.

"You're gonna love this," he snickered.

"What?"

"I could swear I've been here before."

"Really? What makes you think that?"

"The same thing that made me think I knew you. The same thing that makes everything I say sound stupid. A lack of memory."

"Oh, yeah. There is that. Does the place look familiar?"

"No, it *feels* familiar."

"Interesting. Well, why don't we go up? I'm hungry, and maybe it'll come to you by the time we get to the third floor."

"The third floor?"

"Yup."

"Great. If I wasn't already dragging ass, I soon will be."

"I know you're not going to complain in front of somebody offering you dinner and a place to sleep."

"Farthest thing from my mind."

"You swear?"

Gus laughed, "Yes, yes, I swear."

Gus followed the woman up a stairwell to the third-floor landing. The woman tapped lightly on a door and inserted a key into its lock. She pushed the door open a couple of inches before a chain stopped it from swinging farther. She called through the partial opening.

"Jeanie, I'm home. Open up, sweetheart."

"I'm coming. I'm coming," echoed a voice from within.

Gus heard the response growing near. The sound of running footsteps and fingers fumbling with a chain on the opposite side of the door soon followed. The woman turned to Gus.

"Gus, I ask that you watch your language. There's a child inside."

"Oh, yeah. Okay. Bad habit."

The chain flashed past the opening to fall against the jamb. The oversized wooden door swung away to reveal the bright smile of a young green-eyed girl, her face covered with freckles and swamped by a mop of red hair.

"Hi, Mrs. Giordano." The girl turned, "Joseph! Your mother's home!"

Hearing the two names yanked Gus out of the moment. A blended sense of familiarity and dread overwhelmed him. The wave of near recollection brought on a panic attack that would have doubled him over had he been alone.

"Everything okay?"

"I don't know," blurted Gus.

The woman turned to look at him.

"I was talking to the babysitter."

"Oh. Sorry."

The babysitter found the gaffe funny, and laughed as she answered.

"Yes, ma'am. Joseph was good."

"All right, then. Run along. I'll see you tomorrow."

"Good night."

"Good night, sweetheart."

Gus stepped aside, allowing the young girl to exit the apartment. He watched her dance down the staircase in a flurry of legwork. Her innocence warmed his heart. Once the babysitter left his sight, Gus turned to face Mrs. Giordano with an enlightened expression.

"Mrs. Giordano."

"Yes, now you know."

"I know something. Not everything. You have a son. You're married?"

"Was married."

"Oh."

"It's not what you think."

"I wasn't—"

"Hit and run."

Mentally, Gus tripped. "I'm sorry. Forgive me."

"No need to, I'm past it."

"I'm really sorry. I shouldn't have—"

"No, don't be. It wasn't your fault. Like I said, I'm past it. True, I wouldn't wish it on anybody, but there are worse things—even than that. Time heals all, Gus," she said with a raised chin and an air of experience. "I've learned to forgive. That's why you're here. Would you mind putting the fish in the oven to keep it warm? Turn it to one-fifty."

I've learned to forgive. That's why you're here. Another riddle-like comment. Am I supposed to let that slide? What choice have I got?

"Certainly." Gus complied. He walked over to the stove and fiddled with the knobs. "Are you healed then?"

Mrs. Giordano looked up from the counter. She smiled as she answered, "I'm getting close. Who knows, maybe tonight."

Gus blurted out a half-laugh, half-choke. "Oh! *Cough.* Good. That's great." Gus went red-faced. "I'm not sure what if anything to read into that."

"Relax, Gus. I don't bite... hard."

"Okay, good to know. Good to know."

Gus placed the bag of fish in the oven and closed the door just as a young boy came running into the kitchen. The sight of a stranger in the kitchen startled the lad. He veered toward his mother, who was reaching for plates in the cupboard.

"Hi, mom."

"Hello, sweetheart. How are you today?"

"Good."

The boy stared guardedly at Gus as his mother pulled a drawer open and selected a handful of silverware.

"Joseph, this is Gus. He will be our guest for dinner tonight, so I expect you to behave and make me proud. Here put the silverware on the table for me, please."

Gus stayed put but extended his hand. The boy grabbed it and Gus went white.

"Uh... uh... a pleasure to meet you, Joseph. That's a great name. I knew a boy...."

Gus stumbled. He lost his train of thought.

"Are you all right?" asked Mrs. Giordano.

"Wow. Where did that come from?"

"Are you all right?"

"I'm not sure. I guess," said Gus. "I have no idea where that came from. The words just fell out of my mouth. God, I feel like I'm going to throw up."

"Do you have a son or a nephew named Joseph?"

"I don't know. I guess. Why else would I say something like that? No, no. I don't think that's it. I don't think a son. Maybe a kid I knew. Look, can we change the subject? Is there anything else I can do for you?"

"No, not really. I'll finish with this salad and we can eat. Joseph, why don't you show Gus the way to the bathroom. See he has a clean towel to wipe his hands. And be sure to wash yours as well. You hear me?"

"Yes, mom."

Joseph bounded off, clearly unfocused on his role as guide. Gus suffered between the allure of childish innocence and the anxiety that gnawed at his insides when in the boy's presence.

"So tell me, Joseph. How old are you?"

"Eight."

"Eight? And that makes you in what grade?"

"Second."

"No kidding. What do they teach in second grade nowadays?"

"Reading, writing, math... science... and social studies."

"They teach all that in second grade?" asked Gus.

"Un-huh."

"I can't even remember that far back."

"Why? How old are you?"

"Now that's a tough one. Too old. Do you like school?"

"I guess so. I see my friends. I like my teachers."

"That's good. School's good. The more you put in, the more you get out."

Gus found himself feeling somewhat awkward. He was unaccustomed to saying anything more to a child than *you're cute* or *get outta here*. After wiping his hands, he handed the towel to the boy.

"Here you go. Wipe your hands."

Joseph did as told, then tossed the towel onto the counter and ran for the kitchen. Gus held back, welcoming the task of picking up the towel and folding it. He placed it neatly alongside the sink, and then walked back to the kitchen just as Mrs. Giordano stepped over to the table with a large bowl of salad. She placed the bowl at the center of the table.

"You're the guest of honor. You sit here."

She motioned Gus to take a seat. As he pulled back the chair, she went over to the stove and removed the fish from the oven. She placed the filets on a dish and set the plate alongside the salad. A last trip to the counter for bread, and she returned to take a seat.

"Would you care to lead us in prayer?"

"Prayer?"

The surprise in Gus's voice was clear, even comical, but there was no way out of the honor.

"Ah, yeah. Of course." He watched as mother and son lowered their heads—mother doing so with a faint grin. He raised his eyebrows and plowed forward.

"God Almighty, allow me to offer thanks for your blessings so clearly visible this day. Your love is evident in the heart of a Samaritan who has invited this stranger into her home, offering him kindness, a meal, and a place to sleep. Your grace shines through her generosity, and I ask that you bring her lasting peace, and bless all seated at our table. Amen."

"Amen," responded Joseph

"Amen." responded Mrs. Giordano.

The woman looked up and at Gus. She was beaming brightly.

"That was sweet."

"That was the truth."

Her eyes flashed across the table. "Be careful for bones, Joseph. Eat slowly or you'll end up with one of those stuck in your throat, and you won't like it. You hear me? Joseph? Are you listening?"

"Yes, mother. I hear you."

Mrs. Giordano looked toward Gus, smiling, exuding love for her son. For the next half hour, Gus wallowed in happiness similar to what he felt when first in her presence at the breakfast shanty.

I wonder if this is great food times two meals, or two meals times one great woman. Jesus, Gus, why even question it? Enjoy it. Enjoy it while you can because it's gonna be a bitch leaving in the morning. You know it.

"Would you like anything else, Joseph?"

"No, I'm full."

"Very well. You're excused. Time to do your homework. Go."

Joseph rose from the table, slid his chair forward, and left their company.

"And you, Gus? Can I get you anything more?"

"Oh, lord, no. I am fine. I'm embarrassed to know I have no way of repaying you for this wonderful meal... for your hospitality."

"It's my pleasure. If ever I saw a man who looked like he needed it...."

Mrs. Giordano rose from her chair. She reached for the dirty plates. Gus stood up at once.

"Here let me get those."

"No. Absolutely not. I wouldn't have such a thing. Sit down. There are only a couple of plates. It won't take but a second. Now sit down. I insist."

"Never argue with the cook," said Gus sheepishly.

He promptly sat down and watched Mrs. Giordano stack the dishes. She walked across the kitchen and placed them in the sink. She turned on the faucet and reached for a bottle of dish soap. She added a quick squirt to the flowing water. Setting the dish soap aside, she moved to open a cupboard.

Gus studied her figure as she rose to stand on her toes and reach inside the opened cabinet door to search for something. She stepped back and turned to face him.

"I apologize for not having a digestif to offer. My cupboards are bare when it comes to entertaining essentials."

"Oh, please. You're killing me. The meal was perfect. I am content. Believe me, I am fine."

"Do you like Marsala?"

"Marsala?"

"Yes. I have a bottle that I use for cooking. I know you're supposed to use dry, but I like the sweet. That way I can cook it or drink it. Would you like some? It's very good."

"Are you going to join me?"

"Of course."

"In that case, I'd love some. Thank you."

Mrs. Giordano carried the bottle and two glasses to the table. She sat down.

"Allow me."

Gus reached for the bottle, opened it, and filled both glasses halfway. He placed the bottle back on the table, and then raised his glass to his nose. He inhaled the fragrance. His eyes shifted in her direction and, as always, she was smiling.

"Well, what do you think?" she asked.

"I think you have a killer smile."

She laughed. "Well, thank you. But that's not what I meant. How is the Marsala?"

"Oh, that. Smells wonderful. I haven't had it in a long—"

Gus stopped midway and stared off into space.

"What is it?" asked Mrs. Giordano. "Another memory?"

"I just said that I haven't had it in a long time. How do I know that? I *can't* tell you my name, but I *can* tell you I haven't had Marsala in a long time. Are you kidding me? What the hell is that?" Gus frowned. "Sorry. I didn't mean to swear at your table. That wasn't good."

Mrs. Giordano laughed again.

"You're funny. Actually, I miss a bit of that roughness. You know... having a man around. Allow me to be frank and ask; why worry about it? You aren't about to change it. It is what it is, and it remains so until different. The only thing that matters right now is that you and I are sitting here at my kitchen table about to make the best out of booze I cook with. So... my next question is this. Wouldn't this taste better on the veranda?"

Gus laughed. "Undoubtedly. And you're also right to question my worrying, but it's a battle I can't give up, even if I never win. A man, rough or not, needs to know his last name. Right now, I feel like a bastard, a son without a father. Do you understand?"

"Yes. I can imagine. And, I'm sure it will come in time. Probably sooner than you think."

"I hope so."

The conversation halted. Gus found himself hypnotized by the kitchen light flashing across jewels embedded in Mrs. Giordano's earrings. They sparkled as she rotated the earrings around her fingers. First one, and then the other. She was most likely unaware of the endearing habit. There was something so gentle, so feminine, about the ritual that Gus's eyes were transfixed.

"Where's your mind?"

Mrs. Giordano broke the silence. She caught him staring at her. Gus was visibly embarrassed—his hand deep in the cookie jar.

"Sorry," he laughed sheepishly. "I was having one of those moments, you know, when everything seems so perfect. It was.... Hey! Shame on me! Have I lost my sense of social grace or what? A toast is in order! Raise your glass, my dear." Gus insisted as he lifted his glass. "C'mon, c'mon, raise that glass."

Mrs. Giordano broke out in a broad smile. She raised her glass alongside impossibly perfect white teeth as Gus continued.

"To a night made memorable by the heart, hospitality, and grace of a beautiful woman."

"Thank you."

Glasses clinked. Together they sipped. Mrs. Giordano then raised her glass and motioned toward Gus. She stared into his eyes.

"May your memories be as bright as your future."

"Wow. Nice. I'll drink to that."

Glasses clinked. Together they sipped. Mrs. Giordano stood up from her chair. She grabbed the bottle of Marsala from the table and handed it to Gus.

"Here. I want to sit on the veranda. It's nice outside."

Gus followed the woman through the French doors, and onto the balcony. Again, the lines of her figure held him spellbound.

"Doesn't that breeze feel wonderful? I told you, it isn't all dark and dismal out here. Sit down and relax. Look at those stars. Aren't they spectacular?"

Gus looked at the fine line of Mrs. Giordano's neck as she stared upward at the night sky.

You are as spectacular as any star.

"Indeed they are," he said.

They sat across from a small round table and looked out across the night. The heavens were a blaze of swirling color.

Gus wanted no part of any discussion that revolved around him, his loss of memory, his exasperation, or anything that would make him feel anxious. He wanted to finish out the night distracted by the presence of a gorgeous woman, Marsala, and lighthearted conversation.

"I know that I shouldn't go here. It's rude, but I can't help myself. You are a wonderfully attractive and personable woman. Why aren't you married? Why did you not remarry after your husband's death? And don't tell me there were no suiters. I won't believe you."

"You're kind to say as much. It's nice to hear." She looked away and reflected. She then faced Gus directly. "To be truthful, I don't discuss my husband's death or anything associated with anybody. Not to anyone. I never have."

"I apologize. I didn't mean to pry. However, I will take the liberty of saying that doing so might have eased your pain, helped you work through your loss."

"It might have. Or... my recollections might have made it worse. Maybe because you are a stranger, I can finally say my marriage was not what I had envisioned, not what I wanted."

"And?"

"And I've said enough."

"And, I don't think that's true. You said it yourself, I'm a stranger. Tomorrow I will walk out of your life. Why don't you let me take all those pent up secrets with me? Let me lift the smallest part of that burden. Tell me."

"I don't know...."

"Tell me. Please. I'm so egocentric, I forget I'm not the only one with issues," whispered Gus.

The woman looked at Gus and grinned. Then she looked again but deep into his eyes. She was assessing his character, his heart, his soul. Gus gave her the time she needed. And after a prolonged silence, she looked away and unlocked the door to her past.

"I was married to a man...." She looked down at her hands now folded in her lap. "...who was the life of the party." She raised her head and looked up into the night sky with a smile. "Lord, he could make me laugh. He laughed me to the altar, he laughed me into his bed, he laughed me through two pregnancies, and then he laughed as he left. Well... not really, but he turned my marriage into a joke.

"You see, I inferred *he* was killed by a hit and run driver. The truth is it was more like I was killed by a hit and run. He beat me senseless one night and booked. It nearly killed me at the time, not physically, but spiritually. Looking back, I guess I got over it. It was for the best. I got over it."

"He was a fool."

"No, I was the fool. I was worse than a fool. I endangered my son's life by making too many excuses, by standing at his side when I should have left. His good-timing ways got him into bad places. Drugs. Meth. Meth drives you mad. It made him a raving lunatic... a meth monster. It made me a target. I was often the object of his explosive moods, his anger. My husband left the party long ago. He was either high and insane, or low and miserable. Nothing between."

"Why did you stay with him?"

"What can I say? I needed to keep a roof over my head. I could see he was sick. He was an addict. I had so much hope, so much faith in him being able to kick the habit—to pull through. When it didn't happen, when it all came to an end, I hated him as much as I could hate anybody or anything. I blamed him for ruining my dreams, my family, my life, the life of my son. I blamed him for everything. That's probably why he beat me—*guilt*. It wasn't because he hated me. It was because I was all he had left to love, and I betrayed him by exposing the truth of his runaway failing."

"I'm sorry for you. Nobody should have to suffer through that. It hurts me just to think of it."

"Yes. You are right, but we make our own beds. Besides, I forgave him. It took me a long, long time. But I forgave him. You see, eventually, I came to appreciate he was but a shell of the man I fell in love with, the man I married. In time, I understood the bitter truth. He was as much a victim as was I. The difference was that I had hope, albeit misguided, whereas he had none. I remember the look in his eyes the day he realized he was never coming back from his addiction. He cried out of guilt. Mostly he cried out of fear or maybe it was shame.

"I watched him cash out everything we owned, everything we built together. We went broke as the drug dealer sat back and got rich. I watched meth suck away every facet of his character and soul. It sucked away his love for everything, his wife, his son, everything. Eventually, it sucked away his life."

"It takes a long time to heal, Gus. It takes a long time." Mrs. Giordano stood up from her chair and changed the subject. "I always finish my night with a cup of Chamomile tea. Would you care for some?"

"Uhh.... I guess. Why not?"

"It's a mild sedative. It will make you relax. It will make you sleep better."

"Whatever you say."

"I'll put some on. I need a moment to check on Joseph. It's his bedtime."

"Oh, of course. Do what you must. Don't mind me. I can't remember the last time I was this content."

"You can't remember anything."

"True. But... just go with me here. I want to believe I haven't been this relaxed in ages. It makes me feel better."

"In that case, you look very relaxed. In fact, I can't remember the last time you looked this relaxed."

Gus laughed. The spontaneous outburst caught him by surprise.

"So, you do laugh," she said.

"Ma'am, that smile of yours can light up the darkest night."

"Oh yeah? More likely Mr. Marsala is lighting you up. I'll be right back. You stay put."

She pointed at Gus as she made her final demand. She then stepped back through the French doors, leaving Gus to enjoy the stars overhead. He had to pinch himself to see if this marvelous evening was real.

Unfortunately, Gus's night of bliss faltered the moment she departed. He felt his fear creep out from the shadows and work its way toward him. It was closing in. He knew what not to do.

Don't look down. Do anything. Look anywhere, but don't look down.

He knew better than to drop his gaze from the heavens to the pavement, but he had no choice. Gus looked down into the street below. Murkiness isolated the structures, choking out the light and life. He felt his throat grow tight.

I'm going crazy. Nuts. I'm losing it. There is nothing down there but night. Nothing but....

Gus squirmed in his chair. He looked back up to the stars in the sky and prayed for Mrs. Giordano's quick return. He fought his urge to scramble for the lights of the highway. By the time she reappeared, he was in a near fatal state of panic.

Mrs. Giordano noticed his condition at once. He was sitting at attention, straight up in his chair, knuckles whitened by his grip. There was no hiding the sweat breaking across his forehead and bleeding through his shirt.

"My God, Gus. What happened? Are you okay? You look like you saw a ghost."

She showed great concern as she set a tray on the table. Gus focused first on the tea, then on the cream, then on the sugar. He focused lastly on the cake she had brought for his pleasure. These were all good things. She was good. She leaned over and captured his attention. He began to settle.

"Gus? Look at me. Are you okay?"

Gus cleared his throat and swallowed hard. He nodded.

"Yeah. Yeah, I'm better."

"What on earth happened? I was only gone for five minutes."

"I know. I know." Gus took a deep breath. "I can't explain it. It's like the shadows build and I start to suffocate. It's like I have to run for the highway. You know—the lights. I'm sorry. You have been wonderful. You deserve better than this."

"Shush. Enough. You know what I think. I think your loss of memory may well be due to some tragedy, something so traumatic that your mind keeps it from you. I want you to relax. Here, take this tea and come sit with me on the glider. That always makes me feel better. It's like being rocked in a mother's arms. Come. You'll feel better."

Mrs. Giordano poured tea into the cups and handed one to Gus.

"C'mon. Sit with me."

She took his hand and towed him toward the swing. It did not take much coaxing. The closer her presence, the better he felt. She sat down, but when he sat down next to her, the glider swayed more than he expected and caused her cup to spill tea.

"Oh, I'm sorry. I'm a bull in a china—"

"Quiet. Quiet. You worry too much. It's fine. A couple of drops of tea. Nothing more. It's not your fault that this swing is so small. It's true that I can't get anything larger on the veranda, but it's also true that I'm always alone. I curl up my legs, and for one person, it's perfect. Not so much for two, I'm afraid. But it is cozy." She leaned toward him. "Don't you think it's cozy?"

"Cozy border-lining cramped."

"I take it you're not a romantic." She looked up at the stars. "How can you sit under those stars and not be a romantic?"

As Mrs. Giordano stared upward at the stars, Gus stared at her. They sat in silence a moment or two before she dropped her gaze and turned to study him.

"I allowed you a personal question. A very personal question, I might add. In fact, I told you something of my failed marriage that I have been too embarrassed to admit to anyone. Not my friends, not my family. Now I would like to ask the same of you. A personal question that I am certain will be unpleasant. Will you allow me?"

"Uhhh.... I suppose I owe you. Go ahead. Besides, I'm dying to know what kind of question you could possibly have for a man with no memory."

"So it's a yes?"

"Sure. Go for it."

"What was it about my son's name that upset you earlier tonight? You know, before we sat down to eat, when I introduced you to him. What was it about the name Joseph?"

With her shoulders pressed tightly against his, the woman felt his reaction at once.

"Ohhhhh."

Gus stopped the swing. He slid forward to sit up straight. He worked to take in a deep breath.

"Ouch. I guess I shouldn't have asked. Sorry. Are you okay?"

"Yeah...."

Gus barely choked out a response before he began hyperventilating. He started crying. He started crying hard, sobbing. The woman was no longer smiling. She sat silently by his side, taking measure of some horrible thing she had brushed. She studied him. She watched his every move.

"What is it, Gus. Why are you so upset?"

She placed her arm around his shoulder and drew him tightly against her until she felt the tension in his body begin to break. Gus went silent. His breaths were deep but uncontrolled. He looked away as he spoke.

"I can't say. I... I don't know. I feel guilty. It's guilt. All guilt."

"About your brother?"

"I... I... I'm not sure. Maybe. I guess. Maybe it's about you."

"Me?"

"I... I... I don't know."

Gus began to cry again. There was no convulsing. It was more to relieve some inner turmoil. Mrs. Giordano sat and rubbed his shoulders until the episode settled. He regained his composure, at which point she went on to question him in a most gentle manner.

"Were you close to your brother?"

"I don't know. I'm not sure if I had a brother, or a nephew...." Gus halted. "There's something about Joseph. There's something about you. I'm attracted to you, but at the same time I feel like I need to fix something. I can't explain it. This is killing me. Where is all this coming from? Out of nowhere, I am being crucified with guilt for things I can't envision." Again, Gus halted. "I did something terrible. I can feel it. I don't know what. I know it was terrible. I can tell. I can feel it. I can feel it. It moves right through me. It takes away my breath. The sensation is gut-wrenching."

Gus worked to wipe away his tears. Mrs. Giordano leaned forward and kissed him on the side of his face. The tears moistened her lips. She placed her hand on his arm to reassure him.

"I think your memory is returning, Gus..., bit by bit. I suspect the more traumatic events in your past are the ones you fight to suppress. That's why you remember your brother's name, but not what happened. The door to your past opens slowly. That would make sense. Don't you think?"

"It makes sense, but if these are a taste of my memories, what I don't know may be far worse than my knowing nothing. Worse than not knowing my name. Maybe ignorance truly is bliss."

"Maybe. I don't know," said Mrs. Giordano. "I do know I shouldn't have gone there. That's what I get for being nosey. You know, I haven't enjoyed the company of a man in.... I can't remember, it's been so long. I feel like I ruined a wonderful evening."

"Ha! Oh, Jesus, believe me, you're not the kind of person who ruins things. You didn't ask anything outrageous. You just stumbled into the muck of another soul's hell. Wasn't your fault."

"Listen, Gus. All this stress beneath the surface. It's taking a toll. I can see it in your face. I can see it in your hands, the way you shake. You must be exhausted. Let's call it a night. Why don't you come inside and lie down? I told you I'll put you up for the night. I have a spare bed. Why don't you just come inside, lie down, and relax."

Gus nodded. "Yeah, that's probably a good idea. I feel like I've been hit by a truck."

Mrs. Giordano stood up from the glider and looked down at Gus with a smile.

"Give me your hand."

Gus did as she asked.

"Look at me. My hands are shaking terrible."

She pulled him up from the glider.

"C'mon. Let's get you tucked in."

Gus followed Mrs. Giordano through the French doors, past Joseph's room and the kitchen, and into the hallway where she opened a door.

"I'm sorry about the room being so small. I don't have guests as a rule—just Joseph and me. I will say this. The bed is comfortable. You can look forward to a good night's sleep." The woman pulled the blankets back.

"I'll leave you to get undressed. If you like, I can wash your clothes so they'll be clean for tomorrow."

"Oh, lord. No. No, no, no. I won't have you doing my dirty laundry on top of everything else. We have to draw a line here."

"Really? Silly of me to ask. Should've guessed you'd stand on honor. In that case, I insist. Get in the shower, leave your clothes on the floor. I'll put them in the wash. They'll be clean and dry in no time."

"I can't do that. I can't have you washing my clothes. You've—"

"Stop! Just do as I say. Get in the shower. You stink! Did you forget telling me about how you woke up on the floor of a parking garage? You're not clean, my friend. A shower will do you good and save my sheets. I'll put some clean towels out. And a robe. I don't want a smelly you in my spare bed."

She put Gus in his place. He stood silent, unsure of himself.

"Well, that put an entirely different light on the matter," he conceded.

"Good. Now that we've settled that, give me a moment to get my things out of the shower."

Mrs. Giordano left Gus standing in the bedroom. He was not opposed to taking a shower by a long shot. What bothered him was the imposition. However, the idea of being filthy and climbing into a clean bed was just plain disgusting. Especially when it was someone else's bed. Especially when the bed belonged to a woman.

"Bathroom's ready."

"I'm going."

Eyes closed, Gus soaked in the rush of hot water. He allowed the heat enough time to soften the tension in his muscles. Between the tea and the shower, he planned to sleep like a baby.

Mrs. Giordano cracked open the bathroom door.

"Is there anything you need, Gus?"

"No. Thank you. Everything's perfect. I'm just stepping out."

Feeling much better, Gus dried off, wrapped a bath towel around his body and headed for the bedroom. He climbed into bed nude.

Gus left the bedroom door open. He never liked the feeling of being closed in. Even so, Mrs. Giordano knocked lightly out of respect before entering.

"Come in."

"Your clothes are in the wash. As soon as they are done, I'll place them at the foot of your bed."

"Thank you. I wish I could say more or do something to show my appreciation."

"You've said enough. You've made it plenty clear. Besides, you're not the only one who is appreciative. I had my own agenda. I enjoyed your company at dinner."

"Enough to tell me your name?"

The woman did not answer. She only looked at Gus and smiled.

"I don't understand," he said. "You insist on being a stranger, but I could swear we know each other."

"Shushhhh. Go to sleep. Tomorrow will be a better day. I promise."

Mrs. Giordano reached for the switch. The room went dark, and he watched her slip away into the light beyond. Gus lay in bed aware of how deeply he was attracted to this woman. He would have enjoyed her sexually, but the attraction was more than sex. It was about peace in a time of anxiety, tranquility in a time of turmoil. He closed his eyes and gave thought to something useful, like recalling his last name. He was unaware of drifting off to sleep.

A rustling at the foot of the bed awakened Gus. He opened his eyes to see Mrs. Giordano laying clothes across a folded blanket at his feet.

"How long have I been asleep?"

"Oh, I'm sorry. I tried not to awaken you," she whispered.

"What time is it?"

"A little after one. You should go back to sleep."

"One? Why are you up so late?" asked Gus.

Mrs. Giordano walked around to the head of the bed and straightened out the blankets. She leaned over Gus as she tucked him in. Her fragrance filled the air about him.

"Tomorrow's my day off. I can sleep in."

"Question."

"Yes?"

"Would you mind sitting a moment?" he asked.

There was a slight hesitation before she answered.

"For a moment. I was about to get into bed myself."

"I understand."

Gus remained silent until it became awkwardly obvious.

"Was there something else you wished to ask me?"

"Yes. Very much so."

"Well.... I'm listening."

"Mrs. Giordano, I'm about to confess the unthinkable. There is absolutely no way I'm going back to sleep. The fact is I'm burning up with desire to hold you in my arms. After all that you've done for me, it's a terribly insulting admission. I know. I know it's disrespectful, but it's the honest to god's truth."

Mrs. Giordano did not storm out of the room. She did not slice him to pieces for his audacity. Instead, she remained seated on the bed and stared through the dark at his form. Gus watched as she turned her head to study the light beyond the open bedroom door. It glistened off an earring. He viewed her features in the soft light that entered the room.

"Your son sleeps soundly."

Mrs. Giordano turned back to face the sound of his voice.

"And your question...."

"Would you lie with me? I promise I want nothing more than to hold you in my arms. Just the pleasure of holding you close."

Without a word, Mrs. Giordano stood up from the bed and unbuttoned her robe. She let it fall to the floor. She unhooked her bra and dropped it on top of the robe. She slipped her panties down her legs and gracefully stepped free of them. She stood naked before Gus without moving toward him. He waited.

"My name is Veronica. Veronica Giordano. Say it."

"Veronica."

"Say it again."

"Veronica."

"Again."

"Veronica. Veronica Giordano. It's a beautiful name. It fits you perfectly."

"Do you want to kiss me, Gus?"

"More than you could know."

"Do you want to make love to me?"

"I'm too embarrassed to answer that."

"Tell me why."

Gus went silent. He didn't know how to respond.

"I wish I knew. It would be so easy to tell you it was because of the shape and color of your lips, your smile, the flash of your teeth. It would be so easy to tell myself it was because of all those things, but I know it's not. I am driven toward you for a reason I cannot remember. You say you don't know me, Veronica, but I wonder if you're sincere."

"Tell me you want to kiss me."

Gus hesitated a moment.

"Veronica Giordano, I want to crush you in my arms. I want to press my lips hard against yours. I want to suffocate in the heat of your breath. I want to feel the rise of your body against mine. I want to pour my heart into yours. I want to explode. I don't why that is, Veronica. But, I think you do."

"Tell me you have a heart."

"What?"

"Say it. I want to hear you say it. I want you to tell me that you have a heart."

Gus's eyes filled with tears.

"Say it."

"I'm afraid. I'm afraid it would be a lie. I don't—"

"Say it!"

"I have a heart."

Veronica leaned over and pulled back the blankets. She knelt on the bed and straddled Gus. She settled down upon him and slid her hands up across his chest. She leaned forward and kissed the tears about his eyes. She moved down, kissing him lightly at first, slowly. Then as the kisses grew more intense, she lowered her body onto his. Nothing more was said. Nothing else mattered. The lovemaking began.

Gus remained submissive. He did not mount Veronica. He stayed as he lay and drew relief from her attention. He set aside his guilt and allowed himself to savor her desire as he might savor the rarest of pleasures. This was what she wanted. Occasionally, he caressed her breasts, but for the most part, he chose not to interfere.

Gus might have lost himself entirely to the sexual union had it not been for the least perceptible undercurrent of uneasiness.

This was as much an act of respect as of pleasure. Their climax reached in unison, ended without expletives, or accolades, or moans and groans. For Gus, it felt like a reckoning. He watched as Veronica collapsed to curl within his embrace. The woman was satiated to such an extent, Gus wondered if she duped him. He was not about to complain, but the thought lingered until he joined her in sleep.

15

Two things that certainly could bore deep enough to reach the depths of Gus's hard-earned sleep were the screech of brakes on *BUS 7 CHARTERED* and the terrified screams of a frantic woman. They were essentially the same until *BUS 7 CHARTERED* pulled away, leaving only the woman's horrific screams.

Burning sinuses and an orange glow that passed through eyelids yet closed, forcibly awakened Gus. Choking and coughing uncontrollably, he came to his senses in record time. His eyelids opened so fast that they tore across dry pupils, causing a sharp sting and flood of tears. He blinked frantically in order to clear his vision, but in fact, the tears protected his eyes. It was not the light of a lamp that greeted him, but the light of a raging fire.

Gus threw back the blankets and met an unnerving press of heat. He zeroed in on the silhouette in the doorway. More screams snapped his attention to Veronica, fully backlit by flames that turned her earrings into prisms. The kitchen was obviously ablaze. She was screaming hysterically as she tried to confront the heat.

"Joseph! Joseph!"

He could hear the boy responding from the other side of the kitchen. Gus leapt out of the bed and donned his clothes for protection against the heat. As he did so, he yelled to Veronica.

"Get out! Get out, Veronica! I'll get the boy. Get out while you can!"

Gus did not wait for Veronica to think it over. He grabbed her from behind and flung her brutally into the hall, away from direct exposure to the fire and heat. Thrown off balance, she fell hard to the floor and skidded to the base of the front door.

"Get out! Get out!" Gus roared. "I'll get Joseph."

Not wanting to consider consequences, Gus grabbed a pillow to shield him from the heat and plunged into the fire-engulfed kitchen. Holding his breath, and the pillow between face and fire, he bolted through the room. The heat was intense, scorching hot. Flames were scaling the walls and devouring the cabinetry. They puddled as they fanned out across the ceiling.

Gus cleared the inferno and stormed through the doorway to Joseph's bedroom. He slammed the door shut behind him. He ran his fingers through his hair, relieved to find it still there and unburned. He looked at his arms and his clothes, again relieved to see nothing singed or smoking. He carried only the heat that lingered on his skin, and that, he could handle. He looked at the boy.

"Are you—*cough*.... Are you—*cough, cough*.... Are you okay, son?"

"I want my mother. I want my mother."

"I'll bring you–*cough, cough*... to her in a minute. You—must do—*cough*... what I say, okay? *Cough, cough*."

Gus barely got the words out. He had sucked in too much smoke while sleeping, and his sprint through the kitchen only further aggravated lungs he now worked to clear. The boy did not answer him. The smoke was less in the bedroom but filling the space enough to irritate the boy's throat and lungs as well. The child was growing frantic, but Gus had no time to settle him. He stripped two pillows of their cases and flung one toward the boy.

"I want my mom."

"Yes, I know. We'll see her in a minute. But right now you need to breathe through the cloth. It will filter out the smoke. Just like this."

Gus held a pillowcase up to his face. The boy did likewise. Gus understood that the intensity of the fire beyond the bedroom door meant he had but few minutes to save their lives. First, he needed fresh air. The smoke was becoming denser and burning his eyes. The flood of tears made it almost impossible to see. Gus blinked to squeeze out the tears as he looked over to the window. In spite of the darkness, he knew the room.

I remember that bed. Those toys. Am I kidding myself? How can that be? Do I know this boy? Is Veronica lying to me?

There was more about this place than met the eyes—far more. The sense of familiarity sidetracked him when he could ill afford even a second's worth of distraction. Fortunately, the hysteria of a frantic mother reached his ears from beyond a closed door.

"Joseph! Joseph! Gus! Can you hear me? Gus? Answer me! Joseph?"

"Mommy! Mommy! Mommy!"

The terrified appeals of mother and son brought Gus back to what was at hand. Nightlights from the street filtered through the smoke to show Gus the whereabouts of a window that he vaguely remembered. Guided by the feeble light, he found the window. He struggled to open it. It was a historic window, massive in size, stretching from the floor to the ceiling. Gus strained to open it, but routine repainting over the years had sealed the frame shut.

The chair.

Thinking fast, Gus went for a chair that for reasons unknown he remembered was in the corner of the room. Gripping it firmly, he returned to the window and smashed out the glass panes. A rush of cool air blew past him to enter the room and help both Joseph and him to breathe.

Standing before the busted window, he tossed aside the pillowcase, and inhaled deeply to clear out his lungs. At the same time, he bloodied his fingers in an urgent move to clear away jagged shards of glass protruding from the wooden frame through which they would have to climb. Gus leaned out the window and swallowed hard.

Balls ablaze.

His first sight of the pavement was jarring. He wished he could fall upward. The distance looking up was always half the distance looking down, and the distance looking down was something requiring serious consideration. Three stories. Not good. Gus studied the windowsill.

It's close to the floor. If I can lower the kid closer down to the second story, he might survive the fall. Maybe just broken bones and bruises. Isn't anybody down there? Can anybody catch this kid? Where are the fucking gawkers when you need them?

Gus turned and bolted toward Joseph's bed. He flung the blankets from the bed and separated out the top sheet. The mattress slid off the frame as he tore off the fitted sheet. Scooping up the blankets and sheets from the floor, Gus ran back to the window and fresh air where Joseph now stood looking outside. Gus began tying the two sheets together. Something blew up beyond the closed door. The two looked over their shoulders and waited for something worse to happen. It did not. Gus looked at the boy.

"Don't worry, kid. I'll get you out safe and sound. I'm going to lower you closer to the ground with these sheets. Then you're going to have to let go and drop. You'll do fine. Like dropping from the monkey bars. Do they still have monkey bars on playgrounds?"

"Yes."

"I had to ask. You never know. Listen, try to roll out when you hit the ground. It's better than trying to stay on your feet."

The boy said nothing as Gus finished tying the knots. He dropped the sheet to the floor and reached out with his right hand to grab the wall. He leaned out as far as he dared to assess the ground below.

What can't there be grass? Dirt? Anything but concrete and paving stones. Hard as hell. Unforgiving.

Gus was yet leaning out the window when an explosion tore through the bedroom seeking the path of least resistance. The pressure exited the open window. Luckily, Gus's fingers, still wrapped securely around the window frame, held fast as the blast nearly blew him clear of the building.

Fighting off the fright of a near catastrophe, Gus pulled himself back into the building. He saw the boy was knocked against the wall, but safe. He spun around expecting to see a raging inferno at his back. He was not disappointed, but the sight that nearly buckled his knees was that of Veronica standing directly before him. He was mortified.

"Jesus!"

Gus looked behind her and saw the opened bedroom door now acting like an oxygen feed for the inferno. The flames set about at once to devour the doorjambs and adjoining walls. He looked back at Veronica, but had no time to ask how she had managed to pass through the inferno unscathed wearing only a nightie. Everything beyond the open door resembled the guts of a foundry. The room beyond glowed hot enough to melt steel. The heat that reached him was overwhelming. The boy ran to his mother's side.

"Veronica? Wha... wha...? How did...?"

Gus was speechless as he stood before the window staring at the woman. Her hair was pulled back, earrings exposed to the firelight, amplifying it, splitting it into multicolored beams that radiated in all directions, flowing with and piercing through flames to alter reality, framing her face within a halo of light as if sanctified.

She was *smiling*. He was panic stricken, riddled with fear, trembling from the flood of adrenaline, but Veronica Giordano was standing there looking at him and *smiling*. He knew right then that she had lost her mind. She felt no fear. She felt no pain. She had passed through the flames to be with her son.

Gus mumbled something incoherent. The sight of her standing before him, the realization was devastating.

I could have saved the kid, but.... How will she manage the fall? Not the same thing. How will I save her? I gotta lower her down. She'll be heavier. The fall will be worse. I gotta tie blankets to the sheets. Do I have time? Have I got enough time? Shit!

The fire raced along the back wall about to consume what bed clothing remained. The rush of anxiety brought tears to his eyes. He fought off the futility of their predicament.

"Why are you here? Godammit, Veronica. Why did you come back? Why didn't you run? You were at the front door. You were safe. Why? Why? I told you I would save the boy. Why didn't you believe me? I would have died saving that boy. I swear; I would have done that."

Gus broke into tears. He turned away to look out the window. The futility of their situation was emotionally overwhelming. He turned back to face Joseph. He might yet be able to save the boy. He reached for the child, but Joseph backed tighter against his mother's side. A single convulsive plea erupted from Gus's lips.

"Joseph—"

"Thank you, Gus."

Gus looked at Veronica.

"What?"

"I want to say thank you."

Gus stared at Veronica. She was smiling—beaming. She didn't look real.

"Thank you? Thank you for what? For chrissakes, Veronica, we're gonna die here! We die in the fire, or we die jumping. What the fuck are you thanking me for?" he cried.

"Thank you for setting me free."

"What?"

Gus was overcome with despair.

She's lost it, man. Totally lost it.

Veronica babbled on with her eyes, saying little but looking at both her son and him while offering that killer smile. The smile that sucked him into her life—into this mess. He so wanted to do something for her. It prompted him to go down fighting. He felt a final urge to battle the impossibility of their predicament. He spoke to her as much as to himself.

"You're losing it, Veronica. You're losing it. We gotta get out of here, now. Now! Do you understand? Do you understand what I'm saying? We gotta climb down the sheets. It's our only chance. Now! We gotta do it now!"

"It's okay, Gus. I forgive you."

With that and her killer smile, Veronica pushed Gus backward out the window.

He looked like a falling torch as he dropped through the air in freshly washed clothes that smoldered bright in the passing air. His arms were empty. The child remained with his mother, standing in the flames of the inferno.

Gus was beyond bewilderment. His mind went blank from the overload. There was no time to sort out the confusion. There was only time to hear the sound of his ankles breaking, the sound of his femur shattering as it drove a bone spike slicing through his femoral artery. As Gus's legs gave way, he came down on his elbow, turning the joint into powder and particulates of brittle calcium. His head slammed hard into the pavement, untethering itself from the vertebrae in his neck before bouncing to land again.

Gus rested briefly on his side until gravity rolled him slowly over to settle somewhat on his back. He felt nothing. Paralyzed from the neck down, he lay motionless, listening to his heart as it pumped his blood onto the street.

Gus lay with eyes wide open. Out of the corners, he could see how the fearful shadows of the lower street were pushed back, held at bay by the brilliance of the blaze. He could see sparks and fire raining down from above to litter the pavement and his body. Glowing embers burned his clothes, setting his shirt to smolder and flame. He could smell burning flesh but had no feeling. His eyes followed the cascade of glittering embers back up to the broken window where flames now roared. They reached far out the windowless opening for the same fresh air he too once craved.

Gus saw movement on the ground. It proved to be the most mystifying image of all. In stunned silence, he watched Veronica exit the front door of the building with Joseph at her side and walk toward him. She was radiant. Not a hint of harm from the firestorm. He glanced back up at the flames leaping out the window overhead. The cold pavement could not dampen the scorching heat from reaching his face, and in spite of it, he shook uncontrollably as the woman stopped at his side.

Veronica looked down at Gus. She let loose of her son's hand and dropped slowly to her knees. She smiled. Gus watched his severed artery spray blood everywhere, including across the woman he had held with intimacy only hours before. She drew him in close, holding his head firmly in her embrace. She wiped his brow, the smile never leaving her face.

"Thank you, Gus. Thank you for everything. I gotta go."

Gus never closed his eyes. The world simply went dark. His last vision was that of Veronica's smile giving way to form full gorgeous lips, gentle with passion as they descended to meet his—and the glitter of firelight dancing off her dangling earrings.

16

A cloudy haze hung over Gus as he worked crusted eyelids apart. He watched helplessly as unwanted light dug down to his pupils. Light was his second awareness. Before light, there was pain. Pain at the back of his brains that spread like glue to make sure nothing was separated, nothing to fall away and miss out on the hell that pounded the inside of his head.

Gus stared into that gloom overhead. Subconsciously, he began to seek features that might bring the world into perspective. He sensed he was looking upward into an overcast sky. It was a heavy sky. It seemed to be a single, thick, impenetrable gray cloud. A featureless thing that might give one vertigo.

Gus discovered his tongue. He pushed it outward and separated his jaws. They spread far enough for him to slide it back and forth across his lips. His lips were sticky dry. They felt unattached, like cardboard Band-Aids slapped across the opening of his mouth.

A sudden rise of the chest startled him. He felt a cool damp air flow inside and circulate. It brought on a change, an awakening that also coursed within. A hint of smoke wafted through his sinuses. He felt the air, now warmed, now useless, leave. Its departure seemed to take with it much of the gloom suspended overhead. Now, Gus saw *stuff*. Things. Cracks. Lines. Writing.

Peeling paint. All variety of irregularities began to take shape. He found it overwhelming, and so closed his eyes.

Darkness halved the onslaught to his senses. It felt easier to listen than look. It hurt less. His ears hardly felt like they wanted to explode. They did not feel violated. In fact, the intrusion of sounds eased his discomfort. They were distracting. They swirled around him, but tended to sort themselves out.

To anybody else, it was the one-dimensional sound of traffic. A wall of noise that hit like pie in the face. But to Gus, if sound was pie, then it was mixed fruit pie, every color, every texture, every flavor to be savored. Again, he licked his lips. These were sounds that he appreciated, sounds that satiated him. Like warm pie, the indulgence comforted his soul. He would sleep better for it.

Whether by screech of a brake, or blast of a horn, Gus sensed the highway was nearby and working to awake him. It was ready to take him away. It was stirring his mind with glimpses of roads and horizons. The highway was calling, prodding, luring Gus out of a deathlike sleep. It was time to awake, to move. It was time.

Gus re-opened his eyes. He blinked once, twice, three times. He willfully took a long breath.

Okay, I'm awake. Easier to be dead. It is what it is.

Gus turned his head to the side and took note of his surroundings. Bleak was his first impression. Cement floor was his second. A good reason for discomfort. Everything else....

What the hell...?

For a moment or two, Gus remained perfectly still. He was confused. He began searching for memories that might explain what he was doing in a—

Parking garage?

The revelation failed to sink in fully on the first go-round.

A parking garage. I passed out in a parking garage. A parking garage... a parking garage. On the floor? Not even in a back seat? Unbelievable.

Gus forced himself to repeat the fact in order to accept the truth of it.

What the hell was I doing last night?

Gus searched for an answer but nothing came forth. He could not piece it together. There was an echo when he finally spoke aloud.

"Okay. We've been down this road before. Maybe not this bad a road but...."

Too much drinking. Too much of everything.... But memory. I'm probably better off not knowing what I got into last night.

With that supposition, he closed his eyes. His mind went blank. That was fine with Gus. He was happy enough to avoid rushing any strenuous thought, regrets, concerns, or memories that might require taking responsibility or paying for damages.

Balls ablaze, this concrete is cold.

Thoughts of a blanket, mattress, or pillow were just that. Thoughts. Wishful thoughts. A realistic thought had more to do with getting on his feet.

I don't want to stand up. Not going to be fun. I just know it.

Gus rolled over onto his belly. He raised himself to his knees. He struggled for balance. It was slow to come. For that reason, he stayed put, remaining on his knees until certain that if his bent ankles lost any more feeling, there would be no getting up.

"Oooooooooohhh."

Gus moaned as he worked to straighten out his locked-up ankles. He moaned about the numbness in his legs. He moaned about the relentless throbbing that clobbered the inside of his head. To his credit, he did manage to stand up, but not without swaying like the drunken fool he most likely was hours prior. Credit and stability were rightfully due to a concrete column identified by a large red encircled number 7. It was in arm's reach, and already in the business of keeping a building from falling over.

Gus leaned on the column for a moment. He assessed his surroundings from this new vantage point. His overriding impression was one of familiarity. Unfortunately, it was that sense of familiarity that highlighted the total lack of any other impressions. His eyes swept the perimeter of the garage.

Okay. Nothing. I'm getting nothing about what's happening here. I should remember something.

Gus attempted to clear his mind.

"Nothing."

I feel like I been drugged.

Gus's eyes dropped to view his chest. He looked at his arms and his legs, front and back. He patted down his frame until certain; he had not been hurt in some fashion. Gus frowned.

How odd not to have any memories—of any kind.

So odd that a wave of panic washed over him. It came with a rush of adrenaline that caused him to shake. He focused on past events, or intended to, but there were no past events. It was about then that he realized the depth of his affliction.

What the hell is my name? My... name... is—

Nothing.

Instinctively, Gus slid his hands across his pockets. When he reached his back pocket, he frowned.

I don't have my wallet. How can that be? Where would I have left my wallet? Balls ablaze, I can't remember anything.

Gus searched the concrete floor for clues. Anything to shed light on his situation. He spotted a smudge of red. Possibly blood. He reached up to scratch the back of his head, only to discover a wound. He looked at his fingers.

Blood. Interesting.

He passed his fingers across the back of his head a second time.

Humph. That's blood all right. Must have passed out. Fell backward. Hit the concrete. Have amnesia. Makes some kind of sense.

Gus accepted the assumption without much problem. He gave another try at remembering something else, anything. There was nothing.

Great. One big blank slate.

Gus quieted. Ironically, his assumption relaxed him. He fell back gently against the concrete column and stared out across the garage. His mind was empty but calm. A head-wound brought logic to his situation. For now, it worked, but at a much deeper level, Gus sensed something else—something weird. He sensed he had lost something far greater than memories.

The garage seemed to be getting darker. It appeared to be filling with shadows. It felt suffocating. Something was prompting him to leave. He focused on an entrance ramp into the parking garage that sloped downward from the outside. He was below ground level.

"Time to go."

Gus started for the ramp. He staggered up the incline, stopping only long enough to scan the cars.

Is one of those mine?

He stood midway up the ramp thinking about it, but nothing appeared familiar, so he resumed the climb. The ramp winded him badly. He had tackled it too soon after regaining his consciousness. Panting hard, and feeling the sweat break out across his forehead, Gus backed up to lean against a wall at street level. He fought off the discomfort of pressure in his chest. His jaw hung slack, drawing his tongue aside from the inrush of passing air. His lips went from sticky-dry to crusty before he stopped gasping.

Energy drink, anybody? Protein shake? Wheaties? I'll take two.

Gus's sense of humor seemed to be intact, but it wasn't around long enough to be appreciated. He was wary of the street. It was unwelcoming, unfriendly enough to keep him quiet as a mouse until his strength improved. The place was blatantly abnormal. He wasted no time pushing off the wall as soon as strength allowed. Instinctively, he walked through a barren neighborhood headed toward a high ridge lined with old multi-story red brick buildings. They looked equally abandoned from below, but a brighter sky was visible beyond the structures. The light and sounds reassured him that he was going in the best direction.

17

The call of the highway was all that Gus needed. It was the only sound of life in a lifeless world. It permeated every street, every alley, every crack that split pavers. For Gus, the noise was to his ears what beacons of light were to the eyes of lost sailors.

The sounds guided him through the obscurity of this place, this neighborhood that seemed heartless and uncaring. He felt unwelcome, but at the same time forcibly leashed to something that followed, or worse, permanently chained to the shadows he was despairing to escape. The whole of it anguished him.

More than ever, Gus wanted to reach that highway. More than ever, he wanted to run to the sounds that heralded a better place, a place of life, a place of movement and action, a party. A place quite opposite to this, which felt like a party passed, a hangover. A piece of stale pizza crust lying in a box—that unappealing remainder of what was a mouthwatering delight devoured the night before by a rowdy group of celebrating drunks.

Something certainly devoured this place. Something gutted everything good and uplifting ages ago. Only the crust remains. Nothing but a dried out crust of better times passed.

The place seemed to be little more than an extension of the parking garage he had rushed to exit—cold and lifeless. And much like the parking ramp, he now walked up steeply inclined streets that were kicking his ass every bit as bad. The sidewalks should have been stepped. It was much like mounting a cliff, not that extreme, but a fight nonetheless, a battle to rise above the wretched place.

Gus looked back over his shoulder. He looked down into the encroaching gloom that filled the spaces, gloom that flowed like fog to cover his tracks. The street channeled a storm of familiarity that haunted him. Fear was closing in on him, breathing down his neck, whispering in his ear to forewarn that the collector of debts had arrived.

Gus's hair stood on end. He shuddered. He was quick to look ahead, to look at the crest of the hill, to look at the promising light beyond. With renewed vigor, he picked up the pace. Intent on leaving his fears behind, he focused on the roar of traffic. It was overwhelming. It was deafening. It drowned out all thoughts of concern.

It was with great relief that Gus surmounted the hill. Once he had scaled it, he stood on the upper expanse free to pursue the only thing that mattered. The one thing he needed. Each step brought him closer to breaking through the sprawling row of ridge structures that prevented him from seeing the thoroughfare. They resembled a formidable line of defense that contained the essence of life, the pulse of humanity.

As he passed through, he next came upon a second smaller barrier of shops and stands. These edifices catered to untold thousands of wayfarers. He stood awestruck, amazed, by the density of people moving slowly through a channel between the shanties and the shoulder of the road. His eyes moved up the bank of the shoulder in wonder of what lay beyond. The sound overpowered all. It thundered overhead, leaving him lost for any idea of its magnitude.

Wasting no time, Gus climbed the bank and crossed the shoulder in a daze. This monument without end was unlike anything he had ever seen. It defied description.

"Wow...."

A single word, nearly indistinguishable exited on his breath. The highway was dead straight, straight as the beams of sunshine that now came back along its length from a distant horizon. The rising sun burned out all detail, turning everything shaded into silhouettes. Gus was unable to define anything in the distance before him. The light was too bright.

To the side, Gus noted that the freeway, along with its congested shoulder, remained raised above all else. It stood proudly for as far as he could see. The shoulder was wide, and propped up by a sizable bank that fell away to the level of the shanties, and farther out, the brick ridge-line structures that glowed dirty red in the sunlight. Side streets that arose from the shadowy depths beyond the ridge regularly intersected the shoulder and highway.

Gus's fixation broke only once, and for little more than seconds, when he dared to look behind one last time. Briefly, he stared back toward that steep, narrow, barren, side street. It was a tough climb out of the dark swirling nightmare. From the height of the road, he viewed an unending bank of ominous storm clouds that churned violently and concealed everything beneath. It felt like his past.

"Good riddance to your miserable lot."

Gus turned his back on the unholy place with an enormous sense of relief. Now, he absorbed all before him that was alive and upbeat. He looked up and down along the highway and reveled in the midst of life that appeared nonsensically vibrant.

There were thousands of people streaming along the shoulder of the road. Every size and shape, every race, families, couples, friends, people dressed in every fashion imaginable, all bumping into one another, all jostling for space and carrying on, laughing, conversing, engaged in all manner of business and fun. The abnormality of the scene was astounding, a little overwhelming, but certainly consoling when compared to the wasteland of empty streets back in the depths.

In spite of all the commotion and distraction one might envision, the highway itself is what held Gus's attention. He stood with toes to the curb as he studied everything about the thoroughfare. It was like something out of an epic science fiction story. If symmetrical, he estimated the highway to be at least fifty or sixty lanes wide. He could not say for sure because it was difficult to see anything beyond the center lanes.

The traffic in each lane moved at distinctly different speeds. The outside lane was strictly for curbside parking, pick-ups, and delivery. The closer a lane of traffic to center, the faster it moved, faster and faster until reaching the centermost lanes where vehicles were but passing blurs of motion.

They must be traveling four or five hundred miles an hour... or more, maybe a lot more.

The speeding vehicles prevented anyone from crossing the street. Not that anyone would consider such an undertaking in the first place. It was simply too outrageous a distance. It was as if looking across a dozen airport runways butted up side by side with traffic every bit as fast and loud as jetliners.

Whereas it was impossible to identify anything traveling down the center lanes due to their speed, it was equally impossible to identify the vehicles that travelled the slower outer lanes. Cobbled encasements of outlandish decoration, mismatching parts, aftermarket bolt-ons, and untold distances of accumulated dirt hid the original body designs from view. Buses and motorhomes converted for the long haul far outnumbered cars. Gus's thoughts centered on the continent down under.

Australia. Balls ablaze, I'm in Australia. I gotta be in Australia. No shit. I gotta be....

Make it true and I'm a convert. I'm on my knees. Hell, I'll be a nun if it gets my memory back. This has to be Australia. Another clue. Sunday morning in....

18

Gus continued to walk toward the sunlight. The warmth felt wonderful on his face. The heat worked through his clothes to warm his chest and alleviate the stiffness in his frame. He walked calmly amid a thousand strangers as the sky and neighboring countryside warmed under the rising sun. Shoulder to shoulder with men, women, and children, like fish folding into a school for protection, he centered himself within the safety of those souls that surrounded him.

Moving without a mission or the apparent determination of others, Gus was content in allowing the throngs to pull him along in their wake. Their movement was harmonious and hypnotic. It was a unified rhythm that, when combined with the morning sun, made his eyes too heavy to hold open and so they easily succumbed to the warmth and inner peace. He was free of worry, free of fear, free of all things negative. Briefly.

The shredding sound of screeching brakes stopped Gus from walking unknowingly into the path of a bus-like contrivance that jumped the curb. The vehicle appeared bent on running him over. His eyes snapped open a split second before the door of the bus did likewise. Gus jumped backward to safety as he spotted the driver looking directly at him with a big-toothed, carnival-like grin. The man looked like a voodoo freak intent on strangling himself with a silky, multicolored bandana.

The son of a bitch did that on purpose.

The bus held Gus's attention as a file of kids moved forward between the seats to crowd the opened front door. They formed an unintentional barrier between Gus and the grinning driver as they poured out of the vehicle. One by one, they filed off the bus and crashed into each other. Backpacks caused them to teeter as they jammed up on the shoulder.

The pushing and shoving forced Gus away from the bus as the last manic passenger either tripped or intentionally jumped to the shoulder of the road. The jumper's eyes darted erratically, as if searching for a runaway dog. He bolted forward, plowing into the students, bumping into Gus, and barging his way across the flow of the crowd. He apologized to no one.

"Rude. Very rude. What's the hurry, man?"

Gus hollered toward the jumper now out of earshot. He looked back toward the bus and saw the driver grinning in his direction. The man nodded as if he knew Gus, and then closed the door. The vehicle headed back into the torrent of traffic.

Why was he nodding at me? That was weird. Was he telling me something? Did he see something? Was he laughing about the guy bumping into me?

Fully awakened from his sun-induced stupor by the ruckus of kids, Gus looked away from the departing bus and caught a parting glimpse of the jumper's head bobbing up and down within the flow of the crowd. He was fascinated.

Huh. Why the rush? What's he all about? Why was that driver nodding at me? Was he laughing at me? Does he know me? Is all this connected?

Gus unexpectedly broke into a light trot. He elected to keep the jumper in sight. There was no reason to follow the stranger aside from meaningless curiosity, like a cat chasing a shadow. Like most cats, Gus had nothing better to do, whereas the stranger, unlike most cats, unlike Gus, appeared to have a purpose.

He doesn't act like the crowd. He's on a mission of some sort. Like what? What does one do in this place? What the hell's he up to?

The answer came fast. Curiosity dissipated quickly as the jumper made his way directly into a patron-filled shanty belching odors of frying bacon and onion breath.

All that rudeness for breakfast? Seriously?

A little disappointed, Gus fell back from a trot to pace himself. As he slowed to a walk, he gaged the feel of the shanty. It seemed amicable. Nobody staring or paying him notice. The spirited chatter of patrons seated along an endless breakfast counter sufficed to damp Gus's world of paranoia. Enough so, that for one glorious distracted moment, Gus's appetite exploded. Fresh pangs of hunger skewered him with every inhalation.

Coffee. God, I'd kill for coffee.

Gus followed the jumper with caution. A second, closer look confirmed the person was young. Not much older than the kids who had exited the bus. A couple taking their leave barely had time to stand up before the bad-mannered clod crowded in to grab a vacated seat. He sat down on one of the only two stools available at the closest end of the shanty. Gus held back, allowing the couple to pass. The smell of breakfast caused his stomach to groan. He eased up to the second stool and quietly seated himself.

Maybe the jumper isn't an idiot after all. Maybe just starving like me. Maybe not. Oh, oh. I haven't got my wallet. Shit, I forgot about that. No money.

Gus instinctively reached again for his wallet. There was no wallet. This time his hands slid from back around to front, passing over his pockets. The feel was different. He rubbed his pocket, and then slipped his hand inside. Between two fingers, he retrieved a couple of folded five-dollar bills. He held it in front of his eyes.

Now, where did that come from? How did I miss that? I checked my pockets. Huh. Can't believe I missed that. Too thin, I guess. Just didn't notice it.

Pleased by his good fortune, Gus snapped out of his thoughts and noted a hundred or more stools fronting the counter. It stretched as far as he could see. Details of eaters disappeared in the distance. He noted that all the stools were occupied, leaving many to order food and eat while standing behind friends lucky enough to sit. Frequently, a diner would yell, "Gotta go!" and a scramble for his or her seat would ensue. The turnover was fast, patrons rising to stand and squatting to sit in a chaotic show of discordance.

Two servers approached as soon as Gus seated himself. They were both men. The one advancing toward Gus was direct.

"How ya doin', bud?"

"Good, I guess. I think."

"What'll it be?"

"Is it too early for me to get lunch?"

"Not at all."

"What's the lunch special?"

"Half poun' groun' round, sesame bun browned, bacon, cheese, deluxe in a mound."

"That works."

"Fries?"

"Please."

"Drink?"

"Coffee."

"Black?"

"Absolutely."

"On its way."

The server turned and dashed away. Gus raised himself halfway off the stool. He leaned over the counter to look along the length of its backside. He studied the faces of the servers for as far as he could see.

"Looking for something?"

Gus turned to face the other server, who had finished taking the jumper's order.

"Ahh, no. Sorry. Thought I knew somebody who worked here. I think it was a gal. I'm not sure."

I think it was a gal? I'm not sure? I "think" it was a gal? Balls ablaze, what the hell was that? Girls have tits, guys not so much. Why not just scribble "idiot" across my forehead?

The waiter appeared somewhat amused.

"Anything else I can get you?"

"Sorry, that didn't come out right. Bad memory. Meant to say, I thought I knew a gal who worked here. Anyway, I'm good, thanks."

Gus apologized, hoping to nip his blunder in the bud.

"Your order should be up in a minute."

"Great. Thanks."

Gus sat quietly, focused on the particulars of this place. Everything seemed somehow familiar. The sensation was messing with his head. What really bothered him was a notion that he knew a girl connected to the surroundings. He tried hard to focus, to dredge up some memory of her, a vision, but to no avail. He dismissed the effort.

Gus rotated his seat around a few degrees to get a better look at the passing crowd. It was a spellbinding sight, strange in every way—then again, familiar. He had so many questions, and there was no one to ask except possibly the person sitting next to him. The jumper. Gus studied him with some intent until finally sizing him up.

To his surprise, the jumper appeared to be a high-school kid more boyish than manly. Gus pegged him to be late teens or early twenties. He wore a light windbreaker and a baseball cap. Gus was unable to make out the emblem on the cap because the person stared into a cup of coffee held firmly between his hands. He kept rolling his fingers across the cup repeatedly, ringing it with each of his fingernails—*tink-tink-tink-tink*.... *tink-tink-tink-tink*. If Gus was anybody else, he would have left the jumper to his thoughts, but Gus was not anybody else.

"Say, bud.... You from these parts?"

The stranger turned to acknowledge Gus with a quick, confused glance. The emblem on his cap said *QUEER DAZE*. The guy immediately turned back to stare at his coffee. It was obvious to Gus that he had annoyed the man.

"Didn't mean to bother you. I'm lost, simple as that. Thought you might be able to tell me where I am."

The young man turned to face Gus a second time. Now, he studied Gus's face. He said nothing, but his expression changed to one of blunder or possibly shock. He reached up and pulled an ear bud out of his ear. He rolled it between his fingers.

"Sorry."

An apologetic look remained on the young man's face as he spoke.

"I didn't hear you. I was listening to music."

"No problem. Just wanted to know if you can tell me where I am. Long story, short. Had an accident. Got amnesia, and it's a bitch." Gus shook his head in despair. "Anyhow, I'm lost. This place looks familiar, but.... I was hoping you could tell me where I am."

"Veniae."

"Veniae?"

"Yeah. Locum Veniae."

"Where's that? What neighborhood?"

The look of apology shifted to something more pathetic. He turned back to his coffee. Gus persisted.

"Can you tell me what city I'm in?"

This time the jumper did not look at Gus. His eyes remained fixed on his mug of coffee.

"You ain't in any city, man."

"Well, then, what state am I in?" asked Gus.

"State? That's easy. You're in a state of transience. Going from one place to another, just like me, just like the rest of us fools. This place is a tollbooth. You pay the price and you move on. That-a-way. Forever."

The kid flipped a wrist to point out the direction with his thumb and said nothing more. It was for the best because Gus found the young man to be distinctly unpleasant.

Clearly higher than a kite.

Gus twisted about to observe the crowd that, as the kid stated, was headed one way.

That-a-way. Place is frickin' bizarre. Maybe I'm the one higher than a kite.

"Here ya go, sir. Enjoy."

The waiter placed his meal on the counter. Gus cut loose his anxieties. The sight of a steaming hot steak burger overshadowed all else. He grabbed the sandwich with both hands and jammed it into his mouth.

Oh, God, that's good. Jesus. Delicious. Mmmph.

Gus was famished. He could not remember the last time a meal tasted this good. He stuffed himself, but no matter how much he ate, there always seemed to be food left over.

That's it. No more. Can't do it. Another bite and I puke.

He gave up trying to finish the fries on his plate. Gus tossed his napkin across the food that remained on his plate. He leaned back to take a breath. The waiter never missed a beat. He was there with a coffee pot.

"Get ya anything else? Dessert?"

"You know, I gotta tell you. I ate until I felt like I was going to bust open, and I'm still hungry. I'm stuffed, but I'm hungry. No matter how much I eat, I always need something sweet to get my blood sugar up. I crave something sweet. You got any candy back there? You know, like after-dinner mints or something?"

"Candy? Sorry, bud. I got pie, apple, cherry, blueberry—"

"Oh, god, no. I can't do that. Pie will kill me. I need something simple. A piece of candy. A mint. You know. Jell-O. Something like that. A sugar fix."

"What about chocolate?"

The sound of the word sent a wave of adrenaline through Gus's guts. His head snapped to face the jumper.

"Pardon?" asked Gus in surprised shock.

"How about chocolate? You know, *choco, coco.*"

"Yeah, I know. Jesus!" Gus glanced around the shanty to see if anybody overheard the question. "You think you can say that any louder? Are you nuts or what?"

"Just a question, man."

"Oh, yeah. Hell of a question."

"It's a yes or no."

"I've never been opposed to a bit of chocolate now and then," whispered Gus. His guts squirmed at the thought of it. "What's a young guy like you doing messin' around with choco?"

"I'll take that as a yes."

Gus didn't respond.

"I know where you can get a bar. More if you want," said the jumper. "I mean, if you're serious."

"I'm serious, but I don't need a bar. A piece would do."

"Whatever. Let me know."

"I am letting you know. A piece would do. Yeah, that would do it. You carrying or what?"

"No, no-no-no-no. I never carry."

"Okay, so...." Gus waited.

"Did you really lose all of your memory? I mean everything?"

Gus briefly studied the guy before answering.

"Yeah. Pretty much. Why?"

"I guess I was just wondering if you forget everything. What makes you think you'll remember where I tell you to go?"

Gus hadn't really given the matter any thought. The few seconds of delay in his response was enough to tip off the kid.

"Ya know, it's just as easy for me to show you."

"It's not too far, is it?"

"Nah. Down the street a bit."

"Fine. Let's do it."

Gus was quick to get to his feet. He watched the jumper finish his coffee and ease himself off the stool. The man tossed a bill on the counter.

"Lunch is on me."

"Hey, you don't have to do that."

"I wanted to. Ya look like warmed over death. C'mon, I'll get ya dessert."

"Jesus, I really look that bad?"

"Yeah, you do. Stay away from mirrors."

"Nice."

Gus shook his head as he followed the cocky young man out of the shanty. To Gus's surprise, the guy started to walk against the crowd. That was the first time he had seen anybody do so. He hustled to keep up in spite of nervousness in the pit of his stomach.

"Hey! Where you going?"

"Not too far. Just around the corner."

"Yeah, I know. You said that, but you're going against the crowd."

"What?"

"I said, you're going against the crowd. I haven't seen anybody do that. Makes me uncomfortable. Doesn't it bother you?"

"Bother me?"

"Yeah."

"Mmm. No. Not really. Bothers you, huh?"

"Yeah. Either that or it's something I just ate."

"You mean like you feel sick?

"A lot like that. You know that squirming feeling you get just before you toss? It's something like that but worse."

"Not sure what to say. I eat there all the time. Great food. You sure it's not something else?"

"I don't know. Where're we going? How much farther?"

"To see the teacher. Not far."

"The teacher?"

"Yeah, the teacher. That's what the kids call him. Hey, you sure you wanna go? You don't look so hot."

"Thanks for pointing that out—again."

"You having second thoughts?"

"I wasn't till just now. I'm thinking."

"Well, think fast. It's your call. Ya want choco or not? I'm not pissin' my day away watching you puke or something."

Gus looked toward the horizon and noticed a band of black clouds building. In the distance, appendages of soot-like plumes ascended upward to immense heights. A massive pang of adrenaline passed through his insides. He looked away from the horizon.

"Yeah, I guess."

"Ya guess what?"

"I guess we can go. That's what," said Gus with an air of annoyance.

"You're sure."

"Just go."

The jumper nodded. "Okay, this way."

The jumper rounded a corner to his left. The street rolled over the bank in a steep decline that entered a darker shadowy realm. Gus could not make out details at the end of the road, but the severity of his anxiety was becoming unbearable. He called out to the jumper.

"Ah, shit. Don't tell me we're going down there."

"You're giving me some seriously mixed signals."

"I know, but—"

"This is where you get it. The teacher's down there."

Gus found himself torn between the lights, highway, and high ground on the one side, and choco, empty streets, and shadows snaking about on the other.

"How far down do we have to go?"

"Not far, and not long, if you'd quit stopping every two minutes. Now, c'mon."

"What's your name?" asked Gus.

"We don't do names. You know that."

What? What'd he say? I know that? What'd that mean? Why would I know that? Am I a user, a regular?

Unsettled by his thoughts, Gus moved warily into the murkiness. Then to his surprise, groups of teenagers came into view, all scattered, all milling in the streets. A heavy pall seemed to lift. They were self-absorbed, laughing, carrying on, and paying no attention to Gus or the jumper. Gus yelled ahead.

"Hey! What's with all the kids?"

"School."

"School?"

The jumper stopped and turned toward Gus.

"Do you not know where you are?"

Okay. Definitely more to this than meets the eye. Am I supposed to know this place? Anything look familiar?

Gus looked around, trying to make out details within the gloom.

"Uhhh.... No. I don't know. Maybe. No, I guess not. Should I?"

"I don't know. I thought you might."

Gus frowned.

"Why would you think that? Do we know each other?"

"Yeah."

Gus was stunned.

"You're kidding me. Why didn't you tell me that when we were eating?"

"I didn't need you poundin' on me."

"Poundin' on ya. What does that mean?"

The young man removed his cap, wiped his brow with his arm, and looked at Gus.

"You don't recognize me?"

"No."

"Interesting."

He replaced the cap, adjusting it back and forth until the embroidered emblem *QUEER DAZE* appeared properly level above his eyes.

"Interesting, why?" asked Gus.

"Cuz, you don't like me."

Gus noticed the shadows were thickening farther along the street.

"Why don't I like you?"

"Cuz you thought I wronged you."

"Wronged me? Wronged me how?"

"Movin' in on your action."

Gus studied the kid who was now looking at him straight in the eyes as if sizing him up.

"I'm not sure I understand. In fact, I know I don't. What the hell are you talkin' about?"

"It ain't important. This is the place."

The jumper turned away from Gus. He walked directly toward the uninspiring entranceway of an insipid-looking commercial brick building. Gus watched him push a button, or doorbell, or something similar, wait a moment, and disappear inside. Flanking the entrance, Gus noticed small square windows quartered by steel-framed panes of opaque glass dotting the walls overhead as they stretched into the distance. Also upon the sidewalk bordering the entrance were half a dozen unoccupied tables surrounded by chairs.

Gus hesitated outside a moment before following the jumper into the building. He glanced farther down the street and noted shadows milling about. He was certain they were growing darker and reaching higher up the sides of the buildings. He believed the darkness was quietly swallowing up the street and moving slowly toward him.

Gus believed it was the shadows that made his guts churn miserably. He was at a loss to explain his morbid fear of the gloom, but it was enough to drive him toward the entrance doors. He pushed the button on the wall. The door clicked and moved slightly ajar. Gus wasted no time reaching for a handle and slipping inside. He was happy to distance himself from the obscurities lingering down the street.

Upon entering the building, Gus saw the jumper speaking with an older gray-haired man seated at a desk. The man turned his head toward the entrance door with anticipation. An expression of amazement covered his face as he stood up from behind a desk. It changed to a broad grin followed by disbelief as he spoke.

"I'll be damned. I never thought I'd see your sorry ass again. I'd ask how the hell are ya, but by the looks of ya, I'm thinking you been in some sort of dog fight."

"You know me?"

The man's face froze. An expression of bemusement crept across it before ending in a half-grin realization.

"So it's true."

The man's head tilted to one side as his eyes shifted to the jumper, now sitting on top of a nearby desk and adjusting his QUEER DAZE cap.

"He has no idea who we are," said the young man.

"You—got-ta—be—shit-tin'—me."

The old man's words came long and drawn out. He was shaking his head in wonderment. The jumper continued.

"Sat right next to me, shoulder to shoulder, at the breakfast counter. Not a clue."

"All right." Gus interrupted. "You guys win. Like you said, I have no idea who the hell you are, but obviously you know me. So can we move past your great surprise at my expense, and just get down to bringing me up to speed? Knowing my name would be a good place to start."

The two men broke into a fit of laughter.

"Now, that's funny. That's just too funny," said the gray-haired man, still laughing with an air of disbelief. Gus was not amused.

"Guys, this is getting old fast. How about we cease with the hilarity and get on with introductions, maybe tell me what my name is?"

The men laughed all the harder, stopping only after seeing the rage build in Gus's eyes, at which point the old man spoke.

"Don't take it personal. Nobody knows your name. That, my friend, is why we are laughing. It's too outrageous to be true."

"You called me Gus."

"We all call you *Gus*. That's what you go by. Gus," said the gray-haired man.

"And the rest of it?"

The two men looked at each other and back at Gus.

"There is no *rest of it*. You go by Gus. That's it. That's all it's ever been. Gus."

"What? We don't do last names?" asked Gus, unsatisfied.

The men looked at each other and again at Gus.

"*We* do last names. *You* don't do last names," said the older man.

"Why?"

"That's you. Always contrary. Always against the grain. *You* don't do last names."

"Do you know where I live? Anything about me?"

The gray-haired man and the jumper glanced at each other as if to agree they were in accord. The old man exhaled loudly and leaned back in his chair. He shook his head.

"No."

"No," Gus repeated with a sound of defeat.

"No."

"But you guys know me."

"Yeah," the two men said in unison.

"You know me well?"

"Yeah," again a response in unison.

"Let me get this straight," said Gus. "You guys know me well, but you don't know my last name, or where I live, or anything about me."

"Well, we didn't say that we don't know anything about you. We said we only know you as Gus and we have no idea where you live."

"Fair enough," said Gus. "How do you know me?"

"We're all business partners," said the young man.

"Business partners?" repeated Gus with visible disbelief.

"Yeah," said the old man.

"Doin' what?"

"Choc. You deal in choc. We all deal in choc."

"Choc?" Gus repeated thoughtfully, then after a pause, he asked with notable surprise, "I deal in choc?"

The two men were in constant visual communication. They were amazed.

"Yeah, Gus. Choc. You deal in choc, coco," said the gray-haired man. "You deal in high-grade chocolates. You were number one, primo, alpha, the best. Rich. Filthy fuckin' rich. I don't know about your name, but I hope you haven't forgotten where you stashed all your millions. That would truly be a fucking pity."

The gray-haired man snickered and then all three men went silent, all equally amazed by the revelations at hand. The gray-haired man nodded at the conclusion of some inner thought, and then rose from his desk.

"If you have lost your memory, as you say, then you need to see this. Who knows, maybe it will trigger something in your head and get you back to the real world."

The man stepped away from his desk and walked across the large office-lobby-like room toward a door. He turned toward Gus.

"Are you coming?"

"First I want to know your name. Are you the teacher?"

"Some call me that. Mostly the kids around here. The name's Trudel. Carlton Trudel."

Gus said nothing. The name meant nothing. He started across the room. As he neared the man and door, the jumper slid off the desk and followed.

Carlton upturned his palm in a gesture that invited Gus to open the door. He did and stepped through into a warehouse-sized facility filled with stations. A warm, moist blast of air washed over the three men as they entered. The air was heavy with the fragrance of chocolate.

The saliva in Gus's mouth flowed uncontrollably. He found himself inhaling deeply, sucking in the air heavily saturated with the sweet scent. The involuntary act made him somewhat light-headed until he settled down.

Carlton stopped amid the stations and turned toward Gus.

"Well? Do you remember this? Any of it?" he asked with a sweeping motion of his outstretched arm.

Gus followed the sweep of Carlton's arm and peered into the subdued light, the dark gloom intent on concealing the rows of manned stations. Each with a single occupant sitting before a half dozen monitors. Tubing and wires dangled above the stations from the darkness overhead. The monitors provided the only light. The darkness provided privacy and isolated each station.

"Nope."

"Unbeeeelieeeevable," stressed the gray-haired man in a whisper. "Consider my shock in knowing that you paid for half of it. Half of everything you see. You, my friend, were instrumental in most of, no..., in *all* of the design and layout of this facility." Carlton looked at Gus and snickered. "Yup, this is unbelievable. Follow me. I want you to talk to one of the employees. Maybe that'll help."

Carlton headed into the midst of stations with Gus and the jumper in tow. Gus glanced at each of the stations he passed and observed a singularly notable fact. Each of the occupants that operated a station weighed close to a thousand pounds. These employees were freaks of nature.

Carlton came to a halt. He addressed the occupant. "Good afternoon, Jerry. I brought a familiar face. You remember Gus, don't you?"

Jerry's face turned, but his head seemed to remain in place. It was an illusion brought on by his size. The face spit out a transparent feeding tube filled with a brown substance in order to offer up a smile.

"Good afternoon, Mr. Trudell." Then with notable exertion, Jerry rotated his eyes in the direction of Gus. They strained to swivel in their sockets in order to save Jerry's head the effort of moving out of position.

"Oh, gosh, yes. Mr. Gus. How are you, sir? It's nice to see you. It's nice that you're back. It's been a while."

Jerry's speech was peculiar, and it took a following smile to reveal a mouth full of rotted teeth and the reason. Gus winced but quickly concealed his revulsion.

"Likewise, Jerry. How are things going?"

"Not so bad—"

"How's production today?" Carlton interrupted.

Jerry's eyes returned to the glare of the monitors.

"97.4 percent. I apologize for that, Mr. Trudell. A lineman died about four hours ago, just as the day shift was getting under way. It halted production. I had him replaced within seventeen minutes and increased line speed by twelve percent to make up for the lost production. I expect to be at projection by end of shift."

"Excellent, Jerry. You are a credit to the company. That's precisely the kind of performance that warrants a bonus. Let me key-in, Jerry."

Jerry rotated a monitor to face Mr. Trudell. He slid the keyboard toward his boss, who wasted no time. Carlton grabbed a container of antiseptic and sprayed the keyboard. He then ran his fingers across the keys in a blur as cryptic words appeared on the monitor in a password field.

"Your name?" asked the computer.

"Carlton Trudell."

"Please place your hand on the screen."

Carlton did as asked.

"Thank you, Mr. Trudell. How may I assist you?"

"Add five liters of grade 2 choco to Jerry Lambert's allowances."

"Five liters of grade 2 choco have been added to Jerry Lambert's allowances."

"Thank you. Log out."

"You are logged out, Mr. Trudell."

The screen returned to its former view. Jerry was beaming a stub-toothed grin that would have stretched from ear to ear, had there been ears anywhere near his face.

While Jerry passed on his appreciation to Mr. Trudell, Gus turned his attention to the surrounding stations. They reached in both directions forming an orderly grid of rows and columns. All stations had the one common denominator. Occupants of unimaginable size. Each seated beneath a feeding tube that Gus now understood was most likely something far less than grade 2 choco.

19

"Anything?" asked Carlton Trudell.

"Nope. I don't remember any of it. None of it. Wouldn't have recognized Jerry if he sat on me and squeezed my shit out my ears."

Trudell snickered, "You brought Jerry to the firm. Right out of high school. He was a loner, a loser, butt end of every senior class joke. You zeroed in on him, befriended him, got him on choco. And when he could no longer afford to fund his passion, you persuaded him to take a position with the firm."

"He's an asset, Gus. He's one of our best. Not some lost, helpless, homeless scab on a curb. Jerry's mind is sharp. His heart is strong. We'll get years out of him before he explodes. I give you all the credit, my man. You were a hell of a partner."

"What does he weigh?"

Carlton held a finger to his lips and motioned Gus to step away from the cubicle.

He whispered, "Sometimes there can be sensitivity about the whole weight thing. Best to discuss it out of earshot. As for your question... at this point...." Trudell pulled a monitor from his pocket and worked the screen. "Let's see... Jerry Lambert... okay, uhh... that would be... eight-fifty, give or take." Carlton smiled. "The man's got a good three, four, hell, maybe five or even six hundred to go. His heart checks strong, thanks to you."

"How does he move?"

"He doesn't. He never leaves his station."

"Never?"

"Never."

"Unbelievable."

"Not really. Why would he? He's got everything he needs. He wants nothing to do with people. He has his privacy. He has access to all information and current events by way of the infonet. He has a virtually unlimited supply of choco. And besides, by the time they reach six hundred, their legs generally atrophy to a degree that they can't support their own weight."

"So the tubes are...?"

"Feeding tubes. Fortified, Gus. All the vitamins necessary to extend his usefulness. In fact, your brainchild. One of your best. One of many. You extended their lives by forty percent. Brilliant! Trust me, you didn't get filthy fucking rich by being an idiot. Of course, don't take this the wrong way, but only an idiot would forget where he put his stash. That would be humor."

"Yes. And what you see on my face is laughter," quipped Gus.

"You need to work on that a bit."

"I'll keep that in mind. So, you're telling me that Jerry never wants to leave?"

Carlton looked at Gus with a frown.

"Hey, Gus. It's not like he's locked up in here. He can leave anytime he wants. There's no latch on the door. They're all free to go whenever they want. They just don't want to. They're social misfits, weirdoes, ridiculed, square pegs. They have no desire to go out into the world for a fresh reminder of their lot in life. You get what I'm saying?"

"But at eight hundred and fifty pounds, they couldn't go out into the world no matter how they felt."

No one responded. Gus stood motionless, like a marble statue with no guts, no heart, no soul. Empty on the inside. Empty as the existence of those station occupants with nothing to live for.

"I've seen enough. Can we go back?"

"Sure."

Carlton looked over at the jumper. He was troubled. Gus should have been ecstatic over operations and the reminder of his genius. Instead, he appeared appalled. They returned to the office and centered about Carlton's desk.

"Hey, you want some choc? This shit is good. You have my word. Grade AAA Gold. Good as it gets."

Trudell reached into his desk drawer and retrieved an expensively wrapped and wax-sealed bar. Across the face of a premium textured brown wrapper, in brilliant gold stamping read GOLD with bright copper letters, AAA superimposed. He placed it on the desk before Gus. Gus stared at a bar he sensed people would kill for, but he had lost his appetite for something sweet.

"Thanks, but no thanks. I'm good. Actually, I need to step outside for a moment." Gus looked over at the jumper. "What's your name?"

"Berke."

"Berke.... I'll try and remember that."

20

Carlton and Berke looked at each other nervously as Gus headed for the entrance doors. Gus was unaware of that fact as he stepped outside and took a seat at one of the tables. He picked up a placard from the table.

This table provided for your relaxation by the management of G&C Confectionery.

G&C provided tables for the benefit of choco-heads that hung around to buy or use product. Gus sat down, placed his head on his hand, and closed his eyes. He felt depressed. He felt deeply disturbed by the unexpected discovery of his involvement in this illicit affair. Not just his involvement, but also the depth of his involvement.

The vision of Jerry and his one-ton carcass spread out before the electric flicker of monitors in a dark lifeless hole was haunting. Worst of all, Gus suffered to know who he was, to know anything about his past. He wanted his memories back, but feared to know how steep a price he might pay. Gus was not a man to cry. He wanted to cry, but he could not.

The scrape of chair legs across pavement startled him. Gus raised his head, opened his eyes, and saw a high schooler standing alongside the chair with a backpack full of books. The teenager was watching him and sporting an infectious grin.

"Hey, Gus. Where ya been?"

Gus said nothing. He simply stared at the kid and feared what bomb the innocent face would drop.

"Gus! Hey, man. What's up? You mad at me or something?"

"No."

The kid frowned. He removed his backpack, sat it on the table, and settled into a chair. He sat back and studied Gus. The smile disappeared from his face.

"Something wrong?"

"Yeah, you could say that."

"Like what? Something I did to piss ya off?"

"No."

"What then?"

"I had an accident. Don't know where, don't know when, don't know how. In fact, I don't know anything. I don't even know my own name. I mean, I go by Gus. Everybody calls me Gus. But nobody knows my last name, or where I live, or who my friends are. Not even me. In other words, I have absolutely no idea who the hell you are. A rather awkward position considering that clearly you know me."

The kid gave thought to what Gus had told him.

"Now, are you saying that you don't know my name..., or that you don't know me?"

"Your choice."

"Humph. That's different." The kid raised his eyebrows. "Well, for what it's worth, if it makes you feel any better, you always had a thing about names. Not knowing names was a biggy with you. For example, we did a lot of business together, and to this day I still only know you as Mr. Gus."

"What kind of business?"

The kid looked at Gus and frowned.

Speaking with great caution, he said, "I'd rather not say."

Just then, Berke stepped outside and walked over to the table. He nodded toward the kid seated with arms across his backpack. Berke pulled back a chair and sat down. Gus was certain that he understood.

The dreaded bomb dropped.

"You're smart, kid. I don't blame you for being tight lipped. But if it helps, I just walked out of this place." Gus threw his fist up to his shoulder, his thumb pointed at the building behind him. "Berke here gave me the full tour, the entire operation. I saw the stations for monitoring the production of product. In fact, I met an old friend. Jerry Lambert. Do you know Jerry? He can't be more than two or three years older than you."

"Yeah, I knew Jerry. The dude had issues. Haven't seen him around for quite a while. Didn't know he worked for you."

"Neither did I. You feeling a little more comfortable now?"

"A little."

"Listen. If we did any kind of business together, you being a kid and me being way past that, and considering my warm welcome in this place, I'd have to say I was supplying you with choco for your high school parties. Tell me I'm wrong."

"I wouldn't say you were wrong. I would say it was a little more involved than that."

"Is that so?"

The kid said nothing, but looked over at Berke and back.

"Okay, let's move past the suspense. Exactly how *little more involved*?"

"My cut prior to you disappearing was a hundred K."

"What?! Shit! Shit!" Gus shook his head as if to fling out the cuss-words. He took a second to absorb the blow. "Tell me something, kid. What does a high schooler do with a hundred grand?"

"Make you five."

"Balls ablaze." Gus cringed.

"So, what's the deal, Mr. Gus? You disappear for a year and a half. You leave me hanging out there to dry. I bust my balls to hold everything together. Now... now, you're suddenly back. Are you back in or what?"

"Whoa, whoa, son. What's the rush? I know you can't be out of money."

"I'm just as—"

"Hi, Gus. Where ya been?"

A girl called out unexpectedly. Gus saw her expression light up with a broad smile as he turned to face her. She was one of a group strung out along the street. They were all breaking out in smiles.

"We haven't seen you in ages," said another.

"You don't look so good. What have you been doing?" said a third.

"You got anything for us? Hoooooeeeee, we're partying tonight!" howled another.

Schoolgirls that could have passed for a team of cheerleaders broke into a run and approached the table. They interrupted his conversation with Berke and the kid. Directly behind the girls were more school kids, either single or in small groups of two or three. As far as Gus could see there were young teens headed toward the table from a park. Gus's heart sank at the sight of them. Memory or no memory, he could see what was happening. The girls continued to fire off questions, one after another, in an impatient blaze of excitement.

"Hey, slow it down, ladies. Enough. Enough. One thing at a time."

"Okay. You got any choco?" said a more aggressive member of the group as she rolled her shoulders in a sexual manner.

"Seriously?"

"Ah-yeh-yah," another cooed from behind a great smile. Smiles shared by all.

"It's been a long bitter spell," said a third.

"Boring as much as bitter. You got any sweets? You got any choco or what?" blurted out a fourth member of the group.

Gus looked at the girl with an expression of annoyance. "No. I don't," he emphasized with a hard edge to his voice.

The gang of girls quieted at once, folding back as if confronted by a scorching wind. The first girl, least shy of the group, was quick to address Gus with an equal edge.

"What the hell do you mean, *you don't?*"

"Just what I said. If you're looking for choco, I'm out. In fact, I want to know why are you even messing with that stuff? You got any idea how dangerous it is? Have you thought about that? It destroys those girly figures you so love to flaunt. It rots the teeth right out of them smiles you like to flash. It riddles those precious complexions you cherish with disgusting pus-filled pimples. You'll spend everything you earn to satisfy your addiction. Is that what you want? Seriously? You ever think about what the hell you're doing?"

Berke and the seated boy appeared stunned. They said nothing, but the kid pulled his backpack nearer to him as if drawing away, as if putting on a show of space between him and Gus in front of the girls.

"Hey, what are you suddenly? Our dad or something?" smirked a girl.

The question was biting hard.

"Based on what I've seen, if I was your dad, your ass would be chained to a bed."

"Fuck you!" exclaimed a flashy blonde who had been leaning against the edge of the table. She turned away, visibly displeased.

"Girls, I'm not here to run your lives. I'm just telling you that choco will drag you down to hell."

"Hey, we didn't come looking for a preacher," complained one.

"Yeah, yeah, yeah," cried out the crowd in unison.

"Save it for a sermon," voiced another.

With an air of disgust, the frustrated girls turned away and stormed off. One looked back at Gus.

"You know we'll just get it someplace else, right, honey?"

She looked directly at the kid sitting across from Gus and Berke. She blew the boy a kiss. He winked.

"Do what ya gotta do!"

Gus was feeling backstabbed and disagreeable. He looked at Berke and the kid, who were both staring at him. The kid spoke as soon as the girls were out of earshot.

"You're asking *them* what the hell are they doing? How about, hey, what the fuck are *you* doing?"

Gus looked at him.

"Problem?"

"Problem? Ah-yeaaaah. Big problem. That's my income you're messing with." He nodded toward Berke. "That's our income you're messing with. Why the fuck do you want to pump them full of that shit? You sellin' choc now-a-days or recruiting nuns?"

"That's the whole point. I *don't* want to pump them full of *shit*. Especially not *that shit*. I don't want high school kids anywhere near that stuff. As long as I'm around here, it ain't gonna happen, son."

"Well, you ain't gonna be around here long, pops."

The kid pulled a handgun from his backpack, and Gus found himself staring directly down the barrel.

"Balls ablaze, kid! Are you nuts?"

"Nuts? Running your operation, I discovered how much you made off me while I was bustin' my ass doing all your grunt work."

"You're running my operation?"

"Yes sir, Mr. Gus. And I ain't stopping now."

Boom-boom... boom-boom.

21

Boom-boom... boom-boom. Boom-boom... boom-boom. Like a phonograph needle stuck in the final groove of an old 78, over and over, a sound reverberated within the boundless black void that contained Gus's essence. *Boom-boom... boom-boom. Boom-boom... boom-boom.* Over and over and over. It mimicked the rhythm of what might have once been a heartbeat.

Pale gray light pried its way between Gus's barely parted eyelids. Reluctantly, his eyes waded through it. At least it was a soft, gentle sensation, totally opposite the pain in his chest—pain that danced off his ribs like mallets across a xylophone. His chest might well have been an ensemble of broken bones, each fragment a different length, all tuned to sharp pains. At least that is how it felt, and like it or not, it certainly awoke him to reality. Gus's body lurched as he gasped for a breath.

The inside of Gus's mouth was as dry as flour—worse than Geppeto snoring with a plugged nose. He produced all manner of unappealing noises. He smacked his lips together, repeatedly lifting dried spit like lint off a sweater. A dry squeak erupted from the middle of his throat as his lips inflated and then blew apart to form "puh" sounds.

Boom-boom... boom-boom.

The accumulation of sensory input prodded Gus to realize that "he was," but not "what" he was. If based on pain, he was a glob of lacerated leftovers, a crumpled mess beneath a bus. Nothing he wished to see, but he was not afraid to open his eyes, or verify the truth of his condition. It was all about pain. Why add the pain of light? It was so much easier to shut it out.

Eyes closed, Gus lay motionless. Listening. Sounds surrounded him—sounds of traffic, the approaching howl of tires, the screech of brakes, and whine of revving engines. Sounds buried the ever-fainter *booming* noise inside his head. Highway sounds were comforting sounds that called out to him. They penetrated his near un-consciousness to beckon, to awaken, to question where his partying had landed him. The final sound was his own. A pathetic moaning as he slowly re-opened his eyes.

It was not the scenery Gus first recognized, but rather an all-too-familiar confusion greeting him once again after a hard night out.

"Ohhhhh."

Stiff. Stiff. Can't move.

"Man, it's cold."

The words slipped from his mouth as a chill caused Gus to tighten up, which put stress on his ribs, which hurt like hell.

"Balls ablaze. Ohhhhh... ow, ow, ouch! God, I gotta warm up," he whispered with another rib-crunching shudder.

The thought of warmth immediately made him think of a bed partner. *Am I alone?* He wondered. He rolled his head to the left and then to the right. He was alone. Waking up alone was odd. All things odd were generally worrisome. For a moment, curiosity trumped pain and prompted Gus to raise his head. He managed a better look at his surroundings.

A parking garage. I'm lying on the hard, cold-ass floor of a parking garage. Are you kidding me? Ohhh... this is bad. Embarrassing. This better be a dream.

Embarrassing it was, but a dream it was not. His head fell back against the floor.

"Ouch."

Pain shot through the back of Gus's skull. He wedged his fingers between the floor and his head. There was a wound. He pulled his hand back and noticed blood.

"Ohhh... this too is bad. Not good," he moaned.

One touch was enough. His head hurt inside and out. He let it be. Now, only his eyes shifted. Back and forth, they studied the details of the garage and the cars within.

Humph. I know this place. I've been here before. Let me see....

Gus waited for his internal map to zero in location, but it failed miserably. At present, he was totally *un-located*.

Gus's eyes stopped scanning after focusing on a ramp leading up to an outside exit. He wondered what was at street level.

Let's see... that ramp leads up to... what street was that...? Shoot. I should know that. Humph. Strange. Ahhhhhh....

"Time to find out, I guess."

Gus attempted to get on his feet. It did not go well. It felt like he was twisting every cracked rib and then some. He settled back to the floor.

How not to start a day.

Gus let out a long breath while complaining mentally.

This will take time. No need to rush.

He closed his eyes and dismissed the fact that a distracted driver could run over him. He dismissed consciousness altogether. Instead, he slept while stretched out across the garage floor for a day, or a year, or an eternity. He could not say. But at time's end, he awoke with an added strength, a renewed vigor sufficient to sit up and look around with a fresh awareness. He felt better. His ribs felt better. He rolled over onto all fours and stood up, somewhat precariously, but erect.

Filled with a rush of clarity, Gus spun around defensively as if expecting the worse. He looked into the shadows, waiting for something dreadful to appear. He waited. He watched. He waited. He watched. Cautiously, he moved in the direction of the darker corners, the areas in shadow. He was not brave enough to dare something to appear, but he was a man who instinctively faced down his fears. Something made him uncomfortable, but finding nothing more than unfounded suspicions, Gus gained enough confidence to turn his back on the dark.

Gus noted the ramp and headed shakily in that direction. As if to compensate for the slow stride of his feet, his mind raced. The thoughts came without end, all sharing one commonality. All were questions, not one an answer. The notable lack of answers caused Gus to realize that something was woefully amiss. Panic stirred, increasing steadily as Gus began to appreciate how seriously his memory was failing him.

How odd, I have no recollections—of any kind. Am I awake? Yeah, I'm awake. What the hell... I should be remembering something. Balls ablaze, I don't remember my name. Holy shit, I don't know my name.

A full-blown panic attack nailed Gus. Lightheaded, he stopped walking and closed his eyes. He rubbed his face hard within cupped hands to wear away any residual sleep. He took a deep breath and held it. He held it until he hoped the pressure to explode would drive out all the insanity that was clouding his ability to think.

"Puhhhhhhhh!"

A blast of air erupted from his lungs to blow his hands away.

"All right. Let's try this again." *Where the hell am I?*

Eyes still closed, Gus squeezed his eyelids together until a myriad of violet-colored patterns filled his blindness. He then let his face go slack as he rolled his head around and around, believing that at some point the drawbridge to his memory would lower and allow the parade of remembrances to come rolling in.

"Good night. What was I doing?"

Drugs. Clearly, you were doing drugs, you dumb ass. You're never gonna learn.

Gus was dumbfounded and strained to remember anything of what he had been doing.

Anything? A tiny clue? A detail? Too much to ask?

His was a world of alarm and anxiety. This was not about remembering where he was, or what he did last night. This was about remembering *anything*, anything at all. Remembering what his name was for....

"...for chrissakes, c'mon! Who's your mama?"

Gus's brain cramped from frustration, thoughts of mental breakdowns, and insanity, until his insides cramped from adrenaline-fortified fear. Try as it might, his brain was good as dead. Cooked. There was nothing. Nothing.

"Ahhh, shit." This ain't right, my friend. This ain't right."

Gus talked aloud to himself. His voice was the only thing familiar. The sound of it settled him. He needed to keep moving in order to dampen the adrenaline shakes. The ramp was the only option. His mind would not quiet, but his thoughts switched to other concerns. There was something else, something weird. He felt... he felt... utterly disheartened. Something lodged in the back of his mind. It felt like a great secret.

Did I lose something?

He looked back across the garage. He scanned the concrete floor. It was smooth and showed no sign of litter.

"I gotta get outta here."

Gus reached the ramp. Equal to his need to leave was a compulsion to stay. He sensed an inexplicable connection to the garage, a familiarity that befuddled but also stabilized his mind. It was a confusing peace. He glanced about, hoping to spot a parked car he might recognize.

No such luck.

Gus gave up on hopes. He turned his attention to the ramp. He seemed to know beforehand that the climb was a butt-kicker. Memory or not, he was correct. The farther up he walked, the harder it got, and the more certain he was that he had been here before.

At the top of the ramp, Gus stepped over to a wall. It seemed familiar. He leaned in against it. He needed to rest his heart, rehash the few facts in his head, and return to the same questions.

What the heck did I do last night? How did I manage to lose my memory? My name is....

"Shit."

Feeling physically rested, but mentally distraught, Gus pushed himself carefully away from the wall. He steadied himself on legs that felt like mush. He looked in the direction of the highway sounds that reached out for him. They summoned his subconscious like a past lover.

Somewhere out there is the answer.

Gus took a step, and then another. He leaned forward with care until his legs again found the rhythm. His forward progress started out slow and allowed him time to assess what lay ahead. The streets were empty, lifeless, cold, and as uncaring as the concrete floor, as the stone edifices he leaned on. Everything about him sucked the heat and light out of day. There was nothing here for him—or was there? He stopped. He turned his head slightly to the left and listened over his shoulder. The hair on the back of his neck went erect.

22

The roar of the highway overpowered all else. Gus tried to envision such a road. The sounds slammed into the edifices overhead, fell to the street, and bounced back and forth between unlit storefronts and foundations. The noise plowed through shadows that cloaked most of what Gus could see.

Gus was immersed within the barrel-busting booms and escalating pitch of engines roaring to peak rpm. It was music alive with nuances that only a composer or conductor might appreciate. These were sounds he easily deciphered, sounds that inspired and lifted his soul, sounds that pumped life into his weary heart. The sound of the highway stood in stark contrast to the deathly silence of a desolate neighborhood increasingly ill disposed.

Gus was shuffling uphill toward the highway as quickly as he dared. Overexertion seemed less a threat than what he feared he would see closing in from behind.

What was that? Am I being followed? There! There's something in those shadows. I know it. I can feel it. What is that? Jesus, get outta here.

Gus looked at the rash of gooseflesh covering his arms. He shuddered. He looked ahead, up the hill, and hustled forward with renewed vigor. He kept up his guard while adding distance between him and the murkiness following his tracks.

In spite of nagging doubts, Gus made it to the top. His chest burned from exertion. The fear of some *thing* yanking him back lessened. Now he was free to rest. He dared to look downhill into the swirling darkness one last time. A sense of relief settled him as he turned his back on the ungodly place. Now he focused on what he needed.

With a sense of relief, Gus made his way through the tall, unstately brick buildings that crowned the ridge. The edifices stood as guard towers that welcomed him back. Now, he walked unafraid but determined toward the spectacle that emerged beyond a disorderly row of shabby structures. The erections fenced the road in for as far as he could see. He looked up and down the length of the highway and observed the chaos of life. There were untold thousands of people bumping into each other, jostling, and mingling as they marched forward. They were laughing and conversing as they engaged in business and fun. The extent of the commotion was unsettling, but consoling when compared to the wasteland of streets that crisscrossed through the lower shadows he had escaped.

Gus followed the side street through the border of shanties as it rose to scale the bank that would lift him to the shoulder of the road. Working his way through the crowds, he walked across the broad shoulder until the tips of his shoes touched the paved edge of the highway. His face was one of blank amazement.

The expressway was unlike anything he had ever seen. He stood in awe.

"Wow," he whispered in disbelief.

Blank amazement dissolved into mindful scrutiny as Gus worked feelings of familiarity. He knew this highway. He was certain that he had traveled this road before. Maybe more than once. He looked to his left and noticed that all the traffic headed toward him, nothing but windshields and headlights. By all appearances, this was half of a divided highway. Looking to his right, the morning sun forced him to shield his eyes by pressing his hand tightly to his forehead. He watched the taillights of a thousand wheeled extravaganzas disappear into the rays of brilliance.

Gus's struggle to remember ended abruptly at the screech of brakes as a bizarre bus-like motorhome contraption came skidding toward him. He leapt backward from the curb. At the same time the door swung open, the driver, sitting in a captain's chair, was about to say something but didn't get a chance.

"Need a—"

"Christ almighty! Ya tryin' to kill me?"

"I thought you were waiting for a lift?"

Gus looked at the driver. Something about the man was familiar, his face, his dress; something about the man was unsettling. The bus marquee read *BUS 7 CHARTERED* as if identifying or confirming the arrival of a bad omen.

"No, man. No. I'm good."

"You sure?"

"Yeah, yeah, I'm sure. Just watch where you're going."

Gus turned away from the street to lose himself in the mass of the crowd. He began walking with the flow. Walking with the flow made him feel relaxed. It settled him. He watched the bus pull away from the curb and gain speed.

23

Barely seconds passed before Gus again heard the screech of brakes. On guard, he turned quickly to see *BUS 7 CHARTERED* pull up alongside him. The door flew open.

The impossibility of the vehicle's near instant return thoroughly bewildered Gus. If not some colossal magical illusion, or miracle, insanity was the only explanation. This was not about two near fatal bus strikes; this was about his wits and what little remained. A thought that both buses shared the same marquee brought hope until the door opened.

"How ya doin', Gus? Sure I can't give ya a lift?"

Any relief from the suspicion of insanity ended when Gus viewed the same toothy grin and multicolored bandana. In spite of fears he was losing the battle, Gus scrambled to shore up his mental state. For his own sake, he had to block everything out. He had to set aside all that was inexplicable, all that tortured him. Cutting away at his impenetrable mental haze, Gus stared at the driver and asked the most important question.

"You know me?"

"I imagine."

"You look familiar to me," said Gus. "I wanna say I know you."

"Well, this isn't the first time I've given ya a lift down the road."

"Is that so?"

"That's so."

"How the hell did you get back here so fast? I mean, balls ablaze, I see you leave, and a second later, you're pulling up behind me. How did you do that?"

"I only went a couple hundred feet. You walked right past me. You know where you're headed, Gus?"

"Uh... uh...."

"Thought as much. You look a little dazed, a little lost. Come on. Get in. Get yourself out of the crowd. C'mon. Take a seat and take a break. I know where you gotta go, and I'll get ya there.

Besides, got some nice scenery on board." The driver winked as he tucked the color-emblazoned bandana into his shirt.

I walked right past the bus? Could that be true? Did I see the bus park ahead of me? God, I don't remember any of that. Am I awake? Am I dreaming? Am I delusional? Would I have any idea if I was crazy? I'm so fucked up.

In a state of total resignation, Gus looked over at the dust-covered windows. He could make out the silhouette of a woman, but nothing more. She appeared to be watching him watching her. Her mouth was moving.

Is she talking to me? Do I know her? Does it matter? Does anything matter?

Gus looked back at the driver.

"I haven't got any money."

"By the look of ya, I'm not surprised. Tell you what, this one's on me. Come on; get on. We can't be lingering. We gotta go."

"Ah, I don't—" Gus stopped mid-sentence as the sound of the word *lingering* drove a dagger of distress through his chest, staking his lungs to his ribs and preventing him from breathing.

"C'mon. Climb aboard. I'm tellin' ya; this is your bus, Gus."

The driver appeared to know more about Gus than did he. Gus looked to his left, beyond the rear of the bus. He noticed the storm clouds building on the horizon. They looked ominous. The sight of them increased his anxiety—the one thing he did not need. The dagger skewered deeper. He considered the apparent safety of the bus and shrugged.

"I guess."

Gus stepped up into the bus and immediately felt a wave of peace wash over him. His lungs expanded to fill with relief. The sound of the door closing relaxed every muscle in his body. The bus lurched forward to leave all his anxieties behind.

Gus gripped the pole. He looked down the aisle. The bus was full. He assessed the passengers. Male instinct drove his attention to four or five rowdy men in their late twenties or early thirties. It was a primal defensive measure. Another primal instinct drove his focus to a woman, a particularly pretty but frail-looking female. She was chewing gum and staring a hole through him. Her eyes made him uncomfortable, and he glanced her way only long enough to see her push the sticky wad out between her lips.

Pop.

Gus dropped into seat A1.

As soon as he took his seat, the woman stood up and startled him in no small way. He shrank with shock as she approached while calling out loudly in a squeal of delight.

"Hey, how ya doin', stranger!"

Balls ablaze....

The woman tilted her head in a manner that caused her hair to shield her face from view. It also caused a pronounced streak of white to surface.

Is that fake? Who the hell is this nut? Do I know her?

Gus's eyes were full of questions, but before he could conclude anything, the woman plopped down hard to share his seat. Without any reservation, she pressed up against him, and laid her head on his shoulder.

Then... she whispered into his ear.

"Hi. I'm Bonnie, and I'm really sorry to put you through this, but there's four or five guys sitting behind us that have been hasslin' me to no end. They're making me really nervous, and I was wonderin' if you would mind letting me sit next to you and act like we're friends. I know I'm being really rude, but I'm a bit scared. Would you mind?"

Gus leaned back to try and get a look at her.

"Ahhhh...."

"Please, please, pretty please?"

"Ahhhh.... Yeah, I guess. Yeah."

"Oh, thank you. Phew."

The woman pressed her face against his upper arm. She looked up at him and snapped her gum.

Pop.

Really? In my face?

"What a relief. You have no idea how much I appreciate this. Those guys are a bunch of jerks, believe me. Tell you what. I'll just go on pretending I know ya, an' run at the mouth. I'm good at that. Comes natural. You won't have to say anything unless ya want. Okay?"

"Yeah, sure, whatever."

"I already told you my name. Bonnie. And you are? Oh, sorry. You don't have to answer. I was just—"

"Gus."

"Gus," she repeated. *Pop-pop.* "I like that name. One syllable, and to the point. Earthy. Seems like today everybody's named after a country singer or their dog… or their truck."

Gus chuckled. She continued.

"We're so universally mortified of being average we name our kids after tractors. Ya gotta—"

"You mean like John?"

Bonnie looked at Gus. Her mind churning. She started laughing.

"Oh, I get it. John Deere. I guess that is a single syllable. That really was funny. Touché. So what do you do, Gus?" *Pop.*

Gus shrugged his shoulders.

"I—"

"You don't have to answer if you don't feel like talking."

Gus briefly studied her. He was amused.

"I was about to say that I don't know."

"You don't know what?"

"I don't know what I do."

This time Bonnie briefly studied Gus. This time she was amused.

"I don't know," she repeated. "That's kinda weird. Usually people say I'm unemployed, or whatever, or nothin'." *Pop.* "I don't think that—"

"No. Not weird at all. Actually, very simple. I lost my memory. In fact, not only do I not know what I do, I don't even know if Gus is my real name."

"Wow. Humph. So why did you tell me your name was Gus? You just pick it or what?"

"Not exactly. That's what Driver called me. He seemed to know me so I went with it. He said he's picked me up before. I guess it's as good a name as any. Let's face it, you seemed to like it."

The woman looked at him with a queer expression.

"Are you serious?"

"About what?"

"About not knowing your name. You're not just sucking me in to make me look like an idiot?"

"No. I'm dead serious. Why make up a story like that? It doesn't get you anywhere. You don't woo a woman by telling her you have no idea what your name is. Women like men who gain ground, not lose it. Get my point?"

"So, like, you don't remember anything? Like nothing at all?"
Pop.

"Not a thing. No idea where I came from. No idea where I'm going. Well…, let me tweak that. I remember everything necessary to function. You know, like how everything works, like what to eat for breakfast, like how to grab a bus. I remember nothing about me. Nothing. Zero."

"Do you know why you're on this bus?"

"Of course. The driver said, 'Gus, get on the bus.'"

Bonnie laughed aloud. It was an easy laughter that warmed Gus.

"Didn't your mother teach you not to get in cars with strangers?"

"I can't remember. Actually, the driver was quite persuasive. Said he knew where I had to get off. I'm hoping once we get there, maybe something'll click."

"Don't you have a wallet or something with your name an' address in it?"

"Nope. That would've been too easy. Imagine just pulling out my license, looking at my mug shot, and saying; *hey, I know you, ya sonovabitch. Hey, I even know where you live.* You might imagine what my joy would have been."

The girl wore a great amusing grin as she watched Gus.

Pop-pop. "So what happened to ya, Gus? You fall or something? This just happen, or ya always been this way? Or don't you remember?"

"I don't think I fell. The more I think about it, the more I think I got mugged."

"*Really.*" Her tone grew dead serious. *Pop-pop.*

"Yeah. I woke up this morning on the floor of a parking garage. No wallet. Empty pockets. Ribs that feel broken, and a serious owie on the back of my head. See?" Gus turned his head and pointed to the wound. "If those aren't signs of getting mugged, I don't know what is. That's about all I know."

Bonnie looked at his wound.

Pop-pop. "Wow. Good thing you can't see that. I think I'd be scared half to death if I couldn't remember how I got a wound that bad, let alone not knowin' my name, or how to get home. Cripes. Aren't you afraid?"

"Mmmm, not so much afraid as anxious. Maybe you're right. Maybe it is weird. I guess I'm just trying to make sense of it. Trying to find something I recognize, you know, something I can hold on to, get a grip. Unfortunately, in spite of so many things feeling familiar, nothing actually looks familiar to me."

"This is like... killing me. I'm trying to get my arms around it. You can't remember *anything*? Nothing whatsoever? Not the smallest teeny-weeny thing."

"Nope. All I get are these sensations, these impressions that I know—" Gus stopped mid-sentence. Again, he leaned back from the girl. He took a hard look at her features. "Do I know you?"

She shrugged.

Pop. "It's possible. I meet a lotta people riding the bus. I think I've seen ya before."

"You think? Really?"

"Yeah, you look familiar. Where you from? Oh, I forgot, you don't know."

"No. Where are you from?"

"Here. Locum Veniae—"

Bonnie and Gus talked for hours, or days, or maybe years. He could not say, but the next time he looked away from Bonnie's face, it was dark outside. He turned from her to lay his head against the window.

"Have you ever seen anything so magnificent?" he asked.

Bonnie leaned across Gus's lap in order to look outside.

"I know," she said. "Sometimes by the time I get home, I have a crink in my neck from staring up at the stars too long."

"You can't help but to wonder what's out there," said Gus.

The sound of screeching brakes ended their conversation prematurely. They reached out to brace themselves against the force of the stopping bus. Gus looked ahead through the windshield at the glorious display of heavenly color. The door snapped open, allowing cool night air to sweep past them.

The driver turned around to look directly at Gus. He broke into that massive toothy grin.

"This is it, Gus. Your stop. This is where you get off."

Gus looked at the driver most undecidedly.

"My stop?" he repeated.

Gus looked out the window at the passersby walking in the night. He looked back at the driver who was yet watching him and waiting.

"Oh. Oh, okay." Gus looked at the girl. "This is my stop, or at least that's what the driver says. He seems to know."

Gus rose slightly from his seat. Standing half upright, he looked at the girl, expecting her to let him pass into the aisle. That didn't happen. Indifferent to his expectation, she stayed put and commented.

"Now that's interesting."

Gus looked down at her.

"I beg your pardon?"

"We get off at the same stop," she blurted unexpectedly.

"What?"

She stood from her seat and pressed against Gus as she glanced toward the back of the bus.

"Cripes." She turned to Gus. "Hey, maybe this is my lucky day. Can I walk with you? Is that okay? Just for a little ways. I don't want to be alone in the dark." *Pop-pop-pop.*

"Uhhhh.... yeah, sure." Gus then chuckled. "Walk with me where? I don't know where I'm going."

The girl was not the least bit bothered.

"Not a problem. Tell you what. You watch over me for a bit, and I'll watch over you. I know the area real well." *Pop-pop.* "Deal?"

Again, Gus chuckled. "Well, that's not only my best offer for the day, it's my only offer. So... deal."

Bonnie reached for Gus's hand and pulled it across her shoulder. She towed him into the aisle, and then turned into him and whispered.

"Those guys are a bunch of pricks. I can't thank you enough for this."

"I'm surprised the driver didn't say something. You know, tell them to knock it off or something?"

"What's he going to say? Okay, boys, sit down or get detention." *Pop.*

"Mmm. Yeah, I see your point."

Gus also looked toward the back of the bus. He noticed that the rowdies were watching him. He also noticed that they were standing up from their seats and filing into the aisle. He could feel them breathing down the back of his neck. A rush of uneasiness moved through him.

Gus studied Bonnie as he followed her off the bus. He watched her step carefully to the curb. Her frailty lured him. She seemed incapable of confronting the world.

How does someone that fragile manage to get through life?

His instincts to protect her were coming on strong. Too strong.

And I have to feel responsible for this girl... for why? Balls ablaze, she's nothing to me. And that gum popping, Jesus.

There was more swirling about Gus than protective instincts. Something else emerged from beyond his awareness. It was not compassion. It was not fear. It was the subconscious crackling of anger. Flashes that produced heat, sweaty heat under his clothes. This anger was deep-rooted, and hinted of character unknown, maybe flawed, or far worse. Gus was made aware of it.

Meanwhile, Bonnie wasted no time leading the way, stepping quickly away from the bus to walk along one of the side streets that sloped downward into the shadows. A walk in which Gus wanted no part.

"Why are we going down here?" he asked.

"Were you going somewhere else?"

"No. I guess not. I don't like walking down into the shadows."

"What shadows?"

Gus frowned.

"You don't see the shadows?"

"Shadows? You're so dramatic. I see night. I live down here. There's nothing scary around here except for those pricks that followed us off the bus." *Pop-pop.*

"Is that so?"

"That is so. C'mon, keep walking. We don't want to be lingering."

"Ohhhh."

Gus appeared to cramp.

"What? You all right?"

"Yeah. I'm fine. It's nothing."

He lied. His insides squirmed at the mention of lingering.

"Hey. What's going on? Is there a problem?"

"No. Well... maybe one. Could you do me a favor?"

"Sure. I owe you. What do you need?"

"Would you mind spitting out that gum?"

The girl stopped walking. She turned to Gus and started chewing faster.

"Yes." *Pop-pop.* "I would mind." *Pop-pop-pop.*

"Well, can you at least stop popping it? That sound is worse than fingernails on a chalkboard. It kills me—annoying as hell. I'm sorry. It just is."

"Sorry. I pop gum when I'm nervous."

"You're nervous?"

The girl looked over Gus's shoulder.

"Yup." *Pop-pop.*

Gus turned to follow her glance. Four men were gaining on them, closing the distance that offered Bonnie peace of mind. No further explanations were necessary. He understood all that she left unsaid.

The sound of footsteps quickened. Echoes of heels and soles bounced off the buildings, as did the first catcalls and jeers. Gus knew what was going down. He could feel it. He looked around. The darkness was closing in. It was thicker than night.

"Hey! You! Where ya headed in such a hurry?"

The four strangers broke into a sprint, and circled around Gus and Bonnie, preventing them from walking farther into the opening expanse of a cobblestone plaza.

"Get in there," ordered Gus.

He pushed Bonnie into the alcove of a shoe store entrance. The tight entrance offered protection from three sides of attack. He then backed himself up to Bonnie—*protection from the fourth side.* The alcove prevented the stalkers from grabbing her without first going through him.

Gus welcomed the thought of a fight. He broke out in that sweaty heat. He felt lubricated for action, alive, ready to kill. No fear. No thought of failure. He felt normal. Adrenaline damped his fear of the shadows, a thing far worse than the four men he now sized up. He studied the open space in front of him.

"Please don't let them get me." Bonnie whimpered. "Please." *Pop-pop-pop-pop.*

Gus gave thought to Bonnie's terror. He considered how that terror was something only women could appreciate, as he noted every detail of the four men closing in on him. He felt no fear whatsoever. He observed how a fine rain fell from the churning shadows overhead. The ground was wet and glassy, each cobblestone a glistening mound. If he had to go down defending her, so be it. Gus braced himself and smiled.

There's gonna be a blood flood.

"Hey, buddy, we don't want no trouble. The bitch is ours. Walk away, man. Just walk away. She ain't your property; ya get it? She don't belong to you, man. Just walk away."

Gus did not answer. He had no point of reference. He knew nothing.

What's this talk about property? Did I just step between a whore and her pimps? Sounds like it. Hmm. Well, maybe I'm no better. Whore or no whore, what kind of man turns a woman over to dogs? On the other hand, what kind of woman puts a man in this position to begin with—puts me in this position to begin with? Who is she? Why do I even care? It is what it is.

Gus snickered.

"Hey, man. You deaf or something? Ya hear what I said?"

"Yeah."

"Yeah, what?"

"Yeah, I heard what you said."

The spokesman for the group raised his hands and gestured *"what gives."*

"And...?"

"And, I heard what you said."

The leader looked at the others and raised his brows in disbelief. He looked back at Gus.

"Honestly, I'm not sure ya did. Or... ya heard me but didn't get my meanin'. So, I'll make it clear. Get the fuck away from the bitch or your day's gonna end right here, right now."

Gus simply observed the man.

"Hey! You in there?" The man rolled his eyes. "Think about it. What's she to you? A piece of ass for the night. Believe me, she ain't worth it, man. Ya hear me? She ain't worth it. Now, go. Go on about your business. Just leave. Walk away, dude."

Pop-pop-pop.

Gus turned his head slightly and spoke quietly to Bonnie.

"You just keep popping that gum, sweetheart. It really annoys the piss out of me, and right now that's a good thing."

Pop-pop-pop-pop-pop.

Gus returned his attention to the men surrounding him. The stranger cocked his head and scrutinized Gus. He spun slowly around on the heel of his boot to connect with his comrades. He completed his spin, and again faced Gus. His head yet leaned to the side. The stranger stretched his neck, straightened it out, and lunged forward into the alcove behind a hard thrown fist.

Gus grabbed the man's wrist, twisted it underneath, and came up aside him with the attacker's arm pinned against his back. Gus reached for the man's head. He shoved it down with all his might, as he brought up his knee full force, driving it into the stranger's face. The sound of teeth slamming together and a breaking jaw reverberated within the walls of the alcove.

The stranger's head rolled upward and back, fanning a spray of blood through the air. Gus threw out a leg, and pushed the man, causing him to trip and fall backward flat on his back. The sickening thud of his head meeting a paver made his comrades cringe. He lay out cold on the mist-covered pavement. The brute's eyes never closed.

Two seconds. Over.

"Holy shit." *Pop-pop-pop.*

Gus retreated into the alcove. He said nothing. He locked his eyes on the next man lining up to get a piece of him. The man began stepping side to side, and then flicked his wrist. A steel blade snapped outward too fast to see. The gesture ended with a profound click that revealed a wicked-looking switchblade. The man's face broke into a sinister grin.

"Think you're a badass, huh?" The man looked over his shoulder and hollered to his cohorts. "Guys! Drag Gode out o' my way. I got meat to butcher, business to finish."

The other two jumped into action, each taking one of Gode's wrists and hauling the bloodied head across the plaza. Meanwhile, the slasher started tossing his knife back and forth from hand to hand, showing off his skill at wielding a blade. He began bobbing up and down, back and forth, like a boxer. He began making quick stabs in Gus's direction.

"What's the matter, man? Lose your balls? Them puppies slide back up? Can't say I blame 'em. They know I'm gonna slice ya, dice ya, dude. I'm gonna do you up good."

Gus said nothing. He watched the knife with utmost attention. Back and forth, stab-stab, back and forth, stab-stab, back and forth, stab-

As the man reached out to make the predictable second stab, Gus grabbed his wrist and yanked him forcefully toward him while sidestepping the blade. At the same time, he threw his right hand around the back of the man's neck. The surprised attacker instinctively pushed away. He threw his head back, an involuntary move that Gus fully anticipated. Gus took full advantage of the opening and drove his forehead into the stranger's face. The man's nose exploded into a shower of blood.

The attacker, instantly blinded by a flood of tears, stumbled, at which point Gus locked onto his wrist with both hands, spun under and up, twisting the arm around behind him and dislocating it. He next grabbed the man's head, driving it down upon the same battering knee. Again the sound of breaking teeth. The man's head bounced off Gus's knee like a volleyball. The wretched aftermath lay crumpled on the pavement precisely at the spot Gode had occupied a moment earlier.

Gus backed himself into the alcove for a third time.

"Hoooooleeeeeey shit." *Pop-pop-pop.*

Gus said nothing. Instead, he produced the switchblade and began flipping it in the air, end over end. It flashed in the darkness. He never looked at the knife, but it landed squarely in his grip after every toss. The message was clear.

The other two men stood in place. One spoke up.

"It's done, man. You win. If Gode and Baiter can't take you down, we sure as hell can't."

Gus stepped out of the alcove. The remaining two jumped back at once. They watched helplessly from a distance as Gus stepped over to their comrade lying on the pavement unconscious. He grabbed ahold of the man's hair and yanked it upward forcefully, exposing a vulnerable neck. Gus reached down with the blade, and placed it on the man's throat. He looked at the other two men.

"Who shall I say bled out—Baiter?"

"No!" Bonnie screamed. "What are you doing?"

Gus, somewhat startled, looked back at her.

"I'm going to slit this bastard's neck."

"No! No. Why would you do that? That's murder. Cold-blooded murder. Why would you do that?"

Gus was still staring at her.

"I don't know. That's just what I'd do. Keeps you safe, I guess."

"How about we not slit throats, or bleed anybody. How about we just leave and go home. Please. Please. Please. Just let it go. Please, for me. Just let it go."

Bonnie held her breath in alarm. Gus studied her for a moment, and then looked down at the bloodied face. He let it drop to the pavement. The jaw slid out from under the skull as if unattached. He turned to Bonnie.

"Okay. Let's go home."

"Oh, thank God. Thank God."

Bonnie hurried out of the alcove and took Gus by the arm. The knife was yet in his right hand.

"Let's get out of here, Gus. C'mon. Cripes almighty, I'm shakin' so bad, I can hardly walk." *Pop-pop-pop.*

Bonnie struggled with what she had witnessed. Gus listened to her as they disappeared into the shadows.

"For the love of god, Gus. Where did you learn to fight like that?" she asked in a hushed tone. "I've never seen anybody do what you did back there. Were you in Special Forces or something like that?"

"I have no idea."

"No idea at all?"

"None."

"Oh, my god. Unbelievable. So, did you or did you not know you could put the moves on those guys?"

"Did not."

"If you didn't know, then weren't you scared?"

"No."

"Not even a little bit?"

"No. They just really pissed me off."

"Cripes." *Pop-pop.* "I can't imagine. I'm afraid of my own shadow. Unbelieeeeevable. My word, I'm still shaking."

"It'll pass," Gus reassured her.

"At least we're close to home. I just want to get off the street. You should too. I'll make you dinner. It's the least I can do. I owe you. You need to stay out of sight. Yes-no, what do you think?"

"Sounds good to me. It's not like I got plans."

The two walked on. Maybe a block, maybe for miles, maybe they crossed galaxies, Gus could not say. It did not matter. Bonnie was endlessly curious about him, and he enjoyed her attention. He was polite and listened to her many questions and hunches, for she was a talker, but he had few answers to give in return. It seemed to Gus that his lack of memory was possibly more disheartening to Bonnie than to him.

It was clear to Gus that in spite of their fresh acquaintance, they had bonded. He felt as if he had known her since childhood. They might have grown up together, best of friends, kissing cousins.

"This memory thing is killing me, Bonnie."

"I can imagine. Give it time. I'm sure you'll get it back."

"Yeah, when?"

"Be patient."

"Easier said than done. I'm dying here. In my gut, I feel positive that I know you, or that I knew you. You say, no, but I can feel it."

"I didn't say no."

"Then you do know me?"

"I said that we have ridden the bus together."

"No, no, no." Gus expressed his frustration. "It must have been more. I can feel it."

Gus turned his head, wondering why Bonnie stopped walking. He noted her fixation on something ahead. He looked up the road and saw the gang. The whole of it.

"Gus...." *Pop-pop-pop-pop-pop.*

"It's okay."

"No. There's too many."

"It's okay." Gus assessed his surroundings. He needed another alcove or something similar to cover his back. He spotted a firebreak between two buildings at their left.

"Quick, into that alley!"

Bonnie appreciated the potential escape route and ran for the crevice. Gus ran alongside her and they both witnessed the gang break into a run.

"Run! Keep going!"

As Gus yelled out the order, he stopped midway in the crevice. His mind told him that the walls would protect him, but he began to suffer flashbacks of underground caves or foundations that brought on powerful feelings of claustrophobia. He stopped to catch his breath and sort out what was happening.

"What are you doing?" Bonnie cried out.

"Run, Bonnie! Keep going! Don't stop and don't turn around. I can hold them off here better than in the open. Go! Run!"

"But—"

She stopped speaking at first sight of the gang pouring into the crevice. Gus followed her eyes and turned to observe what she feared. He looked back at her.

"Run, Bonnie! It's easier for me if I don't have to worry about you. Run! Now!"

Bonnie fled the space between the buildings. Gus watched her run until she moved outside the tunnel vision view from the crevice. Hoping she was reasonably safe, he turned to face his attackers who were now yelping with excitement.

"Remember, no guns!" one cried out.

"Don't kill him. He's gotta suffer."

"Break his bones like he broke Gode's jaw."

"Baiter's jaw!"

"Yeah, and don't forget about Baiter's teeth! A tooth for a tooth!"

"Yeah!"

They streamed in by single file.

C'mon boys. Make a line. You ain't got space. Stand in line and die one by one. One after another. This is not gonna be a good day, boys.

Gus was unconcerned. He could see that they would bottle up and be unable to attack him in force. One on one, he was confident about his chances. In fact, he was primed to explode. He was going to do some killing, and that fact relaxed him.

The gang attacked without hesitation, and the fight stopped as quickly as it started. Gus pummeled the idiot who elected to be first in line. He fell over like a dead tree. Gus destroyed the second and third in line, the fourth and fifth, letting them fall one upon the other like stacked cordwood. In short time, a wall of bodies protected Gus from the gang.

The attack and commotion fizzled. The gang members looked across the heap of bodies at Gus, and he at them. Gus decided to make a run for it. No sooner had he taken his first dozen steps than a single mountain of a man stepped into the narrow passageway to block his exit. Laughter erupted from those backed up beyond the fallen bodies.

"Get 'im, Block! Get 'im!"

"Take that on, you sonovabitch! Ha!"

"He's dumb, he's clumsy, but he'll squash ya like a bug!"

"Ha-ha-ha!"

The crowd roared. Gus realized he had overstayed his welcome. The rush to attack him was a ploy to stall him long enough for the gang to circle around behind him and block off his escape. Now he faced two fronts.

The gang members poured in from both ends to fight. Each eager to test their strength against Gus. They came wanting a fight and they got it. Gus fought. He fought an unending fight that kept him too focused to see anything but a hail of flying fists and feet.

Gus did not lose the fight, but he lost the battle. The scene slowed to a halt. The remaining gang members lay about panting hard and trying to collect themselves. It was then that Gus had a moment to take in the bigger picture. It was not a picturesque image.

All the while Gus mashed heads, the gang busied themselves blocking up both ends of the passageway until they had constructed walls too high for Gus to scale. He along with two dozen gang members stood imprisoned—walled in on four sides.

Gus could not be at both ends of the passageway at the same time. Because of this, gang members lowered ropes to retrieve their own from whichever side was opposite Gus's position. One by one, the gang snagged individuals and lifted them away until only Gus and one last member remained. The big guy. *Block.*

Appearing dumb and clumsy, the brute touched each wall with a shoulder. He looked like a fifth wall. Moving under his own weight, he was slow. The rest of the gang somehow squeezed by his barn-sized frame in their impatience to get back over the blocked up walls. He wasn't going anywhere. Maybe the gang needed to prove themselves in battle. Maybe he did not.

The world was growing dark. Almost too dark to see. It was all Gus could do to make out the shape of the combatant who stood facing him. Gus felt the onset of concern. The concern might have built had not something landed on Gus's head. He reached up and rubbed his hair. It was wet. Large drops of rain began to fall.

Gus looked up at the sky and saw a most unnerving, writhing boil of black clouds. It was a sky like no other. Gus felt his insides grow shaky as he observed the flashes of reddish lighting skewer the dark swirls overhead. Then to secure Gus's demise, along the top edge of the walls, along the roofline stood two rows of hellhounds. The sight was mesmerizing if for no reason other than the fear it instilled. Gus did not dare look away, and he might not have, if not for the sound of sizzling water.

Gus looked down and along the passageway in the direction of the sound. It came directly from *Block*. The black shape was no longer a dumb, clumsy, slow man. A demon with glowing red eyes now stood unmoving, but watching him with intent. The shape of a crescent moon glowed near white on his forehead. Never had Gus felt such fear, or had he? This fear went so deep that it seemed to pass through lifetimes of existence. Gus was immobilized. He could only stand and look back into the eyes of hell until struck in the back of the head. He lost consciousness.

24

"Gus! Gus! Wake up."

The first awareness was that of pain. Pain from every place that made his being. Excruciating pain.

"Gus. Can you hear me? C'mon. Wake up."

Gus worked to open his swollen eyes. Slowly a shape came into view. It took longer for the shape to form an image that Gus could recognize. At that point, he understood from where came the words he was hearing. He moaned.

"Thank God, you're not dead. I thought for sure they killed you. C'mon, Gus, wake up."

Bonnie patted Gus's face lightly. She did so repeatedly while trying to revive him. She was crying. He felt her tears splash upon his face. Gus came around sufficiently to remember the rain.

"The rain."

"What?"

Gus said nothing more.

"You're gonna make it, Gus. You're gonna make it. You have to try to get on your feet. We can't stay here."

"Yeah."

"Are you awake? Do you understand me?"

"Yeah." Gus began to look around. "How did you get in here?"

"In where?"

"How'd you get in here? Where'd he go?"

"Where'd who go? They're gone. C'mon, Gus. You've gotta wake up."

"Yeah. I'm... I'm awake."

"Good. Now get up. You've got to stand up so we can get out of here. We can't linger, Gus."

The sound of the word *linger* had a measureable effect on Gus. It was enough to prompt him to move regardless of the agony. He struggled against the pain of his beating to do as the woman wanted. He leaned against the brick wall. At least the pain cleared his head.

"Bonnie?"

"Yes, I'm Bonnie. That's good. You recognized me. Are you strong enough to walk? Can you do it? We have to get out of here, Gus. We have to get to my place."

"Yeah, I think I can."

"Let's try."

Bonnie worked herself under Gus's arm and allowed him to support his weight on her small frame. With utmost care, she guided him out of the firebreak and into the opening of a circular plaza intersected by a number of streets. From there, she helped him cross the open ground and disappear deeper into the murkiness. Gus was too beat up to notice or care.

Bonnie walked along the street wearing Gus like a shroud, a cape draped over her. With each passing step, Gus was able to further appreciate the physical burden she carried, *physical* being the key word. Gus broke the silence.

"Why are you crying, Bonnie?"

His mentioning the fact caused Bonnie to convulse with sobs. Gus felt her support giving way, and so he stopped and straightened up to carry his own weight. He turned to face her. He placed his hand on her cheek, forcing her to look up at him.

"What's the matter, girl?"

She shook her head, not wanting to speak, but Gus insisted.

"What is it, Bonnie? Why are you crying like this?"

Bonnie tried to speak.

"Y-y-you c-c-could have d-died."

"Not likely. Besides, I didn't. So... you should be happy, smiling, not bawling."

"You could have died."

"But I didn't."

"But you could have."

"But I didn't."

"I can't believe you would've given your life to save me."

"Well, let's not get carried away here. I didn't go into that fray thinking I was going to give up my life. I'm not a hero."

Bonnie pulled back. She wiped her eyes with her sleeves. She gathered her composure and looked squarely at Gus.

"Say what you want, but you saw that gang. There were at least twenty of those guys, and you stayed behind so I might get away. You knew you could get the shit kicked out of you or worse. You could've been killed. You are more than the man I thought. I needed to know that."

Gus looked at Bonnie and smiled.

"I'm not sure what you're talking about, Bonnie, but honestly, I'm not noble. I wish I was that noble."

"You are. You proved it."

"Hardly. Do you remember those guys from the bus? You asked me if I was afraid. I said no. I was pissed. This was the same. I just got pissed. The more I saw of them, the closer they got, the more I wanted to rip their heads off. There's a part of me..."—Gus shook his head—"that's a monster. I'm sure of it."

Bonnie looked up at him.

"In your own words, *hardly*. Maybe once long ago. Not now. C'mon, let's go home."

Bonnie reached for Gus's hand. They walked arm in arm until reaching the front door of her home. He took one last look along the street before entering.

"This street looks familiar." Gus looked at Bonnie. "Are you certain we've never met? I could swear I know you."

"Like I said on the bus, it's possible. I meet many men. C'mon. Let's go inside."

"Okay, but tell me something first."

Bonnie's eyes raised to meet his, pupils dilated, waiting for his question.

"What happened to the gum?"

"I spit it out."

25

Bonnie held the door open for Gus. Upon closing it, she tossed her keys onto a small side table and pointed.

"I want you to sit down in that easy chair. You relax while I get something to dull the pain."

Gus did as instructed and watched Bonnie walk into the kitchen. He listened as she placed a glass on the countertop. A fridge door opened and closed. The clink of ice followed. She reappeared and walked across the room to a small decorative bar. She reached for a bottle of spiced rum. Returning to Gus, she handed him the glass. She poured the rum over the ice, filling his glass to the brim.

"I'm not sure if I should have put the ice in a glass or on your face."

"Eases pain either way."

"Hopefully, being in the glass, it'll help slow you down enough that I won't have to worry."

"About what?"

"You."

Gus chuckled. "You have nothing to worry about from me."

"That coming from a man who drops creeps like hot potatoes. *And...* doesn't even know how he does it. I'm afraid to learn what else you don't know. I'll bank on the booze."

Gus was grinning. He took no offense.

"Whatever puts you at ease. I'm not complaining."

"Good. Just sit back and be good. I'll get something to clean up those cuts. They don't look pretty."

"Whatever."

Bonnie disappeared briefly into another room and returned with a small blue tub of warm water, a washcloth, antiseptic, and a box of bandages.

"You really don't have to do this," said Gus, feeling a little embarrassed by all the attention.

"Of course, I don't. And you really didn't have to save me from those jerks. You did what you did, and I'm doing what I do. Now, like I said, relax, sit back, and be good. Close your eyes."

Bonnie wrung out the washcloth and gently wiped the blood and grime from Gus's face. She cleaned his bloodied knuckles and hands. With care, she applied antiseptic to each of his open wounds. She moved to apply bandages, but he stopped her.

"No bandages."

"Why?"

"I prefer the wounds to dry fast and scab over. I don't like bandages. They just get stuck in the scabs."

"And you know this how?"

Gus went silent. He looked lost.

She continued. "As you wish. No bandages. Sit up. Let me look you over."

Gus leaned forward in the chair. Bonnie noted the way he flinched when he moved.

"Drink as much rum as you wish. I got plenty."

"I'm good."

Gus closed his eyes and let Bonnie have her way. She rolled his shirt up to his armpits. She studied his tattoos as she ran her hands over his shoulders and chest. She ran her hands gently across his back. They rose and fell on both his muscles and swollen bruises.

Gus caught Bonnie looking over more than just his wounds. He sensed her attraction to him, to his strength. To the possibility that he could protect her, true or not. Her arousal was obvious to him.

"You're a handsome man, Gus. Ruggedly handsome."

"I think you're trying to make me feel better about my nicks and bruises."

"Nicks and bruises? Oh, yeah. That's it. Cripes almighty. Nicks and bruises. You know, you don't look like the kind of person a man would want to tangle with. Even from a distance, I would think a man might figure it unwise."

"And a woman?"

Bonnie failed to respond. She lowered his shirt and encouraged him to settle back into the chair. His eyes parted only enough to watch her finish fussing over him. He appeared gentle, sedated, his eyes heavy with fatigue.

"Are you tired? Would you like to lie down?"

"No. I'm fine. Thank you. It's just the rum. It's making me sleepy. I'd better ease up."

"You probably need some food. Sit tight and I'll fix us something to eat."

"I don't think I'm going anywhere. My head is swimming."

"Yeah. I can see that. Well, a little rest'll do you good. I'll be in the kitchen. Switch on the TV if you like."

"Okay. Thanks," he whispered.

Bonnie left Gus sitting with his near-empty glass of rum. She headed for the kitchen, and set about preparing something quick and hot to eat. She kept looking back at Gus to reassure herself. She did not trust men, even those who fought for her honor. Seeing him nod out from the alcohol eased her wariness. She went about her business putting together a light dinner and placing it on the kitchen table. She arranged the food close to the chair in which she planned to seat him. Looking everything over and feeling satisfied, she called to him from the kitchen.

"Gus! Gus?"

She stepped back to look into the living room. Gus was awakening.

"Yeah, yeah," he responded groggily.

"It's time. Dinner's ready. I set the table. It's easier to eat in here. C'mon."

"Yeah."

Bonnie watched Gus flinch from a fresh wave of pain. He struggled to get up out of the stuffed chair. Finding his bearings, he entered the kitchen as asked.

"How are you feeling? You look a little rough around the edges."

"I'm fine. Stiff. I should probably be moving around more."

"Well, maybe later, we'll risk a walk. We'll see how you feel after you eat. C'mon. Sit down."

Bonnie pulled back a chair. Gus did as told. He sat down. He placed his glass of rum on the table, and watched as Bonnie covered his plate with an impressive amount of food.

"That's quite a dish for such short notice. Are you a chef?"

"No. Not at all. I wish. My mother was a great cook. I always hoped to be. It's not all that fancy. Mostly peppers, onions, and sausage. I diced a potato. I love it because of the color. The peppers just look so crisp and tasty."

Bonnie sat down across the table from Gus.

"Go ahead. Eat."

Gus reached for his fork and dug in. At first, he focused solely on filling himself. He said little. After taking a second helping, he slowed and pursued a light conversation.

"Mmmmm. That was delicious. Trust me, your mother taught you well."

"I wish that were true. Sadly, she died when I was young."

"Did you take classes?"

"No."

"Were you married?"

"No."

"A professional woman."

"Yes, in a manner of speaking."

"What line of work were you in?"

"I satisfied men's sexual needs."

Gus stopped eating. He swallowed his last mouth full of half-chewed food in order to clear his throat. He looked straight at Bonnie.

"You're a prostitute? You belonged to those guys?"

"I don't belong to anyone. And *prostitute* would be the wrong term."

"You're an escort?"

"No, I'm not an escort."

A smile broke across Gus's face.

"Oh, I get it. You're a sex therapist. A counselor."

"Not quite."

"All right, I give up. What are you?" Gus began to laugh.

"What difference does it make as long as the food is good?"

Gus continued to chuckle. He shook his head.

223

"Can't argue that. The food was great. As good as anything I can remember."

Bonnie erupted into laughter. "Oh, now that *is* profound. Coming from an amnesiac."

"Yeah, I suppose. Say, listen, I apologize for the questions. You have to understand, I can't have a proper conversation because I can't remember anything. I can't agree, or disagree. I can't add from personal experience. All I can do is ask questions. It makes me a little too forward, and I'm sorry about that."

"Not a problem. Actions speak louder than words. I'd like to think you saved my life tonight. Maybe for all eternity."

Gus looked at Bonnie and frowned. Her comment was odd.

"All eternity? That's a laugh. I doubt religion is in my DNA. I also doubt your life was at stake. Those guys were probably just bent because I didn't cower and run. You know... egos, male testosterone, and all that."

"Huh. If you only knew."

"Whatever. It's over and you're home safe. No worse for wear."

"To be agreeable, I'll give them the benefit of the doubt. To be appreciative, I'll give you something a great deal better. Have you had your fill?"

"Uhh, yeah. I'm full. Content as a cat. Can you hear me purring?"

Bonnie rose from her chair and walked around to Gus. She took his hand. "Not like you will be. Come with me."

"Where we going?"

"Just follow me."

Gus followed as Bonnie led him into her bedroom.

"Ahhh...."

"C'mon. Don't be shy."

"I'm not so sure about this."

"Would you do this for me?"

"For you?"

"Yes. I want to make you feel good. I want to take your mind off the pain. I want to hold you."

"Uhhhh."

"It's okay."

"No, It's really not necess—"

"I'm not a whore, Gus. I want you to hold me. I want to hold you. Maybe being intimate isn't the best way to show my gratitude, but it's all I have."

"You've already shown me your gratitude. That's enough for me. You don't have to do this."

"I want to do this."

Gus stood silent.

A delicate situation. I don't want to upset her. She's baring her soul for me. Shit. There's always a price for sex. Maybe she has her own agenda. One thing's for sure. She's not about to take no for an answer. What now?

Bonnie tugged on him, pulling him to the side of her bed. She stood before him and pushed him gently onto the mattress. As he sat facing her, she stood over him, and slid her hands under his shirt. She drew the garment up over his head as she placed her lips on his shoulder. She kissed his exposed flesh inch by inch in a slow descent.

Hoo boyeeee.

Gus laughed. There was a hint of nervousness in his voice.

"Where are we going with this?" he asked.

"We aren't going anywhere. You are going to remain respectfully agreeable all the while I give you the most memorable sex you will ever have. Of course, you have no memory, so you'll have to take my word for it."

"Well, judging by what's happening in my pants, I'd say not everything has been forgotten."

"Consider it another unknown facet of your character. I hope you love as well as you fight."

With that, Gus and Bonnie fell silent, saying nothing more as Bonnie moved seamlessly into a gracefully erotic dance.

She slowly teased her way out of her clothes. She did so in a manner that made Gus feel as if he was a boy seeing the innocent beauty of a woman for the first time.

Oh, my god, she's sweet.

At last fully stripped, she turned to him and smiled. He spoke up.

"I can't believe how delicate you are. You look so frail. You remind me of an Asian, or a teenager."

"I know. I suppose I could be either. Do you enjoy fantasy sex?"

"I don't know. Why do you have the number 3 tattooed on your chest? Is this like, what's behind Bonnie number 3?"

Gus could not see the expression on Bonnie's face, but he immediately picked up on the fact she didn't take the bait.

Apparently, she regretted getting that tattoo.

"It's a symbol for a sorry state of affairs. A certain breed of men find the number highly arousing."

"Really?"

"Really."

"Yeah. I guess I've heard some people are superstitious about certain numbers. Can't say I ever connected that with sex. Is that it?"

"Too many questions. It's my turn. Why do you have a ring of flames tattooed all the way around your body?"

"What?"

The ridiculous remark caused Gus to look at his own chest. To his utter shock, he could see flames rising up to his shoulders.

"Balls ablaze!"

Gus was so surprised that he jumped off the bed and ran to a mirror. Astonished, he stood speechless and stared at himself. Tattoos covered his body. He shook his head in disbelief.

"You didn't know about the flames?" asked Bonnie.

"Flames? Are you kidding me? I've never seen any of this."

Gus looked at the collection of images and was not happy.

"I like this one." Bonnie ran her finger across the letters on his chest. *BOOM-BOOM BOOM-BOOM*. "Boom-boom boom-boom. Is that supposed to be your heartbeat?"

"How the hell would I know?" Gus stared at his reflection in the mirror.

"Look at this," said Bonnie. "GOLD AAA."

"I'd rather not," said Gus with eyes yet fixed on his reflection.

"For having so many tattoos you sure don't seem to be particularly fond of them."

"Oh, you noticed? To say I'm unsettled would be a tad understated. Just a tad."

"Well, I probably shouldn't tell you about the one on your back. That would really unsettle you."

Gus twisted his torso abruptly before the mirror. He strained to make out what was there.

"I can see it's big, but what is it?"

"Are you sure you want me to tell you?"

"Would you kindly dispense with the drama and just tell me what's on my back?"

"Well.... It looks like a pack of black dogs or wolves with red eyes. Some are sniffing the ground; others are looking up at a crescent moon. Hold on. I get it. Cripes. I think you've had a pack of hellhounds following you around and never knew it."

"Maybe I didn't, but maybe I did. Maybe I knew it all too well. But I sure as hell didn't know about this. I don't remember ever taking my clothes off until now. In fact, I'm not sure I should be stripping for you."

"What do you mean? You wouldn't like sex with me?"

A reflection of Bonnie reappeared in the mirror, and distracted Gus from the tattoos. His gaze shifted to her naked body walking up behind him. Her frail arms reached around his torso and slowly pushed his trousers down around his thighs in order to fondle his penis. Gus's gaze fell to the bottom of the mirror where he looked at himself.

"I'm so screwed," he lamented. "How do I lie when my dick looks like that? Listen, Bonnie. It's not that I wouldn't enjoy having sex, but something feels.... I don't know... sad."

"Sad?"

"Yeah. Are you sad about something, Bonnie?"

"Not at all. I'm in a great mood. What might have been a terrible night for me turned into a simple but enjoyable dinner, good conversation considering my dinner mate has a bunch of tattoos but no brains, and now hopefully... blissful sex."

"Was that a compliment? I'm not sure."

"The compliment is about to come. Get in bed, Gus. Don't think, and don't try to remember anything. If you have a wife, you won't even know it. The night is young, you're strong as a bull, and I plan on making you as hot as that flaming tattoo."

Face it. There's no way out of this. Go with it, Gus. Just go with it."

Gus inhaled deeply. He let out a tortured breath. He fought to turn away from the reflection of flames encircling his torso. In some inexplicable manner, the sight troubled him. It felt better to focus on Bonnie, especially when she was tugging on his fully erect penis.

Gus stripped off the remainder of his clothes and lay back on the bed. Bonnie leaned over him and commenced to kiss him. As she devoured his lips, she gradually moved across the bed to straddle him. Her talents brought Gus to temperature and then she mounted him. She began rotating her hips. She began grinding him to pulp.

Gus could not remember the last time he had sex, but the intensity of this pleasure seemed beyond anything he thought possible. He felt like he was floating in and out of reality. Liquid euphoria was coursing through his arteries.

"May I turn out the lights?"

"Mmmm. Whatever you want," was all Gus could mumble.

Bonnie reached over and switched off the lights. She stripped Gus of everything but his sense of feel. The grip of her vagina felt like a velvet fist around his penis and drove waves of pleasure through his frame as she rose and fell. Each time she climaxed, he found himself drifting deeper into his subconscious.

Gus was numb with ecstasy. Bonnie's hands glided over his chest and torso, as his did hers. She gripped each of his wrists tightly and coaxed them outward across the pillows, her arms a mirror of his as she began to work up to another orgasm, each more intense than before.

"You had a conscience. I remember," she cooed.

Gus absorbed every nuance of her pleasure until the comment began to take hold.

What did she say? Who cares? What did she remember? Forget about it.

He could not. The distraction annoyed him. Then another disconcerting realization.

My wrists and ankles are bound. Whoa, she's good—wait. How did she do that? She's still riding me.

Gus attempted to move his legs.

Not happening. Am I that drunk? Did I pass out? Did I miss something? How the hell much rum did I drink? Shit, the bitch drugged me. Am I hallucinating?

Gus began to fight the bindings that held his wrists and ankles. Bonnie was unbothered by his pitching.

"Hey, what's going on here? Bonnie?"

The spell was broken. His eyes were wide open.

Gus questioned whether the bedroom lights were on or off, but currents of dark air circled above the bed. They swirled about Bonnie's body like an enormous demonic halo.

Gus focused on Bonnie's face; her eyes were shut, but expressing a forceful fixation to climax again. *That was real*, he thought. He looked into the black cloud swirling overhead. He followed its current as the stream lowered to snake around the bed. The coil of black air undulated about a horror least expected.

Four men stood over him. Gode and Baiter, the two men whom he had beaten bloody unconscious held his outstretched arms firmly against the pillows. The other two held his legs in place against the footboard by the ankles.

Gus struggled anew. He writhed in vain. Bonnie never opened her eyes. Her head hung low as she focused ever more on her own pleasure.

"You had a conscience. I remember."

She spoke just loud enough for him to hear, or maybe he did not hear it. Maybe he thought it, or maybe it was a memory that returned as she gently wove a thick soft rope around his neck.

"Do you know from where the term *angel lust* originates, Gus? It is ironic that for many, the very last seconds of life prove to be a mortal's most euphoric. This is especially true in the case of strangulation."

Bonnie twisted the rope tighter.

"It seems bizarre that both sexes often experience an engorging of the genitals as blood is squeezed off from the brain. I don't know. I guess it has to go someplace. Can you feel it?"

Gus, trapped in a state of total terror, knew his heart was racing at full speed and readying itself to explode. The rope was strangling him slowly, causing the pressure in his head to increase. Adding insult to injury, Gus could feel uncontrollable pressure painfully hardening his penis, just as Bonnie stated. He could still hear her rambling on in a husky, hypnotic voice.

"I was once told, when a man died at the gallows, if he got an erection and ejaculated, it was said that he was well hung. I don't believe it. But they did call his erection angel lust. Then you have those idiot gaspers. Fools willing to flirt with strangulation just to enhance the experience of masturbation.

"And finally, there's that last life experience for those faceless expendable souls. Their last act of financial worth. The final profit for utmost sexual fantasy—*number 3*."

As the last light of consciousness dissipated, Gus watched Bonnie arch her back and thrust her head upward. Her breasts, hardened, thrusted forward. The closing light left him focused on that dark blue, jail-like number 3 tattooed upon her honey-colored chest. In the darkness that now swallowed him whole, he never felt Bonnie collapse from exhaustion onto his frame. All that reached him in this distant place was her final primal squeal, followed by her hot breath and a whisper as she forced the finishing twist of the rope.

"I forgive you, Gus. I gotta go."

26

At the same time a soft gray luminance bathed Gus's barely opened eyes, a miserable pounding slammed back and forth between his temples. The pain was excruciating.

My head. My god. Oh, shiiiiiit, that hurts.

Afraid to move, afraid his head was about to explode, Gus could only stare into the grayish light. Reluctantly, his eyes waded through it. With dulled senses, he observed the minimalistic features that surrounded him. A line overhead. A gray ceiling. A certain dampness that invaded everything but his mouth. The inside of Gus's mouth was sticky dry. It felt as though he had spent the night snoring hard. His throat was raw. His teeth felt coated in dried scum.

In need of oxygen, Gus took five or six deep breaths. The pain began to subside as a basic awareness opened his mind. Gus reached for his neck. It felt badly bruised. It felt swollen. His tongue felt stuck in a constricted throat. He tried to cough out dried phlegm.

Gus might have dwelled on his ravaged neck, wondering why it hurt, had it not been for the distraction of sounds that surrounded him—sounds of traffic—highway sounds. Sounds of comfort. He lay briefly still, allowing the familiar noise to penetrate his awareness.

Gus eventually arrived to that point of wondering where he was lying. The surroundings were odd. It was not the first time he awoke to a splitting headache and state of confusion. It must have been a hell of good night or a hell of a bad drug. He turned his head to the side and sighted along his outstretched arm. Where fingertips ended, there began a broad flat expanse of gray concrete. He stared at it for a long time. He waited for something to pop into his head. Nothing did.

Anything?

"Well...."

He coughed and cleared his throat.

"This is rich."

His voice was hoarse and broken. He rolled his head back and identified the bottom side of a concrete floor. The line of an expansion joint passed directly overhead. The expansion joint triggered something in his subconscious. He squinted as he tried to bring the feature into focus.

Why does that line, that joint, look familiar? Do I know this place? Is this déjà vu?

Gus's curiosity was now getting the best of him. He raised his head to look around.

A parking garage.

His head dropped back against the unforgiving concrete. His eyes drifted shut as he worked to fit the fragments. It then occurred to him that there were no fragments. There was nothing. He opened his eyes.

I know this place. Can't put my finger on it, but....

"What a way to start the day," he whispered. His voice sounded raspy. He took another deep breath.

"Well, guy, let's do it."

Gus was weak. Instead of standing up straight away, he rolled over onto his stomach. His face pressed against the cold surface. He sniffed.

Gas. Oil. Tire rubber. Definitely not perfume. Definitely not silk sheets.

Gus pushed himself up to kneel on folded legs. He placed his hand on the back of his neck. He rubbed it with intent as he rolled his head about. He tried to work out the kink, or the stiffness, or whatever affliction he suffered from sleeping too hard in the wrong position. The discomfort threatened to stay forever.

This is how I get the flu. It always starts this way. Stiff neck and raging headache. Deal with it.

Gus realized his neck felt damp. That prompted him to slide his hand up across the back of his head. His hair was moist and thickly matted. He withdrew his hand and was alarmed to see it covered in lumps of half-coagulated blood.

Balls ablaze. What's with that?

He checked his head a second time and now blood flowed across his fingers. He had disturbed the wound.

Oh, oh. Not good. Just leave it alone.

Gus lowered his hand to his thigh. He wiped his bloody hand dry on his pants. He waited for some explanation, a revelation, anything.

Nope. Nothing.

Getting to his feet was a bear, and doing so made him light-headed and woozy. He stumbled about before gaining control of his legs. He immediately made his way to a support pillar. The column had a large numeral 3 painted in dark blue over a circular beige background. The sign might well have been a target, for the way in which he fell hard against it.

Gus embraced the pillar for safety's sake. As he waited for strength to stiffen wobbly legs, his eyes wandered about the perimeter of the garage. There was no activity in sight. There was only a collection of parked cars that appeared abandoned, a silent connection to the echoes of traffic from afar.

Do I own one of those? Hmm. If I do, I don't know it.

It was one thing to sense this place as familiar, but Gus needed more.

I gotta figure out what I did last night. Can't say I'm proud of myself. Obviously drinking. Drinking in excess. Little bit nerve-racking. Lessons unlearned. Out of control. Doing stupid things. Dangerous things. Busting up my head. Dumb ass. Will I ever grow up?

Gus dislodged dried snot from the back of his throat and spit. The glob landed inches in front of his shoe. He stared at it until his focus moved up his legs and across his chest. His eyes raced along the length of his arms. He examined himself front and back until positive he was unhurt, intact. Some part of him expected a bloody mess, but that was not the case. Not this time.

At least I don't look hurt. Other than my head.

Physically, Gus was intact, but mentally.... Another rush of uneasiness. This one brutal.

All right. Let's try this again. Let me see.... The last thing I remember is.... Let's see....

Gus pressed his eyelids shut hard until little white flashing specks of light danced across a blood-red screen. He was growing irritable.

"Balls ablaze, I can't just lose a whole night. For chrissakes, c'mon!"

Gus was annoyed by the sound of his strained voice echoing. He began to study the vehicles in the garage for a second time.

Are you sure you didn't drive? Maybe I borrowed a car. Maybe I need to remember whose....

His eyes passed back and forth from one vehicle to the next. He struggled to remember anything, taillights, windows, wheels, color, a roof rack—anything.

Damn it. Nothing. How can I not remember anything?

The act of remembering the smallest detail was draining Gus of more energy than he possessed. Even standing still cost him energy. It was as if the gloomy surroundings worked to suck the last few drops of life from his soul.

As Gus assessed his world of discomfort, both inside and out, he found himself ever more repulsed by the lifeless gray structure that caged him. The place was suffocating. A slightly brighter light that flowed down the entrance ramp drew his attention.

"I gotta hit the road."

Gus pushed off the support pillar in quest of the light. He staggered up the incline, a climb that was torturous. At the top, he careened into a wall to rest. The only thing racing faster than his heart was his mind.

I know this place. I just need a minute to figure it out.

Panting hard, Gus closed his eyes and waited for his heart to slow. He looked down the street and viewed shadows collecting below. The streets were empty, not a soul to be seen. The light of day felt scarce. He turned to his right and looked up the grade toward the sounds of the traffic.

Gus was perplexed. He recognized nothing. The most notable details of the street eluded memory, but everything about the place felt inexplicably familiar. For example, he knew before exiting the garage, before seeing the street, he had to head uphill. In likewise manner, he understood there was something sinister about the encroaching shadows that went unseen. A morbidity within the darkness invaded his soul and warned that to linger was unwise.

27

Between light above and dark below, between the roar of a highway and the clutch of silence, the force of opposites propelled Gus over the crest of the hill. He dared to look behind one last time. He needed assurance that nothing would reach from the shadow to rip out his soul. Offering his hidden demons as much time as he dared, he hastily turned his back on the unblessed netherworld.

Gus wasted no time diving into the security of life. He hustled past the ridgeline structures and bordering shanties, to plow directly into the crowd. The masses flooded past him like an outgoing tide. Only the ignorant fought a tide head on, and so he angled his way diagonally across the parade of marchers until breaking free before the curb. At road's edge, he stood and stared assertively at something impossible to forget. Mentally, this was his line in the sand. He raised his fingers to his lips.

No way can I not remember this. Let me see.... This highway goes.... I know this place. Umm.... It's on the tip of my tongue.

The roar of traffic was thunderous. It pounded. It numbed his senses. It drove out all superfluous thought and distraction. It did everything but offer memories. Gus was only able to observe. He looked up and down along the highway. He witnessed a world of souls streaming to some unknown destination.

How could I possibly forget something of this magnitude? But then... how could I possibly forget my name?

The screech of brakes startled Gus. He turned to see one of the bizarre bus-like motorhome contraptions coming toward him. He stepped back from the curb. As the door swung open, the driver hollered out above the din.

"Need a ride, buddy?"

Gus looked at the glowing green number 7 above the door. His eyes dropped to assess the driver.

I know that guy. No... you think you know that guy. Face it; you think you know everybody. Not really. I'm tellin' ya, the man creeps me out. He creeps me out, but I know him. I'm sure of it.

The encounter felt familiar. It felt like an omen, but whether good or bad, Gus could not determine, and so elected to play it safe.

"No, man. No. I'm good."

"You sure?"

"Yeah, yeah, I'm sure."

Gus turned away. He heard the bus doors slap shut, as he started walking toward the bordering shanties. Out the corner of his eye, he watched the bus pull away from the curb. He blended into the flow of the crowd.

28

Gus fell in line with the masses. Walking with the crowds felt agreeable. It was uplifting. It raised his spirits. His lips formed a faint smile as he walked alongside the road and studied the endless line of shanties and lean-tos that corralled him and the crowd against the highway. Glancing back and forth between the eateries, assorted service counters, and the scream of vehicles rushing by on the highway, he happened to spot *BUS 7 CHARTERED* parked ahead at the curb.

Gus neared the vehicle, as the flash of a colorful bandana caught his eye. The driver who had just attempted to pick him up was now assisting an elderly passenger confined to a wheelchair. Gus noticed that the driver was having a problem, and in need of a hand getting the woman and wheelchair on board the bus. He slowed his pace to assess the situation. The driver quite unexpectedly looked up from his challenge and directly at Gus. He hollered out without any hint of reservation.

"Gus! Perfect timing. Give me a hand, would ya? When they fitted push-rings on this chair, they didn't give thought to getting it through bus doors. I swear, you gotta ask what people are thinking when they design this stuff. Obviously, they weren't using their heads or wheelchairs."

"I'm so sorry for the fuss," said the elderly woman.

The driver looked down at the woman seated in her chair.

"On, don't you mind me, Mrs. Wellington. I'm spouting off over nothing. Fact is the door on this bus is too small to be of any use. These handrails get in the way of everything. Don't you worry; we'll have you on the bus before you know it."

If not shocked, Gus was certainly surprised. He had been caught completely off guard. He stopped short to consider the driver. He heard every word the man said, but was battling a tangle of mental questions that began with someone calling him Gus.

Just like that, he picks me out of the crowd? Does that guy know me? Do I know him? Do I ride this bus?

Gus looked back at the glowing green *BUS 7 CHARTERED*. As always, it was about familiarity. He felt answers loomed close enough to kiss. Nonetheless, a veil of some fashion kept him apart from his past. A thin veil.

"Gus?"

"Uh-ummm." Gus cleared his sore throat. "Ahhh.... Yeah, sure. What can I do to help?"

"I'm just gonna back her in. If you can lift the front of her chair that should do it. Watch the push-rings. They get hung up on the handrails. Watch you don't pinch your fingers."

"Got it."

The woman looked up at Gus.

"I'm sorry to be such a bother. Just another old lady who can't do a thing for herself. It's embarrassing."

The driver broke in.

"Mrs. Wellington, you are as light as a feather. Don't fret over nothing. This is all about book-smart idiots."

"I totally agree," said Gus. "How often do we get a chance to be noble? Besides, if the world didn't have little old ladies, where would we get grandmas or chocolate chip cookies? I can't bear to imagine."

"Ha!" Mrs. Wellington erupted into laughter. "You sweet-talking looker, you. Don't you know old people are grumpy?"

"No, no, no. Old men get grumpy, but at the very worst, on rare occasions, elderly ladies might get a tad persnickety."

Again, Mrs. Wellington broke out laughing. "Oh, lord! Persnickety? Ha! That's a diplomatic way of saying fussy, nit-picking, old hoot."

"Never."

"Never, my butt," she howled. "You are a smooth talker. You are."

"Okay, now hold on tight. We're going to lift you. Watch your arms."

Gus assisted the driver in gently lifting the woman and her chair off the curb and into the bus. The driver rolled her to a place designed to park wheelchairs. He strapped the chair securely to anchors on the bus specifically for that purpose. The station allowed a companion to sit alongside in a seat.

"There you go, ma'am," said the driver. "Nothing to it."

"You gentlemen are just too kind."

"Sometimes, it's just nice to do something helpful," said Gus. "Like I said, it's not often I get a chance to prove myself. So, you see, you've helped me do my good deed for the day."

"Well, let me say thank you, Gus. My name is Amanda."

She held out her hand. Gus looked at the woman with a blank expression, and she noticed it.

"Are you all right, son?"

"Pardon? Oh, oh, yes, I'm fine."

"Stop it. I'm old. I'm not blind or senile. I saw the expression on your face. Do you not shake?"

"No." Gus chuckled. "It's not that. You called me Gus. Fact is, I don't really know my name. I'm suffering from amnesia."

The woman gasped, "My word, that's terrible. What makes you think it isn't Gus?"

"Gus?"

"Yes. Gus. What makes you think that's not your name? That's what the driver called you. He seemed to know you. That's what your belt buckle says."

She pointed.

Gus leaned over and studied his belt buckle. He then looked up at the woman.

"Unbelievable."

"Sweetheart, I think your name is Gus. What do you think?"

"I think I've been wandering around all morning trying to remember my name." Gus looked back down at his belt buckle. "Unless that's the name of my gay lover, I must be Gus."

Again, the woman laughed. The sound of her laughter was warm and inviting. It tugged at Gus's heart.

"Well, Gus is a good name. Short for Angus, or Augustus, or Augustine, or Gustave. Are you staying on the bus?"

"Ahhh...."

"He's staying," said the driver. "I know where he has to go. Dropped him off before."

"Wonderful. I like the company of a gentleman. Will you sit with me?"

Amanda patted the seat next to her. Events were swirling around Gus faster than he could handle. Without his memory, he remained clueless about everything. Being agreeable seemed to be the best course to take.

"Why not?"

"Wonderful."

Gus sat down and made himself comfortable. The elderly woman smiled. It put him at ease. Discovering the name *Gus* on his belt buckle might have been a first clue, but it still left him with more questions than answers. He turned to the woman.

"How did you spit out all those names so fast? I was impressed."

"Well, if you were as old as me, those names would be names that you grew up with. They're not like the names of today, which, I swear all come from top movie hits or television. I was raised Catholic. I'm still a practicing Catholic, and St. Augustine was my name saint, or my patron saint. Because of that, I know that he was one of the most revered saints in our faith. He was very influential."

"Augustine. *Augustine,*" repeated Gus. "I like it. Has a nice sound."

"It's a beautiful name. Do you belong to a church?"

"Not sure," answered Gus. "Do you like being Catholic?"

"Well, I was born into it, so I never really questioned the faith until I was older and more cynical. It serves a purpose. Like all things, there's good and bad. It brings one peace. It's inspirational. You know, stories of the saints... like St. Augustine. They make me want to be a better person."

"I suppose."

"So how do you function if you're suffering from amnesia? I mean, how bad is it? Do you know where you are? Do you know where you're headed?"

"It's bad. Really bad. I don't know anything. Things seem very familiar. Like right now, you, the driver, the bus, this place.... You asking me if I belong to a church. I could swear I know it all. But it's.... I don't know. I'm just wandering... waiting... hoping to see something that triggers my memory."

"Do you have any idea how you lost it?"

"Unfortunately, I do not. Woke up flat on my back in a parking garage. I might have tripped, fell, hit my head. I don't know. I've definitely got a wound at the back of my skull. I can tell you this. I don't have my wallet."

"Think you were robbed?"

"Possible."

"Turn your head. Let me see that wound."

Gus did as asked.

"Oh, that is a doozy."

"Yeah. Must have just happened because I had fresh blood on my fingers when I came to. I could hear the sound of traffic and just started walking toward it. And so... here I am."

"Here you are indeed. Well, for what it's worth, you look well."

"Yeah, I don't think I've had a stroke or anything like that. Probably a concussion of some sort that affected my memory."

"Have you been to a doctor?"

"I haven't. Like I said, I just woke up. Maybe two hours ago. I'm still trying to sort everything out. I wouldn't even know where to begin finding a doctor."

"May I suggest a course of action?"

"Absolutely. I'm all ears."

"If you're not pressed for time, and you don't mind being seen with an old lady, why don't you come with me to Redemption? It's the elderly care facility where I live."

"Redemption?" Gus looked at Amanda. His expression said it all. "What kind of name is that for a retirement home?"

"It's a faith-based facility. The focus is on reflection and addressing your life regrets. Helps you to accept death with a peace of mind. At my age, I don't avoid the issue. In fact, most days, I welcome the idea. My time has passed. Unlike you, all I have is memories. Ironic, isn't it?"

"Ahhh...."

"Before you say no, let me just say this. First, there's a doctor on staff. I'm sure in light of what has happened to you, he'll have no objection to giving you a look-over, being you're my guest.

"Secondly, Redemption is renowned for outstanding cuisine. As my guest, you can eat all you want. I promise you will not regret that part of the evening. You have my word."

"Ah, I'm just not sure, Mrs. Wellington."

"Augustine." Amanda addressed him directly. She looked straight into his eyes. "What exactly have you got to lose?"

Gus leaned back to look at this woman. She had an inner strength that belied her frailty.

"Nothing.... Yeah, nothing at all, really."

"Wonderful. Then we'll have dinner."

BUS 7 CHARTERED stopped. This time the driver assisted Gus in getting Amanda off the vehicle safely. The driver wished them a good day, adjusted his bandana, and sped away.

29

The doctor stepped back from his examination. Gus and Amanda only quieted to hear the verdict as the man walked over to a nearby stool and sat down. He retrieved a pen from his lab coat pocket and jotted notes on a form. He replaced his pen, looked up, and spoke.

"Gus, at this point, there's not much I can tell you. Not without further tests. You have a nasty wound at the back of your head, but nothing that appears life-threatening. I don't see any signs of infection, which is good. However, there is a real possibility that you've suffered a concussion that has affected your memory. I'm stating the obvious.

"The problem is we have no idea how long you've been wandering around with this condition. Were you injured a month ago, a year ago, or what? Now, I'm exaggerating, but the point is that because of the amnesia, we don't know. The wound appears recent, you said you were bleeding this morning, but we would have to admit you and schedule a series of tests to get a more accurate prognosis.

"Another possibility is that you had a mild stroke. That seems unlikely. I see none of the telltale signs. Bottom line... your loss of memory is probably due to a concussion related to that wound. I can schedule you for a scan to find out more if you like. Otherwise, the only option is to wait a few days and see if your memory returns."

The doctor walked back over to Gus. He placed his hands on Gus's neck and pressed lightly at points around his neck.

"Have you had any trouble swallowing?"

"No, not really," said Gus. "I started the day out with a horrible stiff neck. Probably from lying on it wrong. Why?"

"I noticed that your neck appears slightly bruised... swollen. Do you have any issues with thyroid?"

"No. I don't believe so."

"Okay. Well, in that case, I can tell you that in every other respect, you are healthy as a horse."

"Wonderful," piped Amanda.

"Do you have friends or family who can keep an eye on you for the next couple of days?"

"I uhh—"

"He can stay here as my guest for as long as he wants," offered Amanda.

"Good. I overheard the two of you say that you're going to the dining room."

"Yes. Amanda tells me that the food is fantastic."

"She knows better than most. Eat well. It's good that you have an appetite. If you decide you want to set something up for additional tests, let one of the nurses know."

"Will do. Thanks again for seeing me, doc. Thanks for everything."

"That's what we do. I'm sorry I can't tell you more at this time. Give it a couple of days and see how you fare. If you feel unusually sleepy or drugged, come back immediately. I'll get you in for a more rigorous exam."

"Will do."

With that, the doctor held open the door as Gus steered Amanda out into the hall. From there she directed him along the corridors until they reached the dining room.

"Wow."

"I told you it was nice. Kind of like being on a cruise, isn't it?"

"I really don't know."

"I love a man who can't argue. Do you see any open tables by the windows?"

"No."

"No? Nothing?"

"Nothing that I can see."

"Wouldn't you know it? The one time I have a guest."

"It's okay. There's no rush. I'm fine. Is that a garden outside those doors?"

"*Garden?* A disappointing word, my dear. Garden might well mean a carrot bed buried under horse manure, whereas

Redemption's collection of flowers is nothing if not magnificent, world-class magnificent. Do you enjoy flowers?"

"Of course, I enjoy flowers. Who doesn't like flowers?"

"Wonderful. While we wait for a table, I'm going to introduce you to our atrium and gardens. You know they say that smell is eighty percent of taste. Allow me to serve you hors d'oeuvres unlike anything you've ever experienced, a feast of color and fragrance that begs to enhance a good wine and cheese."

"Oh, how you toy with my appetite."

Gus navigated the wheelchair between nearby tables until reaching an aisle that led directly to the glass doors of the garden. Before the doors opened automatically, a waiter met them en route and offered each a glass of wine and a small plate of cheese and crackers as if on cue.

"Is the man a mind-reader or what?"

Amanda laughed. "Nothing so mystical. It's one of our customs. I wasn't kidding. Flowers, wine, cheese... they were made for each other." She turned to the server. "If possible, would you notify us as soon as a table facing the garden opens?"

The waiter nodded and stepped back. The doors opened at the wheelchair's approach, allowing Gus and Amanda to pass unhindered. All manner of fragrances were upon them the moment they strolled into the midst of the bedazzling multicolored courtyard.

"Do you have a favorite?" asked Gus.

"Favorite what? Flower, wine, or cheese?"

"Sorry. I was referring to the flowers. I've enjoyed good wines and cheeses, but gardens of this stature are rare. I can't—"

Gus stopped mid-sentence.

"You can't...." Amanda urged him to continue.

"I apologize. It was as if my memory suddenly returned. It was as if I understood the relationship between bouquets of flowers, and the bouquet of wine and cheese from something in my past. Truth is, I am unsure what compelled me to say such a thing."

"I see. Well, to answer your question, if you were referring to a favorite flower, the answer would be no. The more I'm exposed to the splendor of flowers, the less I'm able to have favorites. The best scent may be the faintest. The most beautiful flower may be the smallest and most overlooked. Powerful perfumes are often a gift of the least attractive blossom. Dayflowers are a feast for the eyes. Night flowers are a feast for the nose."

"I see your point. Do you spend a lot of time here in the garden?"

"Oh, my word yes. How can you not? I mean, if flowers aren't the jewels of creation, what else?"

"Oh! Isn't that wonderful? I know that fragrance. It wants to force memories. I can almost see my childhood."

"I assume you picked up a whiff of the lilacs. It was strong on the breeze just then. You probably played about the bushes in your yard as a child. We all did."

"That's just how it felt. Familiar. Carefree. The fragrance fills you with happiness."

"The fragrance of flowers fills you with happiness, with sadness, with all the emotions of life unlike anything other. Nothing brings emotions to bear as do nature's perfumes."

The unending intoxication of the gardens fostered a rich trove of thoughts turned comments and conversation. What started as the wonder of sunflowers, moved to the thrill of yellow tulips, fields of Black-eyed Susans, and the memory of marigolds fastened to a tossed bride's bouquet.

The talk yielded only to the server who summoned Amanda to a table where the garden views were unobstructed. Once seated, the conversations resumed, often accelerated, often reaching a near frenzied exchange. Gus fired off his questions and Amanda eagerly answered every one that didn't pertain to their geographical location. Gus noticed that Amanda seemed always to sidestep that one subject.

"Locum Veniae?"

"Yes, yes, Locum Veniae. Good god, I hate this." Gus shook his head in exasperation. "I know that name. It's right there. It's so familiar that I can feel the reality of it. I just... I just... I just—"

Gus stopped his struggle to explain after seeing Amada looking at him with an enormous glowing smile.

"What?" he asked.

Amanda changed the subject.

"I'm sorry. You know, I haven't answered this many questions since my days raising children. Inquisitive minds. So full of questions. Those were the days when I had worth. Those were my best days."

"Well, don't write yourself off so quickly. I must say that you certainly are sharp upstairs. I keep asking myself how it is you know so much."

Amanda laughed. "I'm old! I've seen it all; I've done it all."

"Yeah, right. Say what you want. There's plenty of old folks who have lived out lives learning nothing. And that ain't you."

"Well, I'm a prolific reader. I'll read anything. I worked as a librarian for a good fifty years. I guess some of it stuck. I'd rather not think about how much has slipped through the cracks of old age."

"Believe me, Amanda, I see no wrinkles, I see no cracks. You've aged gracefully."

Amanda placed her napkin on the table and folded it neatly in place.

"You're much too kind, Augustine. Much too kind. Listen to me. I want to say something. I want you to hear me out before answering rashly. Will you do that?"

"Certainly."

"Very well. Now, listen to what I say. The doctor made it clear that you shouldn't be left alone. We have plenty of guest rooms here at Redemption, but I don't sleep. Well, not much more than a couple of hours at a time—a drawback of aging gracefully. Anyway, what I mean to say is that I would feel much better if you would come to my apartment and spend the night. I have a couple of very comfortable recliners and a hundred channels of TV. I can keep an eye on you. Just to make sure all is well with the head. Would you be interested, or does that make you uncomfortable?"

"No. It doesn't make me uncomfortable at all. What a kind and generous offer. Thank you. It's the perfect ending to an afternoon in the gardens and an evening enjoying culinary perfection. Indeed, the food was everything you promised. Sitting back to relax in a recliner beats every image of going to a guest room without heart, or worse, back onto the street at night."

"Wonderful. If I could ask for an hour of privacy beforehand."

"Of course. Frankly, I need to stretch my legs. I ate way too much. That much I do remember."

"Thank you. Let me just point out that there's a stack of current magazines in the reading room right over there." Amanda pointed across the dining room. "Entertain yourself for an hour or so, and then come up to 305 when you wish. I'll be sure to have some tea waiting."

"Perfect. Just perfect. See you in an hour."

"Wonderful."

"Thank you, Amanda."

Gus rose from his chair as Amanda summoned a staff member to assist her in returning to her room. As a young man rolled her back away from the table, she looked at Gus and smiled as she spoke.

"See you in an hour."

Gus nodded. He watched her leave.

I'm going to spend the night with a wheelchair-bound woman who is forty years older than me. Sex or no sex. Sick. Disgusting. Not thinking about sex, thinking that way about such a fine woman. Cut me some slack. It's a mind game, for chrissakes. A mind game. Nothing more, nothing less. Take everything to the extreme.

Gus chuckled. He headed toward the reading room.

Man, you are a flaming idiot.

An hour passed.

Time to head up. I'm okay with this. Actually, Amanda is very attractive in her own right. Intelligent. Well read. There's something else about her.... Virtues. Personality that draws you into her world. Makes you want to go. An aura of gentility. Like... a mother. That maternal care that makes you feel like there is no place like home. The whole sex thing would be like screwing your mother. Ugh. Balls ablaze, don't you have anything better to think about?

Gus rapped lightly on the door of apartment 305. There was a click and the door opened a crack.

"Come in, Augustine. It's open."

Gus eased the door open with care and entered Amanda's apartment. Instead of a wheelchair, Amanda sat in a recliner. She had a light knitted blanket spread across her legs. There was no indication of her being afflicted in any manner. It was an almost unsettling change of image.

Gus gently closed the door behind him without turning about or taking his eyes off what else he saw.

"I'm stunned. Why am I not surprised? And I wondered why you knew so much."

Amanda smiled. "Please, come in."

Gus walked over to a wall of books.

"You weren't kidding about liking to read. You told me that you were a librarian. You didn't tell me that you *lived* in a library."

"Given a choice, that would be my idea of heaven on earth. Next to family, books can be your closest companions. You cry, you laugh, you travel with the characters within. They take up your cause when everyone else has abandoned you." Amanda looked at Gus queerly. "Sorry, that came out rather depressing, didn't it?"

"No, not at all. In fact, I sense precisely what you mean. I don't know if I was a reader, but I can tell you that I am drawn to these shelves. I can feel my curiosity tugging to take in the titles. Here's one. *Of Guilt and Conscience: The Road to Hell and Back.* Sounds formidably depressing but I am intrigued."

"Well, you may help yourself. Nothing honors a book or author more than a reader. Browse all you want. I am very proud of my collection—lots of signed first editions. But before you get lost in those books, would you mind pouring some tea? It's well steeped, but I'm perfectly comfortable, and would cherish being doted on just this once."

"I would be pleased to dote on you. Men should be lined up to dote on you."

"Oh, you are such a smooth talker. You should be embarrassed."

"Yes, well, maybe. In the meantime, just stay put. In fact, I'll join you if you don't mind."

"Please do."

Gus walked toward a small lamp table situated between two recliners. Amanda sat in the far chair. The closer chair was empty. On the table was a white lace doily, upon which sat a small red Tiffany-style lamp with clear crystal pendants hanging along the bottom rim of the shade. Butted up to the lamp's base was a silver tray that contained a matching silver teapot, two silver-adorned cups and saucers, a silver sugar bowl and creamer, and two silver spoons. Gus picked up the pot and poured.

"Sugar?" he asked.

"Two, please."

Gus picked up the silver spoon and scooped out two mounds of sugar. He stirred the tea and sat the spoon down.

"Cream?"

"Light."

Gus prepared the tea to Amanda's liking.

"Thank you."

"My pleasure." Gus prepared his own cup and took a sip. "Mmm. Tastes good."

"Orange spice."

"Oh, yes. Smells wonderful. Reminds me of the garden."

"Mmm-mmm. I agree," said Amanda after swallowing.

Gus did not sit down. Instead, he carried his tea back to the wall of books.

"Gus?"

"Yes?"

Gus turned about.

"I told you that I sleep very little."

"Yes, I remember."

"If you don't mind, I would like to nap while you browse the books. I don't nap long. Later, when you rest, I can keep an eye on you. Would that be all right? I don't want to be rude."

"It's perfect. To be honest, with all your books calling out to me, I would be a lousy listener. Sleep as long as you like. I won't fear being distracted."

"Wonderful."

Gus watched as Amanda closed her eyes. After a moment, he started down a fresh row of titles. Slowly, one by one, he read the spines as he worked his way from left to right along the wall. After nearly two hours of pulling books and thumbing through pages, Gus browsed his way through the whole of her collection. At that point, he wandered over to three shelving units that were dedicated to photographs of family and friends—memories.

It was not about being nosey, but rather genuine interest in the private life of this remarkable woman that moved Gus to study the images of Amanda's family. He turned to see Amanda still sleeping. He laughed quietly to himself.

I could have predicted Amanda's need for organization and attention to detail. Each frame is placed perfectly.

Each shelf overflowed with family pictures. In short time, Gus understood there was an order to these keepsakes.

Babies... toddlers... adolescents... teens... adults... parents... grandparents.... Huh. Each shelf represents stages in Amanda's family history.

Another characteristic was less obvious. It was only when looking across the shelves as a whole that Gus realized the peculiarity.

Now that's odd. An empty frame for each shelf. Either Amanda procured a frame in preparation for another image, or....

Gus frowned at the other obvious possibility.

Or... there was a frame on every shelf that awaited the image of a missing person. For instance, a lost son.

The empty frames left a disconcerting impression. Gus raised the cup to his lips and discovered the tea was cold. He considered a refill. He turned to consider the teapot on the table. The worry of disturbing Amanda was foremost on his mind, but to his surprise, Amanda was watching him. Their eyes met and she smiled. Gus returned the smile.

"I trust you rested well," he said.

"I did," answered Amanda. "Better than usual. I guess even I enjoy having someone watching over me. That hasn't happened in a long time."

"May I?"

Gus signaled his desire to sit down.

"Oh, of course. You needn't ask."

Gus and Amanda sat comfortably on opposite sides of the small lamp table and floated effortlessly back into conversations that covered a myriad of topics. Gus asked questions to satisfy his curiosity about certain books, mementos, and family portraits. Amanda asked questions that assessed his character.

"And the reason for the empty frames?"

Amanda shrugged. "I like frames."

And that was that, end of subject. Eventually, the conversation slowed and Gus began nodding off.

"Do you need anything, Augustine?"

"No thank you, Amanda. I am perfectly content." Gus's eyes remained closed. "Thank you for everything."

"My pleasure. Thank you for the day and the company. I can't remember the last time I enjoyed so much of both. It was as if you returned me to my past."

"You're welcome."

"I'm going to turn out the lights, if that's okay."

"That's fine," Gus whispered.

30

Gus slept soundly. He did not know how long he had been sleeping. It might have been hours or days. It might have been years. It might well have been an eternity. He could not say. Upon awakening, he opened his eyes to gain his bearings. He saw nothing and was left feeling somewhat disconnected from reality. He raised his hand, passing it back and forth before his eyes. He saw no hint of light. Nothing.

Gus reached over for the lamp on the table.

Where's that stupid lamp?

He fished around but could not find it. He swung his arm in a lower arc, searching for the table, but to no avail.

What the hell? It's got to be here somewhere.

The absence of table and lamp unnerved Gus because they had butted up to the sides of the recliners well within reach. Now, there was nothing but space. He slid his hands along the arms of his recliner, and that brought some reassurance, as if the wings were walls of defense between which he sat stupefied but secure. He attempted to calm himself and figure this out, but was lost for a logical explanation.

This is just plain weird.

In a burst of courage, Gus sat up straight. He began sweeping his arms about in large arcs, but touched nothing. He sat back.

Am I awake, or am I asleep?

He pinched himself hard.

I am definitely awake. I am definitely awake.

Gus repeated the thought in order to bolster his sanity. He resorted to what few memories he had of his surroundings, and assembled a mental image of Amanda's room. He recalled where the chair was in respect to the front door. He recalled where Amanda sat, and where the table and lamp were positioned between the chairs. He recalled where the shelves of books lined the walls. He was hesitant to awake Amanda. He was sure there was an explanation that would make a fool out of him and so elected to work it out quietly, without fuss, on his own. He stood up and stepped carefully in the direction of the front door.

Gus placed one foot before the other, slowly advancing toward the front door as best he recalled. He continued to slide one foot then the next. He knew he had to be close. He stood in place and leaned forward, reaching out with both hands, sweeping the darkness in front of him. He gave thought to how many steps he had taken.

Gus started shuffling cautiously forward again. Again, he made great sweeping motions with his arms.

This is insane, he thought to himself. *Where the hell is the door? How big was this place?*

He should have reached the door or at least the wall by now. Panic began to tighten Gus's chest as if the coils of a demonic snake slowly wrapped around him. Each breath became more of a struggle. He tried to calm himself.

"It's here somewhere. It's gotta be here somewhere," Gus whispered.

Gus knew he had to run into something at some point, unless he was still sleeping, unless he was dreaming. He stopped and took stock of himself. Again, he pinched his arm; he bit his tongue. He spoke aloud.

"Hello. Hello."

Gus listened to his voice. It sounded strange—muffled.

"Hello. Hello."

Gus called out louder. He noticed there was no echo, but also there was no mistaking the fact he was awake. In a fit of annoyance, he determined a bloody nose from an unseen door or wall would be better than creeping along at a snail's pace stuck in oblivion. He reached out with both hands and took off.

There's no wall.

Gus went from a jog to a run.

There's no wall.

There was nothing. Again, Gus pinched his arm. This time painfully. There was no room for doubt. He was fully conscious and awake. His chest caved with the crush of fear. He dropped to the ground. On his knees, he pulled his head down within the embrace of his arms, hands joined, fingers entwined. Riddled with fear, Gus rocked back and forth and cried out pitifully.

"Amanda? Amanda? Are you there? Can you hear me?"

"Yes."

"Oh, god." He nearly wept. "Oh, god." Gus caught his breath and tried to regain his composure. "I'm so embarrassed, Amanda. I was having a nightmare. I think I was sleepwalking. I'm still not sure if I'm awake, but I'm definitely having one hell of a panic attack. Can you turn on a light for me, please?"

"There is no light, Augustine."

"What?"

The answer was unexpected and discomforting.

A blackout. A power outage. Did a storm pass while I slept?

The gentle sound of Amanda's voice broke the stillness to soothe Gus. She ushered in a current of hypnotic fragrances—*night flowers*—Evening Primrose, Queen of the night, Nicotiana, Moonflower, Night Phlox, Jasmine, as if cradling him in the perfume of her embrace. She was close before him. He was overjoyed at the touch of her hand upon his right shoulder. At the same time, he felt her other hand on the left side of his face. He covered her hands with his for reassurance. The feel of her brought much relief. Her lips suddenly touched his cheek. Her breath was fragrant, the smell of orange spice.

"I told you that the brightest showy flowers bloom in the day, but the most fragrant flowers bloom at night to summon those who cannot see. Can you smell the Raganigandha? Can you smell its blossoms in the black of night? I forgive you, Augustine. I gotta go," she whispered.

Gus panicked.

"Go where! Go where, Amanda. Amanda?"

"I gotta go, Gus. Thank you."

"Thank me? Thank me for what? Amanda? Amanda?"

Gus had no idea what was going on or what she meant, but her words frightened him badly. There was something much deeper than the farewell. There was an implication, a revelation of fate beyond Gus's awareness.

"Forgive me for what? Go where? Amanda? Amanda? Forgive me for what? Did I do something wrong? Amanda? Amanda? Are you there? Amanda?"

Gus waited for a response, but none was forthcoming. For one grateful moment, anger crushed his fear.

"Enough of this bullshit, Amanda. I don't know what kind of game you're playing, but it's not funny. Amanda? Do you hear me? Amanda?"

Gus waited.

"Shit."

I guess it's going to be up to me to figure my way out of this piss poor joke. I don't get it. It's sure as hell not funny. But it is what it is.

Gus thought at length about Amanda.

Why would she be so kind, and then so cruel? Where was the wheelchair when she came over and put her hand on my face? Where was it when she kissed my cheek? Did she fake her affliction? Was that another joke at my expense?

Nobody at Redemption or dinner looked surprised when seeing her in a wheelchair. The wheelchair must have been legit.

"I don't know. God help me, I don't know."

His voice had no echo. Gus started walking back in the direction of the recliner as best he could determine. He continued to walk. After five minutes, he realized he must have walked past it. He realized the walls must have been a façade, and he was in some kind of large darkened warehouse.

"Hello! Hello! Anybody there? Hello! Hello! Hellllllooooooo!"

What now unnerved Gus was the total lack of an echo. His voice sounded as if he had a paper bag over his head. Everything about this place was simultaneously suffocating and wide open.

Gus felt himself drop back helplessly into the world of confusion he so desperately hoped to escape. He did not understand. He could not decipher any of it. He did not know from where he came or to where he would go. He could only assume that to stand or sit and wait would gain him nothing. He had to keep moving.

Gus journeyed forward into the black. He walked for hours. He walked until his hips, and knees, and shins, and ankles ached unbearably. He walked while suffering all manner of fears.

Maybe I'm walking into the bowels of an enormous machine. Maybe there's other lifeforms wandering about aimlessly in this blackness. Would I hear them howl or screech? Would they be able to find me? Could they smell me? Maybe they had infrared vision. What if I walked off a cliff, or the unseen ledge of a bottomless pit? There would be no warning, just a step into air.

The fear of an unseen pit forced Gus down to his hands and knees. He crawled. He crawled until his raw knees slipped and skidded across his own blood. He crawled until his back gave out to pain that forced him to collapse. Gus collapsed many times. Each time, he awoke in fits of fear. Eventually there was no way to determine if he was awake or asleep. His experience was a nightmare either way and insanity was the only given.

Gus attempted to stand and walk on weak and painful legs. Keeping his balance was difficult. He fell over many times, always picking himself back up for no logical reason. He might have walked a straight line. He might have walked in endless circles. He might have walked for weeks, or years, or time eternal. He could not say.

Gus ran until he could only walk. He walked until he could only crawl. He crawled until he could only push himself along the infinite, uninterrupted, glass-like surface. It was the only feature in his existence other than his thoughts. It was the only constant in his awareness. His only attachment. It was predictable and therefore comforting. Although he could not see it, he pressed his lips hard against its smooth texture. The kiss was passionate. He then rolled over onto his back, feeling secure no threat would come from behind. Gus was grateful for the blessing of its presence, and the endless invisible plane remained faithfully beneath him to the end.

31

Gus awoke on his back. The surface beneath him was hard and flat. It pained him. He worked to split his eyelids, then waited for the focus to sharpen. Slowly, details of his surroundings grew sufficiently clear for him to realize he was not in his bed, or anybody's bed for that matter.

Ouch. Ouch, ouch.

Gus slipped his hand behind his head and worked to rub out the discomfort. His fingers felt wet. He looked at them and noted a thick coating of blood.

Balls ablaze. That can't be good.

A second check produced more blood and the impression that there was a hole in the back of his head.

What the hell did I do to my head? Huh.

Gus stared at his fingers unable to explain the wound. Not that it made a difference. What could he do about it? He twisted his frame to work out the stiffness that crippled him.

Holy shit, it's cold.

A shudder passed through Gus. It compelled him to get off the floor that sucked the heat from his frame. He raised himself onto his elbows and looked around. He straightened his arms and sat up higher to better survey his surroundings.

Cars. Pillars. A ramp. Concrete everything, everywhere.

He was digesting details. He cleared his throat.

"Ah-hm. Ah-hmmm. A parking garage. A parking garage. Why am I lying in a parking garage?"

Gus frowned. He started sniffing the air. He zeroed in on his shirt. He reached for his collar and smelled the fabric.

Perfume. Flowery. Citrusy. Hint of orange. Maybe. Obviously a woman. Who was I with? Mmmm. Not coming. Not coming. Do I hurt from a head wound or a hangover? It'll come.

Gus rolled over onto his side before rising awkwardly onto his hands and knees. He hesitated briefly as an urge to vomit tightened his guts. Only after his stomach settled did he elect to get on his feet. It took more than just standing up. He teetered upon quivering limbs and noted the extent of his weakness. He moved his legs with guarded ambition as he slowly made way toward a pillar against which to lean. He checked the back of his head again.

Jesus, what a mess.

Gus wiped the blood on his pants as he took in his surroundings a second time from this higher vantage point.

No need to get embarrassed. It's just me and my lonesome.

A few cars sat positioned between yellow lines. No owners walking to or from their vehicles. Gus scrutinized the cars, but claimed none.

I don't think I drove. Maybe I walked or got dropped off here. I'm sure I know this place. I've been here before. It'll come to me. It's coming.... C'mon, c'mon, c'mon....

Gus's head rolled back. His eyes closed as he sought to pull in memories.

There's a street. A hill—there's a hill. He listened to the distant sounds of traffic. *A highway. Yes, yes. The highway.... I remember.*

Gus dropped his head and opened his eyes.

"I have to find the highway. That's the only way out of here," he whispered.

Gus glanced around and found himself drawn to an anemic glow of light, a spill of overcast that flowed down the ramp and into the garage.

Yeah. The ramp.

Slowly but steadily, strength returned to Gus's legs, to his arms, to his body as a whole. He was winded, but still walking after scaling the ramp. He wandered into the middle of the road.

Gus turned to his right and looked at the glow of morning light beaming across the crest of a high ridge. To his left, the remnants of night. He watched warily as a troubling smog slinked about in the distance where the street descended. An immediate gut reaction warned him that this was more than just a city's bad air. What hovered in the distance below obscured all light, color, and detail. It suppressed everything that might lift his spirits. It suffocated life.

"The *Lingering*."

Gus spoke aloud. The word formed out of nothing; it came out of nowhere. The term sounded as foreign as it did familiar. He found the word puzzling, its meaning alien, but its utterance brought forth a vile emotion that cored down to his deepest place within.

32

Unnerved by shadows that appeared to be approaching, Gus turned toward the ridge. His fear was his motivation. He struggled at length to reach his objective. His strength, drained to the point of exhaustion, barely lifted his feet to crest the ridge above. However, once he arrived, the view, the commotion, the insanity of life above the abominable pit revitalized his store of energy.

Feelings of familiarity brought strength with every step, as Gus walked toward the roar of traffic. He passed through the tall brick structures that fenced the ridge to force back nightmarish things unwanted. He passed through the myriad of shanties and lean-tos that paralleled the monumental thoroughfare.

Shedding his wretched morning start, Gus gladly moved into the flow of humanity as it meandered between the highway and fence-like string of shanties, huts, and lean-tos. He was awestruck.

Gus scaled the bank of the shoulder, which along with its accompanying paved lanes stood proudly above all else. Without obstruction, the warmth of a glorious morning light flowed the length of the pathway and permeated every fiber in Gus's being. He stopped his advance in order to close his eyes and allow the sun's rays to find him. He stood still as the heat pressed upon his forehead, forcing his eyes to close. It crossed cheeks to kiss his lips and course down his fragile frame.

Gus opened his eyes only after the sun forced out the last of his cold and desperation. He took in a deep breath, and then another, and another. Each time he exhaled, he purged himself of anxiety and opened his world to inner peace and simple pleasure. Joy and wonder now washed over him in a pulsing parade of waves.

Drawn by the outlandish collection of vehicles that whizzed past him, Gus worked his way toward the road's edge to experience the chorus of whines and whistles, roars and rumbles, all colluding to drown out everything but the most determined thought.

The only thing that succeeded in drowning out the din was the horrific screech of a bus braking to stop. Its doors flung open and nearly slapped Gus across the face. Alarmed, he jumped backward so fast that he lost balance and fell flat upon the shoulder's fine dusty earth. As the unconcerned crowd sidestepped him, he stared upward at the bus marquee. It displayed a bright green *BUS 7 CHARTERED.*

Gus's gaze dropped from the marquee to the parted bus doors. The driver stared directly at him lying in the dirt. Instead of exploding with anger, Gus, overtaken by a sense of familiarity regarding the bus, the marquee, the driver, his ridiculous bandana, the street, the whole of the setting, simply laid where he'd fallen and struggled to sort it out.

"Good morning, Gus! Sorry about the scare. C'mon, get on your feet, man. There's no time to linger in Locum Veniae."

It was a close miss. One that startled Gus terribly. And yet, most surprisingly, he held his temper in check.

"Hey, Driver, you trying to kill me or what?"

"Sorry about that. Didn't mean to put you in the dirt."

"I'll let it go, if you'll help me out. I know we know each other. You called me Gus. But as familiar as your face is to me, I can't for the life of me remember your name. You are who?"

"Don't feel bad. I've never given you or any passenger my name. I go by Driver. Call me Driver. Now, get off your ass, and let's go. I haven't got all day. Neither do you."

Gus's mind raced at break-neck speed. Thoroughly confused but unafraid, he understood he was suffering from some kind of amnesia. He had no idea what had brought it on, but everything was happening so fast, and everything about this place was so familiar, that he had scant reason to dwell in fear of his condition. He was confident that something would soon trigger the return of his memories.

For now, if nothing else, the driver was direct and convincing. Having no plans, or anything better to do, Gus stood up from the bed of dusty yellow ochre. He brushed himself off, causing clouds to float about his frame until sucked away by the breeze of the passing crowd. The driver's recommendation seemed the path of least resistance, and so Gus reached through the bus door, grabbed the railing, and pulled himself up the step. He looked back along the aisle.

"Sit down, before you fall," commanded the driver.

33

Gus gripped the vertical chrome post tightly as the bus lurched forward. He glanced at the passenger's faces and quickly noticed that they were all staring at him. It made him uncomfortable and he wasted no time dropping into seat A1, happy to focus on his feet and nothing more.

"Hey, Gus."

Gus looked up to see a small Asian man in a seat across the aisle looking at him. The man was smiling. So were the passengers seated alongside him.

"You talking to me?" Gus asked with genuine surprise.

The group of passengers broke out in laughter. Gus did not feel as if he were the butt end of a joke because the man addressed him by name. In fact, he felt surrounded by an air of affection that invited him to question the crowd.

"Why are you all laughing?" he asked with a grin.

Clearly amused, the group laughed louder.

"Are you all right?" asked a woman. "We saw you lying in the dirt. Are your shoes filled with sand?"

Shoes filled with sand....

Gus hesitated. He sighed.

"Sand? I'm not sure what you mean, but I guess I'm all right. I feel a lot better now than I did when I woke up. That much I know."

"Well, on the subject of knowing.... Do you know who I am? Do you know any of us?"

Gus studied the faces of those in the seats nearest him. He could not identify any of them with clarity. There was only a sense of familiarity.

"There's something about your voices. I don't recall your faces, but your voices sound familiar to me."

"That's not surprising. It was dark when we last met."

"I'm sorry. I apologize." Gus sighed. "You seem familiar, I could swear I've met you all, but I... I just can't place you. Bear with me, I got off to a bad start. I woke up on the floor of a parking garage. I hit my head on the concrete. When I came to, I didn't know my name. In fact, I just now learned it when Driver called me Gus. Bad day."

The bus slowed and pulled over to the curb. An air of excitement coursed through the passengers as they rose to take their leave. Not one remained seated.

This can't be the end of the line. I just got on.

Confused, Gus stood up only minutes after sitting down. Unsure of where the bus stopped, or where he was to go next, he chose not to move into the aisle. The riders, in contrast, poured into the aisle.

Where are all these people going? Are they all part of a tour group or something?

Questions and answers evaporated as soon as the first passenger filed past. He was an older man of large build who had a prominent scar on his forehead shaped like a crescent moon. He was the first to address Gus.

"My turn, Gus. I gotta go. I knew you'd make it. Never doubted it for a moment. Does my heart good. Take care of yourself."

The man extended his hand. Bewildered, Gus accepted the handshake, but couldn't take his eyes off the scar. He had no idea what the man was talking about. Gus had little chance to reply because a small Asian man stepped across the aisle and pushed in toward him. He was nodding as if conveying his thoughts and feelings without the use of speech.

"I wait long time, man. I t'ank you now. I t'ank you. Now, I gotta go. Bye, Gus. I gotta go."

"But—"

"Hello, Gus. You probably don't remember me. I'm Veronica Giordano. This is my boy, Joseph. You did the right thing. You showed me what I needed to see. Thank you for everything."

"But what did I—"

As Mrs. Giordano spoke her last word, she raised her fingers to her lips. As Gus began to speak, she pressed her fingers against his lips to silence him. He remained silent as he accepted her indirect kiss.

"It took a long time, longer than you know. But thanks to you, we're free. We gotta go."

As Veronica turned to walk away, her fingers were still on Gus's lips when he reached up and grabbed her wrist firmly. She turned to look back at him and gently shook her head no. She smiled and whispered.

"You'll know in time. I gotta go, Gus. I gotta go."

In spite of enormous attraction to the woman, Gus was helpless to do anything but release her. While watching her and Joseph descend to the street, a number of other individuals approached to pat him on the shoulder or shake his hand. All said thanks and stated that they had "to go."

"Hey, there, Gus."

"Hey! I know you. Gary, right?"

"Jerry. Jerry Lambert."

"Oh, yes. Jerry." Gus grimaced. "Sorry, memory...."

"No problem." The man looked down as he focused on peeling back the wrapper of a candy bar. "Just wanted to say thank you before I step off the bus. I appreciate you coming here. Facing you wasn't easy. You like chocolate? Here, I've had my fill. Enjoy. I gotta go."

The man handed Gus a chocolate bar. Gus stood dumbfounded, his hand outstretched with the GOLD AAA chocolate bar face up. He might have dwelled on Jerry Lambert as the man moved toward the door had it not been for the voice of another.

"Hello, Gus." *Pop-pop.*

Gus didn't answer. He stared at this young woman with a streak of white hair and a tattoo on her chest as she popped her gum. Her presence moved him immeasurably.

"Jesus, I know I know you. I know it inside. I just can't remember. Just give me a minute. Please. Just a moment."

"There is a part of you that is warm and caring and wonderful. I needed to see that. Thank you for coming. I understand that you don't remember anything, but you will. It won't be easy, but it'll be for the better. You'll see."

Bonnie rose to her tiptoes and placed her arms around his neck. She crushed him with her embrace and kissed him on the lips.

"You had a conscience. I remember," she whispered. "I gotta go. We'll meet again."

The woman trotted lightly to the bus steps and bounced down to the street. Gus watched her continue to prance as she laughed with the others. He might never have taken his eyes off her frail figure had he not been drawn to another voice.

"Augustine."

Gus turned to face an elderly woman.

"I brought you a present."

Gus looked down at a book. He frowned.

"Of Guilt and Conscience?"

"Yes. Take it. I promise you will enjoy it. It's one of your favorites."

"You know me?"

"Of course I do. We all do. We're happy you came."

"How do you all—"

"Shhh. It's not my place to say, Gus. Besides, I'm holding up the line. Take care of yourself. I gotta go."

She looked back over her shoulder as the file of passengers nudged her on. But it wasn't enough. Gus needed more, much more. He called out to her in desperation.

"Ma'am! Ma'am. Please. I beg...."

The elderly woman turned toward him as she stepped down.

"Oh, please don't call me ma'am. Amanda Wellington. My name is Amanda Wellington." She smiled and disappeared through the door. At first, Gus hollered out in her direction, then he turned to speak to those yet filing past.

"I told you that I suffer from amnesia. I'm standing here like an idiot, or worse, a fool wondering why you are all thanking me. Why won't you tell me? What's the point of all this? Why such a big deal? If I did something wonderful, why wouldn't you want me to know? This can't be right. There has to be some misunderstanding."

"There is no misunderstanding, Gus. We have traveled on this wheeled contraption for nearly an eternity awaiting your arrival. You offered us the way to salvation. Now that we have it, we can move on. We're grateful, Gus. Eternally grateful. You played an important role in our destiny. That's all I can say. Like the others, I gotta go."

A man patted Gus on the shoulder, and moved to step around him, but Gus reached out to stop him. He stared into the man's eyes. His final emotional plea bled from every portal of his soul.

"Please. Sir. I want to be noble. I'm thrilled to think I have done something or things honorable, something that warrants all of this, but all I get from this experience is frustration. What could I have possibly offered you and the others to deserve such praise?"

The man turned from Gus to face the driver. Gus watched as the driver nodded some form of approval. The passenger turned back to face Gus.

"A chance to forgive you."

"What?"

"A chance to forgive you. A chance to purge our souls of negatives. A chance to merge. Salvation, Gus. You opened the last gate closed to our salvation. And that's where we're going. I've said more than I should. I am grateful. I gotta go."

The man intentionally swung around the grab bar, descended the steps, and exited the bus so fast that Gus had no time to question him further. Not that it would have mattered. He knew nothing more would be forthcoming. There was nothing left to do but stand alone, confused, and frustrated as the remainder of passengers nodded their appreciation and thanked him.

When the last of many stepped off the bus, Gus looked to the back of the bus. It was empty. Only he and the driver remained. He turned slowly to confront the driver, who had overheard every word of the passenger's bizarre explanation. More importantly, the person who gave a nod of approval. A man who undoubtedly knew well what this was all about. A man who had no problem calling him out by name.

Gus cracked. His frustration bled out. Memories were scratching away at his mind, ripping slits into the veil of concealment. He was so close to knowing the passengers that he could cry with exasperation. The fact drove him insane with anger that visibly rippled across his expression. His voice flared as he asked questions and demanded answers.

"Driver, I think it's about fucking time for you to spit it out. What the hell did he mean? What the hell did any of this mean? I saw you nod at that guy. I saw the way he looked to you for permission or whatever. I know you, and I know these people, but I don't know them, do I? Why don't I know them? Don't tell me that you don't know what the fuck's going on. You've got answers. I fucking know you've got answers, and I want some."

34

The driver said nothing. He stood unassertive as he assessed the depth of Gus's anger. His expression might have been one of understanding, or concern, or....

Contempt. What's with this guy? A Good Samaritan? Helping me off the street? Working for my betterment? Or something entirely different? That expression. Those eyes. I know contempt when I see it. Don't fucking tell me he's here for me. Bullshit.

"Driver?"

"Yeah."

"You're smirking, man. You're smirking. You got something to say?"

"No, not really."

"Not really? You're certain."

"I'm certain I'm not smirking."

"Then what *are* you doing? Why do I get the feeling you're holding back? You know, *anger... hatred.* I've seen it in your eyes, man. The look of a killer. It comes and goes in a flash. I just saw it. Don't tell me different. It's something I know. Something you can't hide. You wanna tell me I'm dreaming? You wanna tell me it's all part of my paranoia, my confused state of mind? You wanna tell me you picked me up because you know me, because you have a bleeding heart? Really? You harboring secrets, Driver? Something I should know? Why don't you tell me what the fuck this is really about?"

The driver answered Gus in a controlled voice.

"It's *all* about secrets, Gus. But you got it wrong—all wrong. It's not about my secrets. It's about your secrets. The secrets you keep from yourself. The secrets that torture you eternally. Truths you've hidden from yourself. Truths you're beginning to suspect, but choose not to accept."

The driver blindsided Gus. The answer wasn't what he expected. Being knocked off balance, he quickly became defensive.

"Is that so? Well, then, why don't you save me the trouble of working through this pathetic conundrum of secrets I refuse to face? Why waste our time? If you know something, secrets about me, good or bad, then just tell me. Just spit it out. If not, then shut the fuck up. Quit with the bullshit. Don't look at me. Don't smile at me. Don't do whatever the hell it is you're doing. I remember zip, and I'm not gonna get your jokes. And I'm not gonna get your riddles. I don't even know your name. And if you and I got history, I ain't got a clue. You understand? You hear what I'm saying? Why don't *you* face *that?*"

Gus was itching for the driver to make a move, to confront him. Instead, the driver eased back slowly, reached down to the dashboard of the bus, and flipped a switch. He turned a key. The engine killed. He pushed a button two or three times, sending the marquee above the windshield into a flashing blur until it changed from *BUS 7 CHARTERED* to *OUT OF SERVICE*. Finally, the driver turned back to face Gus.

"Are you hungry?"

"What?"

"I said, are you hungry?"

"Hungry?"

"Yeah. Hungry. I've been driving all damn day, and I need a break. Thought I'd stop for a burger and some coffee. Are you hungry? I'll buy."

The invitation caught Gus off guard. Why would the driver offer to buy him lunch after his testy gush of resentment and insulting tone? Just as strange was the realization that he had not given a thought to eating. Only when the driver mentioned eating did he suddenly feel famished.

"You wanna buy me lunch after I just chewed on you."

"I do."

Gus wanted to read the driver. He wanted to make sense of the stranger and his offer, but the only thing making sense was his having no idea about anything, except that the driver had answers, and that he was *hungry*—intensely hungry.

I can beat this to death and get nowhere, or eat and maybe get answers. Damn, I'm hungry.

"All right. Yeah. Sure. Why not? Let's face it, we both know I got issues. I'm screwed up and irritable. Maybe a burger'll do me good. Maybe food'll settle me down a bit."

"Can't hurt," said the driver as he nodded in agreement. "C'mon. Let's go. I know a great little place."

The two men stepped off the bus, leaving the doors open to the public. They worked their way through the stream of strange faces focused on a distant horizon. The driver led Gus past the boundary of shanties and stalls. He led him through the ridgeline structures, and over the crest of the scarp to descend along a route that Gus had traveled many times unknowingly.

Gus only remembered walking this path once, a couple of hours ago, but his loathing of the place ran deep. For him, the road worsened with each step. Following the driver into the depths did nothing but increase his anxiety and the crushing weight of despair.

There's no way, I can do this. I can't go down. No way.

"Balls ablaze...." Gus moaned. "Tell me something, Driver. Why would you go down there?" He looked around warily. The gloom was fast to close in. Occasionally, the hint of a lamp or light would stab through the thickening murkiness to reach Gus.

"Why would anybody go down here? This place is morbid at best. It makes my guts churn," complained Gus.

"Relax. There's this little burger joint just down the hill on the right. You'll love it. Been there many a time. Haven't had a bad burger yet. Not a one."

The two men continued to walk, but Gus worsened.

"I don't know about the burgers, but my memories, or feelings, or whatever it is that I have about this place aren't that hot.

Seems like I was always trying to get the hell out of here. And for good reason, I'm sure."

The driver stopped. He looked at Gus and pointed.

"There. See, like I said, nice little place. No need to worry. Besides, I'm buying. Now stop complaining."

The driver walked up to a window. A server glanced his way and smiled. She immediately approached.

"Hey, Driver. Haven't seen you in a while. How've you been?"

"Been great, Sugar. You're looking pretty as ever."

"Well, thank you. Always nice to hear. What can I get you?"

"How about a couple of house burgers? One for me, and one for my friend."

"Coming right up."

Gus stood alongside the driver, but instead of focusing on the food, his attention centered on the street. His concentration was interrupted only when the driver handed him his food.

"Eat up, Gus. You won't regret a mouthful of this."

"Thanks."

Gus unwrapped the burger and took a large bite, but his near feverish fascination for the street damped the pleasure of eating. He swallowed, and then confided in the driver.

"Do you realize this is the road I followed to reach the highway when you first picked me up on the bus?"

Gus took another bite of the burger, unaware of how the words that rolled off his tongue matter-of-factly impacted the driver. The driver stopped chewing and swallowed. He cleared his throat and turned toward Gus. The driver's expression was one of amazement.

"Yeah, I do remember," said the driver. "I'm surprised to hear that you do. You said, *first* picked me up, spoken as if you remember being here more than once. That's good. Must be your time has come."

"I'm telling you, Driver, this place feels very familiar. What do you mean, 'my time'? Time come for what?"

"To remember."

The driver's suggestion enlightened Gus before his own recognition even thought to form. He chewed on his food, all the while giving thought to what the driver had said.

Huh. You think? Am I remembering? It that possible? Am I getting my life back?

Gus was clearly aware of this increasing familiarity. It was strengthening in places where none had been before. He swallowed and concurred.

"Yeah... you may be right," he thought aloud. "Maybe I *am* starting to remember. Maybe I really have been on this street before just as I thought. I mean, you know, before this morning. Maybe more than once. Yeah, I think maybe...."

Gus frowned. He turned and looked at the driver suspiciously. He struggled to capture glimpses of his past—other times and places. He spoke in a slower manner that reflected his efforts to plunge deeper into the vault that hid away his past.

"You picked me up on the corner of this street... where it meets the highway.... Yeah, I remember that. I remember getting on your bus. We drove for...I don't know—*forever*. It seemed like weeks or months.... It's all murky, vague, but it feels like we traveled for the whole of my life. We went places. I don't remember where all we went, but I remember we were on the road for a long time...a very long time."

Gus observed the driver's reactions. The driver did as much in return.

"What's bad about remembering.... Now, correct me if I'm wrong, but that highway is one way—*one way*," asserted Gus. "How would we end up back here after all the time we spent heading out of this place? Did I lose my memory out there somewhere? Is that what you know? Was it gone all the while we drove back? I mean, why do I have vague memories of driving away from here, but nothing about driving back? How did I get back here? Is there another road or—"

"Gus."

"What?"

"You're thinking way too hard. You need to calm down, and concentrate on your burger before it gets cold."

Gus's expression turned hard. Without warning, he threw his half-eaten burger into the trash, and spun around to glare at the driver.

"Calm down? *Calm down?* What are you—my mother? Calm down...." Gus glanced about the street with a sense of foreboding. "That's easy for you to say. You know what you're doing down here. You know what you did yesterday, last week, last month, last year. I, on the other hand, remember nothing. I have no idea about anything except that maybe you and I have done some serious traveling. And that maybe you know a shitload about me that you aren't saying."

Gus went expressionless. He slipped into another distant thought.

"Hold on.... I remember something else. It just came to me. You... I remember... you... pulling away from the curb on that highway. And just like that, a second later, you're back at the curb. But the road goes one way—*one way.*"

Gus turned away to speak under his breath as he gave thought to another memorable incident.

"That was impossible. It was *impossible*.... That's just one thing. Just one of a zillion things I can't make sense of. My head is so screwed up. So please, don't tell me to *calm down*. Don't tell me that because it only pisses me off more."

Gus looked along the street into the distance as he reflected.

"Freaked me right out. You pulled away from the curb, and *bam*, you're right back. No way. *That* stuck in my head big time. I feel like all of this, everything that's happening right now, is a similar sort of thing. I'm coming and going at the same time. I can't wrap my head around...uhhh...time. Yeah, I've got no sense of time."

The driver responded cautiously.

"You can't very well expect to grasp time if you lost your memory. You've lost all your reference points."

Gus's mind was churning. It was unsettled. It felt driven for answers to questions that were yet beyond his awareness to ask. A cynical laugh erupted as he forwarded a final thought.

"You ain't sayin' shit, Driver. You ain't sayin' shit. There's more to it than that. I know you're part of this. Maybe you're the constant. You and maybe this street. This street feels like a part of me—a bad growth or something. And you... you were driving back then, and you're driving now. You say you know me, but I think you know a lot more about me than you let on. Am I right or what? Tell me I'm wrong, Driver. Tell me I'm wrong, or tell me why I feel some sort of connection to you and this godforsaken hell hole."

The two men continued to face each other, but did so at a guarded distance. There was palpable mistrust in the air.

"No, you're not wrong. We do have history."

Gus half expected the answer, but felt shaken nonetheless.

"I knew it. I fucking knew it."

The words came out low and strained. The driver continued to speak.

"I've driven this bus for as long as I can remember, and like I said, I've faced you more times than I can recall. It's only natural that I might know your name."

"Oh, I get that. Oh, yeah. You *might* know my name after having—how did you put that—*faced* me so many times. No question there, but what else? What about the rest of it? What about... I don't know... time—places? Especially time. I don't get time. How long were we on the road? Where did you take me? Maybe you'd like to fill me in. Maybe you'd like to explain. I mean, I'm all ears."

"Yeah, well, explaining.... Explaining's not so easy," said the driver. "You're in Locum Veniae. Time and space act different here. They're not always linear like you would expect. You could be two places at the same time. Stuff like that. It's too hard to put into words, and frankly, I haven't got that kind of time."

Gus looked down at his feet. He ran his fingers through hair at the back of his head and neck. Fresh blood coated his hand.

The wound remained and reminded him of how sick and tired he was of feeling irrelevant.

"Great play on words. I love it. I love all of it. Two places at once? Too hard to put into words? You think? Either spewing that crap makes you nuts, or I'm crazy for listening. Two places at once? What kind of bullshit is that? I may not remember my own name, but I'm not an idiot. Not by a long shot."

"No, you're not an idiot, Gus. And no, it's not bullshit. I just don't know how to explain it. It's like being asked if you know where a circle begins and ends. Do you?"

"That's a mind game for a six-year-old."

"Maybe so," said the driver. "But it sums up our situation. For the sake of conversation, let's just say the road is one way just as you said, and that it looks straight as an arrow just as you said, but looks can be deceiving. Assume we actually traveled a large circle. A very large circle. A circle as big as the universe itself. Too large to detect a change in direction, but follow it long enough and you end up where you started."

"There's no other street? No one-way street in the opposite direction?" asked Gus.

"No."

"I know you'd like me to believe that, but I don't think so. You could never have pulled away from that curb and returned in the blink of an eye. You didn't drive around the universe in five seconds. Besides, your face tells me different. I got an idea that I've been back here more than just once or twice. I been here a number of times, hundreds of times, thousands of times, but it wasn't from driving around in circles. Where the hell is Locum Veniae?"

"Good question."

"And...."

"And what?"

"What do you mean, *and what*? And where the hell is Locum Veniae?"

The driver looked directly at Gus. He was annoyed.

"What difference does it make? What the hell difference does it make? None. And nothing I'm gonna say will change anything. I'm not the one with the answers. You are. And you're here... *in Locum Veniae.* End of discussion."

The driver stuffed the last of the burger into his mouth and wadded up the wrapper. He headed toward the trash bin. He then started down the street heading farther downward into gloom. Gus remained standing with clenched fists. He foundered within a cloud of unbearable frustration. Obviously, the driver knew where Locum Veniae was, where this street was, where he was.

Balls ablaze. What's the big deal? Why the secrets? Pisses me off. Just pisses me off. He knows where Locum Veniae is. He knows where this street is. He knows about all of this.

The suspicion left Gus bleeding doubt and mistrust. He was drowning in it. However, because he was perpetually confused, because right now he couldn't win an argument with a two-year-old about anything, he let it slide.

"Screw it."

As far as he could see, arguing or pressing the issue was not going to make things different. He was in no position to call the shots.

"Screw it, screw it, screw it."

Gus stepped out into the street. The driver was walking away with or without him.

I'm not hanging around in this gloom alone. No way in hell.

"Hey! Wait up!"

Gus hustled to catch the driver. Upon catching up, he began to reflect aloud.

"Hey! Here's something. I walked through this neighborhood and it was bloody awful. It was dark and miserable. The place was a wasteland. Nobody lived here. It creeped me out so bad, I had all I could do to reach that ridge back there and put it behind me. Now look. It's got some life and color. Not a lot, but it wasn't like this the first time I walked through here. It wasn't like this earlier today. Actually, it wasn't like this twenty minutes ago. What's with that?"

The driver did not respond. Gus continued to ramble.

"Hmm. Something's going on. My memories are returning before I even realize it. That building over there, the one with the massive wood doors and barred windows was a bank—or is a bank. If it isn't a bank, it has something to do with money. I don't actually remember that. I sort of know it. I think I was on the roof of that place."

"Could very well be," said the driver. "I have no idea, but you are right about the neighborhood. Things have come a long way." The driver pointed ahead. "That building over there was the first to rise from the blight of despair. I remember the day it reopened. *Uplifting* is what I thought to myself. The road was uncivil, filled with shadows and fear, but the building glowed like the sun. It stood out like a beacon, drawing others to the light."

"The owners did a good job of restoring it," said Gus as he studied the multi-story building. "You know what else just came to mind?"

"What's that?" asked the driver.

"There was fire in that building. I think somebody jumped from the window."

"Again, I have no idea," said the driver. "You probably know better than me, but I'd pass on *that* memory."

"I only said it because of something in the back of my head. I might have heard about it or read it somewhere."

"You seem to be suddenly remembering a great deal. Is it because of this street?"

Gus stopped and turned slowly to observe details of the buildings on the street.

"I'm beginning to get bits and pieces. It's more like vague perceptions about these places. You'd think I'd remember something about me. I can remember a fire and somebody jumping out of a window, but I can't remember my own stupid name. Go figure. Oh well. I guess it'll come when it damn well pleases."

"No doubt." The driver took in a deep breath. "Can you feel the energy around here? Fresh energy."

"Fresh energy?" asked Gus.

"Yeah, can't you feel it? It's all around us. People are moving back, making investments here. They're bringing back the light, the warmth. The place is coming alive. Can't you feel it?"

"Not really."

"Oh. Too bad."

The driver ended their conversation as he stopped at a storefront and leaned backward to look up the face of the building.

"You remember this place?" asked the driver.

"This place?" Gus responded in surprise.

"Yeah. It's one of the last offerings available for repair. You sort out this mess and you could be well on your way to a redeeming future. Great opportunity."

Gus took one look at the place and was overwhelmed with depression.

"Jesus, Driver. Are you kidding? This place is too far gone. This dump isn't a fixer-up. It's firewood. I feel dirty just looking at it. Feels like it wants to suck the life right out of me." Gus studied the driver. "Oh, wait.... No way. Don't tell me you're honestly thinking about buying this wreck?"

"Close. Spiritually, I'm already invested. My heart says go for it."

"Hoo, boy. You got one twisted heart," said Gus.

"Don't be so fast to jump to conclusions. I think investing some blood and sweat this place could prove to be rewarding. A good return. Wouldn't be easy. Nothing worth having ever comes easy. Would take a person with determination. A soul with stamina. The sort who could see light at the end of the tunnel. I've traveled a good long time, Gus, been through a lot of tunnels, and I know a good thing when I see it. The street's coming back to life. It's a great place to end out our days. What d'ya say we sneak inside and have a look? We'll see how bad it really is."

"What? Are you nuts? It's all boarded up. Undoubtedly for the safety of the public. Only a blind man would have a vision of this being anything more than firewood. This isn't a place to *end out* your days; it's a place to end them *period*."

"So you aren't even a little bit curious? Nothing nudging you to go inside?"

"Hell no. Why would I wanna go in there?"

"Why not? These old buildings are great opportunities to peek into the past. Who knows what you'll find? What's it gonna hurt? I can't believe you're not even a little curious."

No thank you. Nothing about this place has appeal. In fact, it's the opposite. It's lifeless, dreary, suffocating. An oversized coffin awaiting a tenant. Nobody in their right mind would want to go in here. Driver has too many miles under his belt. He would settle for anything just to get out of that bus.

"Don't you have to get back to your bus?" asked Gus.

"I do. But a moment of poking around isn't going to hold up traffic. Not the way they drive. I say we go inside just long enough to have a look'n see. Afterward, back on the bus, we discuss the merits and pitfalls. I'm interested in what you'll have to say." The driver turned toward Gus. "Besides…to be honest, you really don't have anything better to do, and we both know it. Whether I wait an hour or a week to return to the bus, what are you gonna do?"

"I'll work out something."

"C'mon, Gus, where's your sense of adventure?"

Gus rolled his eyes.

"Don't talk to me about adventure. My entire wretched existence is an adventure. Just so you know; I've had a gut full of adventure." Gus suddenly relented. "Fine. Fine. I'm game. But only because you bought me lunch. This is for you. Payback. Debt free. I owe you nothing. You got that?"

"I got that."

Gus settled down.

Maybe a little diversion will do me good.

"You think we'll be able to get in?" asked Gus.

"Yeah, I'm pretty sure we can. Let's see."

The driver reached for the knob on the front door and gave it a twist. The door immediately moved back and away.

"You *are* kidding me, right?" said Gus.

"Why so surprised? Like you said, who would want to go in here?"

"I didn't say that."

"It's what you were thinking. After you," said the driver with an outstretched arm.

35

Gus walked in. He started looking around.

"I guess this was a small grocery store. All the shelves. Look," he pointed. "That was probably a meat counter. Looks like one. I think this was a butcher shop."

"I think you're right."

"Funny isn't it," said Gus. "At one time, this place was probably filled with people, locals, all living in the neighborhood, all knowing each other, gossiping, telling jokes, passing around pictures of their kids, making plans for get-togethers.... And look at it now. I feel like it wants to drag me to hell. Can you feel it? It wants to rip the soul right out of me. The place is packed with ghosts, Driver. I can feel them breathing down my neck, sucking up all the air. God, this place is depressing. Is it just me, or is it hard to breathe in here?"

"You're overreacting."

"Not really. I'm telling you it's hard to breathe in here. Maybe it's the dust. I might be allergic."

"I doubt you got allergies."

"How would you know?"

"Your nose isn't running. Your eyes are clear."

"Whatever." Gus reflected, and then continued.

"You gotta wonder why these places fall to ruin. Why folks abandon them. Do the owners just grow old? Do the neighbors all grow old together and then die together? The whole street dies because all their kids pack up and move away for newer, brighter, roomier lifestyles. Maybe a recession killed business, or made the place too costly to update. Looking around at all these empty shelves, it's hard to imagine that at one time this place held promise."

"This place held a lot of promise. It did good business in its day."

"You sound like you know the place."

"I do," said the driver. "This was a family business. I knew the owner. He lived with his family upstairs. In fact, I can probably still find the stairway."

"Why didn't you tell me straight away that you knew the place?"

"I wanted your honest opinion of it."

"Well, I guess you got that. A dump. You knowing him isn't changing anything. It's still a dump. Are you sure that we should be poking around in here? What if somebody catches us?" asked Gus.

"I'll tell 'em I know the owner, and that I'm looking for an investment property. But like you said, there isn't a soul around. I doubt there'll be a problem. Besides, I'm kind of curious to see the place again. I'm convinced there's a lot to be had here."

"Each to his own. You know what they say.... One man's junk...."

Gus followed the driver, and as predicted, the man found a door that concealed a stairway leading to an upper floor. The two men climbed the steps to a second-story hallway.

"Not too bad," said the driver as he looked around.

"Not bad at all," said Gus in amazement. "Nice woodwork. Look at this oak. They don't build them like this anymore. Nobody wants to spend the time or the money for quality."

"Amen, brother."

Gus remained a couple of steps behind the driver as they ventured down the hallway. They stopped at the kitchen and peered inside.

"Now *that's* weird," said Gus. "Look at those plates on the table. They've got food on them. Totally dried out. Petrified. How long you think they've been sitting there? Years? Decades? Currrrazy. You would almost think something happened. You know, like everybody cleared out in a hurry. Like an emergency.

"They dropped the bomb...," said Gus in a deliberately deep and foreboding voice.

Gus entered the kitchen. He moved toward the table for a closer look at the settings.

"Strange."

He shook his head and then looked up from the table and glanced around the room. Gus walked over to the cupboards and opened one up. He looked at the dry goods yet stacked and stored on the shelves. He looked down at the counter and yanked on a drawer pull. The drawer slid open and revealed an assortment of toss-aways. He pulled open another drawer. Silverware sorted in an orderly fashion came to light. Dried food no longer occupied his thoughts. Gus turned to the driver.

"I know you're talking about buying this place, but as old as this stuff is, we could make a killing just selling this shit to an antiques shop. They pay good money for everyday things like these. I mean the oats and cereal boxes haven't even been opened. Macaroni. Look at all the cans of soup. This is old, old, stuff."

Gus reached for a jar. He moved to untwist the top. It came off with a spin.

"Look at that. Peanut butter. Extra crunchy. Still sealed. Unbelievable. Makes you wonder how long that stuff stays good. Makes you almost want to break the seal and taste it."

"Be my guest," offered the driver.

Gus's eyes returned to look upward and across the assortment of dry goods in the cupboards.

Wow! Look at all this stuff.

"Man, there's a whole bunch of new old stock here. I wonder what else is around here. Let's look in some of the other rooms."

Excited, Gus moved to leave the kitchen. This time the driver followed Gus as he entered the living room.

"Wow. Look at that old TV. I knew it. There's probably a ton of great finds in this place. C'mon, man, you're a bus driver. You get around. Don't you know where there's an antique shop? Look at the books..., and this furniture. This is really nice stuff."

Gus turned about slowly as he surveyed the room. "Like I said, at one time this place was doing good business. Had to be good and profitable for the owner to live like this."

"What the hell is that?" asked the driver.

"What?" asked Gus.

"Right there. Sticking out of that chair? Is that a knife?"

Gus walked over to the chair and leaned over to look closer.

"Sure as hell is. Now, that's a bit bizarre."

Gus went silent as he scrutinized the blade.

"What are you looking at?" asked the driver.

Gus twisted his head around to get a better look.

"Why would anybody want to ruin a perfectly good chair? Vandals. Kids. Shoot the little bast—"

Gus went white. He stopped short as an unexpected wave of apprehension blistered its way through him. He glanced around for something unseen. He saw no one aside from the driver, who appeared intrigued as he walked over to where Gus stood, and leaned in to have a look himself. Gus backed away from the knife. He worked to catch his breath.

"You hear that?" he whispered.

"Hear what?" asked the driver.

"I don't know. I thought I heard somebody. Did you hear somebody?"

"No."

The two stood motionless and quiet. After a long moment, the driver nodded at Gus.

"You're just hearing things. These old buildings creak. Either that or it's your imagination. Either way you can get spooked."

Gus wasn't quick to move. He was listening for anything outside the room. He never took his eyes off the driver, just in case the driver picked up on something as well. But the driver wasn't nearly as concerned about noises or being quiet, and asked Gus a question.

"What's carved into that handle? Is that a name? Looks like a name from here." The driver pointed carefully, taking care not to touch the instrument.

The question distracted Gus. He leaned over to get a better look. At first, he didn't stand back up or look at the driver. He answered with a hard edge to his voice.

"Ya think?"

"It says... *Gus Beretta*," said the driver.

"Yes, it does.... Maybe you thought I was blind. Maybe you thought I couldn't read."

The expression on Gus's face was a mix of anger and impending doom. He looked at the driver, who was staring back at him.

"You okay, Gus? You're white as a ghost. Literally."

Gus was too overwhelmed to answer. A sheen of sweat erupted across his brow. His eyes began darting around the room. He was deathly afraid of something. Something unseen that was strangling the sanity out of him.

"What is this place?"

"What d'ya mean?"

"You heard me. I said, what is this place?"

"Just another old abandoned apartment. Like you said."

"No. No. It's more than that. I felt it in the street. This place is...." Gus looked directly at the driver. An expression of anger crossed his face. "You know what this place is. You know exactly what this place is. You sonovabitch. You brought me here. You brought me here for a reason. Why am I here? Why am I here?" Gus glared at the driver. "Tell me! You sonova... bitch! Why am I here?!"

The driver stood silent, his face expressing deep contemplation. The man's eyes bore through Gus, but he remained composed.

"I brought you here because I had no choice. I *had* to bring you here."

"Great." Gus felt betrayed. "The shit just doesn't end, does it? You *had* to bring me here. For what?"

"So I could be free. So you could be free. So both of us can get the hell out of Locum Veniae."

"Locum Veniae? So *we* could be free," Gus repeated sarcastically.

"Yeah," the driver nodded. "I've tried to leave for as long as I can remember. Like I said, I've faced you many times."

"For God's sake. Free of what?"

"Free of hatred. Free of guilt."

"What the hell are you talking about?"

"You were my final obstacle," said the driver.

"Obstacle to what?"

"To my salvation."

For a moment, Gus just stood and stared at the driver. Then the full fury of his frustration exploded. "Fuck you! I've so had my fill of this bullshit double-talk dribble—this crap. This bloody crap. I don't know what your story is, but fuck you and the bus you rode in on. I'm outta here."

Gus stormed past the driver and ran out of the living room. He stomped down the hallway and stairwell. He hustled through the store, burst through the front door, and plowed recklessly into the gloom. He staggered about blindly before leaning back against the outside of the building.

Ahhhhhhhhhhhhhh. Ahhhhhhhhhhhhhh. Oh.... Please. Shoot me. End it. End all of it. I'm just too damned tired to go on. Just end it. Now.

Gus wished he had a cigarette. He looked down to see the long ash of a half spent butt between his fingers. He brought it up to his lips and sucked in the nicotine. He exhaled a long plume of smoke that the gloom quickly turned invisible.

Gus stood empty-headed. He was desperate for a way out of his nightmare. He studied the renovated buildings that surrounded him. There was more to them than met the eye, as was everything that filled his miserably unmemorable existence. He sensed secrets looming behind every door, every window, every wall—every feature that confronted him.

There had to be a key, something that unlocked the mysteries of his being, the purpose of his existence. There had to be something to untangle the confusion that overpowered everything, that stifled any hope of sensibility.

On the other hand, there did not have to be anything. In fact, the total absence of keys and revelations was the norm. Gus's soul sank as he resigned himself to a reality of no keys, no revelation, and no reprieve. Only more of the same unending frustration. Except for....

"Gus Beretta," he whispered.

Gus closed his eyes. He could sense memories making an approach, closer, much closer, circling about him so close that he begged for clarity, knowing it was about to arrive.

What is all of this about? Who am I? Where am I? Why am I wandering around this stupid place?

A feeling of sickening dread began to creep up on him.

Was this to be the price of memories?

Gus immediately opened his eyes. Frightened, he looked around. His gaze widened until looking down the street where he noticed the approach of black vine-like tentacles—liquid shadows. He choked out a residual puff of smoke.

"The Lingering."

Gus whispered the troubling words. They came from the place where memories hid, but unlike memories, they broke out to chill his soul, to freeze him in place. He wanted to disappear, but he could not. He wanted to run, but in what direction?

Run. Run. Run, you fool. Run.

Gus was out of time. He needed to get away fast. He needed to get back on the bus, back on the highway and headed out before it was too late.

Driver. Get to Driver before it's too late. We have to leave. We have to leave now.

Gus flicked away the cigarette as he pushed himself off the wall. He bolted for the front door of the shop. Far more fearful of the Lingering than anything inside, he stampeded across the old wooden floors, past the meat counter, and over to the concealed doorway. He launched himself up the stairwell steps at a time. He ran the length of the hallway and entered the living room yelling at the top of his lungs.

"We gotta go! Driver! We gotta go!

When Gus reached the driver, he found him sitting peacefully on the couch. The man was entirely unbothered.

"We gotta go! The Lingering. It's here. We gotta go, man. We gotta go, now!"

As if to amplify Gus's concerns, approaching shadows worked to snuff out light entering the room from windows that overlooked the street. The air within stirred and singular currents of unpleasant cold slithered across the back of his neck. He panicked.

"Driver. What are you doing? It's the Lingering. Get up! We gotta go. Now!"

"This is the end for me, Gus. This is where it all began, and where it all ends for me."

"Balls ablaze!" Gus cried out. "Are you fucking nuts?!"

Gus clapped his hands to his head and began walking around in a tight circle.

"For once, just once, would you say something that makes sense to me? And please make it quick. What the fuck are you talking about?"

Gus dropped his head and drew his fists up to his lips. He closed his eyes and resigned himself to the impossibility of his life. He looked at the blackness gathering outside the window. He looked down at the driver.

"Are you deaf, man? Are you not listening to me? It's the *Lingering*. Whatever problems you got mean nothing. We gotta get the hell outta here now. Jesus, get off your ass. We gotta go. We gotta get back to the bus, now!"

The driver was unmoved.

"You go. I stay. This is it for me. This is where it ends."

Gus froze in disbelief. He tried to make something sensible register, but it was hopeless. He threw up his arms in exasperation.

"I can't win. I get it. I'll never win. Fine. You wanna end it? Screw it! Let's end it. I'll end it with you. I'll sit right here, with you, and we can end it together. We can hold hands like a couple of schoolgirls if you want. What's the point of prolonging this misery? I asked to end it in the street and now I get my chance."

Gus dropped onto the couch alongside the driver. The two men sat in silence as the winds of fear howled furiously outside. There were other noises, unsettling, and best unheard. Inside, the room vibrated from forces beyond, forces that beat and pressed hard against the walls, forces hell-bent on invading their space.

36

The Lingering was relentless. It existed to force movement. It existed to suffocate sanity by means of terror-filled dread. It existed to eliminate all thought, all contemplation, and all but one decision—*to flee.* All the while suns were born in glory, burned to cinder, and stars changed the constellations, the Lingering pressed the masses forward—and crushed against the walls of their room. There was no sanctuary within the Lingering, no chance of peace or tranquility for those who whiled away time no matter how infinite. This the driver knew.

"Gus."

"What?"

"You once said that you remembered me pulling up to the curb and scaring the shit out of you. You thought I was going to run you over with my bus."

The driver's comment raised a curtain. A clear vision of the event entered Gus's head. He did not turn to face the driver. He sat and stared straight ahead, as he had done for eons.

"Yes. Now that you've said it, I remember it clearly, like it was yesterday."

"Do you remember how confused and angry you were when I called you by your name?"

"Yes. I didn't realize it was embroidered on my shirt. I felt like a complete idiot, a fool."

"It wasn't."

"I don't understand," answered Gus without emotion.

"It was only on your shirt because I said it was. If I hadn't said it, it wouldn't have been there."

Whatever thoughts passed through Gus's head posed little if any emotional response.

"Even now, after all this time, you insist on doing that thing where you push words out your mouth that leave me clueless. I have no idea what you're talking about. I can't even get mad. I feel nothing. But, if we're going to sit together and die above an old butcher shop... please... in my final moments, spare me."

"I don't believe dying is an option, but that is another matter. The point is... things aren't always what you believe. Your memories are returning, but memory is fluid from an unstable reservoir, prone to all variety of suggestion and influence. Not to mention those times it remains buried, unreachable, as you well know. At its worst, it returns twisted, scrambled, and entirely inaccurate renditions of truth just to deceive you. Still you can only work with what you have.

"Right now, I suggest you think about the first building that you saw renovated. You know the one I mean? We talked about it."

"Yes. I remember. But again, I don't understand. Why would you want me to tell you about that?"

The driver let out a long breath as if coming to terms with his own demons.

"Because you're lost. Because your memories are fighting for reclamation, and I believe I can help you. I want to help you."

Gus turned to look at the driver. His face bore a clear expression of suspicion.

"You wanna help *me*? I'm not so sure that's a good thing. To be honest, you don't strike me as the helping type. Besides, why would you help me? People rarely give without the take. Rarely. So what's your take? What's in it for you?"

The driver smiled.

"You're right. It's true. I'm not the benevolent type. Never have been. Let's just say I carry my own baggage, my own guilt. But unlike you, my memory is intact, and there's plenty of things I wish I didn't remember. Things I sorely regret. You might say that if I can find it in myself to help you, do something good without expectation, then I've become better. A meager act on my part to improve myself. At least that's how I like to think of it. So.... Tell me what happened in that building."

Gus was astonished to hear the driver open up about himself, especially to voice a suggested weakness of character. The man was allowing Gus to breech his defenses, a heretofore-impenetrable barrier. The act disarmed Gus, and so he began to speak with reservation, but later, with far less concern.

"Mostly, I remember there was a fire. There was a woman. There was a child. Her son, I think. I don't know. I remember a fire—I think I was trying to help them get out.... I got hurt. Hurt bad. At least that's what.... I fell. Out a window. No. Wait. Maybe not a window. A ladder. It might have been off a ladder. I want to say I fell into a hole. A deep hole. There were people at the bottom standing around. I don't know what that has to do with the fire. Do you see what I mean? Don't ask me. My memories are so screwed up that nothing ever makes sense."

"I want you to try again. Try really hard to remember what's happened to you."

"I just told you. I can't remember. My memories won't come back. And when they do, they're a scrambled mess."

"Gus. Listen to me. This isn't about you not being able to remember. It's about you not wanting to remember. Fires and falling, those aren't pleasant experiences. You need to face these things if you want to find peace. I want you to try again. Try hard to remember and tell me what else you recall."

Gus looked at the driver with great apprehension. He looked around the room and felt the approach of something wicked.

He looked out the windows and saw what appeared to be black snow. A blizzard of black snow. It was the first time he wondered if he was in Hell. He turned to ask the driver a question.

"Where is Locum Veniae?"

"I really don't know."

"Are you the devil?" Gus asked in spite of believing it impossible, for the man's presence had a way of calming his fears.

"Not to you. But this isn't about me. I need you to remember. Try to remember... please."

"Okay."

As soon as he agreed, a veil lifted, and all manner of visions flowed back into Gus's mind. A vast array of inexplicable emotions and scenes began to collate and culminate into lucid streams of recollections, one after another.

Gus stared into space as he watched past events play out in his mind's eye. He began to narrate, giving accounts of his many rides on the driver's bus. He remembered Bonnie and the old woman in the wheelchair. He dredged up the horrors of addiction, of being abandoned, beaten, stabbed, and strangled. He conveyed one nightmare after another, an endless train of miseries and sufferings until exhaustion overtook him. The reawakening of this plethora of memories, each remarkably miserable in its own right, caused Gus to grow weak. His eyes appeared heavy, sickly, and sunken when the driver's voice moved him to look his way.

"I'm impressed. I wonder what other dreadfulness you harbor. I would say your memory is rebounding at a good pace."

It was only with great effort that Gus broke free of a paralytic state induced by the shock of revelations. It was hard to speak at first, but he responded to the driver.

"So it seems." There was long pause. "I've been thinking. All this time, I've been trying to remember my name. Trying to remember who I am. And yet, you tell me to remember, and everything comes back as if it happened yesterday. How did you do that?"

"I didn't."

"Really. Then who did?"

"You did."

"Bullshit."

"It's true. It was a matter of you making the effort. It's also true I encouraged you, but that's because we've traveled the road together for a long time. It was important for me that you remember. More than important. It was vital for my own salvation, but allowing your past back in was all your doing. You and only you."

"If it's all my doing, then why couldn't I remember my name? I wanted that in the worst of ways. It was such a simple need."

"I don't know, Gus. My guess would be that your name represents your worst association with your past. Other than that, I can't say."

"Did you know about these things, the strangling, the addiction? Any of it?"

"No."

"Are these events the reason I have no memories?"

"To some extent. Yes," said the driver.

"Why? To protect me from the pain?"

"No. Not really."

"Oh. Well…. For what reason?"

"So you could fulfill your purpose."

"My purpose?"

"Yes."

"And what purpose could I possibly have?"

"To be forgiven."

Gus turned a second time to look at the driver. He was bewildered.

"To be forgiven."

"Yes."

"Has anybody forgiven me?"

"Everybody has."

"Everybody?"

"Yes."

"Who's everybody?"

"Certainly, everybody on the bus traveling with you. Obviously, all those who thanked you before getting off the bus. But I'm sure there were many more. Many who never got on. They were passing glimpses. Bumps in the night. Ghosts."

As Gus heard the driver's words, his mind drifted. He recalled precisely the faces of those who had passed by him in the bus aisle to thank him for his help as they stepped down to the street. He thought about the throngs that walked along the highway—the crowds, the jostling and elbowing, the bumping. How many did he not recognize or remember? His attention returned to the driver who was still speaking.

"Everybody on this street. Every time a building is renovated, each time it fills with life, it marks those who found the way to forgive you. They required your presence in order to accomplish their obligation to forgive all transgressors, all transgressions. Those who find salvation find it when free of emotion—guilt, regrets, fear. They carry no hatred, no negatives, or any of the torment that needs to be shed. Those places come alive; they shine for you in the gloom. Even in the bowels of the Lingering you can see the beacons, the way forward."

It was hard for Gus to grasp the driver's meaning, let alone put forth any comment of value. After a pause, he responded thoughtfully, hoping to convey his dark perspective.

"Maybe a beacon for you, Driver. But I can't tell forward from backward or side to side. I can only see fear and confusion at every step, every turn, every direction. If there's a beacon out there somewhere, it didn't beckon me."

"You've been lost a long time, Gus. Far longer than most. On the one hand, you're unable to find your way. On the other, you're forbidden to reach it."

"Find my way to what? What do you mean forbidden?"

"I mean, in order to find salvation, you cannot possess negatives. You cannot remain soiled by your transgressions.

You must be pure for acceptance. A large part of that process is others forgiving your trespasses, so they as well might proceed forward. That is also your purpose. You must remain in Locum Veniae until forgiven by all. Emotions are neutralized in Locum Veniae. It's a place where interactions transition from emotional to logical."

"Forgiven? Salvation?" Gus studied the driver. "When you say *salvation*... are you talking about getting my life in order, or is *life* not even part of the equation?"

The driver said nothing. He watched Gus mull over the reckoning.

"Are you talking about Heaven or Hell?"

The driver said nothing.

"Am I dead?"

"Depends on your point of view."

Gus thought about that for a moment.

"That did *not* sound promising. I noticed you didn't say I wasn't dead. Okay, tell me this, Driver. Why are you here?"

The driver let out a long breath.

"I'm here for you, and because of you."

"You're here for me, and because of me." Gus repeated the words slowly, giving them much consideration. "In other words... based on what you've been trying to explain to me... you're here to forgive me for my sake, you're here to forgive me for your sake... we're both here because I wronged you."

"Because we wronged each other."

Gus looked around. His face suddenly revealed a revelation.

"This is the only building in disrepair. The only place on the street that remains lifeless. Are you my ghost of Christmas to come?"

"No."

"What then? There must be some reckoning, otherwise this place would be filled with the love of life and all the joy it brings," said Gus with an air of sarcasm. "It would stand as another beacon of light to show me the way through the gloom. I believe that was how you—"

Gus stopped speaking. He looked at the driver with an expression of immense surprise. Another revelation.

"Wait a minute.... Hold on one bloody minute. Now, I get it. I know what's happening here. You haven't forgiven me. Balls ablaze.... *You haven't forgiven me*.... That's what this is all about. That's why this place is dreary and lifeless. You haven't been able to do it."

A look of mutual understanding passed between both men.

"So if you're not my ghost of Christmas to come, what's next?" Gus snickered.

"I'm going to offer you the last of the memories that cause your soul to suffer. The grand finale. Like those before me, I offer you a chance to redeem yourself, while at the same time freeing me from my torments. At least that's my hope."

"What torments you?"

"My hatred for you."

"Finally! Finally! Something I can understand. Finally, something that adds up. Something straightforward minus all the meaningless verbal bullshit. It's true. I can feel it in my gut. You hate me! Yes! Yes! So.... Driver.... What if you *can't* forgive me? Then what?"

"Then I'm bound to you. Then we'll never go. Then I'll never go."

"Go where?"

"To my salva—"

"To your salvation?" Gus cut him off mid-sentence. "What makes you think *you've* been forgiven? What makes you think you can forgive me?"

"I've already been forgiven by all I trespassed. Even you've forgiven me."

"What!"

"Bet that's a shocker, but it's true. You've forgiven many, but by no means all. You've forgiven those whose transgressions weren't so egregious. The tough ones are yet to come, and trust me; they will be a bitch. I know firsthand.

"You see, getting here was for me a long, arduous trek to say the least. One I'm sure you'll come to fully appreciate. I saved you for last, Gus. Not that I had a choice. I needed all of eternity and every opportunity to learn how to forgive you. I needed all the practice I could endure in order to face you. As I've said, I've faced you many times, and I've failed as many times."

Gus sat silent on the sofa. He had one final question. A question, which to his surprise, he was reluctant, almost disheartened, to ask. It took all he could muster to face the man.

"I guess it's time to shit or get off the pot. So...," Gus hesitated. "...what did I do to you?"

"You destroyed me."

The driver's answer startled Gus. He knew there was a darker side to his own character, but the remark was unexpected. Gus was beginning to believe that the driver was a force to be reckoned and likely untouchable.

"How?"

"If you wish to know, then you must go over to that chair, grab hold of that knife, and pull it out. But I must warn you. Unlike your other events, this memory will not be vague, twisted, or inaccurate. It will not be a fabrication of your guilt-ridden imagination."

Gus swallowed hard.

"And if I don't?"

"Then we remain here in the jaws of the Lingering, mauled by our emotional connection for as long as suns are born and die. For however long it takes."

"Why must I remove the knife?"

"A gesture that appeases me. An effort that proves to me you truly want to free your soul from the burden it bears. A move that strengthens my resolve to work in your behalf. I need to see that knife in your hands to believe *I have the strength,* the resolve, to forgive you."

Gus sat in judgment of the driver and struggled to determine whether he should do as the man directed. Gus may have thought this over for a month, or a year, or thousands of years. He may have thought longer than it took the universe to play out its existence. He could not say, but a time came.

"Fine. I'll do it."

Gus stood up from the sofa. He walked over to the chair. He stood behind it and placed his hands on its back. He stared down at the protruding knife handle for some time while nervously contemplating what might be unleashed. He moved his hand closer. His fingers began to hide the name, *Gus Beretta*. His palm hovered barely above as he looked back at the driver. The man's eyes bored through him, daring him to proceed. Gus's eyes shifted to observe the violence of the black storm beyond the windows. His feet absorbed the vibration of trembling floors shuddering from the approach of something worse, something yet unknown.

"It's done."

Gus gripped the knife and yanked it out of the chair.

37

The room filled with life—*people*. There was confusion, hysteria, and expressions of terror. At Gus's side, the driver was now sitting in the chair, gagged and bound with blue duct tape. A visibly traumatized woman sat across the room shaking with fear, holding a young girl tightly within her embrace. The young girl was shocked into a near comatose state. Their faces were smeared with tears and snot. There were three other men in the room. Gus recognized them at once as his subordinates.

In a manner that defied explanation, Gus was observing himself as he went through the motion of leaning over the chair-back with the *Baretta* knife in hand. He waved the blade menacingly close to the driver's face. He lowered himself in order to speak into the driver's ear.

"You stupid fuck. What'd you think I was gonna to do? Just stand by and watch you drive away all my business, ruin years of hard work? Let you drive a wedge between me and my suppliers—drive a wedge between me and my customers?

"You *stupid* fuck. The only driving you were supposed to do was behind the wheel of my Lincoln. But chauffeuring wasn't good enough for you, was it? Making enough money to buy this store, give your wife and family a good life, just wasn't enough, was it? You got greedy. You didn't just betray me. You didn't just take advantage of me; you worked to take me down. You, a driver. A dumb fucking driver.

"Now, I'm going to show you what happens to greedy goons who think they're going to drive me out of business. You stupid pitiful fuck."

Gus looked at one of his men.

"Joby. Grab the girl."

"Noooooo! Please, no!" screamed the woman. The driver strained to escape as he jerked against his restraints. He moaned loudly from behind the gag. Gus watched the driver's fruitless attempts and snickered. He reached over and tore the gag off his mouth. The driver's lips trembled as he spoke.

"Please, I beg you. Please. Don't hurt the girl. She's innocent. She's just a child. She's got nothing to do with this."

"You should have thought about that long before now, Driver. I know a couple of little girls, along with sisters and brothers, mothers and fathers, aunts and uncles, all dead at the hands of your gorillas. Uzis are indiscriminate. But I doubt you shed a tear over any one of them. Tell me, Driver. Is your little girl somehow better than all the other little girls? Is that what you think?" Gus waited for an answer. "I can't hear you. Is that what you think?"

The driver lowered his head and began to sob.

"No."

The woman rose to her feet, struggling frantically against two men in order to hold on to her daughter. Her daughter's clothes were clenched tightly in her fists. Gus walked around from behind the chair. He slipped the knife between his belt and pants, and then drew out a pistol and pointed it at the child's head.

"Lady, you pitch one more fit, and I'm gonna paint your face with your daughter's brains."

The woman went white, frozen in place and time as if an ice sculpture. Then as if to thaw, she began shaking uncontrollably, crumbling, cracking, babbling.

"Shut up! Shut the fuck up! You got about one second to let go of that kid."

The woman released the child. A high-pitched involuntary squeal escaped from her throat. Gus wrapped the girl's hair around his fist and held her tight. She was crying. He looked at the mother.

"Are you a good mother?"

The woman nodded.

"Are you willing to give up your life for your daughter?"

The woman's face went blank. Her eyes grew wide. She nodded.

"Is that a yes?"

"Yes."

"I respect that."

Gus raised his gun and shot the woman in the forehead. She dropped to the floor. He spoke to her as a final breath faded.

"I give you my word, your daughter will live. That's more than your husband offered the mothers of other little girls. However, I won't stand for her listening to lies about what a great caring provider her father was. I don't want her to ever forget that he was every bit the butcher that I am."

Gus put his gun away. Still clutching the girl's hair fast above her head, in one quick motion he pulled his knife and sliced an ear off the side of her head. The driver cried out in agony as Gus tossed the ear into his lap. He let loose of the heavily blooded girl, who, having succumbed to the shock, fell hard to the floor.

Gus knelt down alongside her at the foot of the driver's chair. He tapped his blade at the featureless wall of her skull, where once was an ear. He looked up at a sobbing father's face. It was painfully twisted as if wringing out every last drop of tear.

"Tell me something, Driver. Would you give up your life for your daughter?"

"Yes, yes," the driver sobbed.

"I respect that."

Gus stood back up and walked around to the back of the chair. He pulled the driver's head back and leaned down to whisper in his ear.

"You fucked up, Driver. Big time."

Gus dragged the knife across the driver's throat in a slow and deliberate motion. The driver coughed once, blowing a red cloud of blood across the room from his neck. Gus listened to the sound of blood gurgling in the man's lungs. Having concluded his business with satisfaction, Gus pulled out a handkerchief and wiped blood and prints off the handle of his knife.

"Let's go."

"What about the girl?" asked Joby.

"What about her? I gave her mother my word. She lives. I don't go back on my word."

Gus drove his knife deep into the chair alongside the driver's head. He left the knife behind with his name inscribed on the handle. It would remain as a call to fellow drivers. The message was loud and clear. Gus needed a new chauffeur.

38

Gus appreciated the irony of the message—*loud and clear*—now returned to his own hand, albeit with a different take. He looked down at the knife still within his grip. The clarity of the associated memory prevented any denial. The driver had forewarned him that this time nothing would be vague, twisted, or inaccurate.

"You should have been a prophet, Driver."

Gus looked at the driver, who, now seated on the couch, had removed the outlandish multicolored bandana from around his neck to reveal a gash that should have caused his head to topple. Gus swallowed hard.

"In all the other events, I was a victim. This time, I'm a cold-blooded murderer."

"Aren't we all," said the driver nonchalantly.

"How were you able to stand the sight of me? All this time...."

"I couldn't. Not for as long as galaxies collide. It wasn't easy, Gus. I had to face you more times than there are numbers, more times than you can perceive."

"And yet, you managed. No unkind words. Not a one. Only a helping hand and a smile. Was it all a façade? Is the hammer about to drop?"

"No," said the driver. "Nothing so dramatic. I managed by finally accepting the truth about what happened. It took a long time for me to realize that I didn't lose my family because of you. That was by far my most difficult and rewarding test.

"I came to accept how I lost everything because of outcomes driven by random energy. You could say it was my own doing. You could say I decided what lifestyle I chose to lead. But then, I could say that is was your doing, your selected lifestyle. Which of us was really to blame?

"The truth is neither your lifestyle nor mine sealed the fate of me or my wife and daughter. Their demise was not entirely my doing, nor was it yours. We were simply the last actors in a singular culmination of random energy."

"And the point of all this is...?"

"Same as always. Forgiveness. Shedding. I must face you and forgive you. I do this not only for my well-being, but for yours. As you are forgiven so shall you forgive."

"All this time, I thought you were called Driver because of the bus."

"The bus is only a framework of understanding that you need to make sense of your journey toward salvation. It exists only in your awareness."

"Are you telling me that you don't drive a bus?"

"I do not."

"Is there a bus?"

"There is for you. What else matters?"

"So when I get on the bus, are you on it or not?

"Only in your awareness, not in mine."

"So I meet you in other places?"

"You do in my awareness. Like I've said, I faced you many times."

"What happened all the other times?"

"I killed you."

"Jesus! Whose awareness am I in now?"

"Ours."

"Are you going to kill me?"

The driver broke into a broad grin that displayed his mouthful of square teeth. The emotion spread across his face was one of unmistakable joy.

"I'm happy to say, no, not anymore. Goddammit, I'm happy to say that. Not anymore. This time you live."

"Good to know," quipped Gus."

"I got past it. I can't believe I'm saying it. It's been such a long, long journey, so much effort, so many failures. So many, many, many failures. The emotional intensity of our relationship was too powerful for me to overcome. But when stripped of your baggage, your cruelties, your past, when all I see is the inner you, the witness, I find nothing to hate. The choice to forgive becomes easy.

"You are a witness, Gus, nothing more, nothing less, and for that reason, I have finally forgiven you. I hardly believe what I hear when I say the words. *I forgive you.* I forgive you, Gus. I forgive you."

"A witness? A witness to what?" asked Gus.

The driver paid Gus no mind. He sank into his thoughts.

"I grew tired of hating, Gus. I grew tired. I've hated you for so long.... Hating you was the sole purpose of my existence. I wasn't sure who or what I would be without hatred."

The two men went silent. They had much to ponder. Gus finally broke the stillness.

"You'd think I have an axe to grind, but honestly, I feel no ill will toward you whatsoever. Quite the opposite, I feel as if you have been my support, secretive, frustrating, but supportive. Do understand that slitting your throat balanced things out for me. I felt disappointment, but not hate. Does that make sense?"

"It does. Remember, I told you before that you have already forgiven me."

"So, what am I supposed to do now?" asked Gus.

"Whatever you wish. We are free to depart company. Free to go our own ways. I mine, you yours. I can tell you this. You'll work it out, Gus. You'll find your way. But you must move on of your own accord. Don't await the Lingering."

"What about you?"

"I'll be fine. I'm at peace." The driver nodded. "I'm at peace. I've forgiven, and I've been forgiven. I understand that I was a witness, and nothing more. It was never about sins, or good and evil. It was about the chain reaction of choices and decisions. It was about logic, cause and effect, interplay within the stream of random energy. I was a voyager, Gus, as are you."

A great beaming smile crossed the driver's face. The man glowed. He looked as if he was about to cry. His eyes teared with emotion. He nodded, acknowledging a private understanding. His eyes never left Gus.

"I'm being summoned, Gus. The pull is growing intense. With all my heart, I thank you. I gotta go."

The driver arose from the sofa and moved to Gus's side. He reached for Gus's hand and removed the knife. The weapon vanished. He understood Gus's surprise.

"It never existed until I said it was there in the chair for you to see."

The driver smiled. He looked at Gus with the gentle eyes of a mentor and spoke.

"I gotta go. Before I do, allow me to leave you this. If we are but witnesses, then in reality our journey draws us into situations that may be pleasant or horrid, but always random, and strangely enough—predictable. Our random encounters might distract with emotions, feelings of love, hatred, revenge, or in your case—*guilt*. All insufferable. All irrelevant."

39

The driver's departure left Gus feeling alone, somewhat discarded, and surprisingly... *betrayed*. Guided by the toothy-grinned man through later and more traumatic events, Gus came to realize how much time he had spent in the driver's company. He reviewed countless occasions wherein the driver plucked him off the curb, saving him from the insanity of the crowds to enjoy the peace, warmth, and security of the bus. Indeed, it was undeniable that the driver pursued his own agenda, but now Gus found the man's self-seeking ways preferable to feelings of abandonment and vulnerability.

Clouded in uncertainty, Gus arose from the couch to take his leave. He walked through the tomblike apartment shouldering the full burden of his guilt. He halted briefly for a final look into the kitchen. He now understood why the desiccated meal spread across the kitchen table endured un-eaten. Gus turned away to descend stairs that creaked. He walked across old wood floors that squeaked loudly to emphasize the absence of life. He passed by the long-unused meat counter and shelving gondolas empty of goods.

The results of his barbaric, murdering ways were evident in every corner, every space of invaded silence. He had no choice but to face his accomplishments—deeds that devastated more than the life of a man and his family. He had unraveled the thread connecting a community. He had erased a haven where people gathered to share stories about the trivial triumphs of daily life while enjoying treats and planning home-cooked meals.

Gus recalled asking aloud of the driver: *You gotta wonder why these places fall to ruin. Why folks abandon them. Do the owners just grow old? Do the neighbors all grow old together and then die together?*

Now, he had answers. Now, he had the unblemished truth. Now, something more than a premonition was unveiled to reveal how the driver's ruination was merely the tip of terror enacted upon this place. It was his doing that emptied the shelves and streets; his doing that smothered this neighborhood's vitality. It was he who had extinguished the lights. It was he who brought the gloom.

Wishing to rid himself of the haunting verity encased permanently within the discolored walls and dust-covered floor planks, verity that clung to him like body odor, Gus sprinted what distance remained between him and the entrance. He hurled himself past the partially boarded-up front door and into a street disappearing beneath the fast fading light of day.

The gloom he perpetrated was settling in, returning to threaten him with his past and worse should he dawdle. Whereas a higher cause summoned the driver, Gus remained far behind, far from reaching his destination. For him, the lighthouse of salvation appeared dimmer and more distant than ever.

As if washed onto an unknown beach, Gus drifted toward a dull, pitted, stretch of sidewalk swept by the sand and litter of a timeless wind. He strolled its length mindlessly. He dragged himself across a damp masonry wall, its stacked rows of bricks tucked with endless clumps of mold in various hues of greens and grays. The wall fronted a structure abandoned for years beyond count. It supported the remnants of a monument in sordid disrepair. To see the once majestic edifice so neglected served to plunge Gus deeper into downheartedness. The gloom of his making was now fully upon him.

The memories Gus longed to have back were proving to be a burden as distressful as his inability to remember. The irony crucified him. He fell against the scarred masonry façade. He wondered how truly evil people found salvation. He wondered what lay in wait. He longed for direction now that the driver had moved on.

The outflow of emotion grew worse as he slid slowly down to the sidewalk. He shrank from the world, twisting as he collapsed until seated on the clammy concrete, his back scraped raw by the abrasive brick. He welcomed the pain. He deserved it.

Gus dropped his head slowly into the fold of his elbows. He suffered through gut-wrenching recollections of what had occurred in the apartment. The visions were inescapable and he prayed they stemmed from nothing more than dreams or hallucinations because he feared the monster he observed.

He abhorred accepting these visions as real happenings from his past. But the alternative, *not* to accept them, returned him to the black hole empty of everything but unending confusion and frustration—the void that would remain forever unsorted and tormenting. The choice was bleak, and for that reason, Gus cried for hours, days, or maybe years. He could not say. He cried until—

"Hey. Having a bad time of it, are we?"

The sensual voice of a woman interrupted Gus's agony. He stopped crying at once out of sheer embarrassment. He kept his face covered with a hand in order to hide his tortured eyes and tear-smeared cheeks. Something inside admonished him for acting like a blubbering idiot.

"Anything I can do?" asked the woman.

"No, I'm fine."

"You're certain?"

"Yeah, thanks. I'm fine."

Gus was blatantly dismissive, but the woman was not so easily put off.

"Hard to believe. You don't look fine. You've been bawling harder'n a brat dragging a burst balloon. You know, that crumpled little green thing on the end of a fallen string still knotted to a broken child. One massive pop that obliterates all the good in life. Will the kid ever recover? Who knows? What about you? You gonna make it?"

Gus clenched his teeth. It was obvious that this meddler with her unwanted insight was not about to go away. He felt his anger stir. He dropped his hand, thereby exposing his stressed features. He raised his face to stare down this nuisance and simultaneously let his feelings fly.

"Why are you bugging me?"

"You looked like you could use a distraction."

"Well, I'm distracted. Sensational balloon story. Who the hell cares? And for that matter, who the hell are you?"

"Who the hell am I? Hmmm.... Well.... You know what a patron saint is?"

Gus's brow raised as he nodded. He wore a mixed expression of restrained sarcasm and disbelief.

"Yeah, I know exactly what a patron saint is. I started life as a Catholic." Gus immediately frowned and looked away in surprise as he thought to himself.

Where did that come from? Another useless memory?

That was not the only surprise. Gus took a second look at the woman through eyes no longer drowning. This time he was unable to stop looking at her. He wanted only to run his hands across her breasts, across the curves of her hips, along the lines of her legs. His insides rocked with desire.

The attraction was irresistible. She was stunning. She was intoxicating. There was an aura, a glow about her. She brightened everything. He glanced around and realized that the gloom was thinning, the mold vanishing, the damp dissipating from the concrete beneath his buttocks. Even rays of sunshine were finding their way down to a street breaking out in a kaleidoscope of color. It seemed everything good awakened in her presence.

Again, she spoke, and if her beauty was not captivating enough, the call of her voice carried to the farthest reaches of his soul.

Is this the song of a siren?

"A Cath-o-lic," she enunciated as if singing a hymn. "Well, this should be easy, no explanations needed. I'm the Patron Saint of Underdogs and Losers."

"Underdogs?" Gus asked quizzically. He almost wanted to laugh. "Underdogs and Losers? Are you for real?"

"I get it... sounds crazy. Has sort of a... *Hollywood* ring. Don't you think?"

"How could I not?" asked Gus sardonically.

"I know...," she whispered in amazed agreement. "Remember how there were patron saints for the blind, the deaf, the dumb, the sick, the dying.... A saint for every affliction. There's probably a patron saint for uninsured motorists.

"It's funny how things play out. Imagine a patron saint for everybody and everything... *everything except underdogs and losers,*" she paused. "Now that I think about it... that probably would include uninsured motorists.

"Anyway, I brought the matter up with my superiors. They asked me to investigate this anomaly, overlooked as it was. Turned out the position was wide open. In fact, when it came to canonization for that category, there was no competition whatsoever. Can you believe that?"

"Frankly, I can't. Who'd a guessed," answered Gus dryly.

"I know," she whispered again in continued amazement. "That's just what I thought." The woman beamed. "Whereas my colleagues seemed to shun the opportunity, I said, 'Hey, how cool is this? Why not?'"

"How many reasons do you want?" Gus sighed.

She frowned. "Oh, don't be dull. Think about it. My would-be charges were so *out there,* so screwed up, anything but *dull*—not a collection of morons, or boring idiots like you might think. No sir, not at all.... Well, not to exaggerate, yes, I suspect some were mundane, maybe uninsured motorists, but most were brilliantly corrupt, derisive, devious, despicable, or in the least, unlucky to the extreme. How could anybody say no?"

"I can't imagine," retorted Gus.

"They sanctified me on the spot."

The woman looked upward with an expression of elation. Gus looked upward at the woman.

"The Patron Saint of Underdogs," said Gus slowly, giving the title enough time to mature into full-blown absurdity. "Whatever blows your hair back."

The woman's gaze fell promptly. "And Losers," she added.

Gus paid no mind to the correction. He went on pondering her title; his thoughts soon voiced.

"You know, I grew up in a neighborhood built on losers. The church was the only reasonably honest place that—" He halted.

There I go again, coughing up something else from my past. Stuff's coming back for sure. If only something worthwhile.

"What was I saying?" Gus continued. "Ahhh.... Never mind, doesn't really matter. Point is...God *had* to be open-minded in that place. So maybe you truly are the patron saint of bums and drifters."

"Underdogs and Losers," she corrected.

"Whatever."

Gus was fine with it. He was not in the mood to bicker over titles as he began to recall how janitors became *Facility Maintenance Technicians*, receptionists were *Office Ambassadors,* and paperboys ascended to *Media Distribution Officers*. More importantly, interests shifted as his hidden nature began to show, his misogyny and cynicism in full bloom.

"And... you are talking to me for what reason?" he asked. "Do I know you? Did we—"

She cut him off.

"We're distantly connected, and no we didn't. Maybe in one of your fabricated events, I don't know. All that matters is I'm here because of you."

"Ahh, then I take it *you* need to be forgiven," Gus shot back.

"Hardly."

"Oh, so *I* need to be forgiven. And you're sure we didn't—"

"Again. *Hardly.*"

She put a quick stop to his tongue, but his attitude remained testy.

"*Hardly?* Hmm. Would that be your politically correct way of calling me out as an underdog, a loser, below your station, and *specifically* not your type?"

"You figure it out. How are those memories coming along?"

No sooner had she asked the question when a flood of horrific memories flashed through Gus's head—scenes that knocked the wind out of him. They drove him into immediate submission. He went silent as his soul grappled with the blow. It took more than a few minutes for him to regain his mental balance. When he did, he was not about to look upward and see his innermost secrets revealed within her eyes. The fact that she might know how despicable were his past transgressions could prove humiliating beyond unbearable.

"Not at all pleasant, is it?" she said. "Yes, in the past you were a true bastard, well... most of the time. Hence your present position of being a true underdog. Honestly, I'm not sure how you manage to survive beneath the weight of your crimes. The burdens you bear, my-my. A righteous man would have collapsed eons ago."

The woman beat Gus to pulp with little more than her verbal quips. He understood immediately that, like it or not, she commanded a higher level of respect. The fact annoyed him, but rather than bow before her, he cut to the quick.

"What is it you want from me?"

"I want nothing from you. I'm only here to help."

"Help? Funny. The guy who just left said he was here to help. He's gone. Best example of tough love I've ever seen." Gus sniggered. "How would you help me? Take away my confusion? Take away my misery? Charm me? Screw my socks off? Let me hold and kiss those spectacular breasts? Is that what you're saying? Use present pleasure to bury past pain?"

"If that's what it takes."

Her response wiped the leer off Gus's face. He snapped his head as if waking himself up. For a man who did not know his past, and only now began to sense the depth of his lust, he was nearly lost for words.

"You're kidding. I mean you *are* kidding. Right?"

"Why would I? Your request is a simple enough. A brief moment of carnal pleasure—a good fleshy romp. I understand that even now to you a woman represents peace, serenity, pleasure. You've never felt threatened by a woman. You ask me for a sexual union, which you see as the utmost reward for staying alive, for managing to survive one day to the next. Other than a highway, a woman embraced is what settles you most. I'm yours."

The enchantress had Gus's undivided attention.

It's a trick, pure and simple. No goddess just saunters up to a guy and let's him have his way, not without a hefty price tag.

Maybe she's diseased, and no one will touch her. Maybe she's spreading syph to all mankind out of revenge. Maybe she's insane.

On the other hand, maybe she's not any of those things. Maybe she just wants to get laid.

Gus stared at the beauty standing over him.

"You would have to be an angel. Only an angel would say something like that." He shook his head, still unbelieving. "You gotta be some sort of angel... or the worst embodiment of Satan."

"Satan? No. But viewed from the framework with which you are most closely associated at this time, I get how you might think of me as *angel*. Yes. However, *guide* is far more accurate."

"Guide?"

"It better describes me."

"Not from where I'm sitting. If ever there were a perfect word for a perfect woman, it would be *angel*. Besides, what is it with guides? The last guy said he was a guide. Why do I need a guide? Unless, you mean to guide me in," he smirked.

"*Hardly.*"

She dismissed Gus with a flick of her wrist.

"Let's not overlook *where-you-are-sitting*," she emphasized. "Your pants are soaking up puddles and sidewalk scum. You said something about your station.... Believe me, by comparison, *anything* above your station is angelic.

"Let's get to the point, Gus. This isn't about getting laid. This is about salvation. All about salvation. Time to realize there is only one way to salvation my friend. One way. One road only and you *aren't* on it," she admonished while glaring at him.

"You need a guide, Gus. I suppose in some remote place, some clueless clod might think that maybe you're gaining ground, getting there, making progress, but lord, the truth of it is... that for you... it's been slow going. And I mean *sloooow* going—a slog. *That's* why you need a guide. Either that or a nose ring."

40

The idea that someone with answers, a person with explanations, stood before him was frightening. It reeked of hope, a dangerous attraction.

What says this woman won't disappear as fast as she showed up? Disappear like Driver? Then what? Then you're screwed. You can't trust a broad with a body like that. No way. They play men for suckers every day of the week. Just ask.

However, in some odd and inexplicable way, Gus sensed scattered pieces of a puzzle falling into place. He felt her sifting through a dark and dismal life that portrayed him both good and bad. He could feel her reaching through the scrambled mess to find him. Gus paid attention. He listened. Enough so that he returned repeatedly to contemplate a comment that held dreadful consequences. He forwarded his concern.

"You made specific mention of the road to salvation. Why is everybody talking to me about salvation? Salvation from what? My sinful ways, or...."

Gus was asking apprehensively as his mind prepared for the worst. He began to decipher her expression.

"Oh, no, no, no. No, no, no," he retreated. He shook his head. "Don't be telling me I'm dead or something. Don't give me that bullshit. I've been down that road. Everybody wants to tell me I'm dead. Don't need to hear it again."

The woman smiled.

"Do you feel dead?" she asked.

"No. *Absolutely* not. Period. I do not feel dead. No way in hell."

"I didn't think so. *Dead* would *not* be a particularly accurate term in this place. But you could call it *something*."

"Something like what?" asked Gus.

"Like *transition*. You *are* in a state of transition."

"Transition?" Gus repeated. "And from what to what, or where to where, would I be transitioning?"

"From one existence to another. For lack of a term you might better understand, right now you are a ghost."

"A ghost?"

"A ghost," she confirmed.

"No. No, I don't think so. Doesn't make sense. Ghosts *are* dead people. Dead as damned doornails. They haunt places, you know, houses, or woods, or whatever. Ghosts are anchored, stuck for eternity in a hole. Or at least wandering around a hole—*a well*. I'm not stuck. I'm not dead. I'm no ghost."

The woman broke out in laughter. The sound of it filled Gus with both comfort and concern.

"Oh, but you are. You are *so very stuck*. You are a ghost, Gus. A *ghost*. A snippet of conscious energy. An insignificant snippet of conscious energy that belongs someplace else."

She continued to laugh. It was gentle and contagious. It softened the blow of her message.

"Stuck is an understatement. You, my friend, are mired. Mired in the trauma of your mission. Yes, conscious energy may remain attached to a place, or a time, where it must resolve issues, where it must shed negatives before returning to the ALL. You know.

The often-told midnight tale of an apparition visible in an upper-story window. A woman wronged by her man. Well, it's not always a love gone sour.

"In your case, trauma existed everywhere. Not in just one place or at one time. For you, there was no single traumatic event. You see, your entire mortal existence was horrific. You don't haunt houses or places, you haunt yourself. You endlessly relive the traumas of your mortal existence through fabricated events in order to resolve your many associated negatives. The sufferings you've perpetrated on others, you perpetrate on yourself. And I gotta say, you don't hold back.

"Oh, Gus. Dearest Gus. You are so very stuck, my friend."

Gus found it difficult to either make sense of or accept what the woman was telling him. It was so much easier to write it off as garbage, or be belligerent.

"Well, if I'm *so very stuck*, how can I be transitioning? Am I transitioning, or am I stuck? Can't be both."

"Ha! So *you* say. But it can. You're proof enough. You are transitioning, but every time you manage to make two steps forward, you take two steps back. Ev-ry sin-gle time. We've watched you do it over and over, and over, and over, again and again. You're hopelessly looped.

"You were on a mission and returning. *Scratch that*. That's way too positive. Let's say, you were on a mission and are *supposed* to be returning."

"Returning to where?"

"Mmm.... Not so much *where* as *what*."

"Okay! Okay, returning to what, for chrissakes?"

"The ALL."

"The ALL? The *ALL*. Oh, my god. That's it," blurted Gus indignantly. "The ALL, the ghosts, the missions.... Does everybody on the street drool nonsense? Is it like super-contagious? Tell me, I'm curious. Do you find my speech mentally challenging? Do we speak different languages? Because I can't relate to anything you're saying.

"I don't know what your name is, I don't know what your game is, but I've had a gut full of double-talk dribble, and I don't like being played. I don't care how gorgeous you are. I don't care if you bleed pure estrogen. I've got enough issues as it is, and I don't need some smart-ass, insanely beautiful bitch making my head hurt more than it already does. You understand?"

In spite of his awkward position, sitting on the sidewalk, Gus effectively inflated with arrogance. A fact the woman noted.

"I apologize. Let me refresh your memories."

No sooner said than another rush of horrendous memories blasted through Gus's being. Again, the brutality of what he viewed in his mind hammered his soul mercilessly. She dredged up more of the pain he had inflicted on others and returned it to him. He gagged. Physically he was compelled to vomit. He leaned away from the woman and fell over onto his side. His head landed on the concrete as he convulsed. He choked. He struggled for breath, and swallowed hard. He curled up to keep his cramping stomach from retching. Gus desperately sought a mental foothold to step away from his past sins and return to the present. He managed a few words.

"What... are you... what are you... doing to me?"

"I'm helping you."

"Helping me?" Gus choked out a weak laugh. "Help like that... friends like you—"

She cut him off.

"I never said I was a friend. I said I'm here to guide you through a transition from one existence to another."

Gus slowly recovered from the blow.

"Yeah, and I heard you say it the first time. It sounded like mumbo-jumbo then, and it sounds like it now. You said I wasn't dead, so what am I, where am I? I can't be in Hell if I'm not dead, but I sure feel like you just sent me there. Is this why you crucify me with memories of my past? So I understand the reason for my inevitable damnation? Screw you."

Not the least bit offended, the woman continued.

"Oh my-my, no, no, no. No damnation. Hell is nothing more than an overdone bit of theater. The ALL wastes nothing, especially not a soul. Not a soul. Not ever. I already told you what you are. For the lack of a better term, you are a ghost. A ghost stuck in Locum Veniae."

"Locum Veniae. You know, I keep asking *where in god's creation is Locum Veniae?* Never heard of the place, and I been around. Believe me, I been around." Gus paused. "At least I think I have. No! I know I have. Do me a favor. Just tell me, where in hell am I? Where is Locum Veniae?"

"Locum Veniae? Locum Veniae isn't so much where, as what. Locum Veniae means place of forgiveness."

"Jesus. I can't win." Gus closed his eyes in frustration.

"You said you started life as a Catholic—"

"And...?"

"And... I was about to say that as a Catholic you might view Locum Veniae as purgatory."

"Purgatory?" Gus frowned. The concept was too whacked out to register.

"In a manner of speaking."

His curiosity pushed him past the notion. He opened his eyes and looked up at her to ask.

"And the ALL? You keep referring to the ALL. Is the ALL... God?"

"Yes, you could say that. Why not?"

The woman shrugged.

"But you don't say that," noted Gus. "You don't say *God*."

"Merely semantics. ALL is short for ALL THAT IS. All logic. All knowledge. All knowing. When *you* think of God, you think all knowing. When I think all knowing, I don't think of God. For me, gods suggest beings, limited singularities. To say ALL, or ALL THAT IS, removes that personification, but don't worry about it. For the purpose of this conversation, and to the average Joe, it's basically the same. No harm done, nobody's insulted."

Gus calmed down and took a moment to gather his thoughts.

"You said I was on a mission. What mission? What did you mean by that? And please don't give me one of your cryptic, abstract answers. I don't have that much brain power, at least not rational brain power."

Gus walked a tightrope between his explosive anger and the fresh memory of what this woman could do to him without as much as lifting a finger. He felt like she was about to heap more confusion atop the unbearable load he already endured. He felt himself becoming unhinged and wished desperately to let loose his temper for relief. He wanted a storm of anger to bury, to obliterate, all traces of erupting memories and visions that scraped his soul raw. He wanted his rage to leave the land stilled. It might well have turned into a nasty *who-gives-a-shit* moment had the woman not made an unexpected request.

"Stand up."

"What?"

"I said, stand up."

Gus hesitated.

"Why?"

"Don't why me. Just stand up."

"You make me nervous. Why would I want to stand up?"

"Don't be such a scaredy-cat. C'mon, stand up. I don't bite. I promise."

"You *do* bite. That's the whole problem," Gus complained.

Balls ablaze, I know I'm gonna regret this.

Gus slowly pushed himself up off the sidewalk.

"There. Standing. Happy?"

Gus watched the woman nervously.

"You look like a broken man, ravaged, all slumped over."

"And you look like an angel, radiant, leggy. I haven't seen breasts stand that proud in...in.... Point is—looks can be deceiving," Gus asserted.

"Yes, well your looks aren't at all deceiving," she snapped.

As if reading his mind, as if understanding his torment, the woman stepped forward to take Gus into her embrace. Instinctively, he backed away.

"Stay still," she commanded.

She then pressed against him, holding him firmly within her arms. In some inexplicable manner, the feel of her extracted all the fury and frustration from his being. Whatever she was doing, it was better than sex. It deflated all the hype about orgasms. Far better. Gus lost all hint of aggression as his unrealized pleas drifted softly through his mind.

Ohhh. Ohhhhh. Don't let go. Please... don't let go. Hold me. Hold me. Please.... Don't stop. Don't....

Gus entirely succumbed to the euphoria. Emotionally, he spun in a whirlwind of bliss. Instead of crawling under the weight of retribution, he floated. He soared. When finally opening his eyes to find his bearings, he realized that he was no longer within her embrace. He was on his own, energized, refreshed, and standing tall.

"Bet you liked that," she quipped.

At first, too immersed in rapture to answer, Gus remained silent. Eventually the sensation slowly faded and he came around. He could not take his eyes off this orgastic streetwalker, this pandering peddler of ecstasy.

"I can't imagine what that's gonna cost me." Gus shook his head. "I can't imagine. But however much, it was worth it." Gus savored the residual elation. "I don't remember the last time I felt so free. Not like that. Free. Free and blissfully happy. Are my feet on the ground? Honestly, I can't tell." Seconds later, his eyes narrowed. "How did you do that? What did you do to me?"

"Oh, nothing special. To keep it simple and gooey-feel-good, think of kindred spirits. I merged with your soul to assess your anxiety. I helped you shed some of your baggage, nothing outrageous—negatives of no consequence. I infused a little love, a little harmony, you might say." The woman let out a breath of accomplishment. "If all was right in your world, you'd feel like that pretty much always. Bummer, huh? Take heart in knowing things *will* eventually get better, Gus. I promise. Take it to the bank."

Gus took a deep breath. His eyes remained fixed upon the woman as he responded in a slow, settled manner.

"So I've heard... so I've heard." He paused. "Soooo... you simply merged with my soul, huh? Really? Like simply stopping time, or simply creating the universe in seven days. *That* kind of simple? Is that what you mean? I am impressed.

"As for bummer? Bummer falls short. More like premature ejaculation. Felt incredible, but ended way too soon." Gus grinned. "You remind me of some metaphysical happy-go-lucky-sixties-era flower child. A perfect fit for my acid-trip life.

"So, answer me this one insignificant question. I beg. Please. Being that you *merged* with my soul, and I assume know me better than I know me, let me ask about one thing that's really been bugging me. You called me *Gus* a couple of times. Is Gus really my name, or something Driver made up, something carved into the handle of a killer's knife?"

"Your mission name was Gus Beretta. Yes. It was your name. It wasn't made up by the driver."

"*Gus Beretta.* Humph. I was hoping for something else. Any name not chiseled into the handle of a killer's knife.

"It's disappointing when one's own name sounds alien—which reminds me."

Gus focused on the woman.

"You're still alien to me. I don't believe you ever told me *your* name. I mean, even patron saints have names as I recall from my altar boy days."

"They do. Up to this point, I would have just handed you your favorite woman's name, you know, something fit for a table dancer like Kitty or Carly—"

"Carly is not a name for a table dancer," blurted Gus. His expression hardened and then went blank.

And I would know that, how?

"You're right, I suppose not. Make it Candy, or Cherry...."

The guide shrugged her shoulders after noting that Gus had slipped into some private thought. He emerged slowly to correct her by stressing the long e sound.

"*Cherrieeeee.* Has to be French sounding."

"Mmmm," she nodded. "Of course. Pardon my oversight. However, now that you are calm and temporarily coherent, I'll explain a thing or two slightly more complex. With your permission, of course."

"My permission? I don't think that's the way this works."

The woman winked. "Hold on to your seat, sweetie, because I have many names. Nothing as flashy as a table dancer, but you might have called me Mary, or Terri, or David, or William. We go by whatever name is needed."

Gus did not miss the last comment. Not by a long shot.

"We?"

"Yes. We."

Gus felt the bottom of normality fall out from under him.

Balls ablaze, I'm dealing with a lunatic lady—spirit—whatever…for sure, a stir-crazy patron saint. Now who's the loser? She's nuts; it's nuts; they're nuts.

He needed further proof.

"How many is we?" he asked purposely.

"More than one."

"How many more than one?"

"Enough."

"Enough for what?"

"Enough to get the job done."

"Interesting."

Gus nodded because he did not know what else to do. He did not know what else to say. He kept his cool on the outside, but inside….

More than one? I knew it! That's why she offered to scrape my bone. Just plain whacko. I knew it, I knew it, I knew it.

Why am I not the least bit surprised? Crazy as a bitch on black Friday.

The guide studied Gus. She was clearly amused and her smile reflected as much.

"Hardly."

"Hardly what?"

"Hardly what you're thinking."

"How would you know what I'm thinking?"

"It's all over your face."

"Well, if you can read my face that precisely then I don't have to tell you how you just creeped me out. Sounded a whole lot like demonic possession or something unholy. Didn't go over well at all—*at all*. Really, it didn't. I'm not lying. I've already seen too much of that bullshit, or at least I think I have. I'm pretty sure I have."

The woman started laughing.

"My-my. You are a mess."

Possessed or not, demonic or not, the sound of her laughter was so light and free that Gus could not help but laugh with her about his totally screwed situation.

"Don't take this personally, but from our perspective your reservation is quite funny. We are here as interventionists. Guides. Helping hands. Anything but demonic. You're in a rut, Gus. Simple as that. We will give you this. It's an *impressive* rut. We all agree on that point. We would like to explain. Do you mind?"

"Mind? *Mind?* I'm on my knees begging for explanations. Explanations are the only thing I live for now-a-days."

"Are you comfortable?"

Gus stopped short. He thought briefly before answering.

"Right now, I'm not sure. Maybe. I think so. I guess. Well, actually, I would feel much more at ease if you all referred to your collective selves as me or I. The whole *we* thing is really disturbing."

"As you wish," said the woman with a soothing exuberance. "Nothing we... I... say should be alarming, so do your best to remain calm. All right?"

"You are kidding me, right?" Gus sounded appalled.

The woman laughed. Gus relaxed. The allure of her voice forced him to settle and listen.

"You, my friend, did not only miss all the markers, all the signs, or take all the wrong turns; you completely skidded off the road to return. You found the ditch of all ditches."

"If you say so."

"I say so, and I don't wish to complicate things at this point by diving into detailed explanations. Right now that would be pointless. It would be meaningless to you, opening doors to more questions than answers. Just bear with me when we say that you applied for a mission to observe the flow of random energy. It's what we do. It's what you do. We are all witnesses. Let me explain further."

41

"In your particular case, the flow of random energy— *catholic* chance, if you will—was most unkind, and carried you into a succession of experiences that were entirely contrary to your sense of morality. Instead of engaging in logic and harmony with the occasional hiccup, you experienced an unending existence of conflict. The flow channeled you into becoming a perpetrator of this conflict. Your hand brought misery to many.

"The problem at hand arose when your mission ended and you were in the process of disengaging from your assignment to transition back to ALL. Normally, as you become one with ALL, the influx of logic fills you. It overpowers everything. Emotions are shed, logic prevails, the transition is harmonious and complete. That is... *normally.*

"In your case, the intensity of your emotional state was so overwhelming when you began to transition that the influx of logic failed to prevail and you were unable to disengage. Your return stalled and left you stranded in Locum Veniae. A netherworld. A place between the harmony and bliss of logic—the *ALL*, and the clutches of your mission, an engagement beleaguered by confusion and emotional irrationality.

"Post-traumatic stress disorder best describes it. Normally, a witness passes through Locum Veniae only long enough to debrief, for lack of a better word, but not you.

"Not you. Not even close. In fact, your mortal experiences so profoundly anchored you to Locum Veniae that we could only communicate with you in that frame of reference. We bring ourselves to your place in order to enlighten you, in order to explain your situation and guide you through the steps necessary to resolve it and move on.

"Are you finding what we say confusing? What *I* say?"

"More unbelievable than confusing. Maybe less confusing than waking up on a garage floor completely clueless, or talking to multiple personalities at once."

The woman laughed and extended Gus's calm.

"That's good. Keep that sense of humor. You'll need it."

"Don't say that. Makes me nervous about what's coming. Should I fear my future?"

"Ahhh. Glad you asked. From here forward, you can take heart in knowing you will no longer fear for your future or your well-being for any reason. Understand your own hand delivered your suffering, and your enlightenment ends your fear. Fear is of the past. Lucky you. There is no longer a need for the Lingering. You can't rush forgiveness."

Gus could hardly believe his ears.

Does this woman, or whatever, really wield that kind of power?

"Thank God for that," he answered.

"You may if you wish. It may also help your frame of mind to know that your experience, although far from common, is not unheard of. In fact, it's a textbook case—Transitional Setbacks 101—Transitional Abortions Due to Emotional Detachment Failures. We wrote a book about you."

"You mean, I'm famous?"

"*Hardly.* You might be in a buried footnote. Maybe."

"Wow. Who would have figured?"

"Right now, for you, it's a catch-22. If you don't attempt to transition, you won't find salvation. If you do attempt to transition, you still won't find salvation because of your emotional anchors. Either way you end up stranded in Locum Veniae. Purgatory."

"I see. Funny how a memory of my old dog-eared catechism book just surfaced."

"Mmm. Well, joking aside, keep this in mind. A two-minute explanation of mortal to immortal transitions is anything but a road map to salvation. It certainly does not capture the insidious nature of your guilt or illustrate the eventual deterioration of your soul, not the Gus Beretta of your mission, but the essence of you as an extension of ALL. A most unwanted outcome. That is what we're here to prevent."

The woman smiled to lighten the mood. It was for his benefit, but unnecessary, because Gus felt at peace just as she said he would. He was growing eager to move on.

"Okay, I'm not sure I get all that, but I can get past it. Let's get down to how you fix me. How does that happen?"

"It doesn't happen with a snap of the fingers, so don't go getting all impatient and stuff. True, we're here to help, but also true, you need lots of it."

"Okay. Is there something that I should be doing?"

"You'll have plenty to do in time. For now, let me reacquaint you with some truths that you understood before you lost your way, before your mission, back when you were merged with ALL. These facts will play an important role in understanding your final phase of shedding."

"Okay."

"Humor me by going along with the notion that ALL is the fusion of logic, knowledge, and awareness—*souls*. This meld of souls, per se, separates to become singular entities when accepting assignments or missions to witness the logical effects of random energy.

"Our supreme truth asserts that only when the logic of random energy is witnessed does it become knowledge. You, Gus, are a witness. We are all, at one time or another, witnesses. We seek logic. We promote knowledge. It was for this reason that you separated from the ALL to undertake a mission as a singular soul.

"Once transitioned back from a mission, a soul can remain single, it can merge with ALL, or it can merge with any lesser number of souls, just as I have presently. What is important in *this* time and space is that I am one of many merged souls here to guide you."

Gus interrupted her explanations.

"I'm certain I don't want to know, but how many is many? How many does it take to get the job done? Does it have to be a secret?"

"No. At the moment, we are seventeen, give or take."

Gus choked. His face reflected his shock, even though surprises were having increasingly less impact upon his numbed countenance.

"Seventeen?" he repeated.

"Give or take."

"In one body."

"One body."

"That body."

"This body."

"So, from your point of view, earlier, you were talking group sex," he kidded.

The woman's lips tightened. She shook her head in futility.

"My-my," she said. "I must admit, I'm starting to wonder if you truly are irredeemable."

"Well, there are quite a few of you in there. I mean, I never ventured to think past a threesome. But a seventeensome—"

"If we could play down the sexual fantasies, it behooves you to know that our number is to your advantage. You see, Gus, souls are here to support you. Some come from before and after your mission to assist. We are all here to rescue you. To get you back on the road to merging."

"Like guardian angels."

"Why not?"

"So did you take the best parts of all seventeen to make a body look like that? The *ultimate* guardian angel to hover over me at night. Sweet dreams."

Gus could not help himself. The vision of the woman was impossibly perfect.

"Obviously, you're still deep in that ditch." The guide looked at Gus with mild disdain, but she possessed a mandate, and therefore a higher understanding. "The answer to your question is *no*. It was you who made this body. Chew on that for a while. You can masturbate eternally to your own vision of perfection if you wish."

"*I* made *that* body?" Gus exclaimed. "How is that even possible? You're flawless. Perfect. It's killing me just to look at you."

"Why the surprise? I'm built to *your* standards. How could I not be perfect? After all, beauty is in the eye of the beholder, is it not? And speaking of perfect, what better time than now to say what next you need to know? I suggest you get your mind off sex and listen. This information is best heard without distraction. All right?"

"As if I have a choice."

42

"Let's begin by my saying that you created my perfect body out of need. We have already concluded that the sight of your creation brings you much pleasure during this time of stress, or distress if you prefer. Yes?"

"Totally."

"Totally. Just keep one thing in mind. You did *not* create us. You did not make *me*. We presented ourselves as the least confrontational image. An image you revealed to us the moment we merged. For the sake of your sanity, we introduced ourselves by assuming a vision you have fantasized as desirable. You see only one, but I am many. Does that make sense?"

"Yes, I guess so... if you're God."

"God? Yes! Brilliant! The Father, the Son, the Holy Ghost. Three spirits in the one god. Was that what you meant?"

"Uhhh.... Unfortunately, mostly that just rolled off my tongue. I'm really not that sharp."

"Well, the example is exquisite. So, keeping the concept of your creations in mind, let's take this one step farther. Everything that surrounds you, everything you see in Locum Veniae, is an illusion, a world you have conjured up out of desperation to find logic, a world that meets your need to maintain sanity. I only see your illusion, your world, when we're merged. When not merged, I see nothing but you.

"The highway you are desperate to find, the highway you hear at the top of this street, is also a fabrication, a construct of your making. It brings you comfort and a sense of security. To see it, to hear it, to walk or travel it, all these things bring you relief. You need a means of escape. That highway is the only necessary feature in your world. You need a highway in order to navigate your way out of Locum Veniae, and so there it exists in all its mindboggling magnificence. It entices you to move on, to leave Locum Veniae. Does anything I say ring true?"

Gus nodded. "Yeah, I guess. The road tugs at me. I know it does. Watching traffic flow to distant horizons has always given me hope. It frees me from whatever weighs me down, whatever holds me back. It means freedom. Freedom that allows me to breathe. I can't disagree. It's true."

"Excellent. Now, what comes next will push the limits. Are you game?"

Lord, she's staring right at me. She's daring me. Am I game? Memory or no memory, I'm not backing down to a woman. One soul, seventeen, fifty, what difference does it make? If she walks like a woman, quacks like a woman, then she's a.... Gus... you better rethink that.

"I wish I could say hell yeah, bring it on, but I'm nervous. How much of a push is this going to be? Should I be worried or what?" asked Gus.

"You know what it's like when I restore your memories—"

"Oh, hell no. I can't do that again. There's—"

The guide held up her hand to silence him.

"It won't be anything like that."

"Promise."

"I promise, but that doesn't mean it will be pleasant. We're still dealing with memories and emotions. However, it will be bearable. You see, Gus, all of this is a matter of perspective. To break you free of these endless loops, these detours, these barricades between you and your salvation, we must draw you back a safe distance from the intensity of those negatives you dragged to Locum Veniae from your mission.

"We must return you to the objective of the mission. Witnessing the logical flow of random energy and its effects. We must perform alignments. This means you must overlay what actually happened during your mission to what you fabricated here in Locum Veniae, or vice versa. In this way, you can separate fact from fabrication.

"There is no figure that might tally the number of attempts made by the driver to forgive you. But when he finally succeeded, when he was within reach of salvation, we directed him to open your mind to most of what you fabricated.

"We needed you to see the many ways you attempted to reconcile your transgressions. We needed you to see and understand how you replicated the pain you caused others in order to inflict it upon yourself. We needed you to see the hell you created in order to redeem yourself.

"We wanted you to understand that you never feel as though you've paid a price sufficient to earn forgiveness. For that reason, you continue to succumb to your guilt by constructing endless rounds of hellish events to cleanse your soul through suffering. Self-flagellation by every definition of the word. Did they teach you about that bit of morbid psychosis in catechism?"

"I'm thinking probably not," answered Gus.

"Think again of ghosts. Souls that inhabit places and never leave. Think of yourself as a ghost trapped within your transition, stuck between two places as you work to shed guilt. Do you understand?"

"I...I don't know," said Gus. "I understand what you're saying, but I don't fully grasp the fact that I am doing this to myself. It's true that you have opened my mind up to many of my memories, apparently those associated with Locum Veniae, but what is real to me is that I started my day on the floor of a parking garage. These memories you've given me feel more like stories that I've read about somebody else, not so much about me. They're distant."

"Yes, that's understandable. The fabricated events could be dreamlike, slightly less expansive, slightly less connected to reality. Also, remember that you went from no memories to a flood of memories. It's a bit much to swallow in one gulp. The important thing is that you must understand why the blocking of your memory is a critical step in transitioning.

"You see, Gus, your past learned experiences, your memories, dictate every action you take, every decision you make. Past predicts the future. To a certain degree, eliminating your past eliminates your future. Past, present, future, prophecies, choices, decisions, fate, they are all intertwined.

"You believe that having free will, you made evil choices. Sinful choices. When in actuality, that was not entirely the case. You see, choices are only free to recognize or contemplate. Decisions are not at all free to make. Decisions are often made long before the choice is presented."

"How can I not make free choices? A choice is a choice. Free will... isn't that the roadbed we travel through life?"

"It would seem so, yes. But that is mostly an illusion much like your world in Locum Veniae."

"No, that can't be. It's either free choice or fate, and I don't buy into fate."

"There's more to fate than you think. The faiths encountered during your mission routinely referred to prophets and prophecies. How is prophecy not fate?

"A prophecy, the prediction of random energy's path of least resistance or the outcome of energy's path, is a reflection of the knowledge gained by observation of random energy in the past. A prediction of the future will only be as accurate as the magnitude of knowledge from the past. Knowledge always follows a future unfolding as long as it's observed. Knowledge always hints of the future to unfold. The prophecy. Fate.

"The best of prophets cannot alter the flow of random energy, but can change the future. If they warn of a flood, others may build boats. The best prophets are souls that failed to segregate fully from the ALL while transitioning to their missions. This is the exact opposite of retaining emotions while transitioning back to the ALL. In both cases, to some extent, an anomaly has occurred.

"However, prophets are not always anomalies. All prophets use knowledge. It's a matter of the depth and accuracy of that knowledge. Consider the fact that a child is far more intelligent than an adult. But a child might not protect itself. It might grab a hot pan off the stove and get badly burned. An adult would not do this. How can that be if the child is more intelligent?

"The reason is simple. To witness is to record. A record or memory is knowledge. The child has no memory, therefore no knowledge of a hot pan causing injury or pain. For that reason, the child is as apt to grab the hot pan as not. Now, had the child been burned by a hot pan prior, then the child would likely leave it be.

"This means that knowledge ensured a decision before the choice was presented. That could be viewed as prophecy or prediction. More interestingly, it shows the choice may only be free to recognize, and the decision uncontrollable. In other words, the child is controlled by *fate*.

"The newborn is unable to recognize its first choice. Whether or not to take the nipple. It is unable to make a conscious decision because it has no experience, no memory, no realization of consequence. It has no conscious knowledge. However, it does possess subconscious knowledge—*instinct*. The subconscious decision formed before the child latched onto the nipple again is controlled by fate.

"This is one explanation of how past predicts future. It explains prophets and prophecies, and their ability to foretell the future. Most importantly, it explains fate. Had you grown up in a loving environment, odds are you would be a loving, giving person. Unfortunately, the opposite holds true as well.

"In your case, your mission commenced in a turbulent and destructive each-man-for-himself setting for survival. You found yourself fighting from day one to survive. Random energy set the course that produced a fighter: ruthless, brutal, an unconscionable bastard by any measure. But your actions were responses based on memories of your experiences within the flow of that energy.

"In other words, you made few free decisions. In spite of what you think, your past spelled out your fate. Your character is a product of the generations of events that preceded you in your mission.

"Memories can make the shedding process in Locum Veniae impossible because they continue to force a false and unwanted portrait of who and what you are spiritually, and specifically who you will be. So they are often blocked, and you wake up on the garage floor of a world you constructed, naive, lost, confused, but with a clear conscience and a somewhat neutral perspective. You actually are making as close to a free decision, when confronted with choice, as you will ever make. Those first moments following your re-awakening find you most reminiscent of the unbiased witness that once was you.

"By stripping you of your memories, your emotions of hatred, fear, suspicion, anger, those things that stained your soul, you are reduced to an untarnished essence that others are able to observe with clarity. Beneath all these negatives, you are pure. You are logical. You are a witness, pristine in every way.

"When those whom you have transgressed see the core of you, it enables them. When they realize what decisions you would have made when not forced by your past, not forced by fate, it assists them to shed their negative emotions, their desires for revenge, their hatred for you. It allows them to recognize their own obstacles to salvation, their need to shed, and when they have succeeded, they thank you for the opportunity you have brought to them. It is then that they forgive you. You both benefit. To forgive, and to be forgiven. Oftentimes it is simultaneous."

"I forgive you. I gotta go," injected Gus.

"Yes. Exactly. On the other hand, oftentimes it is not simultaneous. Take you, for example. You suffer through your guilt to the point of dying, so to speak, in order to earn forgiveness. The ultimate sacrifice in hopes of someone saying, *I forgive you*, at which point you awake on the floor of the garage without memory in order to repent for another transgression that haunts you. Or to repeat the process a thousand times because your guilt prevents you from believing you deserved the forgiveness and—"

"So waking on the garage floor was the end of an event?" asked Gus.

"No. Not your awakening. Your fabricated death marks the end of an event. You hoped dying would prove your contrition, and it did prove to others that you were worthy of forgiveness. Unfortunately, Gus, you never accepted their forgiveness. You will never suffer enough. You can't die enough times because you can't let go of the guilt. And that will never happen unless you face the actual transgressions, the source of your mythical constructs here in Locum Veniae.

"Your first awakening to an actual transgression, one you didn't fabricate, occurred with the driver. The killing of the driver and his wife was not an event of your making, but the authentic crime itself. In all your previous events, you were the victim, but this last time you were the perpetrator. This last time, you witnessed one of the genuine crimes that drives you to fabricate events necessary for contrition.

"In order for you to understand this you must clearly remember both actual events and fabricated events. You must align both to untangle the confusion between real and illusion. It's the one way, the only way, you will reach a state of logic, shed your emotions, and find salvation. Give me your hand."

"Hoo, boy."

Gus held out his hand with much reluctance. The guide gripped it firmly and gave him a final instruction.

"I warn you. Do not become emotional about what you see. As a witness, you observe only the result of energy spreading randomly. Ignore the pitfalls of illusion, whether by chance or the deceptions of coincidence. Don't dismiss fate. Observe logic and enjoy clarity. All else holds you prisoner in Locum Veniae.

"Are you ready?"

Gus took a deep breath.

"I guess."

43

The guide drew back curtains that concealed the few remaining events Gus fabricated while in Locum Veniae. She monitored his ability to maintain a stoical attitude, to be aware of every detail, but distant from the pain of direct participation. For Gus, the scenes were unpleasant, troubling, like watching fire from a distance. He could imagine the heat. He would squirm with discomfort to think of the suffering, but felt nothing of the burn.

By revisiting the last of his self-defeating constructs, the once black, featureless void of his existence began to dissipate. His recollections were substantive. He was confused but no longer blind. At the conclusion of the observations, Gus saw clearly the hell he had inflicted upon himself. He sorted out the many events he had constructed. He separated each of his awakenings on the garage floor.

Most importantly, he now recognized the loops of fictitious tragedies from which he was unable to escape. A rehabilitation of his self was under way. Knowledge and insight were breaking down fear and falsities, allowing Gus long overdue relief.

"How do you feel?"

"Weak."

"I expect. But hopefully enlightened and less burdened?"

"Enlightened? I suppose. I feel less fearful. I do sense something of inner peace. I don't know how else to describe it. But as for the burden.... Now, unlike before, I have a head full of memories. Dark, sickening memories that weigh me down. If the burden is less, it remains agonizing."

"I apologize. I was presumptuous. What you've said is to be expected. I wish I could take away these scars and leave you euphoric as before, but these aren't the same trivial matters, and at this point without the memories, you are doomed."

"Of course." Gus was pensive. "I do have a question."

"Excellent. Ask."

"I understand that I constructed these many elaborate scenarios to punish myself out of guilt that I carry back from my mission as a witness. I get that. What I can't seem to make sense of is my being murdered by many of these persons that I am determined to appease. There are times that someone I've offended actually says I forgive you, but it seems a thousand to one, they kill me anyhow. I don't get it. How are they gaining salvation by murdering me? If that isn't a dichotomy, I'm clearly missing something."

The guide smiled and then reached down for Gus's hand. She placed it flat on her chest, holding her hands firm across the back of his. She closed her eyes and lowered her head seemingly to meditate. As if commanded, his eyes closed in kind. The guide lifted him again above the tribulations that engulfed him. He was again free and joyous. Sometime later, an hour, a day, an eternity, he could not say, he opened his eyes to see the guide watching him. She was smiling. Gus said nothing. He only returned the smile. He was beginning to appreciate, or maybe remember, the immense inspiration of the ALL.

"Just to settle you," she smiled. "As for your question. A thousand times over, they don't find salvation. They murder you out of hatred and revenge, and wander about Locum Veniae as lost as you. They might watch you suffer and die a thousand times over before they learn to forgive.

"The less obvious answer is that they have learned to forgive, and so kill you out of kindness to speed you on to your next event. If they don't, you will never stop torturing yourself in spite of being pardoned. By killing you, they favor you; they end the event quickly, so you might try again. That should make sense now that you've seen how you torture yourself endlessly in loops."

"Mmm." Gus nodded but remained silent.

"There is one last thing I need to explain. Something that you already know, but lost sight of since going on your mission. It is simply this: In this dimension of Locum Veniae, and the dimension of ALL, time does not exist as a string of occurrences. It is not chronological. It only behaves in that manner as a means of order during certain missions, such as yours, and in the reality that you created here in Locum Veniae.

"Your perception of time is nothing more than a carryover of baggage from your mission when you transitioned. Time as a string of occurrences exists for you locally in your fabricated world, but only for you, and even then, not always. Outside of your construct, in Locum Veniae, the future, the present, and the past are simultaneous.

"The reason you must know this is because it is true that you constructed a world and events to suit your needs, but the souls with whom you merged were not a fabrication of your doing. You did not make them, as you did not make me. They did not wait for you to fabricate an event, and you did not wait for them to make themselves available. There is no waiting when there is no time to mark.

"They do not arrive in Locum Veniae before or after you. They arrive when the door to an event opens to offer resolution. That is how the driver returned to pick you up at the curb after having just pulled away. His pulling away and returning were unmarked by time as you know it. The occurrences were simultaneous, and that fact greatly disturbed the order of your world. You thought you were losing your mind.

"Imagine you are traveling on your highway with its hundreds of lanes. Imagine that everybody you have offended or has offended you is traveling in each of the other lanes. No matter how fast or slow you go, time as a string of events seems normal to the travelers in each of the lanes and in all lanes. However, what if the vehicles traveled at various speeds or changed speeds? Often, you would be ahead of the pack, and often you would be behind the pack. Most importantly, occasionally your position would perfectly flank another. At that point, you could share an event or merge. You might think of this as the way you engage with others who you believe transitioned before or after you.

"Do you understand?"

"I'm working on it. You're telling me that it makes no difference if somebody died before me or after me because time is irrelevant. Without time, souls are free to merge."

"Precisely. Yes."

"I do have another question, if you don't mind."

"Of course. The purpose of my being here is to enlighten you."

"You knew about the cave that swallowed me?" Gus asked.

"We know about many things. About most things actually."

Gus's brow wrinkled. "You're telling me that you witnessed my terror and suffering and did nothing to come to my aid. Why would you put me through that? If you wouldn't save me at that time, then why now?"

"The short answer is... there was nothing to save you from. Remember, the event was of your making. From your perspective, death, and the way you died, overshadows all. From our perspective, it was merely one of an infinite variety of ways to end an event.

"Now, a far more fulfilling and possibly humorous explanation of your ordeal would be one that illuminates the necessity of instilling a fear of inaction, dawdling, lingering.

"More times than not, souls need a gentle or not so gentle nudge to move ahead. Some souls have the ability to forgive all their trespassers, to shed all their emotional baggage, to repent on their deathbed per se prior to transitioning. Some do not. For some, it doesn't click. They transition to Locum Veniae with emotions that are irrelevant if not illogical and blind them from seeing their way home. They go in circles. They would remain to become another *spurned old-lady-apparition* in an upper-story window. For that reason, we intervene. We give them a little nudge, a pinch in the ass, if you will.

"As long as they persist in holding on to emotions, we use that to our advantage. We tap into the alpha emotion. Fear. For those sharing your mission, it could be water, heights, spiders or snakes, rapists, murderers. It doesn't matter what the fear, as long as it's overwhelming and effective. Essentially, we scare the ever-loving sanity out of them. Trust me; they don't linger much after that. In your case, the Lingering was personified by one of us as the man in white who offered you lemon ice water in front of the old stucco tavern."

Gus's jaw dropped, "The demon?" he asked fully astonished.

"Yes, the demon. He was a soulmate of yours during your mission."

"A soulmate?"

"A friend."

"He was a friend of mine?"

Impossible. Inconceivable.

"He was a good friend—a protector. He had no wish to see you mired down in Locum Veniae. He was intent on keeping you moving forward. He was there with you in the catacombs."

"Who? Who was he? Can you tell me how I knew him, who he was in my mission?"

"Yes. If you like. During your mission, his name was Arthur Blake."

"Arthur Blake? Arthur Blake.... I don't know anybody named Arthur Blake."

"You were a young boy. Do you recall sleeping under a blanket made from grain sacks?"

"Grain sacks?"

Gus drifted into another existence.

"Yes.... Yes, I do.... A pile of grain sacks in the corner of an old abandoned building. Stenciled in faded blue. Patterned in large letters—*OWO*. Letters that repeated across the burlap.

Old Western Oats. I remember. Balls ablaze, Mr. Blake. I do remember."

"Yes. I thought you would. Tell me about the memory."

Gus again drifted into his past existence.

"I ran away from home. The difference between my stepfather and me was that I was born a bastard, whereas he lived to be one. One day, I was watching him beat on my mother, and something snapped inside. I grabbed a skillet and crowned him. I slammed it into the back of his head with all the strength I could muster. On the one hand, I thought I killed him. On the other, I didn't believe anything could take him down. He was too mean.

"That single act sealed my fate. I ran for my life. Literally. Scared was an understatement. I didn't dare look back. I ran until my lungs were on fire. I ran until I got tunnel vision, until I was ready to pass out. I reached my physical limit. I was thirsty and worn out, but still scared as hell. I needed a safe place to hide, and soon discovered an old abandoned building where a bunch of bums and homeless people were gathered."

Gus's face suddenly lit up.

"No shit. The water. I remember."

He continued to speak.

"I was walking through the place, sort of mingling with the others, when this grubby old duffer called out to me. I must've looked different from the rest. I'm sure I did. I was only eleven or twelve. He spotted me in the crowd staring his way. He could see I craved something to drink, my attention fixed on a whiskey bottle filled with water and bits of lemon. I knew it was water because I recognized the label. It was my stepfather's favorite booze. It should have been a tawny color, not clear. He raised the bottle in my direction and asked if I was thirsty.

"I wouldn't have gone within fifty feet of a stranger, but I was so damned thirsty. Between cracked lips and a shrunken tongue, I could barely talk, but my eyes cried out for that bottle. I remember.

"Mr. Blake could see it, and tossed the bottle in my direction. That was good enough for me. I ran in and grabbed it. I knew I was too fast on my feet to worry about an old man lying across a bunch of grain sacks. He wasn't about to grab me. I drank that bottle down in two seconds. He started laughing. He asked if I just come in from the desert, and reached into one of his bags to produce another bottle, a plastic one, which he again tossed out to me.

"He never enticed me to approach him. He just spoke to me in friendly manner. He had a soothing voice. It settled me, and I drifted toward him. I put away both bottles of water before quenching my thirst. I think that bottled water was the only thing in the world he owned. I thanked him and walked away to take a piss. I guess it was because he didn't call me back that I returned to stay.

"One day, I swiped a coat. It was a nice navy-blue flannel bridge coat that I spotted hanging in the back of a dry-cleaner's truck. I waited for the driver to walk an armful of laundered items to a customer's house, and then I yanked it from the truck and ran off with it.

"I brought the coat to Mr. Blake. The building was cold and dark, and I thought he could use it. He cried. The man wasn't a pervert. He wasn't mean. He used to tell me stories about his wife and son. He hadn't seen them in years. He said I reminded him of his boy.

"I asked him why he lived in an old building with no heat."

"There's a demon inside me."

"I later realized he was an alcoholic. Same as my stepdad. That was something I understood. I knew that demon well, but Mr. Blake knew of others.

"He warned me to stay off the streets at night, to stay out of the shadows. He had me so scared of the dark that I avoided it at all cost. He said bad men lurked in the night that would do a young boy no good. Even worse, he said there were packs of wild dogs that roamed the unlit places looking to eat. Mr. Blake said the red-eyed devils could shred a boy to the bone in the blink of an eye. I was never to doubt his words or forget them. I never did.

"Mr. Blake always welcomed me back at day's end to rest near him. He promised to watch over me, and saw to it that I had a share of his burlap blanket. Yes, grain sacks stitched together. The bags kept us warm.

"I talked to that old man every night for weeks on end. He wanted to know why I was running around with the homeless. He wanted to know everything about me. He showed me caring, what a father was supposed to be.

"I never knew if it was because the weather warmed or what, but one night I returned to find Mr. Blake, his bags, his bottles, and his grain sacks gone. I never saw him again. I know he wouldn't have just left without saying goodbye. Maybe his demon…. I never knew, but demon or not, he was nothing like my stepfather. He was everything my stepfather was not. Mr. Blake was kind. He was soft-spoken. He liked to read discarded paperbacks. I remember."

Gus went silent. A smile crossed his face before he chuckled.

"Well, I gotta say. He did a hell of a job. Scared the ever-loving piss right out of me. How do I thank him?"

"You already have."

44

"Did he send me into that cave where I drowned?"

"No. You sent yourself there with a little help from us."

"Really. Wow. What great friends," mused Gus.

"Remember when souls merge, they become like one, a shared consciousness. We knew your fears. The demon. The dogs. And one other. You were terrified of tight spaces. Claustrophobia. A narrowing cave that slowly filled with water was the final embedded terror, frosting on the cake, before we terminated the event. Bottom line is we had our arsenal of fear. We were confident that you wouldn't be one to face down the Lingering in Locum Veniae."

"You got that right," Gus concurred.

"Now you should think about why you constructed the catacombs," said the guide. "Why you entered with a party of lost souls to wander the depths. They would never reach the top. Their only choice was to wait for rescue. It was your selfless act and your willingness to die for them that earned their forgiveness. And they did forgive you, time, and time, and time again to no avail. You couldn't accept it. You could not release your guilt, and so you continued to fabricate thousands of similar events. Always forgiven. Always dying. Always awaking in the garage. Always heading back down into the catacombs. The endless loop."

"The bus crash."

"Yes, Gus! Yes! The bus crash! We have an alignment. Very good, Gus. Look for the parallels. Tell me what you see. What do you remember?"

Gus broke from the conversation to look around. He was no longer in front of the crumbling masonry wall. He was now sitting at a street table in front of a café. He looked at the guide quizzically. She smiled and answered his thoughts.

"Your spirits are lifting. You are pulling yourself free of the gloom and entering the light. Feels good, doesn't it? Enjoy the coffee, enjoy your surroundings, relax. It's important to stay relaxed, unemotional, but remember everything, actual and fabricated. Search your memory," said the guide. "Search for the alignment, the parallels, and tell me what you find."

Gus returned his attention to focus on his memories and soon gave accounts of what he saw.

"I remember the bus plunging down the face of the mountain. I was stoned out of my head. A bug that splattered across the windshield startled me. I stared at it for what I thought was a split second, but the next thing I knew we were airborne. I barely touched the brakes. Time seemed to stop as the earth dropped away in slow motion. We went down, down, down. Always down. There was no end to it. Just like the catacombs. The valley appeared dark, shadowed beneath peaks the sun had long since passed over.

"The few passengers that survived the break-up of the bus, the ones that made it to the bottom, began to wander aimlessly along the floor of the ravine. They were searching for a way back up, but being all busted up, and physically incapable of scaling cliffs, climbing was out of the question. They had no choice but to remain below and wait for help.

"I was too far gone to say anything coherent. I had eaten some unexpectedly potent cookies made with canabutter. The problem for me was that as more time passed, the more stoned I got. I couldn't just stop digesting cookies. I was in for the long haul, and at that point, being mentally comatose, it didn't take much effort to play dead.

"As night came on, the bottoms of the canyon cooled down. The survivors started to suffer from exposure, as did I. The passengers huddled for warmth, but to no avail. Finally, one of survivors, walking about to stay warm, discovered a small cave-like crevice. Nobody argued about going inside. The rock was warmer than the air, and the cave seemed safer than the shadows of night and what lurked unseen. They went in as far as they could and huddled.

"As for me, I laid on my back for hours looking up at the walls of the ravine. Heat lightning strobed off the sandstone surfaces. It flickered in bright white flashes. It reminded me of an old black-and-white television.

"I'm not sure how long I watched the lightning flicker along the ravine. When it stopped, I saw nothing but black and stars beyond count. Then as the moon changed position, the bluish lunar glow seeped down into the depths.

"The problem was I hadn't been watching heat lightning. Instead, what I observed were flashes from a thunderstorm off in the distance. Eventually, I heard the booming of the thunder echoing through the canyon."

"Just as you heard in the caves."

"Yes."

"Logical."

"Yes."

Gus went silent.

"Go on, Gus. You must continue."

Gus nodded and continued to recount the tragedy.

"There never was any rain. There was nothing but a sudden explosive roar, after which a torrent of water came rushing through the canyon. It swept me away along with the corpses and wreckage. Only the passengers in the cave escaped the flow. They weren't swept away. The rescue workers found them huddled at the farthest point back in the cave. The rising water first sealed off the entrance preventing them from escaping. Then it drowned them.

"The thought of how they died, the horror of it kept me awake at night for most of my life. I would lie in bed and hold my breath. My heart would race and send me into a full-blown panic attack. I couldn't escape them. I guess that's the fear you pumped into the Lingering."

"Yes," acknowledged the guide. "You never overcame thoughts of their drowning in that confined space. Most likely, they would have drowned in the turbulence of the current had they not been in the cave, but that wasn't an issue. It was drowning in the darkness of a confined space that haunted you. The worst death you could imagine. You carried that horror with you into Locum Veniae. Do you see why you fabricated the flow of water that carried you into the cave?"

"Yes."

"Logical."

"Very."

Gus went on giving a recount of the tragedy, after which the guide assisted him in sorting out the realities and ramifications.

"In the catacombs you elected to climb the ladder. You knew in your heart that your chances were nil, but you never thought twice about it. You would die in an attempt to save the others if it meant righting your wrong. And for all intents and purposes, you did. Many times.

"Remember when you fell, just as you hit the ground, you said the souls were there. They expressed their gratitude and forgave you. They needed to forgive, after which they said they had to go. By offering them your life, you proved you were worthy of forgiveness and freed them to move on. You didn't offer them revenge, you offered them a chance to rid themselves of hate. You removed their burdens. Do you understand that they needed you as much you needed them? Only you could open the door to their salvation. Only you."

The woman smiled. "You have no need to return to the catacombs, Gus. Tell me that doesn't make you feel better."

"I'm getting there," said Gus in honest amazement as he let loose a deep breath. "I'll be damned."

"You were... a thousand times over. Now let us proceed with another alignment."

45

Gus could feel the empty places in his soul begin to fill with substance as merged remembrances sorted out. Damping emotional memories, one after another, allowed for expanding logical realizations.

"The fire."

That was all the guide had to say.

"Veronica Giordano," he whispered.

"Yes. Look back, Gus. Understand your guilt. Face it. Tell us who she was."

Gus stared off into space.

"I thought I knew her the first time I saw her—her and Joseph."

Gus began to weep.

"Stop!" The guide purposely startled Gus.

"What?"

"I said stop. If you can't remove yourself from the emotional ties then we move on to something else."

"I'm sorry," said Gus.

"What would you like to do?"

"I prefer to continue."

"Very well. I only want facts, Gus. No tears. No drama. You're a witness. Tell me who she was. Tell me what you did. Tell me what happened. Just facts. Do you understand?"

"Yes."

Gus's head began to swim as another stream of visions entered his awareness to mingle with his memories of Veronica. He forced himself to settle down each time he felt tears approach his eyes.

"I know what you're saying. Just give me a minute."

"Take your time."

"Victoria Grace Pendyke." Gus stated flatly. "Victoria and Joseph."

"Yes."

"How do I know that name?" he asked.

"Look back to your mission, Gus. Who is Victoria Grace Pendyke? Who is Joseph?"

"Victoria... Grace...." An expression of enlightenment moved across his face. "She often went by Vicky. She was married to Bruce Pendyke. Joseph was their son. Smart. Good-looking kid. I knew Bruce.... Socially. We partied at their apartment all the time. Crazy parties. I sold him drugs. Victoria didn't much care for me. Veronica was good to me. She was a sweetheart, but Victoria hated my guts. I remember now. It was... it was...."

"It was what, Gus? Sort it out. What do you see?"

"Victoria and Veronica both lived in the same apartment."

"Yes. That's the alignment," said the guide. "That's perfect. What else?"

"I don't know. I don't know. It wasn't good."

"What happened, Gus? You must face your guilt logically. Tell us what happened."

Gus was again becoming visibly upset, at which point the guide interrupted.

"Relax, Gus. Relax. There is no place here for emotions. Settle down and sort out the facts."

Gus settled down as directed.

"That's better. Now... tell me what you see. Be factual."

"Fire. I see fire. Flames. I can feel the heat—"

"Step back."

The guide was adamant. Gus continued.

"The place is on fire. I can see it. It's Veronica's apartment... no... Victoria's apartment.... Wait. I'm not sure. Everything is mixed, tangled. They're both... fire. I'm trying to help Veronica. Yes. I know I was trying to help."

"Relax, Gus. Calm yourself. Don't get sucked—"

"Something's wrong. It's Victoria. She's trapped in the apartment! She's crying out! I can see her from the street. She's screaming out the window! Oh, no. No! No! Don't jump!" Gus blurted out. His chest was heaving.

"Stop! Stop! That's it. That's enough. No more."

The guide commanded Gus to stop. Her forceful voice was followed by silence. Gus returned from a dark place and focused on the beauty of the woman. She then spoke soothingly.

"Let's take a break. Emotionally, you're still too close to this experience to shed it. Sit back, Gus. I'll tell you what. Let me change the subject. Do you mind?"

Frustrated by his lack of control, Gus agreed.

"I guess. Whatever."

"It's best to give that one a rest. How about we go back to the bus wreck. What did you do afterward, after you fled the scene?"

"Lemme see. Not much. I hitchhiked home. The cops were already at my apartment waiting."

"What happened?"

"What happened was 195.5A. Five to ten in club fed. I got paroled after eight for good behavior, but.... They should have kept me locked up."

"Why?"

"Well... for one thing, anything of me that was decent was stripped away. Good guys are considered pretentious in the pound. They're despised. Bad likes bad. Bad makes you invisible.

And should you live until comes the day you walk, well... felons don't get jobs. First-time offender, ten-time offender, makes no difference. Felons don't get jobs."

"So, what did you do?"

Gus thought back along memories that were streaming into his awareness.

"A lot. I was hungry. I had no place to stay. I had a choice of stealing mostly worthless junk, possibly getting caught and going back to prison. Or dealing in drugs for a shitload of money, possibly getting caught and going back to prison. I knew all about prison and so the fear of incarceration was no longer there. The risk versus return heavily favored dealing. At least I wouldn't have to worry about fencing goods. Fences were as bad as narcs."

"In fact, dealing is exactly how I met Veronica, or I should say Victoria."

"Okay. How about we go back to Victoria. Want to give it another go? Can you do that without getting upset?"

Gus exhaled. "I can try."

"Good enough. Go for it."

"Okay. Ahh... Veronica... Wait." Gus struggled with a memory. "I just realized that it was Victoria Grace who jumped. It's Victoria who jumped, not Veronica. Veronica pushed me out the window. I tried to save her, and she went and pushed me out the window. Go figure. Stupid. I wanted only to save her son. I could've done it. I could have saved him. Instead, she pushed me out the fucking window."

"Gus! Listen to me. Nobody pushed you out the window. You concocted all of it. This is what needs sorting out. This is why I am here."

"I'm telling you, I laid there on the pavement watching my flesh fry—my skin smoke. I listened to her tell me how she forgave me. I remember her kneeling at my side, looking down at me. She bent over and kissed me. Can you believe that? Who pushes someone out a window and then kisses them?"

"Oh, my-my-my." The guide shook her head. "Okay. Let's go over this again. I want you to listen because I don't think you're getting it. You are dead. Dead. For the sake of keeping it simple, you are dead. Deal with it.

"You are stuck in Locum Veniae just like other floundering fools who need to take care of some last-minute details before passing through the pearly gates—"

"Merging with ALL."

"Yes. Yes. Merging with ALL."

"Again, I repeat. In Locum Veniae, souls need to shed emotional baggage. For the most part that means forgiving another soul, or awaiting another soul's forgiveness.

"In your fabricated event, you set the scene so you could prove your contrition and earn forgiveness by showing a willingness to die for Veronica. She leaned over you and forgave you. She kissed you and said she had to go. She had found her way home. In fact, it was Victoria who was merged with you in that event. It was Victoria who was able to finally shed her hatred for you and move on. I imagine she watched you fall out that window for eons before she could do it. She needed to forgive. You needed to be forgiven. Do you get it? Gus... do you get it?"

Gus sat at the table and stared at the guide. He didn't see her beauty. He didn't see her at all. He was lost in the meaning of her words. Slowly, he came around to answering.

"The problem is that sometimes these fabricated events are foggy and distant, and then there are times that they are as real as me talking to you. I can't tell the difference between what's made up and what isn't. It's clear when *you* point it out, but otherwise it's a bitch convincing myself that my take on the world is distorted, delusional. You try digesting that."

"I'd choke on it. It's true," said the guide. "I did say that you needed lots of help. If it were easy, you wouldn't be here. If it were easy, we wouldn't be here. But we are. It's a struggle, but we move forward. Your existence depends on it. So, let's keep going.

"Now..., you said that you socialized with Bruce Pendyke. But for you, the get-togethers weren't only about good times, were they? They were also about business. Sales. You visited Bruce many times at his apartment to party. He always invited you because you were his dealer. Correct?"

"Correct."

"What was his drug of choice?"

"His only drug. Meth. It got him killed."

"Go on. Tell me about it," the guide encouraged Gus to uncover details of his mission.

"Mmm. Where to start.... For Bruce, it began as great times, raising holy hell. Partying, drinking, the usual. In the beginning, Vicky ran a close second. Back then, she wasn't opposed to having a good time herself.

"But all of that changed one night while Bruce watched a group of guys railing rocks and slamming. Vicky backed off like she'd been burned, but Bruce was really curious, asking lots of questions. He finally came over and asked me to sell him a point so he could give it a try. *Ooooo. Not good stuff,* I told him. *Very, very addictive.*

"You know, to be honest, I liked Bruce. Bruce was all about smoke and beer. He liked his pot; he liked his IPAs. I didn't want him to get into meth. It's dirty. Nasty, nasty stuff. I mean, he had a great wife, a good life. He wasn't an ex like me or addicted like those guys sitting there snorting shards into their heads. I told him to stick with the weed if he wanted to get high. It was safe.

"Well... I guess I bruised his ego. Instead of taking my advice, he got pissed. Really pissed. It was the booze talking. You know how drinking makes some people belligerent, especially if they think you're babysitting them. You know, it's like I said... ego. Anyway, to keep the peace, I gave him what he wanted. Didn't make me happy. Not at all."

"Why do you say that?"

"I say that because make no mistake about it, I was no saint. I was big into dealing. I was all about making killer money. But unlike a lot of dealers, I didn't grow up on the streets in the drug culture. Maybe for that reason, I drew a line between supplying product and introducing someone to anything other than weed. I saw way too much heartbreak. Heard way too much horror in the big house. Don't misunderstand me. If my pushers expanded the customer base with noobs, more power to them. It's just not something I did."

"But you did with Bruce."

"Yeah... unfortunately, I did. But to be honest, I was hoping that between burning the piss out of his sinuses and a likely killer crash, ouch! It would be the last time he messed with that stuff. Coming down from meth is cruel. It's a hard fall."

"And?"

"And he turned out to be a noob that gets first-time addicted. I was right about the snorting. He didn't like the burn. To his credit, he never slammed as far as I know, but he lived to smoke. Meth affects everyone differently. I tend to think smoking is the most addictive. Some say slamming, but I tend to disagree. Most ROAs involve specific doses, but with smoking, as far as doses go, no one has a clue.

"I'll tell you this much, I always sold the largest quantities of meth to smokers. Smoking is smooth, but you always chase the high. You're too far gone to stop picking up the pipe. You fiend through a couple of Gs or an 8 before you know it. It's the quantity of meth that smokers use to maintain a high. That's what seals their addiction.

"And then there's the one last curse. I often think the worst. Withdrawal symptoms from meth may not show up until months after getting off the stuff. You never see it coming. You're feeling all good about yourself getting clean and three months later—*wham*. Just like that, it drops ya.

"Now you're not using to get high, you're using just to maintain normal, which gets ever more elusive—and *expensive*. And that's where people get desperate and do desperate things."

"People, as in Bruce?"

"Yup. As in Bruce. Bruce sold off everything he owned. I heard he even tried pimping Vicky. I think he got into more than just meth. I mean he could shake n' bake for a few hits and maybe get by without blowing his head off, but the only way to get quantity reasonably safe was to start cooking his own. Not a difficult thing to do, and certainly a lot less expensive than paying me.

Anybody can make a load of meth and push it for profit. But few ever see the profit. That's because all the while you're cooking meth, it's cooking you. Your brains get baked, you make bad decisions, you don't learn from your mistakes. You end up dead."

"That's what happened to Bruce?"

"That's what happened to Bruce. He was cooking a shitload of meth and dumping his product all over my turf. Losing sales isn't nearly as bad as losing respect. You can always build sales back up. But respect? If your organization senses weakness in the management, you're finished. They'll run over you like a ten-ton truck.

"I knew for a while that Bruce was cooking in a storage space on the first floor of his apartment building. My guys had been keeping tabs on him for a couple of months. In view of our past friendship, I gave him three or four opportunities to move his operation or shut down. But he had no brains left. He went on doing business as usual.

"Bruce gave me no choice but to pay him a visit in person. We knew from the stakeout when the apartments were full or vacant. We knew when best to slip in and out unnoticed just in case things got messy.

"So, I had my guys meet me at the storage space. We busted in and to my dismay, found Bruce busy cooking. I wished he hadn't been there. He was so jacked up on meth that I expected to die in an explosion at any moment. Lucky or not, the only thing to explode was Bruce. In typical meth-monster fashion, he flew into a rage and came at me swinging a blade the size of a machete. My guy pulled his piece and parted his hair. What a fucking mess.

"Imagine my joy at having to fish through Bruce's skull to retrieve that round. I had the guys drop a fifty-five gallon drum across his head. We made it look like it fell off a stack and crushed him. After that, it was just a matter of setting the place on fire. Meth labs go up in smoke more often than Cuban cigars. The authorities would have never thought anything more of it. Guy gets crushed by falling drum, lab goes unattended, catches fire, end of story. Or more likely, lab explodes, falling drum kills man, end of story. When a meth lab burns, it burns big.

"We stuck around and watched from the street as the place went up. Once the fire reached those chemicals, it was a chain reaction of explosions. Blew out the south wing of that building. Half the ground floor. I remember staring into those flames and thinking how Bruce once had the world. A beautiful wife, a family, a home. Now he was just dead. Dead as hell. Meth dead.

"Right then, the most god-awful scream ever snapped me out of my thoughts to look up and see Victoria holding her son at the window of their apartment on the third floor. I turned to my guy.

"'Balls ablaze! What the fuck, Jake. You said nobody was in the building. That don't look like nobody to me.'

"'Boss, there weren't nobody in that place when we walked in. I promise. I stake my life on it. She must've showed while we were torching the lab.'

"Vicky must have come home while we were in the storage space covering our tracks. Instead of being there ten minutes, between fishing through Bruce's head for that round, and prepping the place to burn, we were there more like half an hour, probably longer.

"I'll tell ya, I was sick to my stomach. There was no getting to her from the street. She was dead as Bruce. Just a matter of time. She was looking down at the street and staring death and me in the face. It wasn't that she recognized me. I was just one of a crowd looking up at her helpless to do anything but watch the inevitable unfold.

"I watched her jump to her death with Joseph in her arms. There was no way I would ever walk away from that. Victoria knew how to raise hell, but she understood boundaries. She knew when to stop. I respected her determination to hold her family together against all the odds. I liked her as a person in spite of the fact that she loathed me. I probably like her more because of it. I respected Vicky.

"Let's be honest, I took away everything of value in her life, but I never wanted to. After that, I took away her life. I took the life of her son. I didn't want that either."

Gus sat stoic. No emotion, numb. He looked at the guide and added. "Just the facts."

"Those things happen. Random energy." She attempted to console him.

Gus said nothing.

"Do you see the alignment?" she asked.

"Yes."

"And what did you get from it?"

Gus considered the memories that were at both times separate and unified.

"I see that Victoria and Veronica are one and the same."

"Yes."

"I understand that Victoria was unable to merge with ALL because of her hatred for me."

"Yes."

"My guilt constructed an event whereby Victoria could partake in my attempt to overcome my guilt in order to overcome her hatred. She needed to forgive me in order to merge. She had to be there, a part of my event, witnessing my efforts to save both her and her son."

"Yes," agreed the guide. "She had to believe in your sincerity, your self-sacrifice, your willingness to trade your life for theirs. And *that* is what she saw, Gus. That is what she saw."

"And she thanked me, said she had to go, and kissed me good-bye."

"Precisely. Thanks to you, Victoria Grace Pendyke merged."

"And I did not. I still feel remorse."

"Not for long. The remorse is residual. It will quickly dissipate. You would prefer to believe in your free choice to take the higher road while on your mission, but your experiences drive every decision you make, no matter how despicable. Your choices are far from being as free as you might think. You will eventually see the truth of it.

"Uncovering the original event, the source of guilt, has allowed you to appreciate the illusions you created in order to repent. Now that you have aligned events real and imagined, you can see that

that logic has no right or wrong. Only random energy running its course, random energy that you volunteered to observe.

"No witness, no record, no knowledge.

"You are the witness, for better or worse, as is every soul involved in your mission. Each soul a different perspective on the same event. Let this guilt go, Gus. Free yourself and move on."

46

"Let's consider Bonnie. You remember Bonnie."

The mention of Bonnie's name brought a fresh flurry of emotions—*intense emotions*. Memories of the fight, the dinner she made, the lovemaking, and the fact that... *she strangled him to death*.

"Yes. I remember Bonnie all too well."

"Which Bonnie?"

"What?"

"I said, which Bonnie do you recall? The one you fabricated, or the Bonnie from your mission?"

"I only know one Bonnie."

"Okay. But there has to be another Bonnie or a girl much like her. A similar name. A similar face. A Brenda, or Barbara, or Belinda. Try to remember. Look back and remember, Gus. Search for her."

The guide not only held the keys to Gus's memory, she also understood the pathways into his past, even if that past was in a different dimension, a different existence. At the mere suggestion to look back and remember, everything about the original event during his mission emerged from the void that plagued him. The memories streamed in a fashion that kept him moving from one to another in a sequence that would align with his fabrications.

"What really happened, Gus?"

"Huh?"

"What do you see? Who is the girl you call Bonnie?"

"I'm not sure. I remember walking down a street. The street seems familiar."

Gus broke from the spell that bound him. He looked past the angel standing before him and studied the street that extended in both directions behind her.

"Is this the street?" he asked.

"I don't know. This place is of your making. I see it through you. It's in continual flux. Changing with your thoughts and moods. Changing as necessary to meet your needs. It is no place I know."

"What is happening on this street? Tell me."

Gus stared past the guide. His eyes peered into an unseen world. The words came slowly at first. Measured.

"I'm with someone. A guy. I'm leading him, escorting him, I think. We're walking down an alleyway. It's late. Nighttime. The alley is dark. There's a dim light in the distance. A porch light of sorts.

"The man is asking me, *'Are you sure this is safe?'*

"I tell him, *'It's safe, man. I do business here all the time.'*

"We stop at a trailer hidden in the shadows, a mobile office that needs to be condemned. I knock on the door. A curtain moves slightly in an adjacent window. I listen to the latches releasing. The door opens partway to reveal a scrubby, unshaven face. The occupant nods and releases the inside chains. He acknowledges me.

"*'Hey.'*

"I do the same in kind. *'Macky.'*

"Then I turn to the john I escorted.

"*'Follow me.'* I say.

"We step inside the trailer.

"*'This your john?'* Macky asks me. He's naturally cautious, suspicious.

" *'Yeah.'*

"*'Got the money?'* he asks me.

"*'Yeah,'* I answer. *'My man would like to see the goods first.'*

"'No problem. This way,' he says.

"Macky leads both of us through a dingy reception room illuminated by a single desk light on a card table. Two folding chairs and an over-stuffed maroon fabric chair show scars of surviving the place. We walk down a hall lined with closely spaced doors. On the outside of each door is taped a photograph of a woman. Obviously images of past beauty. Times that warranted a smile.

"The john says to me, '*Lemme see this one.*'

"Macky opens the door and flips a switch. The light was intentionally worthless. No different than restaurants where you eat in the dark to keep from getting grossed out. Who wants to see dried food on a fork?

"A young woman is lying on a bed. Maybe she's eighteen, twenty, twenty-five, who knows. She appears to be sleeping or drugged. The john walks into the room and rolls her over onto her back. He pushes on her breasts.

"'*They're real. I like that.*'

"Macky starts to laugh.

"The john asks, '*I say something funny?*'

"'*Yeah, man. You ever run into a working girl that could afford a tit-kit?*'

"Macky's kidding around, but the john doesn't think he's funny.

"He says, '*Too many times. For me bolt-ons are a turn-off.*'

"Macky says, '*I totally agree, man. We got nothing here but natural. Squeeze 'em to believe 'em.*' He's still laughing.

"The john looks at me and throws his head to the side, signaling his desire to move on.

"'*Next.*'

"The john peers into the adjoining room and those that customers don't occupy. We skip the rooms where you could hear bedframes slamming into the walls. The last door at the end of the hall has no picture taped to it. Only a glossy flyer with the white unprinted backside facing out. Written with a quick hand, a broad-tipped red marker highlights the number 3.

"My mark frowns. The number confuses him. You can see it on his face, so Macky explains.

"*'It's like this. We move the girls from group to group. The first group, the smallest, is nothing but virgins, the younger the better. The second group are the workhorses. They're the mainstay of the business. Experienced. If you find a virgin in the second group, it's only because she's too old. The regulars work until they get sick and die or gleegasm, you know, OD. Nobody here ever makes it to a hospital.*

"*'If they're that far gone, then they might end up in 3. You see there's a lot o' sick fucks out there that only get off if they're strangling a piece of ass. Erotophonophiliacs. They only want threes. Virgins are big bucks, but nothing compared to what lust murder brings in. I heard one guy dropped ten K to strangle a cunt in 3.'*

"So the john asks Macky, '*Wow. These dudes actually murder the bitches?*'

"*'Oh, yeah. They like the feel of 'em tightening up. But only if they pay for it. Otherwise, if they die, the proprietor loses big time. So, you gotta be careful. If you kill one, you're in deep shit. You'll lose your balls, your life, or your money. In fact, you will probably lose all three. On the other hand, if you wanna kill one, that can be arranged, but you better be able to bankroll it.'*

"The john turns to look at me and asks. '*When was the last time one died?*'

"I threw up my hands and shrugged.

"'*I don't know, man. That's not my business.*'

"Macky starts to laugh.

"'*What's so funny?*' I ask.

"'*You.*'

"'*What?*'

"'*Bonnie.*'

"'*Bonnie?*'

"'Yeah, man. You remember her. She was that wee one. Remember? There was nothing to her. Bonnie. Bonnie. She was kinda cute in spite of being all whored out.'

"I told him I didn't remember. 'I don't remember any Bonnie. There's been too many.'

"'Nah, nah, you remember,' he says to me. 'You thought she was a real cutie. She had that streak of white hair.'

"'Oh, yeah, Bonnie. Yeah, she was cute. What the hell does this have to do with Bonnie?' I ask.

"Macky just pointed at the number 3 on the door.

"I'm standing there not believing it. So, I tell him, 'You're kidding me. I don't remember her being sick.'

"Macky shrugged his shoulders.

"'You remember the dude that drove the SL, the silver one? The guy with the cufflinks?'

"It didn't take me long to remember. Not many johns drive cars like that.

"'You gotta know him,' said Macky. 'You brought him in. Jesus, you made one huge chunk o' change off him.'

"'Okay…. Yeah…, I know who you're talking about. So what are you sayin'?'

"'He paid the price. Took her out. Big, big, bucks. She was still a looker, a moneymaker. Kept her right on the edge for a good three hours. Oh, yeah. He paid through the wazoo for that rush.'

"I looked at Macky. I just looked at him. Honestly, I didn't know what to say. My stomach was turning. I could fish through a dead man's skull for a round, but this…. Made me sick.

"'I'll be damned. So this is where she checked out, huh.'

"'Yup.'

"The drugs, the murder, the prostitution; it was all dirty. My life was dirty. I have no idea why I couldn't turn away from the door—why I was riveted to that number. I suppose having never been weak, for one brief pause, I tried to imagine it. I tried to imagine the helplessness in that room.

"Room 3."

47

"Gus?"

Silence.

"Gus? You okay?"

Silence.

"Gus. You gotta open up. Don't keep your thoughts inside. Not blurting out your emotions doesn't mean you've shedded. Talk to me. What are you thinking? C'mon, Gus. Talk to me."

Gus's eyes shifted from a blank stare at something in the background of the street to the woman's face. With all its angelic beauty, it did nothing to ease his condition.

"I'm not thinking anything. I'm afraid to think."

The woman studied him as looked down at his hands. They were trembling. She spoke to him.

"I noticed you didn't say anything about guilt."

Gus folded his hands and bowed in an unconsciously reverent manner. He confessed.

"The shock took me way past guilt. It made me numb. I have no feeling. I'm emotionally dead."

She smiled.

"Perfect."

48

Gus appeared troubled. More so than the guide preferred. She gave him time to collect himself, but he appeared to be sinking too deep into thought.

"Gus—"

"The old lady in the wheelchair was my mother."

The words erupted from within. There was no warning. A moment of silence passed before the guide responded to the revelation.

"You're certain?" she asked.

"Positive."

"That's a quick alignment. What made you so sure?"

"It wasn't anything I had to remember. I could feel it. It wasn't so much an alignment or comparison. It was more like an extension of something familiar bridging from my mission to my fabrication. The fragrance of the garden."

"Go on. Finish it out."

"I think that's the whole of it. There are no memories that align. Only the feeling of love or caring. The old woman knew me unlike any other. I was at ease in her presence.

"The alignment...."

Gus slipped into his thoughts.

"I understand the alignment. It's about loneliness. I never saw my mother after I ran away from home. I was afraid to go back home for years. At first, it was out of fear. Later, I resented her for letting my stepdad beat on the two of us. I resented her for not taking us away. I was young and clueless to the difficulties she faced.

"Then it was all about time. So many years had gone by that it was easier not to open the door to our past. Every time I considered it, it was like staring at Pandora's box. I viewed a reunion as awkward and likely full of attached strings—my stepfather being a rope. I knew if he was still there, I would want nothing more than to kill him. I didn't care how old, how decrepit, I didn't care if he was blind or sitting in a wheelchair. Whatever he was, he was better dead. So, you see, going back wasn't worth the stress. It wasn't worth the feelings of repression. It wasn't worth doing time for murder. I wanted my freedom, and I had it. No strings.

"I don't know what all became of my mother other than what I was told about her final years. More importantly, she never knew what became of me. She was fortunate. I was told that she had a massive stroke. They told me that she couldn't see, or speak, or even hear. She existed between life and death for seven years, having no contact with the outside world other than touch. She remained locked inside her consciousness, wandering within the dreams or the darkness of her mind.

"I heard that mom would always hold her arms up, reaching out in hopes somebody would take her hand. They said if she grabbed you, she wouldn't let go. It was all she had. I never went to her. Can you believe that? What kind of son abandons his mother to that hell?"

There was silence between Gus and the guide as each reflected on the alignment. This time she allowed him all the time he needed before moving on.

"I will tell you this," said the guide. "This alignment is different from the ones prior. You fabricated your events as usual, and your mother merged to observe your contrition, but she brought her own negatives. Emotional anchors that weighed her down in Locum Veniae. Your mother drew you into her own fabrication as well. You wandered in the infinite emptiness of her existence. You both sought forgiveness, and eventually found it simultaneously."

"Of course."

For Gus, there was no misunderstanding, no confusion about the alignment. It depressed him. The guide tolerated this emotion for Gus's sake. She allowed him to work it out on his own before reaching out to him. She stood up from the table and walked around to embrace him from behind. She placed her arms around his shoulders, pressing her head against his. He was submissive.

The guide lifted Gus from his depression. She did so gently, freeing him spiritually, un-clouding his mind so he might again focus on his duty as a witness, and return knowledge to ALL. The traumas of his mission were peeling away one layer after another. The doors to his emotional prison fully opened. The guide finished by helping Gus align what few events remained in order to exorcize them forever and close this chapter in Gus's transition. He was free to move on.

49

The guide stood up from the table and looked down at Gus with a smile. She reached out to him with her hand.

"Come on. Let's walk back up toward the ridge, back to the highway that brings you peace. While we walk, we can discuss the truths necessary for you to continue unhindered on your highway out of this place."

Gus rose from his chair and took her hand. Together they strolled the street, and lastly the steep escarpment that led to the ridge. There was one profound difference about his walk along the street. The sidewalks were alive with people. The voices of laughter and conversation crept out from every shop. Colorful nightlights began to appear here and there at sidewalk cafés, as dusk settled on the community. Instead of a barren and fearful place where the black of something worse than night awaited the unsuspecting, the street welcomed all. Gus looked back over his shoulder frequently, but there was nothing fearful in sight. The warmth of happiness filled him while he walked in the woman's company and listened to her lecture.

"The first truth, Gus. There is no right or wrong beyond your mission."

She stopped walking and turned to face him. She continued to hold his hand.

"Listen to me carefully. There is no right or wrong beyond your mission."

She looked straight into his eyes. He said nothing, but offered his undivided attention, awaiting her every word.

"Right and wrong are the most basic emotional values that exist in the environment you witnessed. In that place, to end a life is the highest form of evil, and yet, it is acceptable to kill an animal. It is acceptable for one man to kill another during a time of war. It is acceptable for a customer to kill Bonnie as a matter of business. Sacrificing the lives of others to appease the gods is as human as copulating.

"In the environment of your mission, right and wrong are merely perspectives. It is by the consensus of a few that these acts and all others are deemed good or evil. More importantly, such determinations are expressly fluid, changing dramatically with time and events."

She turned from him, squeezed his hand, and continued to lead him up the hill—and through her sermon.

"The ALL is random energy. Existence is energy and only energy. There are no places empty of energy. The darkest void in creation is merely energy undetected or unrecorded. You witnessed a philosophy that expressed a universe created from nothing, but nothing is a state of energy awaiting creativity unrealized. The feat was no miracle.

"We are all energy, Gus. We are all knowledge. Our purpose is to expand and preserve the actuality of knowledge. Individually, we are a dispersion of focal points tasked to observe the random flow of energy from different perspectives, all that it creates or destroys along with the repercussions of those actions, saintly or sinful. This is necessary because only by observation can knowledge exist.

"You must always remember that random energy is pure logic, and therefore beyond judgment. For that reason alone, you cannot describe its actions, impacts, or effects as good or evil. You cannot attach personal interpretations to what you witness. You cannot distort the truth. It will render your information unacceptable or worse, contaminate the bank of knowledge, the essence of the ALL. The first order of transition is the shedding of emotions, personal interpretations, to keep pure the logic.

"Am I clear?" asked the guide.

"Yes."

"Do you understand the folly of your guilt?"

"I believe so."

"Do you have any doubt that you were on a mission of your choosing?"

"No."

"Do you have any doubt that the mission of your choosing is concluded, and you are no longer a participant?"

"No."

"Finally, do you have any doubt that during your mission you served as a witness to the random flow of energy, and that your obligation was to return an account of its effects in your presence? Nothing more, nothing less?"

"No, I have no doubts."

"Gus, you understand the necessity of being a witness?"

"Yes."

I exist by means of my own observation.

50

The guide towed Gus by the hand up the incline of the street, now far less strenuous an ordeal. At times, it felt as though he floated. As they conversed, they walked past the ridgeline buildings and the unending border of shanties, lean-tos, and eateries catering to the migration of souls walking away from the failing light of a passing sun.

"The truths are a lot to digest for a soul that has veered so far from the road," said the guide.

"An understatement," said Gus. "However, the parallels were clear, and the alignments clarified a good deal. I understood, and it made me feel full, complete. But I also sense I am far from salvation. Is that true?"

"The road is long," concurred the guide.

"Am I allowed more questions?"

"Of course. Anything that I am able to answer."

"May I ask you more about ALL?"

"You may ask."

"Do you know him...or her? Have you ever seen him? Will I ever be able to see him?" Gus stopped mid-thought. He frowned. "Wait, I'm not sure I know how to ask this question."

"You can't ask that question because it is based on your interpretation of a god, an entity, a being that was revered in the reality of your mission. It was a different place.

"In this existence, there is no god, no entity, to know or adore. ALL is not a singular being. ALL is a state that you understand as opposed to the specificity of a fatherly or motherly deity.

"When all things are in accord, efficient, merging unhindered, we say they are harmonious. When I merged with you, we were in harmony. In one respect, ALL represents the harmonious merging of an infinite number of souls. That is why the cleansing of souls is necessary. Souls must be free of burdens, all worries, all concerns, souls must forgive and be forgiven of every transgression, every misdeed before merging with others or ALL. This is why we are focused on you."

"Humph." Gus gave thought to all she said. He had no desire to interrupt. He felt starved for answers.

"Understand, ALL is immeasurably more than just a harmonious merging of souls. ALL is energy. You are energy. We are energy. On the grandest scale, there is only energy. And it is random. It knows no boundaries. It flows, it changes, it creates eternally.

"What we witness of its action becomes knowledge. ALL is knowledge in its entirety. ALL has a single purpose, which is to amass knowledge as it occurs. It does so actively. Sometimes collectively, sometimes singularly. We observe on the scale of universes and dimensions. We observe on the scale of atoms and quarks. Knowledge is the record of energy in whatever form it takes. You are matter, you are energy, you are individual, you are ALL.

"You took on a mission of your choosing. You transitioned from energy to matter. You have now transitioned back from matter to energy. You carry knowledge with you. We seventeen were able to access all that you acquired when we merged. When you are free to merge with others, you will access all that they have acquired. This happens fast. You might say that ALL gains access simultaneously."

"So, once I am cleansed, I will merge with ALL."

"Yes. And once you merge, you will possess clarity. All that you have forgotten, all knowledge that is amassed, will be accessible to you."

"When does this happen?"

"*When* is only sensible in a reality that defines past, present, and future as different. The question here is not when but how. You are forgiven by those you transgressed. They are free of their burdens. They thanked you and moved on to merge."

"I gotta go. I gotta go." Gus looked at the woman.

"Yes. Precisely. Now it is your turn to forgive. You must release all the negativities you harbor against those who wronged you."

"How do I do that?"

The guide stopped at the edge of the highway. She stared across traffic that flooded untold numbers of lanes. Gus remained at her side awaiting the answer. Out of a setting sun, the headlights of a million vehicles raced toward them, taillights of equal number left them to find a distant horizon quickly erupting into a show of splendor.

"You follow the road, Gus. It only goes one way. There."

She pointed toward the silent shimmering starlight. At that instant, the horrible ear-splitting screech of brakes shattered the already hectic and noisy passing of vehicles and pedestrians.

Gus jumped back from the curb, but the guide was unmoved. The doors snapped open to reveal the driver grinning with his massive toothy grin. He was sporting the same outrageous psychedelic-colored bandana. Only now, instead of wearing it around his neck, he wore it around his forehead to crown a pair of sunglasses framing lightly tinted bronze lenses.

The driver looked as though he was chaperoning a party bus. The man was clearly in a great mood. He slapped the bus lever into park. He shut down the engine as he stood up from his seat. He was clearly impatient, but holding back, looking into the bus, when a young girl appeared whose hand he held to assist off the vehicle. He escorted her over to where Gus and the guide stood.

Letting go of the girl's hand, he took Gus into his embrace. He squeezed him heartily.

"It's good to see you, Gus. How you doing?"

"Okay. Better."

"You look better. In fact, you look a hell of a lot better than the last time I saw you."

"What are you doing here? I never expected to see you again."

"I never left, Gus. I was your guide. Don't you remember?"

Gus turned to question the woman, but she was gone. Vanished into the night. He directed his attention back to the driver.

"You mean like one of the seventeen?" Gus's mind raced.

"Yup. Surprised?"

"Ya think?"

The driver broke out in unrestrained laughter. He howled. He slapped Gus on the back.

"We've been through a lot, Gus. Many missions, many planes, many dimensions. I'm not about to leave you now. I was barely a step ahead of you, but it was enough for me to reach out and pull you along."

Gus was nearly lost for words. He could do little more than look at this flamboyant figure dancing about him.

"So what now?" asked Gus.

The driver's face was flush with pride. He turned from Gus to the young girl.

"Gus, I want you to meet my daughter, Azalia."

It was impossible for Gus to be anything but apprehensive as he looked at the child. She wore her hair pulled over to fall on one side. The other side exposed an ear with a large and colorful earing. The silence that followed was palatable and the driver laughed unrestrained. He wasn't alone. The daughter laughed as well.

"It's okay, Gus. My daughter forgave me eons ago. Just as she did you. In fact, she has something for you. A present."

"A present?"

Azalia raised her hand and opened it. She dangled a set of keys, which she was clearly offering to him. Gus was perplexed.

"Okay.... Keys to...?" he asked.

"The bus," answered the driver.

"You're giving me the keys to the bus?"

"You earned them."

"I don't understand."

"It's simple. For you the highway is the way to all that is good. It's the constant in your life. So, this is the road. The road to your salvation. I'm giving you the keys to the bus. You can follow the road to complete the second leg of your journey. You must forgive all those who seek it. I must warn you, it isn't easy. Often far more difficult than asking to be forgiven. Paybacks seem seriously rewarding. As you well remember.

"Take the keys, Gus."

Gus accepted the keys from Azalia.

"Now go. Get on the bus and head out. There's nothing for you here, Gus. It's time to go. Don't linger."

Gus stepped toward the bus. He stopped at the door and turned around. The guide was nowhere to be seen. Only the driver and his daughter remained to see him on his way.

"What are you waiting for? You ain't getting laid by that angel. She's long gone."

Gus grinned. He grabbed the hand bar and pulled himself aboard. He sat down in the driver's seat. He inserted the key and started the engine. The driver called out.

"The gearshift is there on your left. That lever with the orange ball closes the door."

Gus stepped on the brake and shifted the transmission into drive. He placed his hand on the door lever.

"Where am I going?" asked Gus.

"The road only goes one way. Do us all a favor and stay on it."

"I'll do my best. Thanks."

With that, the driver raised two fingers to his bandana and snapped off a salute. He then turned to pull his daughter tightly to his side and disappear into the shadows of night and the hustling crowd.

51

Gus closed the door. He turned to look behind him at the rows of empty seats. He was alone, but felt safe. He looked into the side mirror and noticed that no sign of the Lingering lay upon the horizon. He remembered the guide's words.

There's no need for the Lingering. You can't rush forgiveness.

Gus was pleased. As the bus pulled away from the curb, he wished a final glimpse of the driver walking somewhere within the multitudes. The man and his daughter had merged into the glow of a thousand yellowish-amber nightlights, which at a distance turned into stars.

I suppose he merged with his wife, with ALL.

Gus stomped hard on the gas, pressing the antiquated eight-wheeled contraption to respond to his impatience. As the old girl whined with complaint about the strain to gain speed, he switched lanes, moving closer to center. Eventually, the vehicle was moving so fast that everything beyond the side windows streamed by as dashing lines of dim light.

Gus drove in peace. That was the way of the road. Whether for days, months, years, or eons, he could not say. He was content to follow it forever. Ahead of the bus, which was now screaming along at unthinkable speeds and still sounding like a washing machine full of beer cans, was the universe or universes, or dimensions fiercely illuminated in glorious prisms of color against the blackness. The radiance pressed down hard upon souls traveling the solitary road that never wavered.

It shot ahead straight as an arrow to the point of singularity where it lost itself to the brilliance of a billion galaxies exploding across the nocturnal sky. The beauty of the heavens hypnotized him. The beauty spared him from worrying about whatever else awaited. The vistas were majestic, spellbinding distractions from the anxiety of existing. So was the woman's counsel that he recounted repeatedly for strength and guidance.

"You are forgiven by all you offended. Walk free of guilt for you have paid back in full your real debt as well as the false debt you imposed upon yourself.

"What goes around comes around. Now, you must forgive. Now you must face your offenders. Beware. The task is no less demanding. You carry yet the stains of anger, of hatred and revenge. You desire yet to balance scales, even scores, collect what is due, and administer your own justice—eye for an eye.

Beware.

"To forgive, you must confront yourself as you would your transgressor. Only then, might you succeed and move on to merge with others and ALL.

"Know that the road to salvation is short for some, long for others, but straight for all. For there is only one way."

Time was meaningless and distance infinite. Gus could not say if he had driven a thousand miles, thousands of miles, or millions of miles before the first passenger entered his awareness. The passenger was presently unseen, but he could sense the rider waiting at a curb in the not too far future.

Gus piloted the bus toward the outer lanes and allowed the vehicle to slow. As soon as he edged over to the curb lane, this passenger, his first rider, came into view. Gus studied the individual now wincing from the horrendous screech of brakes that brought the bus to a halt. He opened the door.

"Need a lift?"

The man, looking thoroughly bewildered, stood in place staring at Gus.

"C'mon. Get on. I know where you're headed."

The person's face was one of dazed distress. Zombie-like. Mindlessly, he followed Gus's instruction and stepped up into the doorway... at which point Gus screamed.

"To bloody hell!"

A shotgun discharged and blew the man's head off. His body stood erect before slowly keeling backward to land with a puff of dust on the dirt-packed shoulder of the road.

Amazed, Gus looked down through a thick bluish-white cloud of smoke at the short-barreled weapon. He then reached up and touched the back of his head. He looked at the fresh blood dripping off his fingers. He raised his eyes to study the corpse now backed against the ground, floating in a pool of blood that spread out across the impenetrable roadside dust. A chunk of skull rested nearby.

"Ha, ha! *You motherfucker!* Ain't paybacks a bitch? Ha, ha!"

Gus laughed louder than ever.

He closed the bus door, stood on the gas, and began humming an old familiar Hollies song.

The road is lo-ong, with many a winding turn....

Heart-felt thanks to Martha Hart, Cynthia Guy, Samantha Newland, Nancy Burke Smith, and Gerrie Vennesland for generously offering their time and assistance.

Most importantly, I thank my wife, Nancy, for allowing me to act on my dreams instead of my responsibilities. God bless her.

OTHER BOOKS IN PRINT BY
C. JOHN COOMBES

CLAUS: A CHRISTMAS INCARNATION; THE CHILD VOLUME 1
ISBN 978-0-9822213-2-7
CLAUS: A CHRISTMAS INCARNATION; THE WOMAN V2B1
ISBN 978-0-9822213-6-5
CLAUS: A CHRISTMAS INCARNATION; THE WOMAN V2B2
ISBN 978-0-9822213-7-2
CLAUS: A CHRISTMAS INCARNATION; THE DISCIPLE V3B1
ISBN 978-0-9822213-8-9
CLAUS: A CHRISTMAS INCARNATION; THE DISCIPLE V3B2
ISBN 978-0-9822213-9-6
FULL MOON STO
ISBN 978-1-941623-90-9
JACK CREEK HORROR
ISBN 978-1-941623-70-1

Made in the USA
Columbia, SC
22 May 2017